Denise N. Wheatley loves storytelling. Her novels ru strives to pen entertaining books that embody matters of the heart. She's an RWA member and holds a BA in English from the University of Illinois. When Denise isn't writing, she enjoys watching true-crime TV and chatting with readers. Follow her on social media. Instagram @Denise_Wheatley_Writer, Twitter @DeniseWheatley, BookBub @DeniseNWheatley, Goodreads Denise N. Wheatley.

Amber Leigh Williams is an author, wife, mother of two and dog mum. She has been writing sexy, small-town romance with memorable characters since 2006. She lives on the Alabama Gulf Coast, where she loves being outdoors with her family and a good book. Visit her on the web at amberleighwilliams.com

HOMICIDE AT VINCENT VINEYARD

DENISE N. WHEATLEY

OLLERO CREEK CONSPIRACY

AMBER LEIGH WILLIAMS

MILLS & BOON

First Published in Great Britain 2023
by Mills & Boon, an imprint of HarperCollins*Publishers* Ltd
1 London Bridge Street, London, SE1 9GF

www.harpercollins.co.uk

HarperCollins*Publishers*
Macken House, 39/40 Mayor Street Upper,
Dublin 1, D01 C9W8, Ireland

Homicide at Vincent Vineyard © 2023 Denise N. Wheatley
Ollero Creek Conspiracy © 2023 Amber Leigh Williams

ISBN: 978-0-263-30751-1

1123

MIX
Paper | Supporting
responsible forestry
FSC
www.fsc.org
FSC™ C007454

This book is produced from independently certified FSC™ paper
to ensure responsible forest management.

For more information visit: www.harpercollins.co.uk/green

Printed and Bound in the UK using 100% Renewable Electricity at
CPI Group (UK) Ltd, Croydon, CR0 4YY

HOMICIDE AT VINCENT VINEYARD

DENISE N. WHEATLEY

To my little besties, Nina and Brooke Heintzelman.
Thank you for helping me plot out this book.
Also, please do not tell your parents about this...

Chapter One

"You're late," Ella murmured into her cell phone.

She eyed the entrance of Clemmington, California's fall harvest festival, making sure Jake wasn't walking through the iron arbor as she spoke. A group of rowdy teenagers appeared, leaping in the air to see who could reach the maple leaf vines hanging from the ten-foot-tall archway first. But there was no sign of Jake.

"I'll be leaving the station soon!" he yelled so loudly that Ella pulled the phone away from her ear. "I promise!"

She chuckled at his enthusiasm. While their relationship was still fairly new, Ella felt as though she'd known him for years. They had grown close after Jake's brother, Miles, and her sister, Charlotte, apprehended Nevada's Numeric Serial Killer—the man who also happened to be Ella's ex-boyfriend. It had taken Ella some time to recuperate from the ordeal. Soon after the arrest, she submitted a leave of absence from her job as a traveling nurse, left River Valley behind and moved to Clemmington temporarily to be closer to Jake and Charlotte.

"You know," he continued, "considering I'm Clemmington's newly appointed chief of police, you're lucky I even have time to attend the festival."

"*Extremely* lucky. Your dedication to the force is awe-inspiring. But I think even the former chief would approve of you taking a break every now and then," Ella said, referring to his father, Kennedy, who'd retired from the position before recommending that his eldest son take over.

"I know he would. And I'm only kidding. *I'm* the lucky one. I hope you know how happy I am that you're here with me."

"And I'm happy to be here," Ella purred, her golden-brown cheeks tingling from the warmth of his words. "Spending time with you, Charlotte and the baby has really helped me get through everything. Your whole family has, really."

"Well, just know that the Loves are always here for you."

"Thanks, babe."

A gust of wind blew Ella's long dark hair across her face. She pulled a few loose waves behind her ears and pushed through the crowd, observing long lines of festival-goers wrapped around bucket-toss, Skee-Ball and duck-pond game booths. Laughter mixed with screams flew overhead as colorful amusement rides twirled in the air. The scents of freshly popped popcorn and hot apple cider mingled with beef chili and funnel cake. But the mouthwatering smell of french fries sent Ella's stomach rumbling.

"Uh-oh," she uttered as the delicious aroma rerouted her black combat boots in the direction of the food stalls. "All these yummy eats they're serving have me in a trance. I see Pauline's Potato Pit Stop up ahead, and I haven't eaten since breakfast. I was trying to hold out and wait for you to get here. But I am starving, and these potatoes are calling my name."

"Please don't wait for me. Go ahead. Enjoy yourself. Eat, play a few games and make sure you stop by Sofia's Home-made Wine stand. She does a curated flight sampler that you have got to try. It contains a little bit of everything. Sparking, white, red, sweet... You'll love it. It's pricey, but worth it. I'll text you as soon as I'm on my way. I shouldn't be much longer."

"Okay, babe. See you soon."

Ella approached Pauline's, debating what to get. From smoked and loaded baked potatoes to sweet potato waffle fries and garlic mashed potatoes, the choices ran the gamut. She settled on an order of cheesy taco fries, then set out to explore the rest of the event.

"Hey, El!"

Pivoting in the direction of the familiar voice, Ella spotted Officer Underwood, who was standing in line at the Ferris wheel. "Hey, how are you?"

"Great! Where's Chief Regé-Jean Page?" he joked, referring to Jake's uncanny resemblance to the *Bridgerton* star.

"He's still down at the station. But he'll be here soon."

"That man is such a workaholic. Hopefully I'll see you two before we leave."

"Sounds good. Have fun!"

As Ella continued along the festival trail, the air began to cool. She zipped her beige leather jacket and glanced up at the deep purple sky. Dusk had already descended upon the vast grounds. Dark clouds billowed across the setting sun, marking an eerie desolation on several festival attractions.

The petting zoo pen sat empty as the goats, sheep, ponies and alpacas had already been hauled away. Children had abandoned the wooden crates stacked with pumpkin varieties. Fortune tellers packed up their tarot cards and crystal balls, leaving their bejeweled velvet tents behind. The tractor-pulled wagon carrying attendees on a tour of the scenic orchard sat empty, having unloaded its last group for the evening.

I hope they all made it back safely, Ella thought, remembering how Jake once told her that fifteen thousand people disappear from festival hayride wagons each year.

"Hello, young lady," someone croaked behind her.

Ella jumped, turning toward the creepy voice. A tall slender man swung his lanky arm to the side and smiled, revealing a row of jagged gray teeth. "How would you like to try your luck at making it out of Abel's Amazing Corn Maze alive?"

Her wide-set amber eyes narrowed at the sight of his spotty pale skin and gaunt cheeks. Strands of long white hair stuck out from underneath his distressed straw hat. His frail frame barely held his dingy overalls in place. A sign above him read Wander Your Way Through To The End. Or Die Trying... It was a scene straight out of a horror movie.

"I—I think I'll pass," Ella stammered, backing away from the maze.

"Oh, come on," he grunted, taking a step toward her. "What have you got to lose? This is the easiest maze in all of California. Even children have made their way out, all alone."

No sooner than the words had escaped his hollow mouth, a group of kids came running over. They shoved their tickets inside his skeletal hand, then darted inside.

"Those little ones are my regulars," he said. "This is their third time through the maze today. Oh, and one thing I forgot to mention. If you do make it to the other side, there's a prize. Depending on your preference, you'll receive either a free hot chocolate from Beatrice's Bakery, or a glass of wine from Sofia's Winery. Your choice."

Ella could hear the children who'd entered the corn maze laughing hysterically.

Now you have been known to conquer a maze or two during your festival days back in River Valley.

She glanced at her watch, remembering that she also had time to kill while waiting on Jake to arrive.

"*Well*, why not," Ella said before taking a quick bite of fries, then shoving the bag inside her tote. "I could certainly go for a glass of Zinfandel from Sofia's."

"Ahh, yes. Now that's what I like to hear. Admission for adults is ten dollars. But for you, my dear, it's free. Don't fall into a daze as you walk through the maze, and I'll see you on the other side. I hope…"

Ella side-eyed the strange man. "You're good, you know that? You almost had me scared to walk through this thing. *Almost*…"

He gave her a slow wink that sent chills up her back. "The only thing to fear is fear itself. Isn't that what Franklin D. Roosevelt once said? Good luck, ma'am."

She quickly slipped past the man and entered the maze, ignoring pangs of uneasiness banging around inside her chest. Playing it safe with a game of Whac-A-Mole or even axe-throwing would've been just fine. But she'd never been one to turn down a challenge. Or a free glass of wine.

The moment Ella hit the dirt path, darkness descended upon her. She'd underestimated the height of the cornstalk hovering overhead. Dried leaves blew against her body, slicing at the exposed skin on her face and hands. She pulled out her cell and turned on the flashlight, shining it along the rugged trail.

"What have I gotten myself into?" she muttered, picking up speed as she reached the end of the aisle.

Boom!

Ella ducked down, almost falling to the ground. Slow to stand, she noticed a zombie scarecrow looming up above.

She'd almost knocked over the frightening figure, unable to see its deathly gray makeup and shredded black clothing through the darkness. A faux black crow was perched on a wooden beam, squawking loudly as its red eyes glowed in the dark.

Abel didn't mention this maze being haunted...

Ella scrambled to her feet, suddenly anxious to find the exit. She made a right turn and held her phone in the air, searching for the signs. There were none.

What the...

She jogged to the end of the pathway, then made a quick left, her thick soles skidding across mounds of straw-covered dirt. Within seconds, she reached the corner of that aisle. It was a dead end.

"Dammit!"

Ella spun around and rushed down the long trail, heaving as panic began to tighten her airways. The four-way intersection revealed no signs, and no clues leading to the exit.

Stop. Stay calm. Listen for the voices.

She stood still, waiting to hear the screams and laughter of fellow mazegoers. There were none.

"Just keep going," she muttered, her mind spinning with confusion.

Ella ran full speed ahead, ignoring the clouds of dust kicking up around her and cornstalks slashing against her body.

"Wrong way!" someone yelled.

She fell against a massive object, then dropped to the ground.

"*Ouch*," Ella uttered, grabbing her lower back. She looked up. A spell of dizziness blurred her vision. Within seconds, she was able to make out a heavyset man dressed in a tattered plaid shirt, creeping along the edge of the cornstalks.

"Well hot damn!" he yelled. "That must've hurt." He cackled loudly, then reached for her.

"Get the hell away from me!" she screamed.

"Hey! This is *my* turf, lady. And if I see you again, I can guarantee you won't make it outta here alive. Cuz Abel sure ain't coming to save ya!"

He let out a piercing howl, then ran off. The second he was out of her sight, Ella hopped up and ran in the opposite direction. She grabbed her cell phone and pounded the side button.

"Siri, call Jake!"

"Calling Jake."

It went straight to voice mail.

She disconnected the call and slowed down, gathering her bearings.

Take it easy. Deep breaths. This is an amusement attraction, for God's sake. Just keep going until you find your way out...

Ella moved forward. Another dead end appeared up ahead. This time, she didn't freak out. She simply stopped, slumped down onto a bale of hay and tried Jake again.

"You have reached the voice mail box of Chief Jake Love—"

She hung up.

Why would you let that creepy man talk you into this mess? Ella asked herself, realizing that no glass of wine was worth this type of trauma. *Now you're gonna end up on the five o'clock news—another fall festival victim, gone missing...*

Dialing 9-1-1 crossed her mind. But she couldn't bring herself to do it. If those kids could find their way out of the maze, so could she.

*Come on. Suck it up. Get on your feet and find your way
out of here.*

Ella stood, pulling in a mass of cool air. Just as she set
off toward the end of the aisle, something sharp poked her
in the back.

"*Ow!*" she yelled, swinging her arm in the air. "Look,
man, this is not funny!"

She spun a three-sixty turn, expecting the heavyset zombie farmer to pop out from the behind the cornstalks. He
didn't. No one did.

"I am not amused, you…you *clown*. Come on out! Show
your face."

Silence.

Maybe it was just a cornstalk blowing in the wind.

"Keep moving," Ella told herself right before someone
grabbed her jacket and knocked her to the ground.

"That is *it!*" she screamed. "Abel! Come and get me the
hell out of here!"

Ella pressed her palms against the trail, struggling to
stand. Pellets of dried dirt and splintered stalks tore into
her skin. She didn't care. Escaping the maze was all that
mattered.

The moment she rolled over onto her knees, a figure
dressed in all black emerged from the stalks.

No, no, no!

"Somebody help me!" Ella screamed.

"Miss!" a voice called out in the distance. "Where are
you!"

"I'm over he—"

The figure swooped in and covered her mouth with a
gloved hand. "Shut up!" he rasped, putting her in a head-
lock and dragging her into the cornstalks.

"No! Let me go!" Ella kicked her legs wildly, attempting

to scream. But her mouth was still covered, and her throat was jammed in the crook of the assailant's arm.

"Who are you?" she wheezed. "Why are you doing this to me?"

He remained silent, yanking her body into the stalks. Despite ripping at his arm, the pressure didn't let up. Ella dug her heels into the dirt. Her calves burned as the traction inched her back toward the trail.

Keep fighting. Keep fighting!

Beams of light shined down the aisle.

"Ma'am!" someone called out as footsteps pounded in her direction.

"*Lucky bitch*," the attacker barked in Ella's ear before tossing her off to the side and vanishing into the stalks.

A festival security guard ran over. "Are you okay?"

She gasped, clutching her neck while rolling over. "No, I've been attacked!"

"*Attacked?*" he shouted while helping Ella to her feet. "By who?"

"I have no idea. At first I thought it was one of the carnival workers, playing a joke on me. But it wasn't. This person didn't have on a costume. He was dressed in all black and trying to hurt me."

"Did you see which way he went?"

"That way," she heaved, pointing toward the cornstalks.

Security stared into what appeared to be the dark abyss, his twisted expression weary. "It was probably some kid, pulling a silly prank. I'm sure he's long gone by now. Why don't we get you out of here and call the authorities?"

Ella didn't bother to tell him that she was dating the chief of police. Her only focus was getting to safety.

Maybe he's right. Could've just been a kid playing a prank...

Her phone buzzed.

Jake, finally!

She eyed the screen, desperate to tell him what just happened. But it wasn't Jake. It was a text message sent from an anonymous number.

Ella's heart pounded inside her throat as she swiped open the message.

You may have made it out of the corn maze, but you won't make it out of Clemmington alive. Watch your back. Because I know what you did...

Chapter Two

Jake sat calmly despite shards of anger tearing through his veins. He glared at the man authorities suspected had attacked Ella at the festival.

Deep breaths, he thought, clenching his jaw while his knees bounced against the edge of the table.

The stench of wet paint stung Jake's nostrils as renovations to the Clemmington police station dragged on. Their new state-of-the-art forensics lab had sparked his father's desire to spruce up the entire building right before his retirement. What was meant to be a farewell gift to his team resulted in a huge pain as all the dust, electrical cords, power tools and construction crew members took over their workspace.

"So," Jake began, his tightened lips barely parting, "you *are* admitting that you were at the festival on the evening of the fifteenth?"

"Yeah," the young man mumbled. "I was there. But I didn't attack anybody."

"But you were running through the corn maze, harassing the attendees. Is that correct?"

The short husky suspect leaned back in his chair, balancing himself on its rear legs. He glared at Jake through lowered eyes, his baby face contorting into a menacing snarl.

"Please answer the question, Mr. Montero," Miles chimed in, who'd insisted on participating in the interrogation alongside his big brother.

"I know how much Ella means to you, man," Miles had told Jake right before he entered the room. "You're the chief of police now. All eyes are on you, and there's no room for error. I just wanna be there to make sure everything goes smoothly."

"All right, all right. Fine," Jake had finally agreed.

And now, almost two hours later, the brothers had yet to pull a confession out of their suspect.

"We have eyewitnesses stating that they saw you tearing through those cornstalks," Jake pressed.

"They may have seen *somebody*, but they didn't see me."

Through the corners of his eyes, Jake glanced over at the reflective glass window. Ella and Charlotte were standing on the other side of it. He hated the idea of them watching him fail. Ella had been through enough, having been attacked by her serial killer ex-boyfriend shortly before he was apprehended. This assault could've been enough to send her over the edge. But she was tough and hadn't allowed a prank at a small-town festival to break her.

"We're not getting anywhere with this one," Miles muttered in Jake's ear.

"Yeah, but I'm not ready to give up just yet."

Jake slid his chair closer to the suspect's. "Mr. Montero, you do know that there are security cameras all around the festival grounds, don't you?"

The suspect's snarl morphed into a look of surprise. He stared down at his hands, picking at his dirty fingernails. "No. I didn't."

"Well, there are. So whatever you did, we'll see it. We're just waiting on the surveillance footage."

"Not only that," Miles interjected, "but those eyewitnesses we mentioned will be giving official statements, along with the security guards who were on the premises that night. We'll be doing a lineup as well. So here's your chance, Mr. Montero. Whatever you're not telling us, we're gonna find out. Let us hear it from you first. What was your reasoning behind the—"

The suspect leaned forward and pounded his fist against the steel table. "I'm done trying to convince you all that I'm innocent. I refuse to answer another question. I wanna talk to a lawyer. Now!"

Jake slumped down in his chair. Just as he grabbed his file, there was knock at the door.

"Why don't you get that while I keep an eye on Mr. Montero?" Miles told him.

"What do you mean *keep an eye on me*? I'm not under arrest, am I? I can leave anytime I want, can't I? That's what your boy told me when I first walked in here."

"My *boy*? His name is Chief Love. Show some respect, young man."

Ignoring the suspect, Jake lumbered toward the door on legs that had numbed after sitting for so long. Charlotte was standing on the other side.

"Hey," she whispered. "Can I talk to you for a sec?"

"Of course."

He stepped out and closed the door behind him, flinching at the sight of her weary red eyes. Her downturned lips told him that she wasn't here to deliver good news.

"What's going on?" he asked.

"It's Ella. She said the guy you're interrogating isn't the person who attacked her."

"She did? But it was so dark out there. I thought she didn't get a good look at him."

"She didn't. However, judging by the quick glances that she did get, Ella doesn't remember her attacker being as stocky as this guy."

Jake dropped his head in his hand. "Is she sure? Because we've got witnesses who saw him running through the corn maze, harassing patrons."

"She's sure. The man you're interrogating is shorter and much bulkier than her assailant."

"All right." He sighed, his arms falling by his sides. "Good to know, especially since this guy just lawyered up. Back to the drawing board."

"Have the festival organizers sent over the surveillance footage?"

"Not yet."

"Well, when they do, I'd be more than happy to review it with you, Miles and Ella. Even though I'm technically on a work hiatus from River Valley PD, I can't just shake my sergeant duties. I'm all in on this. I cannot have my sister out here randomly being attacked. Not after everything she's been through."

"I agree. I'm hoping this is all a result of some stupid joke being played by a teenager. I'd heard there were groups of unruly high schoolers acting out during the entire festival. *Dammit*, I should've been there with her. Then this never would've happened in the first place."

"Come on," Charlotte said, giving his arm a reassuring pat. "Don't do that. This isn't your fault. Who would've thought that some goofball would be running around the festival, harassing attendees? Ella understands that you've taken on a big job and can't be by her side twenty-four seven. Chalk this one up as a fluke and let it go. Your team will do their job of catching whoever did it. In the meantime, let's just make sure our girl is okay."

Jake stood straight up and squared his shoulders. "You're right. I just want Ella to know that we're taking her attack seriously. But for now, I'll send Mr. Montero home."

"And I'll get back to Ella. Trust me, she knows you're taking this seriously. She also knows that investigations take time, and most cases don't get solved overnight."

"But does she feel safe?" he asked as they headed down the hallway. "Ella came to Clemmington looking for security. And peace. *I'm* the one who's supposed to give her those things."

"We all are, Jake. And we will. Let's just make an effort to keep a closer eye on her."

The pair entered the observation room. Jake went straight to Ella, wrapping his arms around her. "Hey, how are you holding up?"

"Okay, I guess. I didn't think I'd be back inside a police station this soon. But yet, here I am."

His chest pulled when her body stiffened against his. "I'm so sorry, El. Charlotte told me you don't think this guy is our suspect. But we've got a plan. That surveillance footage from the festival will give us some answers. We'll get the official statements on record from the eyewitnesses and security team. And I'll send my guys out to patrol the streets. You never know. Maybe our perp will get himself into more trouble and we'll apprehend him that way."

"Let's hope so. Like you've been saying, maybe this was all just a silly teenage prank."

He planted a soft kiss on her forehead. "On the bright side, I've got some exciting news to share with you and my family tonight during dinner. Something I've been thinking about ever since I took over as chief of police."

"I could use some good news."

Charlotte gave Ella's hand a squeeze. "Why don't we go back to my place until Jake gets off work?"

"Better yet," Jake interjected, glancing at his watch, "why don't you two meet us at my parents' house later tonight? I don't think Miles and I are getting out of here any time soon. Is that okay with you?" he asked Ella.

"Of course," she murmured, her head falling against his chest.

"Come on. Let's get you out of here."

Jake led her toward the exit, hoping the incident at the festival boiled down to teenage antics and nothing more sinister...

"How are you doing, sweetheart?" Betty asked Ella. The matriarch of the Love family had been fussing over her ever since she'd arrived at the house.

"She's fine, Mom," Jake told her, sensing Ella's discomfort at being the center of attention as she shifted in her seat. "Why don't you have a seat and enjoy this delicious meal you prepared?"

"Yes, honey," her husband, Kennedy, chimed in. "The food is getting cold."

Lena, Jake's sister, pulled out Betty's chair. "You sit down, and I'll make your plate. You've done enough."

"Ugh." Her mother sighed, plopping down into the chair. "Fine, but not too much food now. I'm trying to watch my weight."

Ignoring Betty's request, Lena piled a rib eye steak, lobster tail, roasted corn on the cob and grilled asparagus onto a dish.

"This girl doesn't listen," Betty muttered in her husband's direction.

"So, Mom," Miles said in between bites of a crescent roll, "to what do we owe this fabulous dinner?"

"Well," she began, tapping Lena's hand in an attempt to stop her hefty pour of Cabernet Sauvignon, "your brother said he's got some good news that he'd like to share with the family tonight. I figured what better way to celebrate than with a nice surf and turf and homemade apple cobbler."

"Homemade apple cobbler? *Mmm*," Jake repeated, relishing in the warmth that illuminated throughout the Love family's home. The mood was festive, with Ella even appearing more relaxed as she settled against the back of her chair and gave him a wink.

"All right, son," Kennedy said. "Let's hear it. What's this big news you've been so eager to share?"

After taking a long sip of wine, Jake cleared his throat.

"Remember Don Vincent, the owner of Vincent Vineyard who was murdered last year?"

Kennedy set down his fork. "Of course I remember. How could I forget? Don was a great man. A well-respected pillar of the Clemmington community. His charity efforts helped send underprivileged kids to college, put food on tables, provided gifts for families during the holidays—" He paused, his words catching in his throat.

"It's okay, honey," Betty said, clutching his hand.

"No. It isn't. My one regret in life will always be that I never solved his murder." Kennedy's weary gaze shifted toward Jake. "I'm sorry, son. Please, continue. What about Don?"

"Well, now that I've taken over as chief of police, I'm going to reopen Don's cold case. See if we can get it solved."

Taking a breath, Kennedy pressed his hands together. "*Jake*. I... I don't even know what to say. Except, *wow*. I wasn't expecting that. It would be wonderful for the Vincent family and the entire Clemmington community if you could solve Don's murder. But let me be the first to warn you. It's gonna be tough. We covered a lot of ground during the initial investigation. Where would you even start?"

"The best place would be with your old files. You compiled a ton of information and leads. Persons of interest, surveillance footage from the vineyard, interviews with employees and family members. I'm even planning to pull the evidence that was collected at the crime scene and have it reexamined."

"I like that idea," Lena interjected, who'd moved back to Clemmington after working for the LAPD and now served as the head of Forensics. "Since we have the new lab, I can retest the evidence and see if anything comes up that wasn't discovered during the first go-round."

Kennedy's grin widened. "I am loving this plan of action. It would mean the world to me if we finally captured Don's killer."

"I'm sorry," Betty said, pointing in her husband's direction, "but did I just hear you say *we*?"

He shrugged, glancing around the table as wrinkles of confusion creased his forehead. "Yes. Why?"

"I'm just wondering who exactly is included in this *we*. Because last time I checked, you no longer work for the Clemmington PD. So there will be no *we* when it comes to solving this case. Leave that up to our new chief of police and the rest of the force. You'll be too busy vacationing and taking care of our grandbaby to work on the investigation anyway."

A hushed silence swept through the room. It was disrupted when Kennedy snickered quietly.

"Welp, the lady of the house has spoken. Nevertheless, Jake, I trust that you and the rest of the team will get the case solved. If you need any assistance or advice though, you know where to find me—"

Betty threw him a look that stopped Kennedy mid-sentence. He waved his white linen napkin in the air, declaring defeat.

"Thanks, Dad," Jake said. He turned to David Hudson, a detective with the Clemmington PD and Lena's boyfriend. "What do you think of all this, Dave? You were a big part of the first investigation. Who do you think should be questioned first?"

"I'd say start with Don's wife, Claire. I remember her being a main suspect when the murder first occurred."

"What would've given you *that* impression?" Miles quipped through a sarcastic smirk. "The fact that she was having an affair with Alan Monroe, or that she was draining Don's bank account without putting much work in at the vineyard?"

"C. All the above."

"Wait, who is Alan Monroe?" Charlotte asked. "I am so curious about this case now. Ella, why do I get the feeling you and I are gonna insert ourselves in this investigation to help solve it?"

When Ella remained silent, Jake gave her a playful nudge. "I'd actually love it if you chimed in on this case, babe."

"Mmm-hmm," she muttered while pushing a forkful of asparagus across her plate.

Blaming her dry reaction on the rough day she'd had, Jake propped his arm against the back of her chair and leaned in Charlotte's direction. "To answer your question, Alan is the owner of Creekside Winery."

"Also known as Vincent's Vineyard's main competition," Miles pointed out.

"Exactly. It's located a couple of towns over, and word

on the street is that Alan began having an affair with Don's wife, Claire, a few years ago after they'd met at a wine convention in San Francisco."

"Ooh, that would be pretty scandalous if it's true." Charlotte tapped Ella. "Are you getting all this?"

She replied with a slight nod, her eyes remaining fixated on her plate.

"Hey," Jake whispered in Ella's ear, "are you okay?"

"Yeah...just feeling a little headachy all of a sudden."

Miles held his hand in the air. "Hold on, now. We can't just focus on Claire as our main suspect. What about her two sons, Tyler and Greer?"

A loud gag startled everyone at the table. They turned to Ella, who was gulping down mouthfuls of water.

Jake jumped to his feet and slapped her back. "Are you all right?"

"I—fi... I'm fine! A piece of asparagus must've gotten caught in my throat."

"But you weren't eating any—" Jake stopped abruptly when she threw him a death stare.

Something was definitely off. Was it the attack at the festival? Had it triggered thoughts of being assaulted by her ex? Or was it something deeper?

"Please," Ella said to Miles, "continue with what you were saying."

"I was just asking about Tyler and Greer, who took over the vineyard after their father was killed. Rumor has it they may have been behind his murder."

"I always thought one of them had something to do with it," Kennedy said. "Especially that older one, Tyler."

"Same here," Jake interjected. "He and I went to high school together, and even back then, I remember him being super flashy and arrogant. Once he graduated and worked his way up to vice president of the vineyard, his ego inflated to the point of combustion."

"That it did," Kennedy agreed. "And during the time that I was investigating Don's death, it came out that both sons were at odds with their father. Especially Tyler."

"Why were they at odds?" Charlotte asked. "Were the sons trying to take over the vineyard?"

"Something like that," Jake told her. "Tyler and Greer both serve as vice presidents. But neither of them had the best relationship with Don. The business had begun to tear them apart because the sons wanted to take Vincent Vineyard to the next level. Their goal was to keep up with the current trends and give Creekside Winery a run for its money."

"And let me guess," Lena said. "Don was resistant to that idea."

"Very much so," Kennedy replied. "After investigating the case, I felt like a vineyard expert. I learned all about how the sons wanted to expand the planted grape varieties and incorporate newer technologies, digital trends and winemaking equipment. They were also pushing their father to build a visitor area for tastings and group tours. But Don refused. He'd insisted that his old-school way was the only way. He had achieved success by producing a smaller output of wine while growing limited grape varieties, and felt that his simple, grassroots marketing efforts were bringing in a steady stream of business. So in his mind, he'd thought, why fix what isn't broken?"

"*Humph*," Betty huffed. "Poor man. His unwillingness to broaden the business may have very well cost him his life."

Kennedy polished off the rest of his steak, then reclined in his chair. "We all had our suspicions of a few key family members. Employees too, for that matter. Too bad we couldn't put it all together and prove who'd done it. But I have no doubt that the new Chief Love will. Thank you for reopening this case, son."

"Of course. I'm definitely feeling confident. Especially now that we've got a secret weapon on the team that we didn't have last year."

"And by secret weapon," Lena said, leaning toward Jake, "are you referring to me?"

"I most certainly am." He held his glass in the air, tipping it in her direction. "Thank you. All of you. I appreciate your faith in me. Trust that I won't let you down."

"We've got all the faith in the world in you," Kennedy assured him.

"And on that note," Betty said as she began clearing the table, "why don't I bring out the apple cobbler, vanilla bean ice cream and coffee, then we switch the subject to something a little more pleasant?"

"I'd like that," Ella muttered, hopping up and gathering several dishes.

Jake's brows furrowed with concern. "Here, let me help you." He attempted to take a couple of the plates.

"I got it!" she snapped, jerking away and rushing toward the kitchen.

"Is she all right?" Miles asked.

Charlotte grabbed her plate and went after Ella. "I don't know, but I'll find out. Jake, just relax and finish your dinner."

He took a seat just as Betty reached across the table and patted his forearm. "She's probably still shaken up from the attack at the festival, honey. Not to mention that killer ex-boyfriend of hers."

"I agree," Kennedy added. "All that violence would have a negative effect on anybody. This talk of Don Vincent's murder probably got to her too. Just give her some time, son."

"I will." He peered at the doorway, debating whether he should check on Ella. When Lena grabbed the bottle of wine and refilled his glass, he decided against it.

"Speaking of the attack at the festival," she said, "have you identified a suspect yet?"

"No, unfortunately." Jake paused at the faint sound of Ella sobbing. It burned through his eardrums, igniting a fire deep inside his gut. "But I will. Trust me, I will."

Chapter Three

Ella sat in the passenger seat of Jake's car, twisting the jade cocktail rings adorning her perfectly manicured hands. The pair were headed to an exclusive wine tasting event at Vincent Vineyard. She thought she'd seen the last of the place several years ago. Yet here she was, heading to the venue she'd grown to dread in hopes of gathering new intel before Jake officially reopened Don Vincent's murder investigation.

When Ella learned of Jake's plan during the family dinner, she almost fell from her chair. She'd thought her ties to the Vincent family had been severed for good.

Not so fast, the cruel universe whispered in her ear.

Ella's stomach flipped as Jake pulled into the vineyard's winding driveway. The breathtaking Tuscan-inspired winery, with its tan limestone exterior, terra-cotta rooftop and sprawling hillside greenery, exuded a charming old-world European style. When she'd first laid eyes on the sprawling establishment way back when, Ella had been captivated. But now, it brought on feelings of disgust.

"This place is amazing, isn't it?" Jake asked.

"It is," she replied, her low tone laced with reluctance.

Ella envisioned the Vincent family's reaction upon seeing her. Thoughts of them sent pangs of anxiety flipping through her stomach.

Stop it. You can do this.

Her eyes stung at the sight of the arched wooden doorway. A valet driver opened Ella's door and offered his hand. She paused, far from ready to exit the vehicle.

"You ready?" Jake asked, clearly confused by her hesitancy.

"Yep, I'm ready," she lied.

"Listen, I really appreciate you coming here with me tonight. But if you don't want to be a part of this investigation, you don't have to. I just know how much you enjoyed assisting Charlotte with her cases back in River Valley. Plus, since you're taking a break from nursing, I figured you'd want to occupy your time with something interesting."

"Absolutely. I'm happy to help in any way that I can."

She stiffened underneath Jake's curious stare. It was as if he could sense her dishonesty. The urge to tell him what was bothering her lingered on the tip of Ella's tongue. But she swallowed it down. Now was not the time.

Jake held her close as the pair made their way up the curved stone staircase.

"I remember how tough it was for my sister when she took a break from the LAPD after being attacked," he said. "Lena moved back to Clemmington and got so bored sitting around my parents' house that she started investigating the Heart-Shaped Murders' case on her own. That almost got her killed."

"Well, I certainly won't be doing anything that dangerous to occupy my time. But again, I'm all in on assisting you."

"Good," Jake murmured, covering her lips with a lingering kiss. "I can't tell you how much that means to me."

"Oh, so you're just using me for my investigative skills,

huh?" Ella joked, hoping the light banter would ease her agitated nerves.

"No! Of course not. This is all about the companionship. And the affection. And having the woman I love by my side. Before you, I hadn't been in a serious relationship in years. This is a nice change of pace for me."

"Same here. Especially considering the men of my past..."

The pair stepped inside the winery's vast lobby. A large crowd had already gathered, moving from table to table while sipping reds and nibbling cheeses.

Ella inhaled the fragrant scent of grape varieties. The aroma reminded her of that first visit to the vineyard. She'd been impressed with its shiny walnut interior, elegant leather furnishings and abstract oil paintings. Events were usually filled with overdressed women, and tonight was no exception. Ella had opted for a low-key look—a navy sheath dress, minimal makeup and a low bun. The last thing she wanted was to draw attention to herself. But after eyeing the majority of the attendees, who were decked out in showy designer gear, Ella realized she may stick out for appearing so plain.

"Welcome to Vincent Vineyard," a model-thin hostess said, handing them a glossy menu. "Here is a list of the wines that are being served tonight. Be sure to enter the raffle for a chance to win a bottle of our newest Cabernet Sauvignon."

Jake grabbed both menus and led Ella toward a discreet corner before pulling out his phone. "I'm gonna text Miles. See what time he and Charlotte are planning on getting here."

With her eyes glued to the pristine hardwood floor, Ella was careful not to make eye contact with anyone. She wondered whether any of the Vincents had seen her yet. A quick scan of the room didn't reveal any familiar faces.

"Did Miles respond yet?" she asked, leaning into a high-top table while turning away from the crowd.

"Not yet. But the text just went through a second ago."

No sooner than Jake responded, Miles and Charlotte came strolling through the lobby. Charlotte was decked out in a fitted red tank dress and matching stilettos, while Miles and Jake appeared to have coordinated in advance as they were both wearing pale blue button-down shirts and European cut navy slacks.

Ella raised her hand in the air, waving frantically as relief set in. Charlotte blew her a kiss, then led Miles in their direction.

"Hey!" Ella said, throwing her arms around her sister. "I am so glad that you're here."

"Hi. Umm, didn't I just see you earlier today?"

Charlotte had no clue why being there for moral support meant so much to Ella. For the time being, she planned on keeping it that way.

"It's just nice having you here. That's all."

A server approached carrying a tray filled with wine flights and a charcuterie board. "Good evening, everyone. Would you like to try our collection of reds?"

"Absolutely," Jake told him. "What do we have here?"

"We've got our newest Cabernet Sauvignon, which is a wonderful blend of cherry and spices. If you enjoy rich, fruity flavors, then you'll love the Merlot. Our Zinfandel is a delicious blend of zesty, succulent strawberries. The Pinot Noir is one of my favorites thanks to its light, delicate blend of berries. And lastly, we've got our Malbec. People love the smoky plumlike flavor. All of the grape varieties used to produce these wines were grown right here at Vincent Vineyard. If you taste something you love, which I'm certain you will, please be sure to purchase a bottle before the end of the evening. Enjoy."

The moment the server was out of earshot, Jake turned to the group. "Now that's what I like to call a hard sell."

"Or maybe the man is just passionate about his wines," Miles said, picking up a glass of Zinfandel and taking a sip.

Charlotte gave him a side-eye. "Of course you'd start out with the strongest one."

"And you know it."

"Okay, now," Jake interjected. "Let's not lose sight of why we're here. Miles, have you spotted any of our unofficial persons of interest yet?"

"I have." He nodded at Charlotte, then Ella. "All right, ladies. You've both scoured the Vincent family's social media accounts and know what they look like. But let us give you a quick refresher. There's a portrait of our murder victim, Don Vincent, hanging over the fireplace. His wife, Claire, is standing to the left of it."

Ella leaned into Jake. "The thin older woman with the chignon, dressed in the black-and-white tweed Chanel suit?" she asked, as if she didn't already know.

"Bingo," Jake replied. "The two men she's speaking to are her sons. The oldest, Tyler, is the tall muscular one wearing the bright Burberry suit. His brother, Greer, is standing behind him. He's the short stubby guy with his hands in his pockets, dressed in a white polo shirt and black slacks."

"Well the difference between those two is clear," Charlotte said. "And they're at odds with one another, right?"

"Right," Miles confirmed. "Which is interesting, considering they worked together as a team to go against their father when he was still alive."

Covering his head with his hand, Jake turned away from

the crowd. "Uh-oh. It looks like people are starting to notice us." He took a sip of Cabernet Sauvignon and popped a slice of smoked Gouda inside his mouth. "Just be cool. Act like you're here for the wine and hors d'oeuvres."

Ella followed his wandering gaze. Her eyes landed on Claire, who was staring in their direction.

She gasped, spinning around while praying she hadn't been spotted.

"You're fine, hon," Jake said, caressing her shoulder reassuringly. "Just because Miles and I work in law enforcement doesn't mean we shouldn't be here. Relax. Have some wine."

He pulled a glass of Pinot Noir from the wooden flight and handed it to her. Slowly pivoting, Ella glanced over at the fireplace. Claire was no longer there.

"So, back to the Vincents," Jake continued. "When it came to Don's sons, there was one thing that he did give in to. Don allowed them to arrange those group tours I'd mentioned at dinner, and build a visitors' area where guests could unwind over food, drinks and live music. But that was a decision he quickly grew to regret."

"Why is that?" Charlotte asked.

"Wait," Ella interjected. "I think I saw the answer to that question in one of the case files. Shortly before his death, didn't Don allow a bus full of visitors to come to the vineyard, and they ended up getting into a huge fight?"

"That's exactly right," Miles confirmed. "Not only that, but Don got into a heated confrontation with a few of the guys who'd gotten drunk and wandered off into the business offices. Of course he thought they were looking to steal trade secrets or something."

"Oh, wow," Charlotte uttered. "Whatever came of the situation?"

"Not much," Jake told her. "Don reported the incident

to police. A couple of officers showed up to the scene and investigated the situation. But no one involved in the fight was talking, and the guys who'd wandered into the office area claimed they had gotten lost while searching for the men's room. No arrests were made."

Ella drained her glass, resisting the urge to grab another. "Considering Don was killed shortly after that incident, I think those visitors need to be looked at again."

Nodding in agreement, Jake declared, "Trust me, they are definitely on the list of folks who will be questioned."

A sudden hush fell over the room. All eyes turned toward the mosaic-tile floating staircase. Two women stood at the top of the landing, but only one stood out.

Jada Vincent.

Ella's entire body stiffened at the sight of her. Tyler's stunning wife, whose sense of style was just as flamboyant as his, glided down the stairs in a pair of strappy six-inch heels. Her bone straight extensions appeared longer than the monogrammed Gucci dress clinging to her size-zero frame. Her fingers, which were adorned with a variety of blinding diamond rings, were tipped off with a set of pointy black acrylic nails.

Greer's wife, Faith, skulked closely behind her. She was at least a foot shorter and appeared much wider than her sister-in-law thanks to her run-over ballet flats and over-sized gray shift dress.

"Okay, so…" Charlotte whispered in Ella's ear. "These two look familiar. Remind me who they are again?"

"Did you even *glance* at the case files and social media accounts Jake gave us to review?"

"Hey, talk to me after you become a new mother of a demanding mini diva who insists on constant cuddles and feedings and changing and—"

"All right, all right," Ella interrupted, just noticing the dark circles underneath Charlotte's eyes. "I get it." She discreetly pointed toward the staircase. "The woman in the Gucci dress is Jada Vincent, Tyler's wife. She's the sales director of Vincent Vineyard. The other woman is Faith Vincent, Greer's wife. She works as a sales and marketing rep."

"Geez. Talk about keeping it in the family. I see they're both coupled up with the right brothers. Jada's flashy swag matches Tyler's to a T, and Faith's understated look goes right along with Greer's."

After polishing off a few slices of prosciutto, Jake wiped his mouth and grabbed his cell. "Listen, now that the wives have made their grand entrance, I think we should split up and gather some new intel. Let's go socialize. See what the crowd is buzzing about."

"And by crowd," Miles said to Ella and Charlotte, "Jake primarily means the members of the Vincent family."

"Exactly. Miles, Charlotte, why don't you two take the left side of the room while Ella and I take the right? We'll reconvene somewhere in the middle, let's say, in about thirty minutes?"

"Sounds like a plan, Chief." Miles took Charlotte's hand in his. "Happy mingling!"

The pangs of anxiety that had plagued Ella's stomach upon their arrival came back with a vengeance.

"Shall we?" Jake asked, offering her his arm.

She held onto him tighter than necessary, forcing her laden feet to follow him over to the jazz quartet playing near the back of the lobby.

"See the guy who Claire is talking to?" he asked, gesturing toward the terrace.

"I do. Doesn't he work for the vineyard?"

"He does. His name is Manuel Ruiz, and he man-this place. Word is Claire's been dumping all of her responsibilities off on him. So he knows the inner workings of the vineyard better than anyone. When we brought him in for questioning after Don's murder, he was extremely tight-lipped."

"Do you consider him a suspect?"

"Not at all. But I do think Manuel knows way more than what he's told us. Once I start bringing people in for questioning, he'll be one of the first."

Ella's heartbeat stuttered when Claire looked in their direction, then came sauntering over.

Please don't say anything...

"Chief Love," she said. "How nice to see you here. Last time we spoke, you were still working as a detective. Congratulations on your promotion to chief of police."

"Thank you, Mrs. Vincent. It's nice to see you as well. How have you been?"

Her eyelids, which were heavily embellished with thick false lashes, fluttered toward the floor. "I've been...okay, I guess. Some days are better than others. Knowing Don's killer is still out there makes me feel extremely uneasy—"

Claire paused, her voice cracking underneath the weight of her words. Manuel swooped in and wrapped his arm around her. "It's okay, Mrs. Vincent. Now that Clemmington's got a new chief in place, let's hope we'll get some answers."

Manuel's bushy eyebrows shot up, accentuating the lines running across his leathery sunburned forehead. His chubby jowls trembled with emotion. Ella's chest tightened at the sight. For a brief second, she forgot about her own concerns. But when Claire's attention turned to her, they came rushing back.

"Oh!" Jake uttered, placing a hand on the small of Ella's

back. "My apologies. I'm being rude. Mrs. Vincent, Mr. Ruiz, this is my girlfriend, Ella Bowman."

Shards of jagged nerves crawled from the soles of Ella's feet to the top of her spine. She extended her jittery hand, hoping Claire wouldn't remember her.

"It's nice to meet you, Mrs. Vincent."

"Pleasure to meet you as well, dear."

Claire's handshake was weak. Ella clenched her jaw, bracing herself for what was sure to come next. What would Jake say when he found out they'd met before? Under inappropriate circumstances, no less?

But instead of calling her out, Claire's dainty hand slipped from her grip. The faraway look in Claire's pale gray eyes told her everything she needed to know. Claire had no idea who she was.

The weight of relief almost knocked Ella to the ground. She'd gone unrecognized. At least for the time being…

"Testing, testing, one, two. Testing, one, two."

The crowd's attention shifted to Tyler, who was standing near the fireplace with a microphone in hand. The jazz quartet quieted their rendition of Frank Sinatra's "The Way You Look Tonight" before stopping completely.

"Jada, my love, could you please join me?" Tyler crooned.

His wife sashayed across the room, flinging her hair over her shoulder while giggling like a schoolgirl. Greer, who's fallen expression was riddled with annoyance, hovered in a corner while whispering in Faith's ear.

Sidling up to Claire, Manuel muttered, "Looks like somebody's upset that he's not included in the big speech."

"Well, the boys are just going to have to work things out among themselves."

"I'm sorry, Mrs. Vincent, but I disagree. Respectfully, of course. *You're* the one who's gonna have to work things out and make a decision. You know, choose which of your sons will take over as president of the vineyard."

Jake nudged Ella's arm and pointed toward his ear The pair moved in closer, listening in as Claire emitted a low moan.

"*Yes*," she drawled, crossing her arms over her frail chest. "I do plan on making a decision before one of them strangles the other to death and forces his way into the position."

"Ladies and gentlemen!" Tyler boomed. "Thank you so much for being here this evening. Tonight means the world to my family and I, and we're honored that you've chosen to join us. Since the death of my father, running Vincent Vineyard has been challenging to say the least. But my love of this business, along with the support of the Clemmington community, has helped keep me going."

Manuel rolled his eyes. "Why is this man speaking as if he's operating the vineyard on his own? Or at all for that matter?"

"*Please*," Claire hissed, swatting his shoulder. "Now is not the time. Any issues you have should be tabled for now and addressed at our Monday meeting."

"You let that oldest son of yours get away with murder, Mrs. Vincent. No pun intended. He's getting more and more out of control. You have got to do something about his behavior before he—"

"That's enough!" Claire spat so loudly that several guests turned and stared. She raised her hand, silently apologizing, then leaned toward Manuel. "We will continue this conversation later, privately, inside my office."

"Yes, ma'am."

"Over time," Tyler continued, "I was able to convince my father to open his mind, which in turned helped to expand the Vincent Vineyard brand. He'd even agreed to allow visitor tours and build an outdoor deck shortly before his passing."

"*Passing*?" Manuel whisper-screamed. "The man was murdered!"

The steely look Claire shot at him immediately shut Manuel up.

Tyler strolled to the center of the room while wiping away invisible tears. "Speaking of Don's passing, I am proud to say that I have not allowed this tragedy to stop me from carrying on my father's legacy. The cloud surrounding his death illuminates with a silver lining. We have gathered here tonight to celebrate Vincent Vineyard's newest Cabernet Sauvignon. It was made from one of our more recent grape varieties, one which—which, uh…"

He hesitated, turning to his wife. "Jada, would you like to explain to our guests the details of this mouthwatering new offering?"

Her pointy heels screeched along the floor as she scrambled toward the mic. "Well, umm…this wine is delicious, guys! And it's extremely special to all of us because of—because of the, uh…"

A wave of murmurs rippled through the crowd. Guests peered at one another, their eyes wide and shoulders hunching in confusion.

"What an embarrassment!" Ella whispered to Jake.

The murmurs quieted as Greer trudged across the lobby, only to pick up again when Tyler snatched the mic from Jada.

"I guess it wouldn't be right for me to bask in *all* the celebratory glory," he quipped, a slight scowl peeking through his overly Botoxed face. "My brother, Greer, did play a part in producing this spectacular new wine. I'll let him take a few moments to tell you more about it."

Sweat poured from Greer's temples. He stood next to his brother, shuffling his feet from side to side while staring down at the floor. Without glancing in Tyler's direction, he grabbed the mic and stammered, "He—hello everyone."

"Oh, *Lord*," Claire snipped. "Please don't let my child stand up there and embarrass me."

"Just give him a minute," Manuel assured her. "You know your son. He usually needs time to gather himself."

After finally looking up at the crowd, Greer cleared his throat. "As my brother mentioned, it is an honor to be here celebrating with you. I am so pleased at how we've managed to keep my father's spirit alive through this amazing new Cabernet Sauvignon. It is a full-bodied, deliciously tart wine made from a hybrid grape, formed by the merging of Cabernet Franc and Sauvignon Blanc."

A soft smile spread across Claire's face. She held her hand to her mouth, whispering to Manuel, "Gold star for Greer!"

"See, I told you. The man is good. Good enough to be the president of Vincent Vineyard if you ask me. And before you even say it, I know. You don't want to make a decision just yet. But what it really boils down to is that Tyler's your favorite. However, you're not ready for that discussion. So I'll leave well enough alone."

Ella's eyes widened at Manuel's boldness. She held her breath, waiting for Claire's response. But the Vincent family matriarch remained silent, turning her attention back to Greer.

"Our wonderful servers will be passing around glasses of this savory full-bodied red. We hope you enjoy the powerful presence of chocolate, pepper, berries and oak. Please leave your feedback on the scorecards, and if you're inclined to take a bottle—"

"Or a case!" Tyler yelled out.

"...of wine home with you," Greer continued, ignoring his brother, "please do so. Thank you again for coming, and my family and I will be walking around to answer any questions you may have. Enjoy the rest of the evening."

He lowered his head humbly as the crowd broke into applause. Tyler pushed his way in front of Greer, as if the praise were for him.

"What a shame," Ella muttered. She eyed the exit, wondering if she'd be lucky enough to leave the tasting without running into the other family members.

As soon as the thought crossed her mind, Tyler and Jada came rushing over.

No, no, no!

They stopped in their tracks when Manuel began clapping loudly.

"Bravo, Greer! Wonderful speech! Simply *marvelous*!"

The crowd followed suit, their cheers growing louder. Tyler grabbed Jada's hand and dragged her back to the middle of the floor. He took a full bow, then raised his arm in the air as if he'd just won an Olympic gold medal. Jada appeared to understand the applause wasn't for her as she slowly backed away, sheepishly joining Greer's wife in the corner.

Claire nudged Manuel's arm. "See, now you're being an instigator."

"Not at all, Mrs. Vincent. I'm just giving props to the man who deserves them. But seriously? You have got to make a decision and name one of your sons president. Who's it gonna be? *Tyler*," Manuel grumbled, his eyes rolling into the back of his head, "or my main man, Greer?"

Claire ignored him, lifting two glasses of wine off a passing server's tray.

"Thank you," Manuel said to her while reaching for a glass.

"Aht aht. These are both for me," she retorted before rushing off into the crowd.

"I'd better take advantage of this moment," Jake whispered to Ella just as Miles and Charlotte walked up.

"Mr. Ruiz," Jake said, "could I please talk to you for a minute?"

"Sure, Chief. I need to check on our VIP guests in the tasting room, but I've got a few minutes. What can I do for you?"

"I've been reviewing the case files from Don Vincent's murder investigation. My father insisted on conducting the majority of the interviews since he'd taken Mr. Vincent's death so personally."

Manuel's head dropped. He blinked rapidly, pressing his fingertips against his eyes.

"Are you all right, Mr. Ruiz?"

"Yep." He sniffled, scanning the room as if to see whether anyone was watching. "You being here just…just takes me back to the moment when Mr. Vincent was found stabbed to death and the fallout afterward. Accusations were being thrown around, business took a huge hit and the entire Vincent family has been at odds ever since. And who's in the middle of it all, fighting to hold everything together? *Me*."

"I understand that. And I'm sorry to hear it. I'm actually in the process of reopening Mr. Vincent's case. The family deserves answers, as do you and the rest of the Clemmington community."

"*The family*," Manuel snorted, grabbing a glass of wine off the nearest tray and downing it in a few gulps. "Good luck with that."

A commotion broke out on the other side of the room. As

a crowd gathered, security stepped in attempting to break it up.

"Let's go," Jake said to Miles, setting off toward the brawl.

"No!" Manuel yelled, grabbing both officers and pulling them back. "Please, I respectfully ask that you stand down and let security handle it. I don't want our guests to see law enforcement confronting the brothers."

"The brothers?" Miles asked.

When the crowd broke, Jake realized it was Tyler and Greer who'd gotten into an altercation.

"Chief Love," Manuel said, "I'll take it from here. But I definitely want to speak with you about Mr. Vincent's murder. There are some things I didn't share after his death that I'm ready to reveal now. I'm tired of covering for people who should probably be behind bars."

Jake reached inside his pocket and pulled out a business card. "Call me. As soon as possible."

"You two need to cool off!" Claire yelled at her sons. "In my office. Now!"

Manuel shook Jake's hand, then slowly backed away. "I need to go and help diffuse this situation. I'll call you soon, Chief."

After he rushed off, Jake rejoined his group. "I think our work here is done. Why don't we head back to my place, exchange notes and discuss our next move?"

The words were barely out of his mouth before Ella linked arms with him and made a beeline for the exit. "Sounds like a plan."

"Charlotte and I got a lot of intel while eavesdropping on Jada and Faith," Miles affirmed.

"Same here," Ella said over her shoulder. "Except ours came from Claire and Manuel."

"Who knew this case would start taking shape at a wine tasting event of all places," Jake quipped.

Who knew I'd escape the event unscathed, Ella thought, ducking her head while rushing out the door.

Chapter Four

"How long have we been out here?" Charlotte panted.

"It hasn't even been twenty minutes, sis."

Ella rounded the corner of Clemmington High School's six-lane track, jogging at a slower pace than normal. Since having the baby, Charlotte had declared it her mission to shed the excess weight. She'd tapped Ella as her personal trainer. But getting Charlotte up and out of the house had proven to be challenging. Ella realized she had to come up with rewards in order to make it happen. That morning, she'd incentivized her sister with a banana smoothie and skinny latte before the day's workout.

"I shouldn't have drank all that coffee," Charlotte huffed. "I think I have to go to the restroom."

"*Again?* You just went five minutes ago!"

Charlotte shrugged, dipping off toward the locker room. Ella grabbed her arm and dragged her back onto the track.

"Oh, no you don't. You are not slick. You're just trying to take another break. Once we hit the two and a half miles mark, you can slow down to a nicely paced walk. But until then, we have to keep moving."

"Ew, you are so annoying."

"Look, I'm just doing what you asked—trying to help

get you back in shape in the event you decide to go back into law enforcement."

"If this is what it's gonna take, I'll opt to remain a stay-at-home mom."

"Yeah, right," Ella muttered. "I'll believe that when I see it. Once you feel comfortable leaving Ari with a nanny, you will be itching to get back on the force. Speaking of which, how would that work with you being a sergeant in River Valley and Miles being a detective here in Clemmington?"

"You know, I haven't even thought that far ahead. For now, I'm just focusing on enjoying motherhood and my engagement. I'll start thinking of wedding ideas once the time is right. But Miles and I have both been through so much. It's nice to concentrate on the good things in life without worry too much about the future. He's gonna be busy anyway now that he and Jake are reopening Don's cold case. But look, enough about me. How are things with you and Jake?"

The question curled Ella's lips into a blushing smile. "Good. *Really* good. I can honestly say that this is the best relationship I've ever been in. I'm talking no toxicity whatsoever. Being friends first really helped. We decided in the beginning to make communication a top priority since that's one of the things that our past relationships were lacking. So, we try our best to be open with one another, and honest…"

Ella's voice trailed off. A whirlwind of thoughts crashed her mind. The statement she'd just made was no longer true. Because she'd been far from honest with Jake as of late. Or anyone else for that matter, considering she had yet to reveal her connection to the Vincent family.

"Hey," Charlotte said, slowing down and nudging her arm. "What's wrong? Where did your mind go just now?"

Ella pulled away, unable to look Charlotte in the eye. She picked the pace back up and clapped her hands. "Come on, let's go! Don't try and distract me from the mission at hand. Keep it moving while we talk."

A loud grunt was all Ella heard behind her as Charlotte jogged to catch up.

"Is there something you're not telling me?" Charlotte asked. "Because you've been acting a bit strange lately. Like something's bothering you, but you're holding it in."

"Nope," Ella lied, the reply shooting out of her mouth so fast that she was certain it sounded disingenuous. "There's nothing going on. My mind does tend to drift toward thoughts of Noel being the Numeric Serial Killer from time to time, and how you and I both almost lost our lives. But, I'm trying to work through all that."

"I still think it would do you some good to go to therapy. Talking with someone could really help. You might—"

"For the thousandth time," Ella interrupted, "I do not need therapy!"

"Okay!"

Ella spun around, not realizing she'd gained enough speed to leave her sister behind.

"I need a break, dammit," Charlotte continued, stumbling toward a nearby water fountain and taking a long drink. "Let's hit the bleachers and talk."

Here we go...

Ella took her time walking off the track. The soles of her black running shoes dragged across the rust-colored rubberized surface. Each freshly painted white line separating the lanes blurred as she thought of all the questions Charlotte may spring on her.

"Have a seat," Charlotte said, plopping down on a steel bench and banging her palm against the spot next to her.

The muscles in Ella's thighs tightened as she sat down. She stared straight ahead at the Go Clemmington Coyotes!

sign planted across the track, already dreading the conversation before it had even begun.

"Hey," Charlotte began, "whatever came of the eyewitnesses and surveillance footage from that incident at the fall festival? Was Jake able to uncover anything that would help catch your attacker?"

"No, unfortunately. Jake did photo lineups for the eyewitnesses who claimed to have seen the suspect running through the corn maze. But none of them could make a definitive choice. As for the surveillance footage that security was supposed to turn over, they sent videos from the wrong day. By the time they tried to retrieve the footage from the night I was there, it had already been recorded over."

"Ugh, are you serious?"

"Yep."

"Well, don't lose hope, El. You know Jake is working hard on the case. Both yours and Don's. By the way, I love that he's including you in the investigation."

"I do too. It's sweet that he's so determined to keep me occupied while I'm on a work hiatus."

Charlotte slid toward the edge of the bleacher, stretching her calves against the row below her. "What do you think is really going on between those Vincent brothers? They have such a strange dynamic."

"They really do. And not only is it strange, but it's destructive. We know why though. They're both vying for that position of president and seem willing to do whatever it takes to get it."

"Even if it means killing for the position?" Charlotte asked.

"I believe so. Especially considering how they—"

You're talking too much!

"And their *wives*," Ella continued, quickly shifting gears. "That Jada seems just as bad a Tyler."

"Oh, for sure. Miles and I overheard her talking to some of the guests at the wine tasting. She is so superficial. All she did was brag about the new red convertible Maserati Tyler just bought her, their lake house in Tahoe and the private jet they're looking to purchase. Throughout the conversation, she kept waving her left hand in the air, flashing that obnoxious wedding ring set. In total, it looked to be about twenty carats!"

"What about Greer's wife, Faith? She seems pretty quiet. But pleasant."

Charlotte nodded in agreement. "She is, from what I could tell. One thing about her though. When it comes to Vincent Vineyard? The woman knows her stuff. I heard her speaking to some guests, and unlike Jada, Faith's conversation was all about the business. She rattled off so many facts about the grape varieties they grow, the distillery's new stainless steel fermentation vessel that doesn't add tannins to the wine, how the shape of a wine glass can affect the flavor. By the time we left the event, I felt like a sommelier!"

"Hmm, interesting. And how about Tyler's big speech? He had all the confidence in the world while addressing the crowd, but nothing prolific to share. Greer had to step in and save him from complete embarrassment."

"Then Tyler repaid him by starting a fight. It's terrible how Tyler seems to be the brother who's always in the forefront, when it should obviously be Greer. Same thing with Jada. She's the sales director, while Faith is a lower ranking sales rep. It should be the other way around."

Ella stood and propped her foot against the bench, stretching her hamstrings. "You know what they say. The squeaky wheel gets the oil. Greer and Faith need to step it up and be more vocal. He's clearly the better man for the job of president. But when Jake and I overheard their mother speaking with Manuel, it sounded as if she didn't want to play favorites by picking one son over the other. Manuel was trying to be the voice of reason and convince her that Greer is the best choice. But she was trying not to hear it."

"*Well*," Charlotte moaned as she dragged herself off the bleacher. "Lucky for us, we don't have to worry about helping Claire figure out better ways to run her business. We're just here to assist our men in finding her husband's killer. My money is on Tyler. He seems like the ruthless type who'd do anything to get ahead, whether he deserves the top spot or not."

"And that wife of his seems like she'd support him in any way she could if it meant beefing up their bank account." Ella broke into a slow jog. "Come on, let's get back to it. Two more laps around the track."

"Grr," Charlotte groaned, her sneakers scuffling against the asphalt. "And what are you gonna treat me to in return for these last laps?"

"How does a Chinese chicken salad from The Dearborn Grill sound?"

"Like something worth running for!" Charlotte picked up the pace, jogging alongside Ella to the rhythm of her steps. "So if you had to take a guess, who do you think is behind Don's murder?"

"Claire," Ella responded without hesitation.

"Really? Why is that?"

"Because technically, she had the most to gain. The vineyard is all hers now. Regardless of who takes over as president, Claire still holds the power. Not to mention if she was in fact having an affair, Don's death would mean she could continue doing so in peace—without worrying about getting busted or threats of a divorce. Plus, I don't know. There was something sketchy about her when she was talking to Manuel at the wine tasting. I just can't put my finger on it."

The urge to share her secret about the Vincents nipped at the back of Ella's throat. She swallowed it down, not ready to deal with the questioning. Or the judgment.

"THANKS AGAIN FOR LUNCH, SIS," Charlotte said as she and Ella exited The Dearborn Grill. "Next time, I'll treat."

"I'd love it if we could just get your workouts in without the promise of a reward. Especially when that reward is tied to food—"

A pinging cell phone stopped Ella mid-sentence.

"Oh, *sorry!*" Charlotte quipped, throwing her hand in the air. "I can't hear you over all the loud beeping."

"Yeah, sure you can't."

While Charlotte checked her phone, Ella glanced down the block, contemplating whether she should walk back to Jake's place or go home with Charlotte and wait for him to pick her up after work.

As autumn settled upon Clemmington, the cozy vibe of the enchanting streets appeared more charming than usual. Leaves on the maidenhair and sweet gum trees had already transformed into eye-popping shades of gold, purple and red. Front porches were decorated with everything from pumpkins and gourds to orange mums and mini haystacks. Residents had switched out their tank tops and tees for oversized cable-knit sweaters. The fall season was in full swing, and Ella was looking forward to soaking up every bit of it—especially with Jake.

"Did you hear me?" Charlotte asked.

Ella spun around, realizing she hadn't heard a word her sister said.

"No, sorry. What'd you say?"

Charlotte propped her hand onto her hip. "Ma'am, what is it with you and all this drifting off into space? Are you sure you're okay?"

"Yes. I'm fine. I'm great, actually. I was just thinking about how happy I am being here in Clemmington. Enjoying my favorite time of the year, being with the man I love…"

"And being here with your sister and niece too, right?"

"Of course! Now, what were you saying?"

"I was asking if you wanna come home with me and wait for Jake to pick you up. I can make us some hot chocolate and light the outdoor firepit, you can visit with Ari and shower her with kisses."

"Ooh, that sounds very tempting. But can I take a rain-check? I'd love to walk home and enjoy the sunset."

"*Walk?* But Jake's place is almost two miles away. I'm less than two minutes away. Wouldn't it make more sense for you to just wait for a ride home? Or I can drive you now if you need to get back sooner."

Ella reached out and embraced Charlotte tightly. "Thanks, sis. But no, I'm good. I'll call you when I get home."

"I've somehow found a way to take offense to this. I think what you're really trying to say is that you need to burn more calories because I slowed you down out there on the track this morning."

"Ha! That isn't even close to what I'm saying. But wait, now that you mention it…"

When Ella pulled away, she noticed a scowl on her sister's face.

"You do know that I was just joking, right?"

"Yeah, I know. I was just thinking about you walking home alone. Are you sure you'll be okay?"

Flashbacks of the attack inside the corn maze raced through Ella's mind.

Stop it. That was just a prank. Don't do that to yourself.

"Of course, Sergeant Bowman. I'll be fine."

"All right." Charlotte threw her a slight wave goodbye but didn't budge from the spot where she was standing.

Slowly backing away, Ella blew her a kiss. "I promise to call as soon as I get to Jake's. Now, don't worry about me. Go on home. I'm sure Ari misses you."

"Call me *as soon as* you get home!" Charlotte insisted before finally turning around and walking off.

Ella pulled out her wireless headphones and connected them to her phone. She tapped her "Autumn on the West Coast" playlist and strolled down the street to the rhythm of "September" by Earth, Wind and Fire.

A sweet vanilla-like scent filled the air. It sparked thoughts of Christmas. Ella took a look around, realizing it was coming from the balsam fir evergreens lining the businesses' doorways.

Before reaching the end of the block, she thought about stopping by the grocery store to pick up something for dinner. She and Jake had been ordering out constantly. Now that he'd officially reopened Don's cold case, Ella figured a home-cooked meal would do him some good.

She forged ahead, putting a little pep in her step as she hit the corner. Ella had stood at the intersection a couple of times before. Instinct told her to make a left and head down Hollow Lane. She peered into the distance, hoping she was going in the right direction.

Or you could just use Google Maps, Ella reminded herself. She opened the app and entered Fox & Sons Gourmet Market. Walking directions popped up. The store was twenty minutes away on foot.

Ugh...

Ella toyed with the idea of heading home and making do with whatever was in the refrigerator. But as far as she could remember, that consisted of a few eggs, a can of tuna, wilted arugula and a box of baking soda.

She envisioned surprising Jake with grilled lamb chops, scalloped potatoes, glazed carrots, strawberry cheesecake and a nice bottle of Bordeaux.

"Yep. Off to the store I go."

Continuing her trek down Hollow Lane, the street appeared fairly desolate—a far cry from busy Yellow Bell Avenue where the restaurant was located. Streetlights were few and far between, darkening the road as the sun quickly set. Front yards were empty as schoolchildren had already been ushered inside. Porch lights on the bungalow houses had yet to be turned on and only small bits of light crept through the looming tree branches.

The eerie scene sent Ella scurrying toward the end of the block. A barricade stood at the corner. Detour signs hung from each end with arrows pointing to the right. She checked Google Maps. The instructions told her to make a right turn. She tapped the screen and pulled up the detailed directions.

Construction up ahead. Reroute through Gateway Park.

Ella crept toward the park's iron gate. A narrow pathway surrounded by unkempt grass appeared. She pushed past the low hanging branches, marching along the trail while hoping that a snake wouldn't slither through the brush and attack.

The path led to a wide open field. Goalposts stood at either end, but there were no soccer players in sight. The park appeared empty. Ella hit the audio tab in Google Maps.

"Keep straight," the voice instructed. "In a half mile, turn right."

"A half mile!" Ella blurted out, her voice traveling through the wind up toward the darkening sky.

Okay, either you're in or you're out. Don't just stand here. Make a decision and go!

Without giving it another thought, Ella took off running. She breathed in through her nose and out through her mouth, laser focused on the other end of the park. If someone was going to come after her, they'd have to be one heck of a runner.

She stumbled, her ankle twisting on the uneven gray asphalt. But Ella took the hobble like a champ, straightening up and forging ahead without skipping a beat.

In two-three-four, out two-three-four, she internally chanted while inhaling and exhaling.

She removed her headphones and tossed them inside her pocket as strong winds threatened to snatch them up. Ella ignored the oddly shaped shadows bouncing off the path, appearing more like ghostly shadows than swaying tree limbs. The one thing she couldn't ignore, however, was the sound of footsteps thumping behind her.

Stinging pricks stabbed at her calves. A numbing fear threatened to send her tumbling to the ground.

"Do not turn around," she panted, struggling to pick up speed. But thoughts of being attacked again took hold of her muscles, subconsciously slowing her down.

The mix of chilled air and terror dampened Ella's eyes. Everything in front of her blurred. She blinked rapidly, a voice inside her head yelling, *No! Fight. Run faster!*

Ella managed to break through the angst weighing her down. She burst into a full sprint, wiping the tears from her eyes as three magic words appeared up ahead.

Gateway Park Exit.

"Yes!" she squealed. "Thank you!"

The footsteps that had been scuffling behind her grew distant. She pushed open the park's iron gate and ran out, then boldly turned around to see who'd been following her.

A man who looked to be at least eighty years old appeared in the near distance. He was hunched over, barely making his way along the path. He waved at Ella, then held his hands to his mouth.

"Nice sprint, young lady! I remember back when I was able to run like that. Nowadays I'm just glad my legs still work!"

"Thank you!" Ella whimpered with relief, giving him a thumbs-up before falling against a brick column.

You're good. Everything's fine. You've just gotta stop letting your imagination run wild.

"Keep straight," the voice directions in Google Maps instructed. "In thirty feet, your destination will be on the right."

Ella stretched her back, then headed toward the store, emitting an exhilarating whoop when Fox & Sons finally came into view. She sent Charlotte a text, letting her know she'd stopped by the grocery store and asking if she wouldn't mind picking her up and taking her home.

"Because there is no way in hell I'm walking back to Jake's from here."

Within seconds, her phone buzzed. Ella expected to see a response from her sister. But instead, an email popped up from anonymous@anonymous.com.

What in the world is this...

She swiped open the message.

You Are One Bold Bitch, the subject read.

The phone almost fell from Ella's hand. She squeezed her eyes shut, willing herself to read the message.

Come on. You can do this. You have to.

Her eyelids gradually lifted as she scanned the bold letters, typed in all caps.

FIRST YOU HAVE THE AUDACITY TO SHOW UP AT VINCENT VINEYARD, THEN YOU FIND THE NERVE TO STRUT THROUGH MY NEIGHBORHOOD, AND MY PARK? ALONE?? YOU'D BETTER BE GLAD THAT OLD MAN CAME OUTTA NOWHERE. HE SAVED YOUR LIFE. JUST LIKE THAT SECURITY GUARD DID INSIDE THE CORN MAZE. BUT TRUST ME. NEXT TIME, YOU WON'T BE SO LUCKY. ELLA BOWMAN, YOU ARE NOT IN NEVADA ANYMORE. HERE IN CLEMMINGTON, THE ODDS WILL NEVER BE IN YOUR FAVOR...

Chapter Five

Jake sped through Vincent Vineyard's parking lot and pulled into a space near the entrance.

"We're late," he said to Miles.

"Yeah, that's because we shouldn't be here. Tyler was supposed to meet us at the station for questioning. Not on his turf, where he'll be cool and calm in his own element."

"Not necessarily," Jake replied, leading the way toward the door. "Maybe he'll be nervous since we're at the scene where his father was murdered. If Tyler did have anything to do with Don's death, I expect him to be extremely uneasy once he finds out we're obtaining a search warrant."

"True. Either way, I just hope we get some answers."

The officers entered the winery. Tyler and Jada were standing in the middle of the lobby, dressed in matching monogrammed Louis Vuitton outfits.

"These two..." Miles muttered under his breath.

"Gentlemen!" Tyler boomed, approaching the men with open arms. "Welcome back to Vincent Vineyard. Can I get you two anything? A glass of Merlot? Pinot Noir? Our fabulous new Cabernet Sauvignon, perhaps?"

"Thank you, Mr. Vincent," Jake responded, "but Detective Love and I are on duty."

Waving him off, Tyler grunted, "Ahh, who cares about

the rules? You're among friends. I won't tell if you won't. Right, hon?"

He pivoted on the heels of his shiny black snakeskin oxfords, stopping in front of Jada.

"That's right, babe," she gushed through a mouth full of stark white veneers. "So what's it gonna be, fellas? I'll bring out whatever you want."

"We're good, thanks," Miles reiterated sternly. "Mr. Vincent, is there somewhere we can talk? Privately?"

Tyler's arms fell by his side as his entire body deflated. "Yeah, we can meet in my office. Jada, could you please excuse us?"

"Of course. But before you all go…" She paused, reaching for Jake's chest. "Are you *sure* I can't get you two a glass of—"

"*Jada*!" Tyler snapped so loudly that she almost jumped out of her shoes. "Excuse us. *Please*. I'll circle back with you later."

Her lower lip trembled as she stormed off, her stilettos screeching against the hardwood floors.

"You're leaving scratches!" Tyler yelled to her back. "Pick up your feet!" He balled his right hand inside the left and cracked his knuckles. "Gentlemen, follow me. I'll show you to my office."

Jake and Miles threw one another exasperated glances on the way there.

"So, Chief Love, you were pretty vague when we spoke on the phone about this meeting. What exactly is it you'd like to speak with me about?"

"We were hoping to discuss your father's murder, in detail. Since you're the one who found his body, we want you to walk us through exactly what happened."

"But I already told your father everything I knew back when he was investigating the case."

"We're well aware of that," Miles interjected. "But now that a year has passed and some of the shock has worn off, you may remember something that slipped your mind during the initial investigation."

Tyler stopped at the bottom of the staircase. "I can guarantee you that this situation is just as traumatizing now as it was back when it first occurred."

Miles peered at him, slowly nodding his head. "I understand."

"However, you may be right. I'm willing to talk about that day. At least what I can remember of it."

As Tyler headed up the stairs, Jake held Miles back.

"Mr. Vincent?" the chief said.

"Yes?"

"Instead of talking us through that day, would you be willing to walk us through it instead?"

"What do you mean?"

"Are you up for taking us out to the grape fields and retracing your steps, showing us exactly what happened when you found your father's body?"

An uncomfortable silence filled the lobby. Tyler's eyes darted from Jake and Miles to the front door, as if he were contemplating making a run for it.

"Look, if you think that would be too much for you to do—"

"Nope," Tyler interrupted, bouncing back down the stairs. "That's not it. I just—this won't be easy. I'm still suffering from PTSD over the whole ordeal." He squared his broad gym-honed shoulders and readjusted the lapel on his fitted blazer. "But I'm up for it. Let's do this."

Faux confidence burst from his feet as Tyler led them

onto the terrace. Jake stepped outside, inhaling the fragrant scent of grapevine flowers. Yellow beams of light streamed from the sky, fading in between layers of fog that had rolled in off the Pacific Ocean. The vast rows of grapes were barely visible underneath the haze.

"Wow, this is stunning," Miles said. "How large is the field?"

"Seventy-two acres," Tyler uttered, staring out at the gentle slopes. "Dad was so proud of what he'd built. From harvesting the grapes to bottling the wine, that man knew how to do it all. He could've run this place alone if he had to. For a short time, right after purchasing it, he actually did—"

When Tyler's voice wavered, Jake placed a hand on his shoulder. "I'm so sorry. Are you sure you're up for this? We can talk in your office if you think that would be easier."

"Nope. I'm up for this. Let's go."

The brothers followed him along the dirt paths tucked between wide rows of grapevines. Gusts of wind sent billows of dust swirling around Tyler's designer ostrich shoes. He didn't seem to care. He was the type who'd toss them in the garbage and order a new pair.

"I found my father's body up ahead," he mumbled, pointing toward an area filled with clusters of small tightly packed purple grapes. "In the middle of his beloved Pinot Noir vines. He was having so much trouble with that variety last year. They were beginning to rot, which, according to Greer, was due to the grapes' thin skin. I kept telling my dad to just let it go. We were losing a ton of money. Pinot Noir isn't even one of our bestsellers. But *no*. That man was determined to make it work. All because Alan Monroe's winery had produced a successful line of it."

Jake was tempted to ask why he was so concerned with

the vineyard's profits rather than his father's death. But he refrained, making a mental note of it instead.

"What time did you arrive at the vineyard that day, Mr. Vincent?" the chief asked.

"Umm…at around 11:00 a.m."

"Is that what time you normally arrive?"

"Yes, for the most part. My father would usually get here at around 7:00 a.m. And Greer comes in soon after, at about 7:30 a.m. or so."

"I guess this is a question I could ask Greer when we speak to him," Miles said, "but is there any reason he didn't find your father's body first, since he was here hours before you'd arrived?"

"*Humph*," Jake huffed, scratching his head in feigned confusion. "Greer claimed he was in the distillery most of the morning, supervising the installation of the new wine press. Key word, *claimed*."

"Duly noted," Jake said, opening the Notes app on his cell phone and typing in his exact words. "And this area here is the precise location of where the body was found?"

Tyler's head fell. He closed his eyes, barely nodding while mouthing the word *yes*.

Despite having plenty of photos from the crime scene inside the case file, Jake used his phone to snap several more. "Can you tell me what condition your father was in when you saw him?"

"He, uh…he was lying on his side, with his back to me. I ran to him, thinking that he may have fallen out under the hot sun, or even had a heart attack. But when I turned him over, there was a pool of blood gathered beneath his body. His shirt was soaked, right in the chest area. When I saw that, I thought a coyote may have attacked him, or he'd fallen into one of the wooden posts. I just couldn't wrap my mind around the thought of my father being killed."

"So it never occurred to you that a knife could've done that damage? Or a bullet even?"

"No," Tyler deadpanned, his left eyelid twitching uncontrollably.

"What did you do after finding your father?"

"I yelled for help. I didn't have my cell phone on me at the time. After a while, I realized no one could hear me all the way out here. I hated leaving my father alone. But I had to call 9-1-1. So, that's what I did. Went straight to my office and called the authorities."

Miles pulled a small notepad from his blazer pocket and flipped through several pages. "If I can recall correctly, when your wife was questioned, she stated that you went running to *her* office, saying you'd found your father's body. This occurred before 9-1-1 was called. Case notes also state that your wife was the one who actually made the 9-1-1 call."

Tyler pulled a monogrammed handkerchief from his pocket and dabbed it over his dampening face. "That could be the case. I'm not sure, Detective. It's been a long time since all that went down. I know you don't expect me to remember every single little detail."

"No," Jake replied. "We don't. But the problem is, that's not what we'd consider a little detail. Not being able to recall whether you were the one who dialed 9-1-1 is pretty significant—"

"Hold on," Tyler interrupted, backing away from the officers. "Did you all come out here to gain new insight? Or accuse me of murder? Because if it's the latter, I'm going to have to ask you to leave and not speak to me again until my attorney is present."

His defensiveness etched a bright red flag into Jake's brain.

Defuse the situation before he lawyers up...

"That's not the case at all, Mr. Vincent," Jake insisted. "Our only goal is to gather as much information as possible and bring justice to your family."

"Yeah, right," Tyler rebutted. "Need I remind you that it was Clemmington PD who dropped the ball on finding my father's killer. Not me. So please refrain from speaking to me in that accusatory tone, inside *my* place of business, and asking incriminating questions while my lawyer isn't here."

"Again, that was not my intention—"

"*Also*," Tyler interrupted, "I do understand that you're the new chief of police. But don't let that go to your head. Trying too hard to score a touchdown could cause you to fumble the ball, *rookie*."

Jake's entire body stiffened. His hands rolled into tight fists as the urge to square up left him shaking.

Raising his watch in the air, Tyler eyed the time. "Sorry to cut this conversation short, or should I say, interrogation?"

"No," Miles replied flatly. "You had it right the first time."

"Okay, well, sorry to cut this *conversation* short, but according to my Hublot Unico, I've got a meeting to get to. A major wine distributor's coming in, and I can't be late. God forbid I allow Greer to handle it on his own. He'd bomb it before the presentation even got started. Yet another reason I should've been named president a long time ago..."

Before either of the brothers could respond, Tyler had already set off toward the main building.

"What an obnoxious piece of—"

Jake gripped Miles's shoulder, stopping him mid-sentence. "Keep your cool, man. Let's just continue to give this guy enough room to incriminate himself."

The brothers peered ahead, watching as Tyler climbed

the marble stairs two at a time while typing away on his cell phone.

"What's the next order of business, Chief?" Miles asked.

"Next order of business? We need to talk to Greer."

Chapter Six

Ella carried one of Don Vincent's case files over to the dining room table, careful not to slip on the freshly waxed floors. She glanced at the clock. It was after 6:30 p.m. Jake would be home any minute.

She cracked open the oven door, checking on the Cornish hens. A whiff of the roasting meat drifted through the air, along with hints of the bell peppers, white mushrooms and sweet yellow onions. After lowering the temperature, she shut the door and sat down at the table, sipping a cup of herbal tea while taking a quick look around.

Jake lived in an industrial style two-bedroom loft located in a refurbished building once used to manufacture medical equipment. Large arched windows allowed in plenty of sunlight, while exposed brick, walnut flooring and timber support beams gave the place a sexy masculine feel. The gourmet kitchen and spa bathroom were a far cry from her modest one-bedroom apartment back home, making her feel as though she were living in the lap of luxury.

I could get used to this, Ella thought the moment she'd walked through the door.

Since reopening Don's cold case, Jake's loft had turned into a war room of sorts. Boxes, files, photos and reports were strewn everywhere. Ella had grown tired of the clutter and managed to gather it all inside the office, vowing to try to maintain some semblance of order as she assisted in the investigation.

But keeping his place intact had become the least of her concerns. After the scare at the park and subsequent email, Ella was struggling to figure out how to tell Jake what was going on. The longer she waited, the wearier she grew. Don's investigation was in full swing. Not only was the Vincent family aware of it, but so was the entire Clemmington community. The news made the front page of *The Daily Herald* earlier that week, the headline reading, *New Police Chief Reopens the Case His Father Couldn't Solve.*

The title was triggering for Kennedy, making him feel as though he'd failed the community despite putting in over thirty-five otherwise successful years on the force. As for Jake, the pressure to solve the case went from zero to one hundred within a matter of days. Ella could already see the signs of stress. He hadn't been eating regularly, and sleep had become challenging since he couldn't turn off his brain at night. Pouring over the same case files time and time again in hopes of uncovering missed details wasn't helping matters.

If Ella told Jake the secret she'd been keeping, it would send him over the edge and probably end their relationship. The mere thought sent pangs of devastation crashing through her head.

Just keep it to yourself. At least for the time being...

In the midst of all the madness, Ella had managed to find one solid lead during her investigation. Buried within a stack of crime scene photos were notes taken the day a group of tourists fought at Vincent Vineyard, shortly before Don's death. Ella pulled the names of the men involved and did an online search. She discovered that one of them had a criminal history.

Ben Foray had been arrested in San Diego on charges of forgery, robbery and false imprisonment a few months prior to the brawl. The accuser, whose identity had been kept anonymous, opted not to press charges. Ben walked away a free man.

Five months after the vineyard incident, he was arrested again and charged with corporal injury to a spouse or intimate partner. The most recent news article reported that Ben was out on bail and awaiting trial. Ella thought it would be a good idea to give him another look.

The sound of Jake's keys jiggling outside the door sent a thrill through Ella that jolted her toward the door. She threw her arms around him the moment he walked inside, greeting him with a warm embrace and lingering kiss.

"Welcome home, babe," she murmured.

"Hey you," he said, chuckling in between kisses. "To what do I owe all this love and affection?"

"Just being the good man that you are. That's all."

Jake slid his hand in hers and glanced around the loft. "Wow. It looks great in here. What did you do, hire a cleaning service? And what is that delicious aroma coming from the kitchen?"

"First, no, I didn't hire a cleaning service. I straightened this place up all by myself after realizing I'd made a mess of it with all the boxes and case files. Second, I prepared a nice home-cooked meal for you since you've been working so hard. Seems as if you needed a little pick-me-up."

"That I did. And in turn, I think *you* deserve a special thank-you."

Ella's body grew warm as Jake ran his fingertips along the small of her back. She leaned into him, her lips tasting traces of cedar cologne lingering on his neck. He pulled her closer, kissing her deeper. As he slowly steered her toward the bedroom, Ella stopped, attempting to lead him in the opposite direction.

"Oh, no you don't," she said, laughing softly. "Didn't you get enough of that this morning?"

"Is that a real question?" Jake's gaze roamed her curvaceous figure, which was on full display in a fitted off-white romper. "Let me be clear about one thing. I can *never* get enough of that."

"You'd better cut it out," Ella warned playfully.

"All right, fine. If you're not gonna indulge me in the bedroom, the least you could do is feed me. What are we having?"

"Roasted Cornish hens, lemon herb quinoa and a shaved Parmesan arugula salad with homemade vinaigrette dressing."

"Mmm, sounds amazing." Jake followed Ella into the kitchen and washed up at the sink, then poured two glasses of wine. The articles she'd printed were still scattered across the table. He took a seat and thumbed through each of them. "What's all this?"

"That, my love, is what I'd like to call a hot new lead in the investigation."

"Ooh, really? Tell me more, Detective Bowman."

"While I was scanning the case files, I came across a stack of photos from the crime scene. Stuck in between them were notes that were taken after the fight incident at the vineyard. The articles you're holding are about one of the men who'd been involved. His name is Ben Foray. Does it ring a bell?"

Peering down at the man's photo, Jake shook his head. "No, it doesn't. But we questioned those guys so briefly. No one was hurt during the scuffle, and there wasn't any damage done to the vineyard. I do remember Don wanting to press charges, but Tyler and Greer convinced him not to do so. Especially Tyler. Neither he nor Greer wanted the negative attention. Claire ended up taking the side of her sons. So, despite his better judgment, Don decided to drop it."

"Well, what do you think? Judging by those charges Ben's been hit with in recent months, wouldn't it be worth bringing him back in for questioning?"

"Absolutely. Thank you. This was an awesome discovery. And it's so ironic…"

"What do you mean?"

"I put a call in to Manuel yesterday asking when we could talk. He said he'd come down to the station, because he didn't want to discuss the case at the vineyard. Problem is, he's busy as hell trying to help Greer keep the place up and running smoothly."

"No surprise there. Seems like Claire and Tyler are too focused on their own agendas to get any work done."

"Exactly. So Manuel and I are in the process of getting a meeting on the calendar. In the meantime, I asked him to send me the surveillance footage from that day the fight broke out. He emailed it over yesterday. But I've been so busy that I haven't had a chance to look at it yet."

"Wait, you've already got the footage in your possession?"

"I do."

"That's great! Why don't we take a look at it over dinner?"

"Good idea," Jake said, pulling his laptop from his brown leather messenger bag.

Ella rushed to prepare their plates, barely sitting down before honing in on the computer screen. She held her breath as Jake pulled up his email. "I cannot believe I'm actually a part of this investigation. Well, *unofficially*, but still. Is it wrong for me to be this excited?"

"No, not at all. Do you know how exhilarating it is to solve a case? You're supposed to be excited. That's why being a member of law enforcement is so fulfilling." He turned the laptop in her direction and opened Manuel's message. "Okay, here we go."

Ella scanned the email. "All right, so Manuel has identified the men in the video by their hair and outfits. Ben Foray has a shoulder-length brown mullet and is wearing a dark green polo shirt, Mitch Wilkerson is in the white button-down and has a short blond crew cut and Dylan Lee is bald, dressed in a black T-shirt. Got it?"

"Got it."

There were two videos attached. Jake double-clicked on the first one. A new screen popped up. He pressed Play.

The upstairs area of the vineyard's main building appeared. Within seconds, three men could be seen creeping up the staircase. The first had long curly hair, the second had a blond crew cut and the third was bald.

"Okay, our culprits have been made their grand entrance," Jake said.

"And look at them, opening all the office doors, peeking inside. The audacity…"

The pair watched closely as the men approached a door at the end of the hallway, cracked it open then went inside.

"The police report stated that Don caught these guys in his office," Ella confirmed. "I'm wondering if that's it."

"If it is, then Don should be showing up any second now. Let's keep watching."

Two minutes passed before Don came into the frame.

Manuel was by his side, along with a man wearing a black chauffeur hat and blazer.

"That's the tour bus driver walking with Don and Manuel," Jake said.

Ella leaned in closer, watching as Manuel threw open each door lining the hallway. When he reached the corner office, Don stormed inside. Manuel followed him while the driver stood in the doorway.

"Uh-oh," she said, her eyes widening. "I'm almost afraid to see what's about to happen next."

No sooner than the words were out of her mouth, the three visitors came charging out of the office. The driver tried to stop them, but they tore away from his reach and flew down the hallway. Right before Ben went out of frame, an envelope fell from his pocket. He quickly bent down and grabbed it, barely escaping the driver's grasp before jetting off. Then, the screen went blank.

"*Whoa*," Ella gasped. "Did you see what I just saw?"

"I sure did."

"I wonder what was inside of that envelope."

"Trust me, that'll be one of the first things I ask Ben when I question him."

Jake clicked on the second video. Another screen popped up. This time, the east side of the vineyard appeared, where the visitor area was located. A billowing tan awning hovered above a stone U-shaped bar. Cushioned cream stools and mahogany table sets lined the perimeter. Within seconds, a group of people emerged.

Ella swallowed a forkful of quinoa, then sipped her drink, watching as a few couples took seats at the bar. Larger groups sat at the tables while servers appeared carrying trays filled with wine glasses and charcuterie boards.

Soon after, Mitch and Dylan came into view, shuffling

sheepishly toward the visitor area. Mitch's head hung low while Dylan's hands were stuffed inside his tapered chinos. When Ben resurfaced, his arms were waving wildly through the air as he gestured toward Don and Manuel, who reappeared moments later.

"That Ben is a problem, isn't he?" Ella asked.

"Problem might be an understatement. Judging by what I'm seeing here, on top of everything you shared regarding his criminal history, I need to bring him in for questioning ASAP. The police report from this incident didn't include all these details."

"Tyler and Greer probably downplayed everything since they didn't want to press charges. Whatever it takes to shine a positive light on the vineyard and keep profits rolling in, right?"

"Apparently so." Jake polished off the last of his Cornish hen and wiped his mouth. "On a side note, this meal is fantastic, babe."

"Thank you. I'm glad you're enjoying it. Wait, look!" Ella pulled the computer closer as Ben pointed his finger in Don's face. "We've got action. Mayhem is about to ensue in five, four, three, two—"

Before she hit one, Don flung Ben's arm in the opposite direction. Ben lunged forward with his fists in the air. Manuel stepped in just in time, blocking a blow that almost connected with Don's jaw.

"Where in the hell are Tyler and Greer?" Jake asked right before both sons emerged. Tyler grabbed Ben, helping Manuel hold him off while Greer led his father back inside the main building. The bus driver kept Mitch and Dylan at bay as the rest of the guests looked on in horror.

Ella shook her head, stabbing at a piece of arugula. "Who

would've thought that this type of chaos would take place at such a nice establishment?"

"Well, it's to be expected when you've got criminals and their cronies on your property. Maybe this is one of the reasons why Don didn't want the visitor area to be built in the first place."

Once the Vincent men and Ben were out of the frame, the video cut off.

"I guess I'll be adding a few more persons of interest to my list," Jake said, downing the last of his wine. "I can't thank you enough for finding those notes. And doing the research on Ben. *And* reviewing this surveillance footage with me. This has been a good night. One that I really needed."

"I think we both really needed it."

The smile on Jake's face faded. He stared off into the living room, his mind clearly roaming into heavier territory.

"And it's not over yet," Ella said, giving his hand an affectionate squeeze before clearing the dishes. "Wait until you see what's for dessert."

Jake pivoted, watching as she walked toward the sink. "I can already see what's for dessert. And I'm giving it five stars in advance."

"I'm saving *that* dessert for later. But in the meantime, how about you try some of this?"

"Mmm," he breathed at the sight of a pumpkin meringue pie. "How did you find out about my obsession with Rita's famous pumpkin pie?"

"Through Miles, of course. Lucky for you, Rita added her seasonal fall desserts to the menu earlier this week. I know you've been having a rough go of things since taking on Don's case. So, I wanted to do something special for you tonight."

"And that you did. Thank you."

Jake walked over and brought Ella close, caressing her neck with his lips.

"Mmm, that tickles," she moaned as the nuzzling turned into deep kisses.

He grabbed her by the waist and whispered, "Let's save the pie for later. There's something tastier that I've gotta have. *Right* now."

"Lead the way," Ella said before following him to the bedroom.

When they reached the doorway, Jake paused. "Oh, by the way, you're gonna have to get yourself a nice cocktail dress. If you don't have one already."

"Oh, really? What's the occasion?"

"I received an invitation to a charity event being held by the Vincent family. And you're my plus-one."

"Wait. You...you received *what*?"

"An invitation to a fundraiser being thrown by the Vincents. It's in support of underprivileged students who don't have the funds to pay for college. I usually go every year. After the way things went down when Miles and I met with Tyler, I honestly didn't expect to be invited. But my guess is that Claire's in charge of the guest list."

Ella barely heard a word that Jake had spoken. She was too wrapped up in the thought of having to face the Vincent family yet again.

Chapter Seven

Ella checked her reflection in the full-length mirror hanging behind the bedroom door one last time. Her strapless velvet burgundy dress hugged every curve. She'd styled her hair into a low bun and molded her bangs into sleek body waves. Her makeup was simple—golden nudes with a deep matte red lipstick. But the highlight of the entire look was her red and black ombré-feathered mask, trimmed in sparkling black sequins.

When Jake first told her about the Vincents' charity event, he was so busy trying to get her inside the bedroom that he'd failed to mention the fundraiser's masquerade theme. It was the one saving grace that would help Ella blend into the crowd while observing the family.

"El!" Jake called out from the living room. "You ready, babe? We're gonna be late. I don't wanna miss the auction. I have got to put in my bid on those Lakers tickets and the players' meet and greet afterward."

"I'm coming!" Ella gave herself one last glance before grabbing her black satin clutch and heading out.

"*Phew phew,*" Jake whistled, embracing her the moment she stepped foot inside the living room. "Woman, don't make me skip out on this event altogether and take you right back into that bedroom. You look...*phenomenal*. I'm feeling a little subpar dressed in this plain ole black suit."

"Subpar? Please. You'll be the most handsome man there. However, if there *is* a way for you to mail in your donation so that we can skip the event, I'd be down with that."

Jake chuckled, not realizing Ella was dead serious.

"Not a chance," he told her. "If nothing else, I wanna show you off. Let the entire town of Clemmington see just how beautiful my lady is."

The response sparked a burning dread that simmered inside Ella's gut.

You've got your mask. You'll be fine, she told herself on the way out the door.

But there was one small factor Ella had forgotten. Everyone knew that she was dating Jake. When they saw him, they'd know it was her by his side—especially after he'd refused to wear a mask.

Just stay low-key and keep your head down...

Ella slid inside the car and immediately rolled down the window, hoping the cool night air would garner some relief. When Jake turned on a smooth jazz satellite station, she closed her eyes and swayed to the music.

Don't worry about tonight. All will be well.

A deep pothole jolted her eyes open. Ella stared out the window. Jake had just made a right turn down the wrong street. "Wait, where are we going? Isn't Vincent Vineyard in the opposite direction?"

"It is. But the charity event isn't being held there. It's at the Hidden Treasure Casino."

"Really? I don't remember you mentioning that."

Jake reached over and laced his fingers within hers. "Sorry. Must've slipped my mind. I've been so focused on

Don's investigation that I'm having trouble remembering whether I'm coming or going."

Ella sank down into her seat, relaxing against the backrest. Relief set in at the thought of avoiding the vineyard. Guests at a casino would be spread all around the gaming floor, making it easier for her to blend in with the crowd.

Bright lights shone up ahead as they approached Hidden Treasure. Jake slowed down, eyeing the long valet line filled with luxury cars.

"I see the Vincents have brought out the who's who among Clemmington," Ella murmured, staring out at the throngs of elaborately dressed attendees crowding the entrance.

"As they do every year. That wait for the valet is probably gonna take forever. I'd better park in the garage. I'll drop you off in front first. Don't think I didn't notice how high those sexy heels are you're wearing. I don't want your feet to start hurting."

"That's sweet of you. But these shoes are pretty comfortable. Go on to the lot. I'll walk back with you."

"Are you sure?"

"I'm positive."

Jake proceeded to the garage, driving up the ramp until they reached the top floor. "It is a packed house tonight. But that's a good thing. The bigger the turnout, the bigger the endowment."

"Uh-huh," Ella muttered, barely listening as a bout of anxiety tightened her chest.

After pulling into a space and helping her out of the car, Jake took a step back, ogling Ella from head to toe. "Whew! Did I mention how beautiful you look tonight?"

"You did. And thank you again." She glanced down

at his hand. It was wrapped in black satin. "What is that you're holding?"

Unwinding the unidentified object, he placed it over his face, secured it behind his head and turned to her.

"It's my swashbuckling mask."

"A *mask*? But I thought you weren't going to wear one."

"I wasn't. However, tonight is for a good cause. Since I'm the chief of police, I figured the least I could do is follow the event rules."

"Well, I'm glad you did. You look great." Ella looped her arm within his. "So great that you just might have to keep that on when we get home."

"Ooh, I think I like the sound of that..."

Ella slipped on her mask before they entered the elevator. When the doors opened onto level one, they squeezed their way out onto the crowded sidewalk and headed toward the casino.

"Wow, this place is nice," she said, staring up at the gold awning and rolling spotlights shining down on the bright red carpet. "Reminds me of Las Vegas."

The thought of her home state reminded Ella of the threatening message she'd received after leaving Gateway Park.

You are not in Nevada anymore. Here in Clemmington, the odds will never be in your favor...

She tightened her grip on Jake's arm. He glided his hand over hers, their fingers instinctively intertwining. The warmth of his touch put her mind at ease, at least for the time being.

Photographers stood outside the casino's grand entryway, snapping candid pictures of guests as they strolled inside. Frank Sinatra's "Luck Be a Lady" blared from multiple speakers hanging from the revolving doorways.

The moment Ella and Jake hit the gaming floor, the music

was drowned out by ringing slot machines and cheering gamblers. Crowds were gathered around blackjack, roulette and poker tables. The energy was electrifying as dealers shuffled cards, bartenders poured craft cocktails and servers passed around glasses of Vincent Vineyard wine.

"What are we drinking tonight?" Jake asked right before they were approached by a couple.

Ella stopped so abruptly that her heel snagged against the pale gold carpet. Had she not been holding onto Jake, she would've stumbled to the floor. She stared down at her feet, barely looking at the pair, whose faces were covered in crystal Venetian masks.

Panic set in. Was it Tyler and Jada? Or maybe Greer and Faith?

"My, oh, my," Ella heard Jake say. "You two really went all out, didn't you? If there's a prize for best masks, you'll definitely win first place."

"And if that prize consists of a case of wine," a familiar voice responded, "we'll take it!"

Someone nudged Ella's shoulder. "What is wrong with you? Why are you just standing there, hiding behind Jake without even saying hello? Could you be any more rude?"

Slowly raising her eyes, Ella grinned sheepishly after realizing it was Charlotte and Miles.

"Oh, sorry!" she squealed, embarrassment flaming her skin as she hugged her sister. "You look great. I'm loving your satin green dress. And those masks. Where'd you get them?"

"Miles and I scoured the internet for these. We found them at a little boutique in New Orleans that specializes in Mardi Gras costumes."

"Well, they look amazing." Ella quickly turned to Jake, feeling as though they were on full display at the casino entrance. "Should we go grab a drink? Then play some slots or a little blackjack?"

"All the above. Charlotte, Miles, would you two like to join us, or are you gonna hit the craps table first, which is all Miles has been talking about for days?"

"I'd love a drink," Charlotte said. "Miles has plenty of time to blow our money playing craps. Let's not encourage him to start early."

The foursome headed toward a bar near the far end of the room where the line was the shortest. On the way there, Ella's eyes darted from wall to wall in search of the Vincents. None of them came into view.

"So what's the game plan for tonight?" Charlotte asked. "Are we going to divide and conquer like we did at the wine tasting? Or follow the old adage *there's strength in numbers* and stick together?"

"Why don't we play it by ear?" Jake suggested. "Get a feel for the Vincents' behavior, then figure it out from there."

Miles nodded in agreement. "I like that idea. Plus, now that the town knows we've reopened Don's murder investigation, we probably need to be a bit more inconspicuous than we were at the wine tasting."

"True." Jake pointed at an empty high-top table off to the side of the main stage. "Why don't I order the drinks and you all grab some food, then snatch up that table?"

"You got it, Chief."

Miles, Charlotte and Ella headed for the buffet, filling plates with salmon tartare, steak bites, stuffed peppers and Asiago cheese. Once the foursome met back up at the table, Jake passed out the drinks and held his high in the air.

"A toast. To the four of us, getting this case solved so that we can bring justice to Don and the entire Clemmington community."

"Cheers," they exclaimed in unison.

The swing music playing in the background quieted. It was replaced by Kool & the Gang's "Celebration." The red velvet stage curtains slowly parted. When Claire, Manuel, Greer and Faith appeared, the crowd broke into applause.

Claire and Greer stepped forward first, waving while positioning themselves at the podium. Manuel and Faith came up behind them, clapping and smiling at the audience.

The sight of the family tightened Ella's throat. She swallowed the chunk of cheese she'd been chewing, quickly chasing it down with a gulp of wine.

"I wonder why Tyler and Jada aren't onstage?" Charlotte said.

Fearful of saying the wrong thing, Ella shrugged but kept her mouth closed.

Claire raised her hand to quiet the crowd. She looked radiant in a silver tuxedo dress and matching heels. Her diamond jewelry threw off laser beams each time they hit the lights, while her nude makeup showcased a smooth face that appeared freshly lifted by a plastic surgeon.

"Hello, everyone," she crooned into the mic. "Thank you very much for being here this evening. As many of you know, this particular charity event was one of Don's favorites. My husband always believed in putting education first, and that everyone should be given the opportunity to attend college. Your attendance tonight means the world to me, my family and especially the students who will have a chance to better themselves thanks to your generosity. It saddens me that Don isn't here to celebrate this joyous occasion. But he is with us in spirit. We dedicate this night to him. Thank you again for—"

A commotion erupted on the other side of the room. Heads swiveled toward the staircase that led to the second floor's high roller games. Tyler and Jada appeared at the top of the landing. He was dressed in a shiny hot pink suit. Her bandeau top and skintight miniskirt had been cut from the same cloth, literally.

"What in the…" Charlotte uttered.

Tyler pointed at the DJ and gave him a thumbs-up. Guns N' Roses' "Welcome to the Jungle" blared through the speakers. The flashy couple floated down the stairs, appearing as though they were starring in a music video rather than attending a scholarship fundraiser.

Several guests whistled and howled with glee. But the majority of the crowd looked on in shocked silence. A tap against the microphone turned everyone's attention back to the stage, where Greer stood at the podium.

"*Excuse* me, everyone," he barked. "Like my mother was saying, we'd like to thank you for being here, and—"

"Yeah!" Tyler shouted over his brother. "Thanks for coming out, everybody!"

He and Jada strutted toward the middle of the casino. Photographers pushed their way through the crowd, falling to their knees in front of the pair while snapping away.

"This is disgusting," Ella hissed.

Once they were done with their paparazzi moment, Tyler took Jada's hand in his, twirling her around before heading to the stage.

Faith, who'd been watching it all from the sidelines, burst into tears and ran off. Claire shook her head in disdain but didn't appear as distraught as she should've. Greer continued to try to turn the crowd's attention back to them. But his chin lowered to his chest in defeat when all eyes remained on his brother and sister-in-law.

"Clemmington, Californiaaa!" Tyler yelled into the mic after shooing Greer away. "How's everybody doing tonight?"

A hesitant round of applause scattered through the crowd.

"Friends, my wife, Jada, and I could not be happier to be here. Yes, this evening is for a great cause. But it also gives us a chance to step out in our best attire, biggest jewels and fanciest cars, all while mingling with the hottest people in town. Not to mention you're sipping on *the* best wine in the country. In the *world* even. Am I right?" He leaned forward, turning his ear toward the crowd. "I said, *am I right?*"

The audience roared in agreement.

Ella grabbed her clutch, digging inside for her cell phone. "Oh, I have got to get a video of this. It is unreal."

There was another disruption near the side of the stage.

"I know, Manuel!" Claire sniffed, climbing down the stairs and rushing ahead of him. But he was hot on her sparkly kitten heels.

"*Please*, Mrs. Vincent, listen to me. You have got to do something about Tyler. The man needs to be put in check. That stunt he just pulled was beyond disrespectful!"

The pair stopped near Ella and her group's table.

"I will speak to my son when and how I see fit." She pointed at the stage, her artificially plumped lips curling into a sly smile. "You've gotta admit though, he does have that wow factor. I mean, look at the crowd. They're completely captivated!"

Manuel's eyes narrowed, his tongue clicking in rapid succession. "With all due respect, Mrs. Vincent? You're delusional."

"You may be right. But you know what else I am? *Rich*. Thanks to who? Tyler. Because ever since he took on a more prominent role, sales have skyrocketed. So if he wants to be a part of tonight's thank-you speech, who am I to stop him?"

"The owner of Vincent Vineyard, that's who. Not to mention Tyler's *mother*. The man needs to show some respect, Mrs. Vincent—"

"Are you done?" she interrupted. "Because I'm being rude. I'd like to go and greet my guests. You should too. We need to be out there personally thanking them for their support."

"One last question before you go, Mrs. Vincent. Was that Alan Monroe I saw in the crowd?"

"Yes," Claire retorted through pursed lips. "Why?"

"This may be none of my business, but don't you think having the man here who you've been accused of cheating on your husband with is a bit...*inappropriate*?"

"You're right, Manuel."

"I am?" he asked, standing a bit taller.

"Yes. You are. That *is* none of your business."

Manuel raised a hand to protest. But Claire had already sauntered off into the crowd. He just stood there, vigorously rubbing his weary red eyes.

"That poor man," Charlotte whispered. "I don't know how he can continue working for her."

"My guess is that it's his loyalty to Don," Ella responded. "But something isn't right with that woman. Her occasional grief seems forced. As if it's more for show."

"What gave it away?" Jake asked. "The fact that she's got her secret lover here, or that she allowed her crass, obnoxious son to practically take over the business?"

Miles downed the rest of his wine, then readjusted his mask. "You know, Tyler and his wife remind me of those over-the-top televangelists. They're both flamboyant, fake, attention-seeking, money hungry—"

"And most importantly," Ella interjected, "untrustworthy."

"That part," Charlotte concurred.

Through the corners of her eyes, Ella noticed Manuel drifting toward their table. They made eye contact. He stared at the group, as if trying to figure out who they were behind their masks. It didn't take long for him to recognize the officers and walk over.

"Chief Love, Detective Love, it's good to see you both here," Manuel said before nodding in Ella and Charlotte's direction. "Ladies, you both look ravishing. Thank you for coming." He didn't wait for a thank-you before turning his attention back to Jake and Miles. "Could I please talk to the two of you? Alone?"

"Of course," Jake said, setting down his glass and grabbing his phone. "We'll follow you." Before walking away, he leaned in and kissed Ella's cheek. "This should be interesting. Be right back."

The minute they were out of earshot, Charlotte grabbed her arm. "This is the best reality show I have ever seen, and it's not even being filmed! Who would've thought that a small town like Clemmington would produce such great drama?"

"Speaking of filming," Ella said, once again rummaging through her purse, "I cannot find my phone. I must've left it in the car. And I have *got* to get some footage of this fiasco before the end of the night."

"Yes, you do," Charlotte agreed. She pointed toward the stage, where Tyler and Jada were now slow dancing to the tune of UB40's "Red Red Wine" while a large crowd gathered in front, staring up at them in awe. "Apparently those two think they're celebrities, with their trashy selves. I'm being blinded by the neon pink outfits. Jada's skirt is barely covering her lady bits. And—wait, where are you going?"

"To the parking garage," Ella told her, dangling Jake's

car fob in the air. "Come on. Walk with me so I can get my cell phone and—"

"*Dammit!*" Charlotte squealed.

"What's wrong?"

"Look at me," she whispered, pointing at her breasts. "I'm leaking!"

"Oh, no," Ella moaned at the sight of two stains that had seeped through her dress. "You should've worn a thicker pair of nursing pads. Did you pack extras?"

"*Extras.* How about I forgot to put any on at all! I blame it on being overly excited to get dressed up and go out. I've gotta run to the ladies room and get this situation under control."

"Do you need help?" Ella asked, following her as she shuffled toward the back of the casino.

"No, I should be fine!"

And then there was one, Ella thought. She tapped her chocolate brown manicured nails against her clutch and scanned the room. Tyler and Jada had finally left the stage. They were now lost in the crowd, along with Claire. Faith never reappeared after fleeing the stage in tears. Considering Greer was nowhere in sight, Ella assumed he was off somewhere consoling her. Being without her phone and the company she'd come with left Ella feeling alone. And vulnerable.

She eyed the entrance. People were still rolling in and out of the casino. There were guests everywhere. Her mask was securely in place, so no one would recognize her if she walked to the car alone.

You'll be fine, she told herself before heading out.

When she reached the sidewalk, Ella realized there wasn't quite as much traffic away from the casino's revolving doors. The building's bright lights grew dimmer the farther away she walked. And the parking garage seemed much closer when they'd arrived.

Just get there, get the phone and hurry back...

Ella picked up the pace, her walk turning into a slight jog as she shuffled on the balls of her feet. When she reached the garage, she flung open the glass door and pounded the elevator's up button. Several moments passed before the doors opened. A large group of people poured out, reassuring her that the lot was still bustling with activity.

"You look gorgeous!" one of the women said as she brushed past her.

"Thanks," Ella panted, rushing inside the elevator and hammering the fifth-floor button. The doors closed, but the elevator didn't move.

She laid on the button. After a few seconds, it finally began to rise. Then it stopped, dropped and stalled.

The lights flickered. Ella gripped the railing and steadied herself, then lunged forward and hit the emergency alarm.

"How may I help you?" a perky voice chirped through the speaker.

"I'm inside the Hidden Treasure Casino's parking garage elevator, and it's stuck!"

"I am so sorry about that, ma'am. We've been having trouble with that elevator for over an hour now."

"And you didn't put up a sign? Or better yet, take it out of service?"

"We are short staffed tonight, ma'am. My apologies. I will put in a call to our service center and see how long it'll take to have someone—"

A loud beep blared through the elevator, drowning out the woman's voice. The lights went out. It took another plunge. Ella backed into a corner and screamed.

"Miss!" the operator yelled. "Are you all right?"

"No!" Ella yelled just as the elevator lit back up. It jerked once more, then rode up to the fifth floor.

The doors opened. Ella tore off her mask and sucked in a huge puff of air.

"Can you tell me exactly what's happening?"

"It looks like the elevator is working again. At least for the time being."

"Wonderful. Someone will be out there to service it as soon as possible. In the meantime, please be sure to take the stairs back down to the first floor."

"Of course," Ella wheezed, stumbling out of the vestibule and into the lot.

Rows and rows of cars blended together. She squinted, peering into the dimly lit distance in search of Jake's.

Per usual, she hadn't paid attention to where they'd parked. Ella struck the alarm fob over and over, waiting to hear a beep or see blinking taillights. Only dark silence filled the air.

The eerie clicking of her heels against the cement echoed off the walls. She darted down one row and up another, still gasping from the panic of being stuck in the confines of a malfunctioning elevator.

Ominous shadows appeared in her peripheral. When she moved, they moved. She stopped, pressing her body against a nearby pillar. And then it dawned on her. The shadows were a reflection of her own body, rushing past the shiny cars' exteriors.

Ella closed her eyes and drew in a deep breath.

Your mind is playing tricks on you. Calm down. Find the car. And get back to the casino.

She stepped away from the column and set off toward the second to last row of cars. Hit the alarm fob again.

Bloop, bloop.

"Thank you!" she shrieked as lights blinked up ahead.

Running at full speed, she somehow managed not to twist her ankle while charging toward the car.

Ella threw open the door. The phone wasn't on the passenger seat. She felt around on the floor until her hand landed on it.

Dread slithered across her skin as she closed the door. Now she had to find her way back to the first floor. Alone. Through the stairwell.

Call Jake. Have him meet you here while you wait inside the car.

Her fingers quivered as she dialed his number. "Please answer..."

Ella held the phone to her ear, anxious to hear his voice. The other end of the line was silent. Several moments passed before three beeps pinged in her ear. She glared at the screen.

Call failed.

No reception.

"Dammit!"

Ella spun around, wishing that a security guard would suddenly appear. No such luck. An exit sign blinked in the far right corner. She set off toward it, willing her aching calves to get her there.

"Hey!" someone barked.

Ella stopped. Pivoted. No one appeared.

A sickening chill settled in her chest.

Keep going!

She charged toward the exit sign, sprinting through the middle of the aisle.

"Hey, you!" the commanding voice called out. "In the burgundy dress. Stop!"

A shadowy figure emerged from behind a purple pickup

truck. Ella prayed that it was a guest of the charity event, and a plus-one would appear. But the person was alone.

Stop looking over your shoulder. Turn around and get to the stairwell!

Footsteps pounded behind her. The faster she ran, the closer they got.

Ella reached the corridor. Grabbed the handle and ripped open the door. Ran down the stairs as if her stilettos were sneakers, gripping the banister while taking them two at a time. She jumped when the door slammed behind her, then winced at the creaking sound of it reopening.

"You thought that mask was gonna hide your identity?" someone yelled from above. "I recognized you the minute you strolled through the door!"

"Leave me alone!" Ella screamed.

"Oh, I will. Once you get the hell out of Clemmington!"

This is a nightmare. I never should've come here. I knew better! I have got to talk to Jake...

Tears streamed down her face. The stairs grew distorted, transforming into what appeared to be gray slopes of dirt. Ella kept going, determined to escape the garage alive.

Her aching feet weakened. The straps on her shoes sliced into her skin. She ignored the pain after seeing that she'd reached level two.

Almost there. Keep going. Faster!

Ella's assailant appeared at the top of the landing. He was getting closer. So was the exit. She sped up until finally, the first floor exit appeared.

"Yes!" she screamed, throwing open the door.

Boom!

Ella slammed into someone standing on the other side. She cried out. How in hell did the attacker beat her there?

The man gripped her arms as she tried to fight him off, then held her upright before she went crumbling to the ground.

"El!" he yelled. "What is going on?"

She froze. Looked up at the man. It was Jake.

Ella grabbed hold of him, then turned to see if her attacker was still in the stairwell. He was gone.

Pull yourself together. Now!

"I... I just got turned around in the lot," she said, straightening her dress. "Then the elevator malfunctioned, and I had to take the stairs back down."

"Okay, well, Charlotte told me you'd come to the car to get your phone. She thought you would've made it back to the casino by now. So I came to check on you."

Thank God...

"Are you okay?"

"Yeah," Ella lied. "I'm fine."

Jake kept an arm wrapped firmly around her shoulders on the way back to the casino. "I've got to catch you up on what happened when Miles and I spoke with Manuel. That Tyler... He is something else."

"Can't wait to hear all about it," Ella mumbled, wondering when she'd get up the nerve to tell Jake the truth.

Chapter Eight

Jake and Miles sat across from one another inside the police station's conference room, waiting on Greer to arrive.
They'd opted to meet with him there instead of the vineyard
so that he could speak freely.

"Let's not rule Greer out as a possible suspect just because his mother and brother appear to have a stronger motive," Jake warned.

"Oh, I'm not ruling anybody out. The Vincents are one
strange family. I can't wait to hear what the brothers' wives
have to say about all this too."

"My guess is that Tyler's wife will ride for him until the
end. Her loyalty seems obsessive, almost cultlike."

"I couldn't agree more," Miles said. "Those two are the
perfect match. Like the male and female version of one another. But both wives have one goal in mind, and that is to
see their husbands take over as president of Vincent Vineyard."

"To the point where one of them may have been complicit
in having Don killed. And not to take the focus off of those
two, but do you have an update on the men who broke into
the vineyard's offices during that tour?"

"I've put in calls to Mitch and Dylan letting them know
we need to speak with them as soon as possible. Still wait-

ing on callbacks. As for that wild one, Ben Foray, I'm having trouble locating him. San Diego PD is helping to track him down since that was his last known place of residence."

Jake tapped his pen against the table, staring at his most recent case notes. "Good. I wish we could've gotten more information out of Manuel at the charity event. But are we surprised that Tyler ran over and interrupted us before the conversation even got started?"

"I certainly wasn't."

"Tyler knows that Manuel holds the key to helping us solve Don's murder. He also knew that Manuel was heated after the stunt he and Jada pulled at the charity event. He made his presence known as an intimidation tactic, just to keep Manuel quiet."

Miles tore open a packet of sugar and poured it inside his World's Best Dad mug of coffee. "And it worked. You see Manuel didn't utter a word about the case after Tyler walked up. Wouldn't it be something if Claire and Tyler were in on all this together, and they conspired to kill Don?"

"It would be. From what I'm seeing, I wouldn't rule that theory out either."

A text message notification from Ella popped up on Jake's buzzing phone.

Hey babe. Hope your day is going well. Charlotte and I are going to grab lunch. I'll wait at her place until you get off work. Can you pick me up from there? XO

Of course, love. Enjoy. See you tonight.

"Judging by that goofy grin on your face," Miles snarked, "I'm guessing that's Ella texting you?"

"You've got a lot of nerve given the way you giggle like a clown every time Charlotte looks your way."

Miles balled up a napkin and threw it in Jake's direction. "Dude, I was only kidding. No need to take low blows!"

Jake caught the napkin right before it hit his forehead, then glanced at the time. Greer was almost thirty minutes late. "I wonder what's taking our guy so long to get here. I hope Tyler didn't find out he was coming in and pull something to deter him."

"I wouldn't put it past him." Miles paused, taking a long sip of coffee. "Hey, what was going on with Ella the night of the charity event? It seemed like after you two came back from the parking garage, she was shaken up."

"Ugh," Jake groaned, running his hand along the back of his neck. "I don't know, man. Your guess is as good as mine. When I got to the garage, I saw that the elevator wasn't working. So I went to the stairwell, and the second I opened the door, *bam!* Ella came flying through the doorway and fell into my arms. She seemed completely disoriented."

"Do you think something happen to her inside the garage?"

"I have no clue. She said she'd gotten stuck in the elevator on her way up to the car, then got freaked out by the dark creepy stairwell on the way back down. The more questions I asked, the more she shut down. So I just left it alone. It was definitely weird though."

"Hmm. Well, after that attack in the corn maze and, of course, Ella's ex-boyfriend being the Numeric Serial Killer, we shouldn't be surprised."

Jake propped his elbows on the table and rubbed his hands together. "Yeah... I've tried talking her into getting therapy, but so far, she's refused. Adamantly."

"Really? I'm surprised. Especially considering she's a

nurse. After everything she has been through, you would
think she'd understand how much counseling would benefit her."

There was a knock at the door.

"*Finally,*" Jake muttered before calling out, "come in!"

Lena cracked open the door and stuck her head inside.
"Hey, sorry to interrupt. No Greer yet?"

"Nope." Miles checked his phone. "Not yet. No call or
text saying he'd be late either."

"I'll text him now to find out his ETA," Jake said. "Let's
just hope Tyler didn't get inside his head and convince him
not to come."

Lena moved farther inside the doorway, balancing a box
with a stack of files on top.

"What's all that?" Miles asked.

"I finally found the evidence from Don's crime scene
that we couldn't locate. It was in the back of the storage
closet Dad used as his personal property room. I think he'd
stored it there for safekeeping, just to make sure it didn't
get misplaced."

"Did you find anything worth being retested?" Jake
asked.

"I did. Don's clothes are here, samples of the soil surrounding the area where his body was found, a pair of thin-
ning shears and a serrated grape knife."

"*Wait!*" Jake jumped up and peering inside the box. "You
said you've got a grape knife?"

"I did. Why?"

"I was just wondering if that could be the—"

"Murder weapon?" Lena interrupted. "I'm way ahead
of you."

The conversation pulled Miles from his chair. He walked
over, his lips twisted with skepticism. "Hold on. If that was

the weapon used to kill Don, don't you think the Definitive Solutions Crime Lab would've discovered that through DNA testing?"

"Possibly," Lena replied. "But it won't hurt for me to run it again and see what I may find since our lab's technology is more advanced than theirs."

"I agree," Jake said. "Let us know if something comes of it."

As Lena turned to walk out, she was stopped by Lucy, the police station's administrative assistant.

"Oops, sorry," Lucy said, quickly stepping aside. "Chief Love, Detective Love, I've got Greer Vincent here to see you."

"Thanks, Lucy," Jake replied, watching as Greer peered inside the room. "Come on in, Mr. Vincent. Have a seat."

Greer shuffled through the door with his head hanging low. His dull skin appeared ashen. Dark bags cradled his puffy eyes. A scruffy beard covered his haggard face, and he appeared about three weeks overdue for a haircut.

"*This should be good*," Lena whispered to Jake before closing the door behind her.

He took a seat at the head of the table. "Thank you for coming in to speak with us, Mr. Vincent. And congratulations on such a successful charity event. I'm sure it'll help a lot of students attend college this year."

Greer snorted loudly, wringing his hands while staring down at the table. "Yeah. Thanks. But I really don't wanna talk about the charity event. You guys called me down here. What can I do for you?"

His flat tone reeked of defeat. Jake pitied him, almost feeling bad for having to question him.

Ignore it. Press on. Find out what he has to say.

"As you know, Clemmington PD has reopened your father's death investigation. We are determined to make an arrest this go-round, and we're hoping you'd be willing to share your thoughts on what was going on around the time of his murder."

An awkward silence filled the room. Greer had yet to make eye contact with Jake or Miles.

"Mr. Vincent," Miles said, "are you all right? Can I get you anything to—"

"Mr. Vincent was my father' name. Please, call me Greer. And no, I don't need anything. I'm fine." He finally looked up and glared at Jake. "What exactly are you going to do differently to find the killer this time? Your dad's investigation came up empty, despite him having years of experience. Better yet, is this really about you bringing justice to my family? Or are you trying to prove that you actually earned the position of police chief? Because rumor has it you bypassed a few more qualified candidates thanks to a little thing called nepotism."

Jake's eyes narrowed as he stared back at Greer. The urge to bite back simmered on his tongue. He bit down on his cheek, refusing to stoop to Greer's level, while flipping open his notebook. "Mr. Vin—my apologies, *Greer*, in your opinion, what was life like for your father around the time of his death? Were things normal? Did he seem down, feel threatened or experience any sort of strange run-in with someone?"

A guttural moan bellowed from Greer's wide open mouth. "I can't do this!" he wailed before bursting into tears.

Miles jumped up and handed him a box of tissues. The unexpected outburst transformed Jake's irritation into concern. When Greer's head hit the mahogany tabletop, the chief placed a hand on his shoulder.

"I cannot believe this has happened to my family," Greer

moaned. "Who would've done this? *Why* would someone have done this?"

"That's what we're working hard on to figure out," Jake assured him. "My sister, Lena, who's an expert forensic scientist, is retesting crime scene evidence inside our new state-of-art lab as we speak."

After Greer failed to raise his head, Miles chimed in. "We're also going to be bringing persons of interest back in for questioning and running polygraph tests. Including the men who broke into your father's office during that tour of the vineyard."

Those words pulled Greer up from the table. "Good," he croaked before wiping his face with a tissue before blowing his nose into it. "I was always suspicious of those jackasses. But your father didn't seem to think they were viable suspects. He was set on the idea of my dad's murder being an inside job. Meaning someone in the family committed it."

Jake propped his chin in his hand, slowly nodding. "Well, I'm leaning into that theory as well. If Mr. Vincent's murder was in fact an inside job, who do you think would've done it?"

An obnoxious laugh crept through Greer's sniffles. "Listen, I hate to throw my own brother under the bus, but Tyler is the only answer. He's the one who'd have the most to gain."

"I hope this doesn't come across as disrespectful," Miles interjected, "but what about your mother?"

"She obviously had something to gain as well."

Jake's neck swiveled at his candidness. But he kept his cool to keep Greer talking. "Do you think it's a possibility that they both had something to do with the murder?"

Several seconds passed before Greer replied, "To be honest, I don't think my mother was involved. She had it made, whether my father was dead or alive. The big house, the fancy cars, the designer clothes and expensive jewelry, not to mention the status of saying she's Vincent Vineyard's COO. My mom even had a lover on the side—"

"Hold on," Miles interrupted while rigorously taking notes. "Your mother's affair was public knowledge?"

"I mean, yes and no. Was it discussed out in the open? No, not really. But did people around town whisper about it behind closed doors? Absolutely. The worst part was that Alan Monroe and my father had been rivals for years. My mom knew that. Of all the men she could've been with, she chose him." Greer hesitated as a few lone tears trickled down his face. "My father did mention divorce a few times, but my mother knew he'd never leave her. So she never took him seriously."

"What are you saying?" Jake asked. "Mrs. Vincent didn't have a strong enough motive to kill your father?"

"In my opinion? No."

"Okay then. Let's get back to Tyler."

A cluster of angry lines formed between Greer's eyebrows. "What about him?"

"You said he'd have the strongest motive. Tell us why."

"Weren't you two at the wine tasting? You saw the man make a complete fool of himself in front of the entire crowd, as if he knows anything about...about *wine*, and...and *harvesting*, and business in general. All the man knows is flamboyance. And attention. Putting on for the cameras. He wants the power. He wants to be the king of Vincent Vineyard. But the problem is, Tyler doesn't possess the knowledge or skill set to do so. What he does possess, however, is the ability to charm the hell out of my mother. And our employees. The patrons. The whole damn community, really."

Greer paused, gulping down a bottle of water until there

was none left. He jumped from his chair and grabbed another off the shelf, then began pacing the floor.

"And don't even get me started on Tyler's wife. Jada is just as bad as he is, if not worse. I'm talking money hungry, power hungry, superficial, cold... I could go on about her all day. What I can't understand is how my wife can tolerate her. They are *complete* opposites."

"Aside from the fact that they're sisters-in-law," Miles said, "does your wife have a significant relationship with Jada outside of the vineyard, or would you consider them to be more like work friends?"

Greer plopped back down into his chair and stared up at the ceiling. "Oh, they definitely have a significant relationship outside of the vineyard. For some odd reason, Faith considers Jada to be one of her closest friends. And all Jada does is take advantage of her. Dumps her work off on Faith. Even forced my wife to take computer courses so she could serve as the vineyard's tech expert after Tyler refused to pay for a consultant. Faith took on all that responsibility with no additional pay too."

"Understood. But that's work-related. What is their personal relationship like?"

"*Tuh,*" Greer sputtered, his lips forming a sour pucker. "It's one-sided, to say the least. Whenever Tyler does something to upset Jada, she comes running to Faith. And Faith is always there to console her. Then Tyler buys Jada some expensive apology gift, and she goes right back to being happy again. Then he messes up once more and she comes running back to Faith, and the cycle continues. All Jada cares about is Tyler, and all Tyler cares about is Tyler. In the meantime, maintaining Vincent Vineyard is left up to my wife, Manuel and, of course, me."

The defeated look in Greer's eyes weighed heavily on

Jake. He knew how close Greer was to his father. To have endured that loss, then deal with a mother, brother and sister-in-law who didn't seem to care had to be excruciating.

"I know this is tough on you, Greer," the chief said. "You have my condolences."

"Mine as well," Miles added quietly.

"Thank you. I appreciate that. And uh...sorry about the outburst—"

Jake held his hand in the air. "Please. Don't apologize. Believe me, we understand. You've been through a lot. I appreciate your raw honesty. And your transparency. You have no idea how many people come in here with a stoic, emotionless wall up. It's as if they don't want to show any sign of humanity for fear of appearing guilty, even when they're not. So we appreciate your candidness."

"I hope at least some of what I shared gave you a little more insight into the vineyard's dynamics."

"It definitely did." Jake cleared his throat, tapping his pen against his palm. "Greer, where were you at the time of your father's murder?"

"I was inside the distillery, overseeing new equipment installation."

Just as Tyler said.

"Okay then," Jake replied. "I guess we can wrap this up..." He hesitated when Greer slid away from the table, sitting up straighter and crossing one leg over the other.

"You know, Chief Love, there is something else weighing heavily on me that I feel compelled to share. If I may."

"Of course. Please do."

"I don't want either of you to be totally fooled by my brother's antics. Tyler may be a clown, but when it comes to doing what's best for Vincent Vineyard? He's all in. I mean, is he the sharpest knife in the drawer? Obviously not. Husband of the year? Never. Do we have our fair share of disagreements? Absolutely. But I blame that on our big brother-little brother dynamic, you know what I mean? I'm sure you both do, considering you're brothers and all, right?"

Jake glanced at Miles, whose expression was just as perplexed as his. "I'm sorry, Greer, but where are you going with all this?"

"Okay, let me break it down in a way that'll be as palatable as possible. Since my father's death, running Vincent Vineyard has been so much easier. I'm talking more pleasant. More productive. More profitable. More...more *everything.* We no longer have to beg, and overexplain and kiss anybody's ass to get what we want. If I pitch an idea that'll enhance the business and increase our profit margin, I get an immediate yes. Oh, and just between us, I talked Tyler into secretly planting several new grape varieties in the vineyard a few years ago, after my father refused to expand the wine selection."

A loud silence filled the room.

Tread carefully, Jake thought, his mind racing with confusion. *This might be the new intel you've been looking for...*

"How did you manage to pull that off behind your father's back? Didn't he keep a close eye on those fields?"

"He did. But I worked around it. I knew Tyler had a ton of extra cash at his disposal, so I convinced him to pay the vine workers hush money to make it happen. They worked late at night, long after my father had gone home. It's a shame how the grapes were ready to be harvested right before his death. He never got a chance to see how profitable the new lines of wine have been."

A sick feeling settled in the pit of Jake's gut. Greer's shift in demeanor was alarming, as was his admission and love/hate relationship with his brother. But none of that was enough to charge him with a crime.

"What did your mother have to say once she found out about all this?" Miles asked.

"Found out? She was in on it from the very beginning. Unlike my father, Claire is extremely business-minded. She didn't give a damn about Don's traditions and old-school way of doing things. She's all about making a profit. Period."

"Did Manuel know about these secret grape varieties that you planted?"

"Of course not. Manuel was way too loyal to my father. Had he known, he would've gone straight to Don and snitched. And then, who knows what would've happened." Greer glanced casually at his watch. "On that note, I need to get out of here. I'm meeting with a wine distributor, and I can't be late. God forbid I let Tyler run it on his own. He'd ruin the sale before it even closed with all his boasting and false promises. Yet *another* reason I should've been named president a long time ago..."

His words felt all too familiar. They were the exact ones Tyler had spoken about him. After his declaration, Greer appeared just as ruthless as his brother.

Maybe he isn't the good stand-up guy he'd portrayed himself to be...

Greer stood, stretching as if he'd just awakened from a long peaceful nap, then headed for the door. "Thanks again for the vent session, officers. Enjoy the rest of your day."

And with that, he walked out.

Jake and Miles peered at the door, then one another, their expressions frozen in shock. Several moments passed before Miles spoke up.

"First of all, what in the hell was *that*? This interview

took a turn that I did not see coming. Secondly, how many different personalities did we just witness in one man?"

"I lost count. I think it's safe to say that Greer has completely lost the plot. We have got to get Manuel in here as soon as possible. He's the one who'll give us some real insight into this entire situation."

"Haven't you reached out to him?"

Jake sat back, sliding his notebook aside in frustration. "I have. He keeps claiming to be too busy to get down here. I think he's afraid of saying something that might incriminate Claire since his loyalty now lies with her."

"Well, if he can't come to us, then we need to go to him."

"Don't worry. I'll get him in here. In the meantime, I'm adding Greer's name to our list of suspects, right next to Tyler's."

Chapter Nine

Ella sat in front of her laptop, eyeing the woman staring back at her through the screen. She had a youthful air despite being well over sixty. Her long fluffy blond hair cascaded down the sides of her pleasant face, outlining dimpled cheeks and a genial smile. The woman's gentle tone and calming demeanor put Ella at ease, enabling her to open up in ways she'd never expected.

"So, Ella, tell me. Why haven't you shared the fact that you're undergoing therapy with Jake?"

Peering blankly at the keyboard, Ella's mind swirled for a response. Telling Jake would mean delving into what she'd been hiding. She still wasn't ready to reveal her secret to him nor to her therapist. All Ella really wanted was help getting through the trauma of her past, and ways to cope with the attacks she'd recently experienced.

"I don't know, Mrs. Lane. Jake is going through so much right now, with this investigation and all the scrutiny. I don't think he realized how challenging reopening this case would be. Now that the cat's out the bag, Clemmington is expecting an arrest. Immediately. That, plus being the new chief of police, is a heavy burden to carry. So to answer your question, I don't want to give him another thing to worry about."

"The fact that you're in therapy is a good thing, Ella. Not

a worry. You're Jake's partner. He loves you. He wants you to heal from all that you've been through. Just like his investigation, you are a high priority as well, just a different kind. Plus, isn't Jake the one who recommended that you seek counseling? That alone tells me that he cares. I can't tell you how many of my clients have sought therapy against their partners' will."

Ella pressed her hands against the sides of her face, ruminating on her words.

She doesn't get it. No one does. Because they don't know the truth...

"Listen," Mrs. Lane continued, "I understand the toll that the attacks have taken on you. We're working through that. But this secret that's haunting you, that you're afraid to share with anyone, do you understand that until *I* know what it is, I cannot help you through it?"

Ella nodded, remaining silent for fear that if she opened her mouth to speak, a sob would come rolling out. When Mrs. Lane sat quietly, awaiting a response, Ella finally whispered, "I'm just not ready to talk about it. I'll open up eventually, but not right now."

"I understand. Well, whenever you're ready, I'll be here. In the meantime, have you worked on any of those coping tactics that we discussed during your last session to help manage the anxiety?"

Sliding her notebook toward her, Ella flipped to the page where she'd written a list of strategies. "I have. I've been taking some time to meditate first thing in the morning and throughout the day whenever I start feeling uneasy. And I'm writing in my journal again, allowing myself to feel whatever emotions I'm dealing with from day to day. If I'm sad, I face the sadness. If I wanna cry, I let it out."

Mrs. Lane broke into applause. "I'm loving the progress, Ella. When I first suggested you begin journaling, you were very much against it. But look at you now. Great work. Do you notice a difference in how you're processing your emotions?"

"I do. I've just been letting them flow, which has enabled me to let them go. Well...not *completely*. But I'm getting there."

After checking her clock, the therapist clasped her hands together. "Some progress is better than no progress at all, my dear. Now, it looks like we're almost out of time. Is there anything else you'd like to share with me, or that you'll be focusing on during this upcoming week?"

"Yes, there is. I've been reading up on how diet and exercise can help reduce stress. Of course I'm aware of that considering I'm a nurse. But I hadn't ever really considered eating in moderation and working out on a regular basis. So I've incorporated those two things into my daily routine, and I'm already seeing a difference in my mental state. I'm thinking more clearly and remaining calmer when issues arise that would normally get me riled up."

"That's wonderful, Ella. A heathy diet and consistent exercise routine can absolutely help curb your stress and anxiety. Speaking of which, what about the work you've been doing to assist in the investigation? Have you discussed with Jake the need to pull back on your involvement since it may be triggering your anxiety?"

Ella bit down on her lip, resisting the urge to lie. She had yet to tell Jake that she needed time away from the case for the sake of her mental health. As far as she was concerned, it wasn't an issue. But her therapist thought otherwise.

While the investigation was interesting and keeping her busy throughout the day, deep down, Ella knew that there could be some truth to Mrs. Lane's suggestion. Maybe pulling back would be a good thing. Because the case was a constant reminder of her ties to the Vincent family, the attacks she'd endured and the fact that someone wanted her dead.

The buzz of Mrs. Lane's alarm rattled the speakers, jolting Ella from her thoughts.

"That's our time, Ella. We can pick up right where we left off next week. Are you still able to keep your standing appointment?"

"I am, thank you. Looking forward to it." Her hand hovered over the top of the computer screen. "See you then—" Ella paused at the sound of sleigh bells jingling outside of the loft.

"Good to see you too, Mr. Stevenson," someone said on the other side of the front door.

Jake.

When the jingling grew louder, Ella realized they weren't sleigh bells. They were his keys, sliding inside the door.

Mrs. Lane threw a finger in the air. "Oh, wait! One more thing. Don't forget to check your email for this week's homework assignment."

Ella pounded the volume button on the laptop until it was practically silent. "Will do," she uttered, her eyes peeled to the doorway.

"I think this assignment will be particularly helpful in reducing your stress levels. It's a visualization exercise that follows the mind-over-matter mantra. The way it works is, when you think of those moments you were attacked in the corn maze, chased through the park, stalked inside the parking garage or received threatening messages, you detach yourself from them. Immediately. And replace them with a visual that's peaceful and safe. Put yourself in a place where you feel calm. And relaxed. What does that look like to you? Is it a sunny beach? A mountainside cabin? A stunning ski slope—"

"*Mrs. Lane*," Ella interrupted just as the door opened, "is all this information included in your email?"

"Yes, it is. And thank you for stopping me. I was on a roll and just realized my next patient is waiting in the queue. I'll send the assignment over as soon as I'm done with—"

"That sounds great. Thanks again for today!"

Ella slammed the laptop shut and scurried into the living room. "Hey, babe! How was your day?"

"Hey." Jake sighed, giving her a kiss so quick that it barely grazed her lips. "My day was unreal, to put it lightly. Greer came in and spoke to Miles and me. You would not believe some of the things that man said to us. Let's just say he is not who we thought he was. That whole mister meek-and-humble act? It's just that. An act." He paused, leaning his head back and pulling in a sharp breath of air. "What is that deliciousness I smell?"

"Blackened chicken."

"Mmm," Jake moaned, following Ella into the kitchen. "That sounds good. What is it with you and all this cooking? You trying to spoil me into putting a ring on it?"

She waved her left hand in the air. "Maybe... But seriously, I'm just trying to keep us fit and healthy."

"Okay, I can respect that. What are we having to go along with the chicken?"

"A Cobb salad. We've got a mix of baby spinach and chopped romaine, hard boiled eggs, cherry tomatoes, cucumbers, red onions, a little blue cheese and a red wine vinaigrette."

Jake leaned against the counter, watching her intently. The soft smile on his face crinkled the corners of his deep-set eyes. The loving expression caused a tinge of guilt to singe her chest.

You'll tell him everything eventually. Just not today.

"I love that we're having a nice salad as a starter," he continued, popping a tomato inside his mouth. "I need more veggies in my life. What side dishes did you whip up?"

"No side dishes. Just the Cobb salad topped with the chicken. Oh! And garlic-flavored protein croutons too."

"What are you trying to do to me, woman? Starve me or something? Can we at least throw in a little mac and cheese or sweet potato fries, some creamy risotto… Hell, *anything* to go along with it!"

"Says Clemmington's new chief of police who needs to be in great shape in order to run down all those criminals," Ella reminded him while pulling down a couple of salad bowls.

"Yeah, okay. Don't be mad if I pop a frozen pizza in the oven later tonight."

"You'd better not!" She bumped her hip against his side as he washed up at the sink, jumping when his cell phone vibrated against her thigh.

He dried his hands and checked the notification. "*Yes,* finally!"

"Good news?"

"Great news. Manuel is ready to come into the station and talk with me. Judging by the tone of this text, he sounds determined this time."

Leaning over his shoulder, Ella peered at the screen and scanned the message. "That is awesome. But wait, what is that he's saying about Greer?"

"Oh, *wow.* So apparently, when Greer left the police station today and returned to the vineyard, Manuel overheard him talking to his wife. Greer told Faith that he'd accomplished his goal of throwing off law enforcement by sprinkling bits of incriminating evidence over everyone close to Don's murder investigation."

"What? Why would he do something like that?"

Hunching his shoulders, Jake scanned the message once again. "I have no idea. You know, he was acting really weird when we questioned him. But it never dawned on me that he was scheming on us. How sad is it that Don's own son would rather play games than bring justice to his killer?"

"Maybe because Greer *is* the killer. Either way, it's disgusting. Don deserves better than this. From what you've told me, he was an upstanding man who was good to his entire family. And what do they do? Push him out to gain control of the business that *he* built. I swear, the Vincents take the phrase *money is the root of all evil* to another level."

"Hold on," Jake interjected as he continued scrolling through the text. "Listen to this. Manuel also overheard Faith tell Greer that he should've pointed the finger directly at the person he thought committed the murder, even if it is his own mother."

The serving spoon fell from Ella's hand. "So what is she saying? That Greer thinks Claire killed Don?"

"That's what it sounds like to me."

As Jake began replying to the message, Ella's mind shifted. Visions of being chased inside that dark dank parking garage stairwell appeared.

She squeezed her eyes shut, her therapist's words popping into her head.

Detach yourself. Immediately.

Thoughts of a warm serene beachside drowned out the noise. She walked along the soft sand, its grainy surface massaging the soles of her bare feet. Ella felt safe, calm, at peace…

"…and I cannot *wait* to hear what he has to say for himself," Jake barked, grabbing the serving spoon and filling their bowls with chicken and salad.

"Wait, I'm sorry. I must've zoned out. You can't wait to hear what who has to say for himself?"

"Ben Foray. Please don't tell me you missed my entire rant."

Ella turned her head, avoiding Jake's curious gaze as she poured two glasses of Riesling. "I believe I did. Sorry, babe. Run it by me again, please?"

"I was saying that Miles received a call from Mitch Wilkerson? Remember him? Ben's friend who broke into Don's office with him?"

"I do. What did he have to say for himself?"

"He's agreed to talk to us. *And*, he confided that Ben isn't in San Diego. He's been hiding out at Mitch's place right here in Clemmington for the past few weeks. Mitch thinks he may try and leave town soon, so we need to catch up with him before that happens."

"That's awesome, babe," Ella said as they sat down at the table. "Despite Greer's strange behavior, you all are making great progress."

"We are. Once I speak with Manuel, things should really start coming together. At least that's my hope."

"Mine too. He's got to be fed up. And things around the vineyard are only going to get more hectic now that the one-year anniversary of Don's death is upon us. It's finally time to name one of the Vincent sons president."

Jake's unblinking eyes stared into his glass as he twirled the stem between his fingertips. "Let's just pray that Manuel doesn't let us down. Because like I told Miles, he holds the key that'll crack this case wide open."

Chapter Ten

Jake pulled open the Hole in the Wall dive bar's flimsy wooden door. Before stepping inside, the stench of mold, cigarettes and marijuana smacked him in the face.

"*Damn*," Miles grunted, waving his hand in front of his nose. "This place is foul."

"And that's putting it nicely."

Clouds of smoke lingered over the trucker hat-covered heads crowding the bar. Country music blared from a run-down jukebox propped in the corner. A group of men were in the throes of a heated pool game near the back. Mugs of beer were being tossed back faster than they could be poured.

It wasn't an ideal location to question Mitch and Ben. But Mitch had tipped Jake off earlier that day, letting him know they'd be there that night. Since Jake wanted to confront Ben before he skipped town, he didn't have much choice.

"Why does it seem like this establishment just popped out of nowhere?" Miles yelled.

"Well, for starters, we're never on this side of town. And when I looked it up online, I found out it had been closed for a while after getting shut down for failing the food health inspection."

"I am not the least bit surprised by that," Miles quipped as he and Jake made their way farther inside.

The rickety wooden tables lining the narrow bar's outdated paneling were packed, making it difficult for the officers to squeeze through the crowd.

"Did Mitch say exactly where he and Ben would be sitting?"

"Far right corner in the back, over by the kitchen."

"I cannot believe they actually serve food here," Miles said as buckets of hot wings filled practically every table.

Holding in a fit of coughs, Jake peered through the haze. He spotted two men hunched over a lopsided pub table, clearly not wanting to be seen. One of them had a blond buzz cut. The other had his long brown hair pulled into a ponytail and a pair of sunglasses propped on top of his head.

"I think I've spotted our guys," Jake told Miles.

"Lead the way."

The chief casually approached the table, tapping Mitch's shoulder and extending his hand. He'd already informed Mitch that they would be keeping things cool so as not to appear suspicious and alarm Ben.

"What's up, Mitch?"

"Hey, how's it going, Chief Love?"

"*Chief,*" Ben slurred, attempting to jump up from his stool but instead falling against the wall. "Chief of *what*?"

"Chief of police. Clemmington's to be exact," he replied, grabbing Ben's arm and helping him back onto his stool. "I'm Jake Love. This is my brother, Detective Miles Love."

Ben ignored Jake's extended hand, glaring across the table at Mitch through bloodshot eyes. "What the hell is this about, man? You setting me up or something?"

"*What*? No! Of course not. I didn't even know these guys were gonna be here."

"Sure you didn't. Damn snitch…"

"Listen," Miles interjected. "Chief Love and I just so happened to be in the area, we're off the clock, and wanted to stop in and grab a couple of beers. Speaking of which, can we buy you two another round?"

Ben snatched up his cell phone and began typing away. "Nope. I'm good. A drink coming from you might be spiked with pig's blood."

Just get down to business, Jake thought, realizing the niceties weren't going to work.

"In case you two hadn't heard," he said, "Clemmington PD has reopened Don Vincent's murder investigation. You're familiar with the case, aren't you?"

Mitch's eyes darted from the officers to Ben, who remained silent while staring down at his phone. "Um…yeah, we're familiar. I'm surprised you all never caught the guy who did it."

"So are we. Mr. Vincent was killed a few days after you two were at the vineyard. On that group tour—"

"*And*?" Ben interrupted, glaring up at Jake. "So what?"

"We reviewed some interesting surveillance footage from that day. You two, along with your friend Dylan, were caught breaking into Mr. Vincent's office. Ben, I believe it was you who left there with an envelope that fell from your pocket. Would you mind telling us what was inside of it?"

Ben snatched up his mug and drained it, then discharged a smelly burp. "Yeah, I do mind. Now what?"

Miles moved closer to Ben and leaned into his ear. "We could always take this conversation down to the police station and have it there, if you think you'd be more comfortable inside an interrogation room. It's up to you."

Suddenly Ben sat straight up, nodding while wiping his eyes. "Nah, I think I'm good here. I do remember being at the vineyard that day. But what I *don't* remember is breaking into some office. Actually, you know what happened? My buddy Mitch here escorted me to a private area, and I just followed his lead, thinking it was all a part of the tour."

The group turned to Mitch. His crooked jaw hung open, but he didn't utter a word.

"*Right*, Mitch?" Ben spat through clenched coffee-stained teeth. When he failed to get a response, Ben pointed at Jake. "Look, what is this really about, man? Back when everything went down at the vineyard, the police showed up and questioned us. Then nothing came of it and we were sent on our way. The owner didn't bother to press charges. So why are you heckling me about it a year later?"

"Because, once again, shortly after that incident, Mr. Vincent turned up stabbed to death in the middle of the grape fields. Which is mighty suspicious, considering you fought with him days prior to the murder—"

Bzzzz...

Ben's cell phone vibrated so forcefully that it almost skidded off the table. Jake caught a glimpse of the screen right before Ben grabbed it. The name that appeared almost knocked him to the sawdust-covered floor.

Jada Vincent.

"What's up, babe?" Ben yelled into the phone. "No, I told you to *text* me back, not call. Why? What do you mean why? Because it's...it's hot in here! Get it? *Really* hot!"

Miles turned his head away from the group and leaned toward Jake. "You know that comment wasn't about the bar's steamy temperature, right?"

"Of course. It was all about us. And you'll never guess who he's talking to."

When Ben shot him a look, Jake pulled out his cell phone and texted Miles.

That's Jada Vincent on the other end of the line!

Miles's shoulders slowly caved as he read the message. He nodded discreetly, replying, We'll get to the bottom of that in due time. For now, let's just stick to the script.

"I don't know if they will!" Ben continued to rant. "But just in case they do, alert my law—my *guy* so that he'll be on call." After a few moments of silence, he yelled out, "No! *Blackman.*"

In his drunken state, Ben failed to realize the overtness of his thinly veiled code words. Blackman & Associates was one of the largest and most well-respected law firms in the area.

"Look, I gotta go," Ben continued. "Yeah, yeah, I'll let you know. Just make sure you hold up *your* end of the bargain."

He slammed the phone against the table and grabbed Mitch's drink, gulping it down in two swallows. Mitch just sat there, slouching in defeat.

"You done with your call?" Jake asked. "Maybe I can proceed with what I was saying?"

"Sure, Chief. You may proceed."

"So, what was inside that envelope you stole from Don Vincent's office?"

Ben's phone buzzed again. Charles Blackman's name appeared on the screen, owner of Blackman & Associates.

"Sorry, gents," Ben said, hopping up so quickly that he stumbled backward. Jake grabbed hold of him right before he fell against a dart board hanging from the wall. He stood and shook it off, then staggered toward the kitchen. "I gotta take this. Mitch, do a little strip tease or something to keep these guys entertained until I get back. *If* I come back."

The moment Ben was out of earshot, Mitch turned to the

officers. "Chief Love, Detective Love, I am so sorry about this. I knew Ben wouldn't be an easy nut to crack, but I had no idea he'd get this wild."

"It's not your fault," Jake told him. "I appreciate you informing us that he'd be here tonight."

Mitch threw his hands in the air as if he were under arrest. "Just so you know, I have *no* idea what was inside that envelope Ben stole. Once we got kicked off the tour and sent home, he sat in the back of the bus without saying a word. And another thing. He was the one who invited us to the vineyard, which was shocking, considering I've never once seen the man drink wine. Places like this are his thing. Grimy dive bars where the beer flows like water and hard drinks are strong and cheap."

"Hold on, back up a minute," Miles said. "Going on the tour of Vincent Vineyard was Ben's idea?"

"Yeah. So was breaking into Don's office. Thing is, Dylan and I didn't know it was a break-in to begin with. Ben told us that he has ties to the Vincent family, and one of them asked him to go in there and get those papers."

"Did he mention which family member?"

"No, not that I can recall."

Jake grabbed a napkin and wiped beads of perspiration from his forehead. Fatigue had begun to set in as the stifling, smoky air constricted his lungs. "Sounds to me like Ben invited you two there to be his fall guys."

"Same thing I was thinking. And we both fell for it. But I shouldn't be surprised. The man is a con artist—" Mitch stopped abruptly when Ben came bursting through the kitchen door.

"Sorry for the interruption, my friends!" he boomed.

"You seem to be in a much better mood than you were before that phone call," Miles said.

"I am. You know why? Because that was my attorney. And he advised me not to say another word to either of you." He pointed across the table at Mitch, his thin lips curled into a snarky smirk. "Hey, man. Did you know that we don't *have* to talk to the police? We can refuse to answer their questions and just refer them to our attorneys!"

Jake looked on in disgust as Ben grabbed a pitcher of beer and guzzled it down. He slammed the empty jug onto the table, then crossed one foot over the other.

"Gonna go grab us another round—"

Bam!

Ben crashed to the floor after attempting a double reverse spin. This time, Jake didn't help him up. Instead, he tossed Miles a nod that indicated *let's get the hell out of here.*

"Mitch," Jake said, extending his hand, "it was good running into you."

"Likewise," he muttered, glancing down at Ben. He was still on the floor, thrashing about on his back like an incapacitated cockroach while struggling to stand.

Jake and Miles stepped over him and made their way toward the exit.

"We need to put Ben under surveillance," Miles suggested. "And bring him into the station to formally be questioned. If he feels the need to bring his lawyer, then so be it."

"I agree. Since he's suddenly caught a case of amnesia, I'll be sure to show them both the video footage of him being chased out of Don's office with that envelope in hand. While I'm at it, I'll bring Jada in for questioning first thing in the morning. I am done playing games with these people."

"I like where your head's at, Chief," Miles said, giving

him a high five. "But quick question. What if Jada refuses to come in?"

"She won't. Especially when she finds out I know about her connection to Ben."

Before reaching the car, Jake's cell phone pinged. A text notification from Manuel popped up.

"Uh-oh," he uttered, tapping the message. "What do we have here…"

Chief, I don't know what's going on, but Jada has lost it. She's screaming, crying, running up and down the hallways and saying she's done. I heard her mention your name. Tyler managed to calm her down, and now they're in the conference room behind closed doors.

"We've got action," Jake told Miles before replying to the message.

I just met with Ben Foray and Mitch Wilkerson. Between us, Ben and Jada are somehow connected. I need to find out how. Do you have any idea what was inside that envelope Ben stole from Don's office?

Manuel replied within seconds.

I do. I wanted to share this with you in person, but, it was an amendment to Don's Will, stating that he wanted Greer to take over as president of the vineyard in the event that he dies. I was the only one who knew about that document. Or so I thought…

Jake nudged Miles's shoulder. "Check this out," he said, turning the screen toward him before typing a response.

I really need for you to get to the station and talk to me. On record. I understand your loyalty to the Vincent family, but info you're holding on to could solve this case. You owe it to Don and everyone else to bring justice to his killer.

You're absolutely right. I will be there before the end of the week. You have my word.

The brothers shared a fist bump before climbing inside the car.

"You were right," Miles said. "Manuel has been holding out on us."

"I'm just glad he's finally willing to talk. Prepare for this case to be blown wide open."

Chapter Eleven

Ella slid her palm across the linen tablecloth and intertwined her fingers with Jake's.

"Thank you," she murmured.

"Thank me? For what?"

"For tonight. Inviting me out to this nice dinner. I needed it. We both needed it."

"I agree. And you don't have to thank me, sweetheart. It's my pleasure."

The week had been a long one, and it was only Wednesday. From Jake's run-in with Ben to Jada lawyering up and refusing a police interview, frustrations were mounting. Ella had practically confined herself to the loft after fear of another attack took over. With Charlotte back in River Valley visiting their parents, she'd been spending her days doing investigative work and practicing new relaxation techniques recommended by her therapist.

"This place is nice, isn't it?" Jake asked, glancing around the restaurant. "Fancy French château with servers dressed in tuxedos, serving up delicious signature dishes and custom wine blends."

"It's beautiful. The silk brocade drapes, crystal chandeliers and stone wood-burning fireplace are definitely giving off castle vibes."

"Well, that would be fitting, considering you're a queen and all."

Ella shifted in her seat at the sight of Jake's sexy half smile. "Why are you giving me that look you know makes me swoon?"

"Because… I was just thinking."

"About what?"

"About us. And our future. I know you came to Clemmington to get away from everything that went down in River Valley. But it seems as though you're enjoying your time here. Am I right?"

"You are. Clemmington is a nice change of pace. I've lived in River Valley my entire life. Even though I move around temporarily for work, it's all I've known. But, yeah," she murmured, staring out at the ornamental garden surrounding a marble tiered fountain. "I'm definitely enjoying being here."

"Good." Jake ran his fingertips along the top of her hand. "That's what I like to hear. I'm serious about this relationship, El. You know how much I love you, and from what I've been told, the feeling is mutual."

"It definitely is."

"I think it's clear that we want to make a life together. We've both been out here long enough to know what a good thing looks like, and that once you get it, you don't let it go. Plus, Clemmington General Hospital is always hiring."

"So what exactly are you saying, Mr. Love?"

"What I'm saying is, I want to settle down. I mean *all* the way down. Get married. Start a family. And I can only see myself doing those things with you."

Same here, Ella wanted to respond. But the words refused to escape her lips. Because she had yet to reveal the news that could change Jake's mind about everything.

He picked up his glass and held it in the air. "Come on, grab your wine. We forgot to make a toast. To us. May our relationship continue to grow, prosper and reach new heights. I am so grateful for you, Ella. Being hired as chief of police, then taking on the biggest case of my career… I don't know if I could've done any of it without you. So, thank you. For being here, for supporting me and, most of all, for loving me."

Ella pressed her napkin against her cheeks, catching tears as they trickled from her eyes. "Babe, thank *you*. For all of that. I don't know if my words will stack up to yours. But I'm happy to be here by your side, loving you, supporting you in any way that I can and experiencing this journey with you. I know it isn't easy. And I hope you realize I wouldn't have made it through all that I have without you. Whether you know it or not, you saved me. So, here's to us as we continue to love, support and cover one another."

"Cheers."

As the pair sipped from their glasses, Ella stared at Jake. The love in his shining eyes punctured a hole of guilt through her chest. She felt like a fraud for claiming to adore someone despite not having been completely honest.

"Hey," Jake said. "Are you okay?"

"I'm fine," she lied, the tears she'd cried transforming from joyous to fearful.

"You sure? Because you just did that thing that you've been doing a lot lately."

"What thing?"

Jake released her hand and pointed at her face, drawing an invisible circle. "That thing where you space out, and your thoughts go somewhere deep inside your head. It's as if you've been hypnotized, and you're in some sort of trance."

"Really? *Hmm*," Ella uttered, her furrowed brows feigning confusion. "I didn't realize I'd been doing that." She slid the last of her seared duck breast and sesame ginger zucchini onto her fork and shoved it inside her mouth to avoid any further explanation. A surge of relief hit when Jake swallowed down the final bite of his elk loin, his expression still filled with happiness.

The server approached with dessert menus in hand. "Mademoiselle, monsieur? I hope that you enjoyed your main courses."

"We certainly did," Jake told him. "Everything was amazing."

"Wonderful. I am delighted to hear that. Can I interest either of you in one of our custom desserts?"

Despite being completely stuffed, Ella scanned the menu, wishing she could order everything from the lime and basil tart to the pecan-crusted coconut cheesecake.

"They all sound delicious to me," Jake said. "Which would you recommend?"

"Every offering is delectable, but if I had to choose one, I'd select the classic vanilla crème brûlée topped with citrus segments."

"Now that sounds scrumptious," Ella said. "I'd love to top off my dinner with it."

"Make that two," Jake told the server.

"Yes, monsieur. I will be back shortly. Oh, and my apologies. I forgot to mention that the desserts are complimentary."

"Really?" Jake replied. "That is so nice of the chef. Please tell him we said thank you."

"Ahh, but these were not gifted by the chef. They are being sent compliments of your friends, Tyler and Jada Vincent."

Ella's stomach dropped to the floor. She swiveled in her chair, frantically searching the restaurant for the pair.

"Oh," Jake uttered, also looking around. "Well then, we'll be sure to thank them personally before we leave. Where are they sitting?"

"Upstairs. In our private dining area. You can't see them, but they can see you. I'll be back shortly with your crème brûlée."

"Thank you." Jake waited until he walked away before turning Ella. "Interesting. And somewhat creepy, right? *You can't see them, but they can see you.* So Tyler and Jada have been watching us the whole time we've been here?"

"Apparently so." Ella shivered at the thought of being spied on. Especially by those two. "Now I feel exposed. Violated even."

"Come on now. Don't let them hold that much power over you."

Easy for you to say, Ella thought. Not only did Tyler and Jada have power over her, but they were using the moment to exert it. Knowing they were there was triggering. It transported Ella's mind back to the attack in the corn maze, the chase through the park, the hunt inside the parking garage...

You're doing it again. Deflect. Deep breaths. Think of a beach, a mountainside, glistening white ski slopes.

"I guess we should still find out where this private dining area is located," Jake said, "and personally thank them for the desserts."

"Why?"

"Because I want them to see that I'm not moved by Jada lawyering up and refusing to talk to law enforcement."

An icy chill spun around Ella at the thought of coming face-to-face with the pair.

Play sick, she thought. *Have the server wrap up the desserts to go and get the hell out of here.*

"I need to run to the men's room. Be right back."

Ella barely acknowledged the soft kiss he planted on her cheek before leaving the table. Once Jake was gone, she discreetly eyed the restaurant's second level. A glass staircase led to a stone wall. The dining area had to be on the other side of it. A couple of narrow tinted windows were encased on either end. But there was no door.

Strange...

Something caught her eye near the corner. A crack in the granite appeared. A server slipped through it, revealing a secret door.

"Mademoiselle..."

Ella flinched at the sound of the server's voice. "Yes?"

"Here is your crème brûlée—"

"I'm sorry," she interrupted, holding her hand out before he set them on the table, "but Jake and I just realized that we need to leave. Would you mind wrapping those to go?"

"I'd be happy to. I'll bring the check as well."

Ella reached inside her purse and pulled out her credit card. "Here you go. You can take care of that now. Thank you."

"You're quite welcome. Also..." He reached inside his jacket pocket and pulled out a white envelope. "This note was left for you at the hostess stand, Ms. Bowman."

How does he know my name?

She glanced down at it. There was her answer. Ella's name had been written on the front.

"Do you know who left this?" she asked.

"My apologies, but I do not. I was in the kitchen when it was delivered. I know you and Chief Love are in a hurry, mademoiselle. I will return with your wrapped desserts momentarily."

She nodded, her chest pounding as she tore open the envelope.

Dear Ms. Bowman,
It was mighty bold of you to rear your ugly head
here tonight at a Vincent family staple. Your days are
numbered. Enjoy the dessert. And know that there is
nothing sweet about what I've got planned for you.
Welcome to the jungle, bitch.

XO,
Me

Ella's vision blurred as she reread the card over and over again.

"The desserts haven't arrived yet?" Jake asked.

She bolted from her chair so abruptly that her head banged against his chin.

"*Ouch!*"

"Jake!" she squealed, clutching the sides of his face. "I am so sorry. I didn't see you come back from the men's room. You...you startled me."

"I was going in for a kiss and instead damn near got knocked out!"

As he wiggled his jaw from side to side, the server came rushing over. "Is everything all right? Monsieur, do you need medical attention?"

"No, no, I'm fine. Maybe an ice pack, but I can take care of that once I get home."

"Very well. Here is your receipt. Once again, thank you for dining with us this evening, and we look forward to see-ing you again. Have a wonderful evening."

"Receipt," Jake said. "But I didn't pay the check yet. And we haven't had dessert."

"Tonight is on me," Ella told him, quickly shoving the note deep inside her purse. "And I suddenly started feeling a little headachy. So I asked to have the desserts wrapped up to go."

"Well, don't I feel special. Thank you, my love."

"You're welcome. Now let's get home so I can pop a couple of aspirin, and you can put some ice on your—"

"Wait!" Jake interrupted, turning to the server. "Before you go, would you mind showing us to the private area where Tyler and Jada are dining?"

Dammit! Ella wanted to scream.

"Monsieur, my apologies. But Mr. and Mrs. Vincent left about five minutes ago."

"Oh, okay then," Jake said. "I guess we'll just have to catch them next time."

Ella's feet almost broke into a happy dance as she and Jake walked hand in hand toward the exit. But then, the thought of running into Tyler and Jada in the parking lot crossed her mind.

Stop it. They should be gone by now.

Nevertheless, Ella knew the past was closing in on her. She'd soon have to admit the truth to Jake. At this point, it wasn't just their relationship at risk. It was her life.

Chapter Twelve

Jake bit down on his thumbnail, his feet tapping rapidly against the floor. He checked his watch again. Manuel was almost an hour late. He promised he'd be at the police station first thing in the morning, before checking in at the vineyard.

The chief glared across the interrogation room table at Miles. "Can you believe this guy? He just emailed me yesterday. Gave me his word that he'd be here today. What type of hold do the Vincents have on him that's preventing this meeting from happening?"

"Money. Job security. Loyalty."

"But what about his loyalty to Don?"

"*Humph*." Miles squinted, staring up at the ceiling as if the answers lay in the white fiberglass tiles. "Not to sound cold, but real talk? Don isn't here anymore. Therefore, Manuel's allegiance is going to be with whoever's signing his paycheck."

"That's just sad."

"It is. But as the saying goes, the truth hurts."

There was a knock at the door.

"*Finally*," Jake said, jumping up from his chair. "Time to get some answers." He swung open the door. Their administrative assistant, Lucy, was standing on the other side.

"Lucy, what's going on?"

"Gina Ruiz is here," she panted, her olive complexion a pale shade of gray.

"Who?"

"Gina Ruiz. Manuel's wife."

"*Okay*," Jake replied, stepping out into the hallway. "Is Manuel with her?"

"No. That's the thing. She said that he's missing."

"Missing? What do you mean *missing*?"

Jake didn't wait for her to respond. He and Miles rushed to the front of the station. When they reached the waiting area, the chief paused at the sight of Gina. She was standing at the front desk, talking to a couple of officers, her body hunched over as tears poured from her swollen eyes.

"But this isn't like him!" she wailed. "Manuel has never spent one night away from me in the twenty-six years that we've been married. I'm telling you, something has happened to him. And I know those evil Vincents had something to do with it!"

"Mrs. Ruiz," Jake interjected, "I'm Chief Love. I was supposed to meet with your husband here at the station this morning. Did you know about that?"

"No," she whimpered. "I didn't. Ever since Mr. Vincent's murder, Manuel has been keeping so many secrets from me—"

When her voice cracked, Jake held out his arm. "Mrs. Ruiz, please. Follow me to the conference room where we can talk privately. Can I get you anything? Coffee, tea, water?"

"The only thing you can do for me right now is find my husband. *Please*. And bring him home safely."

Once inside the conference room, Jake offered Mrs. Ruiz a seat and set a bottle of water and a box of tissues on the table. A sense of dread burned deep in his gut. It was an instinct he'd possessed for years, and it was never wrong. Someone must've caught wind of Manuel's interview with law enforcement and done something to stop it.

Jake grabbed a blank notebook from the cabinet and sat across from Gina. "Mrs. Ruiz, when was the last time you spoke with your husband?"

"Yesterday evening. At around 6:30 p.m. He said he was heading into an operations meeting with Mrs. Vincent and would be home as soon as they were done."

"Mrs. Vincent, as in Claire Vincent?" Miles asked.

"Yes. *Claire.*" The disdain in her tone seeped through stiffened lips.

"Were you and Mrs. Vincent having prob—" Jake began before stopping mid-sentence. He'd find out whether the two women were having issues later. Right now, his number one priority was finding Manuel. "Why didn't you call and report your husband missing at some point during the night since it's so out of character for him not to come home?"

Mrs. Ruiz recoiled in her chair. "Because I… I thought he may have finally given in to Mrs. Vincent's charms and stayed the night with her."

The room fell silent. Only the sound of Jake's creaking chair could be heard as he leaned to the side. "Are you saying that you believe your husband is having some sort of personal relationship with Mrs. Vincent?"

She was slow to respond, first pressing a tissue against her flushed cheeks, then sniffling quietly. "Possibly. I have no proof of it. But those two seem to have grown quite close since Mr. Vincent's murder."

"Well, first things first. We need to find Manuel. We'll start by going to Vincent Vineyard and seeing if any of the family members or employees know of his last whereabouts."

Jake was interrupted when Gina's cell phone pinged. She pulled it from her purse, frantically unlocking the screen while chanting a prayer under her breath.

"Oh, my God!" she screamed.

"What is it, Mrs. Ruiz?"

"It's my son, Daniel. He and his brother Mateo used the location apps on their cell phones to try and locate their father. They're saying he's somewhere near Cypress Creek!"

Muscle spasms ripped through Jake's limbs as he leaped from his chair and hurdled toward the door. "Mrs. Ruiz, please stay here for a moment. Detective Love and I need to alert the other officers."

"No!" she insisted, running after him. "I have to get to that creek and find my husband!"

"It would be much safer if we escort you there. But first I have to pass this information along. Just give me a moment. I'll have Lucy come and sit with you while I assemble my team."

Mrs. Ruiz's head fell as she collapsed against the wall, crying into her hands. After Jake stepped out into the hallway and signaled Lucy inside, he and Miles charged up and down the aisles of the station, alerting his officers of the new development.

"Call the paramedics," Jake said to Officer Underwood. "Tell them to get to Cypress Creek ASAP!"

As the other officers rushed to their squad cars, Jake ran to the crime lab and pounded on the door. Lena threw it open within seconds.

"What's wrong?" she panted, her face covered in goggles and a mask.

"Manuel Ruiz never showed up for his interview. His wife is here, and his sons may have located him somewhere near Cypress Creek. Why don't you ride out there with David and I'll go with Miles. Make sure you bring your master forensics kit. We may have a crime scene on our hands."

JAKE PULLED INTO a clearing near the edge of Cypress Creek's hiking trail. He and Miles hopped out of the car and ran to the trunk, quickly slipping on latex gloves and blue booties before heading toward the woodland.

Officers had already begun stringing yellow crime scene tape along the perimeter. Once Jake and Miles entered the grove, the sun's bright rays disappeared between eighty-foot-tall black oaks' bristled leaves.

The brothers stepped carefully over the trees' oddly shaped roots growing above ground, their feet sinking into the forest floor's damp soil. Echoes of croaking frogs, buzzing insects and chirping birds ricocheted through the damp breeze.

"It feels like I'm walking through a jungle," Miles said.

"Yeah, which is exactly why I'm glad Mrs. Ruiz decided to stay back at the station. She didn't need to be out here. Especially if we end up finding Manuel's body."

The pair approached a group of officers searching the edge of the creek.

"Anything turn up so far?" Jake asked David.

"Nothing yet. We're keeping an eye out for anything viable. A shoe, a pair of glasses, a cell phone...anything that may lead us to Mr. Ruiz."

Jake took a quick look around the vicinity. "Where is Lena? She was supposed to ride here with you."

"She did. But she's gonna hang back in the car for a bit. Just between us, I think she might still be struggling after everything she went through with the Heart-Shaped Murders investigation. Since she spends most of her time in the forensics lab these days, being out here might be triggering. So I told her we'd call if we need her."

"Good idea. But hopefully we won't—"

A gut-wrenching scream whirred through the air.

"Help! *Help!*" someone yelling in the distance.

Jake and his officers took off running in the direction of the shouting.

"Who's there?" Jake called out. "And where are you?"

"It's Daniel and Mateo Ruiz! We're over by the west end of the creek!"

Miles grabbed Jake's arm and pointed up ahead. "This way!"

The excruciating cries grew closer. And louder.

This can't be good, Jake thought, a sick feeling pooling inside his chest.

He and the team continued running at full speed, pushing past low-hanging branches while leaping over hollows hidden within the dirt.

"Should I call Lena and tell her to get out here?" David heaved.

"Yes!" Jake yelled right before his phone buzzed. The call was coming from the police station.

"Chief Love speaking."

"Chief! It's Lucy."

He could barely hear her for all the screaming in the background.

"You're gonna have to speak up, Lucy!"

"Can you hear me now?" she shrieked.

"Yes! What's going on?"

"Mrs. Ruiz's sons just called her. They think they've found their father's body floating in the creek! Where are you?"

"We're looking for them now. Tell Mrs. Ruiz that we're handling it and I'll contact her once we know more."

"Okay, got it."

Jake peered up ahead. Two young men who looked to be in their late teens clung to one another near the water's edge.

"I think I see Mr. Ruiz's sons!" Miles said.

The chief sped up, fighting off the cramps tightening his leg.

When the young men noticed law enforcement heading their way, they charged toward them, jumping wildly in the air while pointing toward the water.

"He's over here!" they yelled.

Daniel and Mateo led them to a body floating near the bank of the creek.

"Oh, my God," Miles choked, covering his mouth.

A swarm of fathead minnows darted around Manuel's thick black hair as it swayed in the current. His white shirt was pulled up to his neck, exposing his bloated pale back. Jagged bite marks covered his skin, inflicted by scavenging creatures feeding on his corpse. An infestation of blowflies hovered over his body, crawling along the flesh in search of a perfect spot to lay eggs.

One of Mr. Ruiz's sons ran toward the water, almost reaching the body before his brother pulled him back.

"Guys!" Jake said, wrapping his arms around both men and guiding them away from the creek. "Please, I know this is tough. But you're gonna have to let us do our jobs and figure out what happened here. By the way, I'm Chief Love. I'll be handling the investigation. And I am so sorry that this has happened to your father."

"Who would've done this to him?" one of the brothers cried. "Why would some maniac kill our dad?"

"That's exactly what we're going to find out. In the meantime, I'd like for you both to head to the police station with Officer Underwood. He's going to ask you some questions. Your mom is there too, and I'm sure she needs you right now. I'll check in with you shortly. Okay?"

They nodded, leaning on one another as Officer Underwood escorted them away from the crime scene.

Miles placed a hand of support on Jake's shoulder. "I just called the medical examiner's office. He's on the way."

"Good, thanks." Jake instructed a couple of officers to continue cordoning off the area, reminding everyone not to disturb the body. Just as Detective Campbell began taking photos of the scene, Lena and David ran up.

She stared out into the creek, shaking her head while eyeing the victim. "What are you thinking? That someone found out Mr. Ruiz was coming to speak with law enforcement and got to him before he got to you?"

"That's exactly what I'm thinking," Jake replied.

"Well, I'd better get in here and start processing the scene. I'll keep you posted and let you know if I find anything worthwhile. Miles, did I just hear you say that the medical examiner is on his way?"

"Yes, he is."

"All right." Lena pulled several brown paper bags and a metal scalpel from her forensics kit. "I'll be over by the water, gathering samples of the soil near Mr. Ruiz's body. Once the medical examiner removes him from the water, I'll collect his clothing along with any trace and biological evidence I can find. Fingernail clippings, blood evidence, wounds, bite marks…"

Jake pulled his father's white monogrammed handkerchief from his pocket, which he'd passed down for good luck, and wiped his face. "Sounds good. I'll be circling the area, searching for evidence and keeping an eye on things. Give me a holler if you need me."

Lena gave him a thumbs-up before setting off toward the creek. "Fingers crossed there's something viable here. We need it. Especially after the reexamination of evidence from Don's crime scene didn't render any new results."

"Yes, we do," Jake grumbled, still disappointed by that news.

He found a quiet area away from all the chaos and called Ella. She picked up on the first ring.

"Hey, babe. How did it go with Manuel this morning?"

He opened his mouth to speak. But the words just wouldn't come out.

"Hello? Jake, are you still here? *Dammit*, I think I lost you."

"No, I'm still here."

"Uh-oh. You don't sound too good. What's wrong? Please don't tell me that Manuel didn't show up."

"No, he didn't show up. Because he's—"

"Wait," Ella interrupted, "don't tell me. Let me guess. Manuel lawyered up too, didn't he? See, I cannot believe how these people are trying to avoid being—"

"*Ella*. Listen to me. Manuel didn't show up because he's… he's dead."

The other end of the phone went silent. Jake waited for her to say something. But after several moments, there was still no response.

"El? You there?"

"I… I'm here," she stammered. "This is just…unreal. Manuel is dead? What is happening? I feel like I'm reliving a nightmare all over again. First it was the Numeric Serial Killer, and now this!"

Jake pressed his fist against his forehead, wondering if he'd made the wrong move.

You shouldn't have called her with this news. You should have waited until you got home. Told her in person.

But he knew it was only a matter of time before the media caught wind of Manuel's death. He'd rather Ella find out about it from him than some random reporter.

"Listen," he said. "I don't want you to get upset. I just want you to be aware of what's going on. We still don't know exactly what happened to him. But his body was found floating in Cypress Creek, by his sons, unfortunately. I've got all of law enforcement out here with me and we're waiting on the medical examiner to arrive. Once he does, I'll know more."

"Does Charlotte know yet?"

"I doubt it. Miles is busy examining the crime scene with Lena, and I'm pretty sure the news hasn't hit the media yet."

"So what's next, Jake? How in the hell are you going to catch whoever's doing this? I mean, it's obviously someone connected to Vincent Vineyard. But who?"

"That's what we're all here working to find out. I said it before and I'll say it again. I'm done playing mister nice guy. I am not doing any more polite rounds of questioning or interviews on anybody else's turf. I'll be conducting interrogations down at the station, with lie detector tests to boot. And you'd better believe I'll be obtaining a search warrant, giving me full access to the vineyard. And if Manuel was in fact murdered, let's just hope the killer left some sort of DNA evidence behind—"

"*Chief!*" Lena called out. "I need you over here. I've got something!"

"I'll be right there!"

Ella moaned into the phone. "I heard all that. Be careful, babe. And please, keep me posted on any new updates that you get. In the meantime, I'll reach out to Charlotte and let her know what's going on."

"Thanks. Love you."

"Love you too."

A surge of energy shot through Jake as he rushed over toward the edge of the creek. He crouched down next to Lena, observing the small coin envelope she was holding.

"What have you got there?" he asked.

"Shell casings. Four of them. Looks like they're twenty-two caliber long rifles."

Jake peered inside the envelope and studied the contents. "So Manuel may have been shot to death?"

"Possibly. Either that, or he drowned. While we wait on the medical examiner to provide that information, I'll test these casings for DNA."

"How can you do that?" an officer asked who'd been hovering behind them.

"Easy," Lena replied. "First, I'll soak them in a tube of mixed chemicals that will break open cells that could identify a suspect. I'll also enter the serial numbers into the National Integrated Ballistics Information Network and compare the cartridges to those that are already in the system. You never know. They may end up connecting to another crime that's been committed."

"That would be great," Jake said. "I'm so glad we're using the NIBIN now. Since those casings look to be made of brass, you may be able to lift fingerprints off of them too, right?"

"That is correct. I've taught you well." Lena turned toward the creek, squinting as she stared out at Manuel's body. "It'll be interesting to hear the results of the autopsy. Speaking of which, I wonder when the medical examiner is going to get here. I really want to start lifting evidence from the body."

No sooner than the words were out of her mouth, Dr. Lynn and two of his transporters were allowed past the crime scene tape.

"Chief Love, Ms. Love, it's good to see you both, despite the grim circumstances, of course."

"Dr. Lynn," Jake said, standing and shaking his hand. "It's good to see you as well."

The medical examiner pointed toward the water. "Has the victim been identified yet?"

"He has. His name is Manuel Ruiz. The body hasn't been disturbed. We're thinking that he was attacked in some way and left for dead. Lena just found several shell casings near the edge of the water, not too far from the body."

"Good to know. Once we remove him from the creek, we'll be able to get a better look and possibly figure out how he lost his life. I'll search for ligature marks, stab wounds, bullet wounds… You know the drill. Of course, I'll have more definitive answers once the body is transferred to my office and a full autopsy is performed."

"Absolutely. I'll get out of your way and let you get to it. Lena will be working with you as she collects biological evidence from the body. If either of you need me, I'll be in the vicinity. Please, keep me updated on any pertinent findings."

"Will do." Lena gave his shoulder a reassuring nudge. He responded with a nod of thanks, then watched as Dr. Lynn photographed Manuel's body. The medical examiner's assistants pulled several white linen sheets from their equipment case, along with a black vinyl body bag, rolls of tape and brown paper bags.

Once Dr. Lynn was done taking pictures, he and his team pulled Manuel's body from the water and laid him on his back. Jake's stomach twisted into knots at the sight of his swollen, disfigured face, which had been mangled by ravenous aquatic creatures. Right below a particularly deep bite mark on the left side of his chest were two small red holes.

Lena turned to Jake and pointed toward the wounds just as Miles walked up.

"What's the latest?" the detective asked.

"Lena found several shell casings near Manuel's body. And there looks to be gunshot wounds in his chest."

"*Humph.* The plot thickens…"

"And all roads are leading back to those Vincent brothers. We just need to figure out which one of them is willing to kill for the vineyard's top spot."

Chapter Thirteen

Charlotte pulled in front of Clemmington General Hospital and put the car in Park.

"Are you sure you don't want me to come inside with you?" she asked Ella.

"I'm positive. I'll be fine. Bringing me here was more than enough."

"Okay, well, I'll be waiting for you when you're done." Before Ella stepped out of the car, Charlotte grabbed her arm. "Wait, do you really think this is a good idea? I mean, you've been through so much already. Taking on a full-time job right now may be too overwhelming, don't you think?"

Ella fell against the back of the seat. "For the tenth time, Charlotte, no. I don't think taking on a full-time job would be too much for me. I need this. I cannot continue to just sit around Jake's loft, digging through the same case files over and over again in search of new leads. Nursing is my passion. It takes me away from all the madness that's happening around me. Even my therapi—" She paused, remembering that she hadn't told Charlotte she'd been in counseling. "I mean, working with patients is therapeutic. It'll be good for me."

"Well, if going back to work is something you need in

your life so badly, why didn't you tell Jake about this meeting with the hospital administrator?"

"I love how you're acting like we haven't been through this already. I'm not one of your suspects, Charlotte. Constantly asking me the same questions isn't going to change my answers. Now, for the last time, I'm planning on surprising Jake with the news once I get the job. He and I talked about me moving to Clemmington permanently and taking on a full-time job. This is my way of showing him that I'm serious about it."

"Okay, fine," Charlotte snipped. "You know, you've been acting really weird lately. Like there's something going on that you're not telling me. Are you sure you're not hiding anything?"

Ella's head swiveled as she stared straight ahead at the hospital's redbrick exterior. Lying to her sister had never come easy. The older they got, the harder it became. "No, Char. I am not hiding anything from you. Now can I please go inside before I'm late?"

"Yes. Go on. I'll try and find a space near the entrance so you won't miss me when you come out. Good luck, Nurse Bowman."

"Thanks, sis."

Ella bolted from the car and practically ran through the hospital's automatic glass doors. The relief of being out from underneath Charlotte's scrutiny was eclipsed by a bout of guilt.

You have got to confess your secret to somebody. Why not let it be your own sister?

But as the Vincent Vineyard murder mystery deepened, Ella grew wearier of discussing her past with anyone. Including Charlotte. After Manuel's murder, the entire town of Clemmington was up in arms, feeling as though they may

have another serial killer on their hands. Ella, however, refused to sit around wondering whether or not she'd be next.
She had to get out and live. Being cooped up alone while
waiting for the next threat to drop had become unbearable.

Just focus on this moment and getting the job, Ella
thought as she approached the reception desk.

"Good morning, ma'am," a plump older woman with a
fire-engine red pixie cut said without looking up from her
computer screen. "How may I help you?"

"Good morning. My name is Ella Bowman. I'm here to
meet with the hospital administrator, Bernadette Stevens."

The woman's acrylic French tips click-clacked across her
keyboard as she searched for the appointment in her system. "All right, Ms. Bowman. Here's a visitor's pass. The
elevators are straight back behind the reception desk and
to your right. Mrs. Stevens's office is located on the third
floor. Once you arrive, please let her assistant know that
you're here for your 10:00 a.m. meeting, and she'll take it
from there."

"Will do. Thank you."

Ella glanced around the facility as she made her way to
the elevator banks. It was modest, with its stark white walls
and speckled beige tile. Scenic watercolor paintings served
as the decor, while artificial birch trees and pale blue furniture filled the lobby. The staff seemed friendly enough,
smiling and greeting everyone from coworkers to visitors
as they passed one another. The vibe was simple, but cozy.

I could get used to this...

When the elevator arrived, Ella stepped on and headed
to the third floor. As soon as the doors opened, a young
blonde woman wearing turquoise cat-eye glasses and a huge
smile bellowed, "Hello, Ella Bowman?" before hopping up
from her chair.

"Yes!" Ella boomed more enthusiastically than she'd intended. She blamed it on the receptionist's big cheerleader energy.

"It's so nice to meet you! But..." She paused, propping her fist underneath her chin while putting on a dramatic pout. "I do have a bit of bad news."

"Oh, no. Don't tell me. The neonatal nurse position has already been filled?"

"No, no, nothing like that. Mrs. Stevens just had a family emergency and left a few minutes ago." The woman plopped back down into her chair, grabbing the desk before she rolled back into the wall. She snatched a sticky note off her computer monitor and slowly read from it. "Mrs. Stevens sends her apologies, asked that I thank you for filling out the job application online, and said she'll email you to reschedule today's meeting."

A pang of disappointment stirred inside Ella's head. The neonatal unit was looking to fill the position immediately. She'd hoped to land the job today and start as soon as possible.

"Okay then," Ella muttered, taking a step back toward the elevator. "Thank you, and I, um... I guess I'll just keep an eye out for Mrs. Stevens's message—"

"Wait!" the woman shouted before jumping back up. "I have an idea. Since you're already here, why don't you go up and take a look at the NICU? You know, so that today won't feel like a wasted visit."

Ella clasped her hands together, her spirits lifting at the suggestion. "I would love to. Thank you. Where is the unit located?"

"Just one floor up. On four. I would take you myself, but we're so short-staffed, and I'm pretty much working this floor alone. But you'll be fine. I'll call and let the receptionist know you're on the way."

"I really appreciate this. Thanks again."

After stepping back onto the elevator, Ella arrived on the fourth floor within seconds. The receptionist was on a call but waved her through the heavy metal door.

She entered the hallway, her ears perking at the familiar sounds of patient monitors ringing and alarms pinging throughout the unit. The bright green walls and shiny hardwood floors appeared more vibrant than the hospital's sterile lobby—a nice touch for parents in distress.

Ella peeked inside the patient rooms, clutching her chest as she eyed the incubators housing newborn babies. Being there felt cathartic, comforting even. It was a reminder of where she belonged.

She tiptoed along the corridor, silencing the loud heels on her shoe boots, while everyone on the floor spoke in hushed voices. Two nurses standing outside a room whispered to one another, their grinning expressions filled with joy.

"Yes!" one of them exclaimed. "Baby Melinda started breathing on her own today and was transferred upstairs to the nursery."

Aww, the nursery! Ella almost blurted out. She smiled at the women and continued down the hallway, staring at a stairwell door once she reached the end of the corridor.

Her feet shuffled back and forth. She was itching to go up to the nursery and lay eyes on the babies.

No one would mind, she thought, already considering herself an employee.

Before giving it another thought, Ella crept into the stairwell and took two steps at a time up to the fifth floor.

She cracked open the door, sticking her head inside and taking a look around the bustling unit before entering. Its green walls and shiny floors resembled that of the NICU. Doctors and nurses scampered up and down the hall, zooming past visitors carrying bouquets of flowers and new moms getting in a little exercise.

Ella approached the nursery, swooning at all the chubby-faced babies swathed in blankets.

"Aww," she breathed, her forehead pressed against the glass.

"They're adorable, aren't they?" someone asked.

She spun around, startled by the question. But when she saw what appeared to be a loving grandmother, her defenses settled.

"They sure are," Ella gushed. "I'm a nurse, hoping to get a job here inside the NICU. This is the part I miss most. The newborns."

The woman came closer, pointing at a little girl swaddled in a fluffy pink blanket. "There's my grandbaby. Bonnie Nicole. She is such a sweet girl. Quiet, already breastfeeding, sleeping well... Nothing like her mother, who was colicky, didn't latch for quite some time and refused to sleep through the night. *Whew!* I certainly don't miss those days."

"Well, at least you'll have a different experience this go round. Congratulations to you."

"Thank you so much. I'd better get back to my daughter's room and check on her. Good luck with that nursing job."

As the woman walked away, Ella suddenly remembered that Charlotte was outside waiting for her.

She set off down the hallway in search of the elevator banks. The west wing corridor's stairwell came into view first. Ella figured she'd stop back down on the third floor and thank Mrs. Stevens's receptionist before leaving.

After giving the unit one last look, Ella slipped inside the stairwell, feeling confident in her decision to return to work. She bounced down the concrete stairs, the sound of her heels echoing loudly off the industrial gray walls. For a brief moment, the memory of being chased inside the casino's parking garage flashed through her mind.

Nope! she told herself, immediately deflecting.

Thoughts of the nursery's sweet babies overrode the chase. Ella focused on the newborns until she reached the third floor. She grabbed the handle and pulled the door. It didn't open. She tried again, a little harder this time. It didn't budge.

What the hell?

Ella gave it a few more yanks before giving up and running to the fourth floor. She tried that door. It too was locked. She felt herself growing hot as her breathing quickened.

Stay calm...

She pulled out her cell phone and called Charlotte. Three beeps chirped in her ear.

Call failed.

Ella looked around. The ceilings, floors and walls were all made of cement. There were no windows. It was as if she were inside a bomb shelter.

Of course. No reception.

She stared at the door. It was painted gray, not white like the one she'd seen on the way up to the fifth floor. The vinyl decal with the floor number was black, not silver like the others.

That's when it dawned on her. Ella had used the east wing stairwell to go up from the third to the fourth and fifth floors, then got turned around in the maternity ward and took the wrong stairwell back down.

"That's okay," she told herself, ignoring the rumble of fear bubbling inside her stomach. "This is an easy fix."

She knocked on the door, praying that someone on the other side could hear her.

"Hello?" Ella called out.

No response.

"Hello!" she tried again, louder this time. Her knocking turned into banging as her anxiety increased.

Once again, nothing.

"Forget this," Ella uttered, charging down the stairs while convincing herself that the first-floor door would be unlocked. It wasn't.

"Hey!" she screamed. Prickling pain shot up her arm as she pounded on the door. "I'm locked in the stairwell! Can anybody hear me?"

Still, no response.

Ella squeezed the burgundy metal railing and glanced down. There were a few more sets of stairs below. After running the three flights, hitting the landing and practically falling into the door, she grabbed the handle.

"*Please* let this one be unlocked," she whispered, twisting the lever and pulling back. This time, it opened.

Her chest heaved with relief. "Thank you!"

Ella stepped inside the room, unable to see through the darkness. The door slammed behind her. She winced, blinking rapidly to adjust her vision.

Several bleak corridors appeared up ahead. The concrete floor was covered in dust, and yellow caution tape hung from the doors. Do Not Enter and Construction Zone signs were scattered everywhere. A flickering exit sign hung above a door in the far distance. Ella made a run for it. She reached the halfway point.

Boom!

A door slammed behind her. She stopped abruptly. And waited.

Silence.

Ella spun around. A sharp gasp caught in her throat. She held the cough threatening to escape her lips, searching for some sign of movement. There was none.

Turn around and get the hell out of here!

She set off toward the exit, her muscles throbbing as her boots pounded the concrete.

"Excuse me, ma'am?" a strange voice rasped behind her.

Do not stop. You're almost there!

"Ma'am! Is everything all right? I heard banging inside the stairwell, and when I checked the second floor, you were already heading down to the basement."

Ella slowed down a bit and glanced over her shoulder. A figure was jogging toward her dressed in scrubs, a white lab coat, surgical hat, mask and gloves.

"*Oh, thank God,*" she cried out, falling against the wall while panting uncontrollably. "I got locked inside the stairwell and freaked out. So I ran down here. All I'm trying to do is leave the hospital."

"You poor thing," the doctor murmured, moving in closer. "I'm so sorry that happened to you. Since this area has been blocked off, all the doors are locked. Come with me. I'll show you where you can exit. It certainly isn't down here. This area is under construction and restricted to the public."

"Thank you so much," Ella breathed, trying to get a better look at the person. The voice sounded strained, as if they had just undergone throat surgery. The scrubs and lab coat were ill-fitting, appearing way too big. But the downturned brown eyes behind the goggles—they appeared somewhat familiar.

"You're welcome. Follow me."

Ella hesitated. The tingling in her gut set off an alarm inside her head. Something wasn't right.

The doctor spun around. "You coming? Or do you wanna stay down here and let the bogeyman get you? Ha!"

Ella jumped at the doctor's sinister laughter. *That wasn't funny*, she almost spewed.

"Sorry," the doctor snorted. "That's a running joke between my kids and me. I guess it just popped into my head since Halloween is right around the corner."

"You know what?" Ella said, slowly backing away. "I think I'm gonna just try this door down here instead of going back upstairs. The sign above it says it's an exit, so I'll take my chances and see where it leads me."

The doctor's head swiveled. Ella didn't wait for a response. She turned and headed toward the door, struggling to walk at a normal pace so as not to appear frightened.

"Suit yourself!" the doctor called out.

Behind her, Ella heard footsteps thumping. But they weren't going in the opposite direction. They were coming after her.

"*Ellaaa*," the doctor sang out. "You're not gonna get away from me this time!"

Her calm stride transformed into a frantic sprint. Tears sprang from Ella's eyes as reality hit. Her attacker was following her every move, even hunting her down inside the hospital.

Will I make it out alive this time?

The exit was a just few feet away. Ella reached out, her fingertips inches away from the handle.

"Gotcha!" the assailant screamed before jumping onto her back.

Ella's body slammed against the concrete floor. She cried out in pain. "Help! *Please*, somebody help me!"

The attacker pressed his mouth against Ella's ear. She cringed as his sharp wet teeth grazed her lobe. "Shut up before I slice your throat open!" The threat was backed up by a cold jagged piece of metal pressed against her neck.

"Why are you doing this to me?" Ella hissed. "What do you *want*?"

"I want you to get the hell out of Clemmington before I tell everyone your nasty little secret. You know what you did." He flipped her over onto her back and took hold of her neck. "Unless you wanna end up like Manuel…"

"No!" Ella screamed, flinching underneath the weight of his body as excruciating pain shot up her spine. She let out one last cry for help before the grip on her throat intensified. Ella choked, her head tightening as the blood vessels in her face pulsated.

The attacker squeezed her lower half between his thighs while his elbows dug into her chest. Barely able to move, she attempted to swing her arms and fight back. But her fists couldn't connect. She was punching the air, wasting her last bits of energy. Her breathing thinned. Ella felt herself fading.

The exit door flew open. Bright sunlight poured into the dimly lit basement. A burly construction worker wearing a red plaid shirt, neon mesh work vest and white hard hat appeared in the doorway.

"Hey!" he yelled. "What are you two doing down here? This area is restricted. Didn't you see all the signs?"

Ella's attacker jumped up and backed away. "Yes, we did. But this woman was in distress. I was attempting CPR. However, she seems fine now."

No! Ella tried to scream. But the hold on her neck had numbed her vocal cords.

"I've got to get back to my patients!" the assailant said before taking off running.

"Yo, Doc!" the construction worker called out. "Didn't I just tell you that you're not supposed to be down here? Exit this way."

But it was too late. He had already ducked back inside the stairwell.

Ella rolled over onto her side, gasping for air while clutching her neck.

"Ma'am, are you all right?"

"No," she whispered. "But I will be."

He bent down and helped her to her feet. She immediately fell against the wall.

"Whoa!" he grabbed her arms, helping to steady her. "Do you need me to escort you up to the emergency room or something?"

"No, I'm fine. Could you just show me the way to the parking lot?"

"Sure," he said. "It's right out here."

He held Ella up as they walked out onto the loading dock, where a group of workers were busy loading wooden planks onto the backs of pickup trucks. She wanted to throw her arms around the man and thank him for saving her life. But she didn't have the energy.

"Are you sure you're okay?" he probed once again. "Do you need me to walk you to your car?"

"I appreciate the offer, but no. I'm fine."

He pointed toward a half-open rolling steel door. "Head straight through there and to the right. The parking lot will be straight ahead."

"Thank you again."

Ella fought through the pain of her attack, struggling to straighten up and appear normal as she searched for Charlotte's car. A fresh batch of tears threatened to fall at the thought of escaping yet another brutal confrontation. But she held them back. She couldn't let her sister see her upset.

Just get to the car, Ella told herself, ducking down in between the vehicles for fear that her attacker may be watching. The moment she reached Charlotte's sedan, Ella tore open the door and fell into the passenger seat.

"Hey!" Charlotte boomed. "How'd it go? It must've been great considering you were gone for so long. Tell me all about it. Wait! Before you start, just let me apologize for questioning whether or not you're ready to go back to work. Only you can make that decision. Not me, or anyone else for that matter. So, I'm sorry. Now go on. I'm listening."

Ella sat straight up, turned to her sister and burst into tears.

"Oh, honey, what's wrong?" Charlotte embraced her tightly. "You didn't get the job?"

"No, that's not it. Remember earlier, when you said it seems like I've been keeping something from you?"

"I do. Why?"

"Because you were right," Ella muttered. "We've got a lot to talk about."

Chapter Fourteen

"Is your name Jada Vincent?" a polygraph examiner asked.

"Yes."

"Are you the president of the United States?"

"No."

"Have you ever stolen anything?"

"I—um…no. *Wait.* Yes."

Jake stood inside the observation room, looking on as Jada underwent a lie detector test in the interrogation room. The examiner had already told her to stop fidgeting three times. But she continued to wiggle her index and ring fingers, which were covered in black electrodes that measured the skin's sweat and ability to conduct energy.

"She's nervous," Miles said. "Notice how she can't keep still? Her legs are bouncing around all over the place. I guess she doesn't realize all that excess movement will affect her results."

"I don't think Jada is taking any of this seriously. She has no idea we're considering her a person of interest. I'm surprised her attorney even agreed to a polygraph."

"He seems pretty convinced that she's innocent, so that could be it."

Jake peered at the examiner's computer screen. He studied the lines measuring her respiratory rate, electrodermal activity and heart rate. So far, only small lines appeared, indicating her answers were truthful.

"Did you have anything to do with Manuel Ruiz's death?" the examiner asked.

"No."

"Were you born on November tenth?"

"Yes."

"Do you know a man named Ben Foray?"

Jada remained silent. The examiner looked up at her, awaiting a response. The lines on the computer screen enlarged significantly, indicating the question had caused her blood pressure, breathing and perspiration rates to increase.

"Do you know a man named Ben Foray?" the examiner repeated.

"Nuh—uhh...*no.*"

"*Wow*," Miles breathed, running his hands down the sides of his face. "I cannot believe she lied about that. What is she hiding?"

"I don't know, but best believe we're gonna find out."

Jada shifted in her chair, the sequins on her yellow bellbottoms jumpsuit blinging off the walls.

"Did you have anything to do with Don Vincent's murder?" the examiner asked.

"No."

"Are you currently in the state of California?"

"Yes."

"Do you know who killed Don Vincent?"

"No."

Once again, Jake monitored the computer screen. The lines were small, indicating Jada was telling the truth.

"Mrs. Vincent, the polygraph test is complete," the examiner said. "Please remain still while I take the instrument out of operation."

She slumped back in her chair, kicking her clear platform wedges out in front of her.

"Thank *God*," she moaned. "Hurry up and get this stuff off of me! How did I do? Did I pass? Wait, what am I saying? I already know the answer to that. Of course I passed!"

The examiner stood over Jada, removing the black rubber tubes from her chest and abdomen. "I need to speak with law enforcement first. Once I do that, I'll come back in and share the results with you."

"What the hell? Well, can I at least speak to my attorney?" Jada jolted from her chair and swung open the door. "Nick? *Nick!* Get in here. I'm done!"

Jake rushed inside the interrogation room. "Mrs. Vincent, I will send your attorney in momentarily. Joseph," he said to the examiner, "I'll show you to the conference room. We can talk there."

Once everyone was situated in their designated locations, Jake and Miles sat across from Joseph.

"So," Miles said, "how did she do?"

The examiner opened his laptop and pulled up the test results. "Well, there was no deception indicated on any of the questions."

"*Really?*" Jake blurted. "But I saw those lines on the screen increase significantly when you asked Mrs. Vincent whether she—"

"Knew Ben Foray," Joseph finished for him. "I was getting to that. It was the only response that rendered an inconclusive result."

"Inconclusive? Not deceptive?"

"That is correct."

"Interesting..." Jake turned to Miles, his wrinkled expression perplexed. "Why don't we bring Mrs. Vincent in? See what she has to say about this?"

"Let's do it."

The minute Jake hit the hallway, he heard Jada screaming at the top of her lungs from behind the interrogation
room's closed door.

"Listen to me, Nick! My heart was thumping out of my
chest the whole damn time! Why would you let me agree
to a lie detector test in the first place?"

Jake stood outside the door, listening for her attorney's
response.

"Because you're innocent, Mrs. Vincent. I'm telling you,
this was a power move on your part. There is not one iota
of a doubt in my mind that you passed the test."

"Oh, please. Stop trying to butter me up. I'm not paying
you five hundred dollars an hour to kiss my ass. I'm paying you to save it!"

Jake had heard enough. He threw open the door and stuck
his head inside. "Mrs. Vincent, Mr. Blackman, the polygraph examiner is ready to reveal the test results. Please,
follow me."

Jada, who'd been standing over her attorney with her
arms crossed, leaned down and stuck her finger in his face.
"You'd better hope these results are in my favor. Because
if they're not, and this town finds out and starts spreading
rumors that I'm some deranged serial killer, I swear I will
beat your—"

"Mrs. Vincent," her attorney interrupted, "why don't we
go with Chief Love and wrap things up so you can get back
to the vineyard? Didn't you say you have a meeting with…
with, um…"

As he headed toward the door, Jada shot visual daggers at
his back. "A meeting? What meeting? I never said I had a—"

"We're right behind you, Chief Love," her lawyer interjected, side-eyeing Jada after she failed to catch the bone he'd thrown.

Once Jake led them inside the conference room, Jada tossed her Chanel bag onto the table and threw her arms in the air. "All right, mister polygraph man. Enough with all the suspense. Let's hear it. How did I do?"

"Well, as I told the officers, the majority of your responses rendered a result of no deception indicated."

"Yay! *Wait...*" she sidled up to her attorney and whispered, "What does that mean?"

"That you passed the test."

"*Yes!*" Jada squealed, her sequin pants swishing loudly as she swayed her hips from side to side.

"There was one question, however," the examiner continued, "where the results rendered inconclusive."

The flurry of yellow sparkles stopped mid-swirl. Once again, Jada turned to her lawyer. "Translation, please?"

"An inconclusive result occurs when neither a truthful nor deceptive result is rendered."

"In English, Nick! Is this man saying I didn't score a hundred percent on the test?" Jada charged the table, hovering over the polygraph examiner's laptop. "Which question did I mess up on?"

"The one where I asked whether you know a man named Ben Foray."

Jake paused, observing Jada's reaction.

She gagged, gripping her stomach while covering her mouth. "Nick, let's go," she choked before snatching up her purse and charging the door. "Now!"

"Hold on, Mrs. Vincent," the examiner said. "You can always retake the test and see if your response registers as no deception indicated next time—"

"I will not be retaking a thing," she shot back. "*Nick.* I'm ready to get out of here!"

Her attorney rushed out the door, chasing after Jada as she ranted down the corridor.

"Let's follow them," Jake told Miles. "I don't wanna miss a word of this."

"Right behind you."

Jada's arms swung wildly, her tirade intensifying. "How the hell did Faith pass her lie detector test with flying colors and I didn't, Nick!" Jada fumed. "And that damn Tyler... He is *always* getting me involved in some mess."

"We'll discuss this later, Mrs. Vincent. Preferably outside of the police station."

"I don't give a damn where I'm at. I am pissed! This is my reputation on the line here. All the shady ass schemes Tyler's involved in are gonna land us both in jail—"

"That is enough, Mrs. Vincent! As your legal counsel, I am advising you to keep quiet before you land *yourself* in jail."

As Nick ushered Jada out the door, Jake and Miles stopped at the reception desk.

"What did we just witness?" Miles asked.

"Quite an incriminating outburst," Jake replied. "All this intel, but not enough evidence to draw up charges on anyone. That's the most frustrating part of this investigation. Everybody's whereabouts checked out during the time that Manuel went missing. Claire and Alan were each other's alibi, Tyler and Jada claimed they had eyes on one another throughout the day and night. So did Greer and Faith. All the other vineyard employees' stories checked out too."

"Yeah, well, somebody is lying."

"I agree. But who though?"

Miles leaned over the desk and pulled a piece of licorice

from Lucy's candy jar. "That's the million-dollar question. What's our next move, Chief?"

"I need to put in another call to Judge Pierce. Find out when he plans on issuing that search warrant. We have got to get inside Vincent Vineyard. Once we do that, we may very well find our answer."

Chapter Fifteen

The Love family was gathered on Kennedy and Betty's backyard deck in celebration of her birthday. The atmosphere was festive as a silver balloon garland hung from the cedar wood fence, multicolored string lights twinkled within the redbud tree's branches, and a huge bouquet of red roses sat in the center of the table.

Betty's favorite restaurant, The Spicy Cajun Kitchen, had catered the event with several of their specialties—jambalaya, a crawfish boil, deep fried okra, French bread rolls and king cake for dessert.

The setting was perfect. The mood, however, was somber. Despite having promised Betty that there would be no talk of the Vincent Vineyard case, whispers of the investigation buzzed throughout the yard.

"Did Miles tell you that Manuel's autopsy results came in this afternoon?" Ella asked Charlotte.

"No, we haven't really had a chance to talk. I was at the pediatrician's office all day with Ari for her shots. What did the medical examiner conclude?"

"That Manuel was shot twice in the chest. Once in the rib cage and once in the lung parenchyma. But it wasn't the bullets that killed him since neither hit a major organ or blood vessels."

"So how did he die?"

"He drowned. There was bloody froth found in his airway and a significant amount of water in his stomach."

"Ooh, that poor man." Charlotte's gaze roamed toward the other side of the deck where Jake, Miles, Lena and David were hovered in a corner. "How is Jake doing? He's gotta be extremely stressed out. Trust me, I know what all this feels like firsthand."

"Stressed isn't even the word for it at this point. This case has become a twenty-four-hours-a-day obsession for him. Sleepless nights, early mornings fueled with black coffee and Excedrin Migraine and incessant brainstorming on his next move. I keep a supply of nitroglycerin on hand just in case the man has a heart attack."

"Wait, stick a pin in that for a sec," Charlotte said as Betty approached.

"Ladies, would either of you like another piece of cake? If so, you'd better grab it now before my husband and sons devour the rest."

Ella moaned, adamantly shaking her head. "Mrs. Love, as delicious as that cake is, I cannot fit another morsel of food inside this stuffed belly. But I will say that The Spicy Cajun Kitchen is my new addiction. They just might find me standing in line tomorrow. As for today, however, I am cutting myself off."

"Same for me," Charlotte chimed in.

"Well, we've got plenty of leftovers, so feel free to take some home if you'd like."

The moment Betty was out of earshot, Charlotte's smile faded. "What's the latest on the evidence that was collected at Manuel's crime scene? Did Lena get the results back yet?"

"She did. Nothing viable came of it."

"None of it?"

"Nope," Ella confirmed, her attention turning to Jake. Even from a distance, she could see the lines of distress etched in his expression. "Any DNA that could've come from Manuel's body or clothing was destroyed by the water. There were no fingerprints on the shell casings, and the serial numbers didn't match any of those stored in the network. The soil that was collected near Manuel's body contained remnants of his blood, but no one else's."

Charlotte stared out into the yard, taking a long sip of ginger beer. "You know, it's funny how life works. Here we were, thinking that the worst was behind us after the Numeric Serial Killer was locked up. We left River Valley behind and came to a new town to be with our significant others. I expected this fresh start to lead to some peace. But instead, we're right smack dab in the middle of another wild murder investigation."

Please don't say it, Ella thought, already knowing the direction her sister was taking the conversation.

"Since this case seems to be going left," Charlotte continued, "wouldn't now be a good time for you to tell Jake your big secret?"

"No," Ella whispered, her eyes darting from her sister to Jake. "It isn't. I already told you that I'll share it with him once the time is right. Now will you please drop it? *Especially* here?"

"Fine. But I'd be remiss if I didn't reiterate that the time was right when you first—"

"Will you *shush!*" Ella grabbed her arm, glad she'd only shared that she was seeing a therapist. Charlotte assumed it was to help her cope with the whole Numeric Serial Killer situation. She had no idea there was a way bigger secret being kept under wraps.

After the attack at the hospital, Ella thought she was

ready to come clean and tell Charlotte the truth about what she'd been hiding. But then, she panicked. Ella wasn't prepared to deal with her sister's reaction, let alone the pressure she would've put on her to confess to Jake. He was at the height of the investigation. The news would ruin his focus, and in turn, wreck the case. The Love family, along with her own, had been through enough. Ella refused to be the cause of yet another devastating blow.

A pinch of her cheek pulled Ella from her thoughts.

"Look," Charlotte said right before Jake and Miles walked over. "I'll drop it. At least for now..."

Ella mouthed the words *thank you* just as Jake moved in, wrapping his arm around her waist.

"What are you two over here whispering about?"

"Probably the same thing you and your Clemmington PD cohorts were buzzing about over in the corner," Charlotte replied. "The Vincent Vineyard investigation."

"Yeah." Miles sighed. "Seems like that's all we're talking about these days." He brushed a few strands of hair away from Charlotte's eyes. "I haven't even had a chance to catch you up on all the latest."

"I think I'm up to date. Ella was just telling me about Manuel's autopsy results, and how nothing came of the DNA evidence collected at the crime scene."

Everyone turned to Jake, who was too busy checking his phone to notice the looks of concern on their faces.

"That's where we're at today," Miles said, giving his brother a reassuring shoulder bump. "But I have no doubt this case is about to take a turn in our favor."

"It sure is," Jake added, holding his cell in the air. "Especially now that Judge Pierce has finally signed the search warrant. Looks like we'll be paying Vincent Vineyard a visit first thing tomorrow morning."

The smile on Jake's face almost lifted Ella off her feet. It was the happiest she'd seen him in weeks.

"That is awesome, babe," she said, standing on her tippy toes and kissing his cheek. "I have a feeling this is gonna be it. Once you get inside those offices and start digging through the files, you'll find everything you need to make an arrest."

"Let's hope so. I certainly appreciate the vote of confidence." Jake raised his vodka tonic in the air. "You all know it wouldn't be right if I didn't make a toast."

"What are we toasting to?" Lena asked as she and David approached.

"Some sensational news," Miles told them while propping his beer bottle next to Jake's glass. "The warrant to search Vincent Vineyard has finally been signed!"

Lena and David responded with a resounding, "Yes!"

"Hey!" Kennedy called out from the sliding glass doorway. "You all better not be out here talking about you-know-what. Tonight is all about celebrating my wife. Remember, *none* of you are too old to be put in a time-out."

"Uh-oh," Jake uttered. "We'd better table this conversation for later."

Lena backed away, her right brow lifting slyly. "Fine. But don't think I'm not about to sneak over there and tell Dad about that search warrant."

"While you're at it," Miles interjected, "be sure to tell him that the renovations on the police station are finally done. You know, just so the conversation won't be *all* about the investigation."

"Good idea." Lena tapped her glass. "And afterward, who wants to grab another round?"

"I do!" Miles, Charlotte and David said in unison before following her toward the house.

Once they were alone, Jake tightened his grip on Ella's waist.

"Hey," he murmured, "have I mentioned lately how glad I am that you're here in Clemmington with me?"

"You haven't. But you can always mention it now if you'd like."

He placed a finger underneath her chin and lifted her head, their lips inches apart. "Ella Bowman, I am over the moon that you came all the way from River Valley, Nevada, to be here with me. And since I'm on the subject, have you given any more thought to moving here permanently?"

"I have."

"Oh, really? And?"

"*And*, I think I love that idea."

Jake squeezed her so tightly that she almost lost her breath. "Are you serious?"

"Yes. I'm serious!" she wheezed, laughing and choking at the same time.

Her moment of joy was interrupted by the sting of shame. Her secret loomed overhead like a violent storm cloud, as did the attacks and the threats—all of which she'd been keeping from the man she claimed to love.

Ella's smile shriveled. She knew there was only one way to fix the problem. And it didn't involve therapy, getting a job or running back to River Valley. It all came down to confessing the truth to Jake and finding the person behind the threats.

Chapter Sixteen

Jake banged on the door of Vincent Vineyard with a search warrant in hand and all of Clemmington PD in tow. Several moments passed. There was no response. He pounded the door once again.

"You're being too courteous," Miles said. "I say we kick that thing in and storm the place."

"I concur," Detective Campbell chimed in.

Jake jiggled the handle. The door opened. He turned to the officers and gave them a thumbs-up. "Let's go!"

The officers stormed the lobby, with Jake holding up his badge while taking a look around.

"Police!" he called out. "Clemmington PD is here to collect evidence as it pertains to the murders of Don Vincent and Manuel Ruiz. If you have any questions, you can meet us in the lobby and we'll be happy to address them."

Silence.

"Where the hell is everybody?" Miles asked.

"I have no idea. I'll do a quick search. See if I can find the family. In the meantime, let's stick to the plan. Lead the team upstairs and start inside the offices, removing any files, electronics, hard drives…anything that might contain pertinent information."

"Will do. If you need me, call me."

As Miles guided the officers upstairs, Jake heard a group of people cheering outside. He jogged toward the back of the lobby and peered out onto the deck. Claire, Tyler, Greer and their wives were standing at the bar in front of a crowd of people. They were each holding a bottle of wine in their hands as onlookers took photos.

Tyler stepped in front of the family and took a bow. "Thank you, everyone, thank you. Now, as you know, we consider all of you to be our Vincent Vineyard VIPs. You get premiere access to our newest offerings, and this group was the first to try the latest Cabernet Sauvignon. Today, I, along with the rest of the Vincent Vineyard staff, present to you that Cabernet's accompanying dessert wine." He turned toward the outdoor staircase and clapped his hands. "Servers!"

A group of staff members dressed in white shirts, burgundy vests and black slacks came rushing up the stairs, carrying trays filled with port glasses.

Jake observed the Vincents closely, watching as Greer stood behind Tyler with a frown on his face. Jada and Faith were whispering frantically with one another while Claire stared out into the crowd in a complete daze. The investigation had clearly taken a toll on them. All except Tyler.

"Prepare your palates, my friends," Tyler continued, strolling through the rows of guests. "What you are about to experience is the perfect blend of warm dark chocolate and smooth ripe raspberries. Close your eyes. Imagine yourselves on a sexy getaway, lying next to your significant other. The mood is set. The energy is buzzing with passion. But instead of making love to your partner, you're sipping on this perfectly sweetened port."

"Oh, *please*," Greer moaned, gripping his stomach while leaning against the bar.

"It's tickling your taste buds," Tyler continued obliviously, "*exploding* inside of your mouth—"

"Mr. Vincent!" Jake interrupted, unable to bear another word.

The crowd turned in their seats, watching as the chief stepped onto the deck.

"Chief Love?" Tyler uttered. "What…what are you doing here? Can't you see I'm in the middle of a presentation? We're hosting an exclusive event for our most valued wine distribution companies. And I do not believe your name was on the guest list."

A few chuckles rippled through the crowd. But the majority of the guests appeared alarmed, as did Claire, Greer and Faith. Jada, however, marched over to Tyler and slipped her hand in his, as if to show her allegiance.

"Mr. Vincent, the reason why I'm here is because Clemmington PD has obtained a warrant to search the premises—"

"*Excuse* me?" Tyler interrupted right before Claire grabbed Greer's arm and yelled, "Go call our attorney! *Now*!"

Several guests turned their cell phones toward Jake and began filming.

"You're here to search the *premises*?" Tyler barked, storming over to Jake. "The hell you are. Let me see this warrant. And who signed it?"

"Judge Pierce," Jake replied coolly, handing him the document.

Greer shuffled over and snatched the paper out of Tyler's hand. "You cannot do this, Chief Love. What right do you have? What grounds are you even doing this on?"

"First of all, we're already doing it. My officers are inside your offices gathering evidence as we speak."

"They're *what*?" Claire screamed, attempting to run back inside before Faith held her back.

"Secondly," Jake continued, "Clemmington PD has reason to believe there is evidence here that's connected to the murders of Don Vincent and Manuel Ruiz. Third, and most importantly, please do not get in the way of my officers as they work to remove said evidence from the premises."

One of the guests recording the confrontation nudged the man sitting next to her, uttering, "Who knew we'd be getting a wine tasting *and* a show?"

"Okay, everyone," Jake said, waving his arms in the air. "The event is over. Please put your phones away and exit the premises. Mr. Vincent, could you show them a way out that doesn't require them to reenter the lobby?"

"You cannot do this," Tyler hissed.

"Chief Love," Claire cried, "could you at least wait until our attorney arrives before starting the search?"

"Too late, Mom," Greer told her, his phone stuck to the side of his face. "I'm still holding for the lawyer. Tyler, aren't you supposed to be showing our guests the way out?"

"I'm busy trying to put a halt to this…this *travesty*! And you should be helping me. Whose side are you even on?"

"The vineyard's, obviously. But this is not a good look! Now get these people the hell out of here!"

"Watch your mouth, little bro. Don't forget who's really running things around here."

"How could I? It's *me*!"

"*Hey*!" Jake interjected. "Just remove your guests from the premises, please. You'll have plenty of time to argue among yourselves once they're gone."

Ignoring their continued rumblings, Jake reentered the building, sending one of his officers outside to monitor the evacuation while he headed upstairs to check on the search.

"Chief!" Miles called out.

Jake jetted toward the end of the hallway. "What's going on?"

"We've got a problem. Manuel's office has already been cleared out. And his computer is gone."

"*No*, come on! That's the main piece of equipment I was looking to seize. Let's make sure the team searches all the offices from top to bottom." Jake peered over the railing, staring down at the Vincents as they clamored inside the lobby. "While you all do that, I'll talk to the usual suspects. See if any of them know of its whereabouts."

As he rushed back down the stairs, there was a commotion near the front entrance.

"I said that Tyler Vincent is expecting me!" a woman yelled before pushing her way past two officers.

Lauren Downs, host of a popular news and entertainment television show on WKMD-TV, came marching through the lobby with her camera crew in tow.

"Tyler!" she called out, flipping her bouncy platinum curls over her shoulder. "What in the hell is going on here? I could barely get inside! Why would you have law enforcement working the door and not tell them I'd be here filming a segment for my show? Did you forget that I'm covering the wine tasting event?"

For the first time, Jake saw Tyler lose his cool. He shooed his family members off to the side and ran over to Lauren, sweat visibly dripping down his face. "This way, guys!" he said to the production team.

"*Ew*," Lauren muttered after Tyler wrapped an arm around her. "Why are you perspiring like that?"

He ignored the question, panting uncontrollably while ushering her toward the deck.

"Excuse me," Jake said, "Ms. Downs, I'm sorry, but I'm

going to have to ask you and your crew to leave. The vineyard is closed to the public at this time."

"*Public*," Lauren shot back. "I'm sorry, Chief Love, but are you aware of who I am? I am not the *public*. I am Clemmington, California's most watched, most influential television host—"

"I know exactly who you are, Ms. Downs. And this is in no way meant to offend you. But again, Vincent Vineyard is not open for business at this time. So I'm going to have to ask you to leave."

"*Chief*," Tyler sniffed, his eyes darting wildly. "Can you please just chill and let me take the crew out onto the deck for a few minutes so that I can speak with them in private?"

"I'm sorry, Mr. Vincent. But no. I cannot."

One of the men on Lauren's team whispered something in her ear. Her mouth fell open as she turned to Tyler, then Jake, then her cameraman. She threw him a hand signal. Within seconds, he began filming.

"Hello, ladies and gentleman," Lauren said into the camera. "I am reporting live from Vincent Vineyard."

"*Hey!*" Tyler yelled, lunging at the cameraman. "Cut that damn camera off!"

The man dodged Tyler's swipe and continued filming.

"We are here today to bring you breaking news."

Jake stepped in front of the camera. "Ms. Downs, please—"

"Vincent Vineyard has been overtaken by the Clemmington Police Department," she interrupted, slowly moving toward the door while her crew followed, "as they continue to investigate the tragic murders involving the family."

Claire came running toward Lauren with her fists in the air. "Get out of my establishment before I—"

"Mom!" Greer yelled, holding her back while Tyler tried to knock the cameraman to the ground.

A couple of officers stepped in, subduing the Vincents while Jake moved the crew toward the exit.

"For the last time, Ms. Downs. I'm going to need for you to leave the premises. *Now.*"

"You heard the man!" Claire shrieked. "Get the hell out of here!"

The crew took their time, inching through the lobby. While the cameraman kept filming, Lauren kept reporting.

"As you can see, I am surrounded by complete and utter chaos. The entire Vincent family is in shambles over the deaths of Don Vincent and Manuel Ruiz. The scariest part of it all is that I may very well be standing in the midst of a cold-blooded killer! Chief Love," she continued, turning to him, "your father worked the Don Vincent murder investigation for *months* before throwing in the towel after he failed to solve it. You, a rookie police chief, recently reopened it. What makes you think you have what it takes to finally crack the case?"

She shoved the microphone in his face. Jake sucked in a sharp breath of air, his skin growing hot with irritation. "Didn't I tell you to—"

Watch it, he told himself. *You're on live television...*

"Ms. Downs, I will not be answering any questions regarding the investigation. Now this is the last time I'm going to ask you to leave. If you do not vacate the premises, I'll have no choice but to take you and your crew into custody."

"You witnessed that, ladies and gentlemen," Lauren said into the camera. "Chief Love has threatened to arrest my team and me as we attempt to report breaking news regarding the latest on the Clemmington serial killer." She shoved the microphone off to the side and leaned into Jake, whispering, "You haven't heard the last of me..."

Don't feed the trolls, he told himself, resisting the urge to kick the camera to the floor.

"Get out of here!" Claire screamed while charging the doorway. She stared out at the lawn, her eyes filling with tears as more reporters hurried up the walkway. "There's more of them! Where are they coming from?"

"Tyler called them here, Mom," Greer told her. "Remember? We wanted to get the town excited about the new dessert wine. We had no idea the cops would show up with a search warrant."

"This is a disaster!" she cried into his shoulder. "And such an...an *embarrassment*. Vincent Vineyard will never recover from this."

Jake ran toward the reporters with his hands in the air. "Everyone, please. The event has been canceled and the vineyard is closed. We're going to have to ask you to leave the premises immediately."

"It doesn't look like it's closed," one of the reporters replied while continuing up the walkway. "What's going on here?"

"The police are raiding the place!" one of Lauren's crew members yelled. "They're looking for Don Vincent and Manuel Ruiz's killer!"

A chaotic scramble ensued as journalists bombarded Jake with questions.

"Chief Love! What new evidence did you find that brought you here today?" someone asked while another called out, "Chief! Who do you think committed the murders? Was it one of the Vincent family members? Are you prepared to make an arrest today?"

Jake marched to his car and popped open the truck, grabbing a roll of caution tape. Just as he headed back toward the building, law enforcement came filing out the door. Their hands were loaded with boxes and brown paper bags filled with evidence.

"*Horrible* timing," he mumbled, wincing as the reporters ambushed the officers. Jake ran back up the walkway and recruited Miles and Officer Underwood to help cordon off the area.

"Get back, please," Miles warned, blocking the microphones and cameras that journalists shoved in their faces. "Keep it up and I *will* take you to jail."

The warning sent reporters scurrying away from the entrance. But their cameras kept rolling, which meant the search and seizure would be all over the news.

"Well, I certainly didn't see this coming," Jake said to Miles. "Who knew today would turn into a damn media circus?"

"You never know. Maybe this is a good thing. All the attention might encourage someone to come forward with some information they've been sitting on."

"That's true. Between that and all this evidence we're collecting, something's got to come to the surface."

For the sake of this town and my reputation, it'd better...

Chapter Seventeen

Jake and Ella rode down Pacific Coast Highway, trailing behind Miles and Charlotte. They had just left a birthday celebration in Malibu thrown by an old high school friend of the Love brothers. Right before the festivities began to boil over, the foursome decided they'd better set off on the long drive back to Clemmington.

"Ooh," Ella groaned, slipping off her black suede booties. "I think I danced for about an hour too long in these shoes. Why didn't you tell me to sit down for a minute? Give my feet a break?"

"Because the DJ wouldn't stop playing all my favorite old school hip-hop songs, back-to-back. When the music's that good, there is no sitting down."

"*Facts*," Ella murmured as she dug her fist into the ball of her foot. "I may have fractured an ankle though. Nevertheless, I had a fantastic time."

She peered out the window, in awe of the rippling silver clouds drifting through the lavender-streaked sky. The sun was setting into the dazzling turquoise water. It brought on a fleeting sense of peace, as did the entire day. Good times were few and far between as the Vincent Vineyard murder investigation had taken over their lives.

Not only had Ella been fighting alongside Jake to help

find the killer, but she'd been battling her own internal demons. The walls were closing in on her. Time was running out as the threats against her were intensifying. She'd be dead if it weren't for the construction worker thwarting the attack at the hospital. Next time, she might not be so lucky.

There shouldn't be a next time. You have got to tell Jake. Now.

"I love how everybody kept commenting on us being dressed alike," he said. "Little did they know we hadn't planned on wearing matching jeans, fitted T-shirts and leather jackets. It was a complete coincidence."

"Mmm-hmm…"

Jake gave Ella a nudge. "Why are you so quiet over there? Too much dancing? Champagne? Both?"

He let off a sexy chuckle—the kind that sent her straight inside the bedroom and in between the sheets. The day had been so perfect. She'd met his old high school crew, blushed when everyone called them the perfect couple and swooned when Jake professed how much he loved her. For the first time, she felt less like a girlfriend and more like a wife.

So why ruin all that now with your confession? Just enjoy the rest of the night. Go home and make love to your man. Save the admission for tomorrow…

"Hey," Jake said softly, reaching over and clutching her hand, "is everything all right?"

Ella turned to him. "Everything is perfect. I was just thinking about how amazing the day has been."

"I second that. And my favorite part of it, aside from you, of course, was *not* talking about the investigation. Today was all about fun, family, friends and us. We need more of this. Which means I have got to get this case solved so that I can focus on my woman and our future together."

When Jake tightened his grip on Ella's hand, the pressure

almost squeezed the confession out of her. But she pursed her lips, allowing the tears that had welled in her eyes to trickle down her cheeks.

"Babe, what's wrong? Why are you crying? Did I say something to upset you?"

"No. Not at all. You said something, several things actually, that just warmed my heart."

And made me realize I probably don't deserve you.

"Good. That's what I like to hear. And if my words warmed your heart, just wait until you feel how my lips are gonna heat up that body of yours once we get home and I take off all your—"

Jake paused when his cell phone pinged through the speakers.

"Dammit! Just when I was getting to the good part." He jabbed the Accept button. "Chief Love."

"Chief!" someone screamed on the other end.

Ella jumped in her seat and checked the caller ID on the car's touch screen. It was Lucy, calling from the police station.

"I'm here," Jake said. "What's going on?"

"I just received a call from Claire Vincent. You need to get to the vineyard. Now!"

"Why? What happened?"

"Greer is dead!"

"Wh…what?" he stammered, pounding the phone's side button to increase the volume. "Greer is *what*?"

"He's dead!"

Ella covered her mouth right before a scream escaped her lips. She turned to Jake, whose arms were visibly shaking as he clutched the steering wheel.

"I'm on my way there now," Jake said before hanging

up and scrolling the call log for Miles's name. The phone barely rang before he picked up.

"What's up, big bro? Did you and El change your minds and decide to come by for a nightcap and game of cards—"

"*Miles*. Listen to me. Greer is dead. Head to Vincent Vineyard. Now!"

JAKE PULLED INTO the vineyard's lot and threw the car into Park. He and Ella jumped out, gazing at the commotion swirling around them. Moments later, Miles and Charlotte arrived.

As the officers went running toward the crime scene, Charlotte grabbed hold of Ella.

"So let me get this straight. Greer's body was found inside the distillery?"

"Yes."

"Floating inside a vat of wine?"

"Yes. At least that's what Officer Underwood told Jake. He was the first one to arrive on the scene."

"*Oh, my God...*"

Law enforcement had blocked off the winery, only allowing a select few in and out. Tyler, who was standing off to the side of the entryway, struggled to keep his crumbling mother on her feet. Faith appeared completely inconsolable as her entire body shook within Jada's embrace.

"Who did this?" Faith screamed at Tyler over and over again. "Did you do this? I *know* you did this!"

He ignored her, focusing solely on his grief-stricken mother while Jada did her best to quiet Faith down.

Charlotte turned away from the family. "*Wow*. And you said that Claire was the one who found Greer's body?"

"Yes. Claire and her alleged lover, Alan Monroe."

"Ooh, that is terrible."

A weary sense of dread swarmed Ella's head. She opened the passenger door of Jake's car and slid down into the seat, begging her fatigued body not to give out on her—especially now that her mind had already begun to slip.

This is too much...

The chill of regret slithered across her skin. Ella should've confided in her sister a long time ago. Because then she could have divulged that after finding out Greer was dead, she'd received a text message saying, YOU'RE NEXT!

Ella jumped when someone tapped her shoulder.

"It's just me," Charlotte said softly. "Are you okay? You're sitting here all hunched over, looking like you're about to pass out. Do you need some water? I think Miles has a case in the trunk."

"I *feel* like I'm about to pass out. But no. I'm fine."

Ella could feel Charlotte watching her intently. Knowing her sister, she saw right through her lie. Relief set in when Charlotte turned her attention back to the winery.

"It's weird that Alan Monroe is Vincent Vineyard's biggest competitor, yet he was here on the premises tonight. I mean, I get that he and Claire are involved or whatever, but what was he doing inside the distillery? Isn't that where their secret winemaking process takes place?"

"It is. Jake was wondering the same thing. Officer Underwood actually explained it all to him while we were on our way here. Which version of the story do you want? The long or the short?"

"The long version since it looks like we're gonna be here for a while."

"Okay, so, remember the day that Clemmington PD executed the search warrant here at the vineyard?" Ella asked.

"Yep, I do."

"Well, when law enforcement arrived, the Vincents were

in the middle of hosting some exclusive tasting for a group of wine distributors. Claire wanted to invite Alan, but Tyler and Greer weren't having it. They thought it would be disrespectful to their father's memory—especially after she went behind their backs and invited Alan to that Cabernet Sauvignon tasting we attended. Plus, they were worried about him stealing their port wine idea and stocking it at his vineyard too."

With a wave of her hand, Charlotte dismissed the statement. "I bet Tyler and Greer were more concerned about Alan stealing the wine idea than they were their father's memory. But anyway, I digress. You may continue."

"Since Alan wasn't allowed to attend the event, Claire snuck him in today and was planning to do a private tasting for just the two of them after everyone went home. While she and Alan were attempting to pour the wine straight from the vat, nothing was coming out. They thought it was clogged. Alan climbed up to check and see what was going on. When he lifted the lid, there Greer was, lying inside."

"Already dead?"

Ella responded with a nod, unable to verbalize that yet another murder had been committed. She shuddered at the memory of lying on that cold hard hospital floor, almost being strangled to death. And that sharp object practically penetrating her skin inside the corn maze. Then the terrifying chase through the parking garage stairwell, the threatening text messages...

"Stop it!" she screamed, pressing her hand against her head, then jumping out of the car.

"El!" Charlotte ran after her. "What's wrong? Is talking about Greer's death too much for you to handle? If so, we can drop it."

"*All* of this is too much for me to handle! I messed up, Charlotte. Bad. *Real* bad."

"You messed up? What are you talking about?"

Ella released a trembling exhale, staring down at the ground while struggling to find the right words.

Just keep it simple. Start from the beginning.

She looked up at her sister. Ella's chest ached at the worry in Charlotte's eyes. "I'm so sorry."

"Sorry…sorry for what?"

"For what I've been hiding."

"Come on, El. Just spit it out. I'll never stop loving you no matter what it is. I bet you're just being dramatic and it isn't even that bad."

"Oh, but it is."

Charlotte grabbed hold of her. "*What* is?"

Say it. Just say it…

"I had an affair with Tyler," she finally blurted.

Hearing the words come out of her own mouth stopped time. Everything around Ella froze. Her vision blurred. She could no longer see Charlotte standing in front of her. But she could feel her sister's supportive grip slip from her shoulders.

"You did *what*?" Charlotte hissed.

"I had an affair with Tyler."

"Tyler *who*?"

Ella turned away, wishing the ground would part ways and swallow her up.

"Tyler Vin—*Vincent*," she sputtered as acid crept up her throat.

"*Ella*! How could you do something like that? When did this happen? *Why* did it happen? Oh, God…" Charlotte pressed her hands against her face, moaning into the night air. "I mean... *Tyler Vincent*? Of all people. Him? *Really*? You cannot be serious—"

"Will you please lower your voice?" Ella pushed Charlotte back inside the car and slammed the door, then climbed into the driver's seat. Her first thought was to start the engine and drive off. But she couldn't. She'd been running from the truth for long enough. It was time to face reality.

"Please tell me this is some sort of sick prank," Charlotte whispered.

"It's not. But I can explain."

"You'd better. Because *dammit*, Ella, this is not good. Especially now that the investigation has completely blown up."

Ella banged her head against the back of the headrest, squeezing her eyes shut. "So, Tyler and I met several years ago at a wine festival in Reno. He wasn't married yet, but he and Jada were engaged. I had no idea though, because when he introduced himself, he told me he was single."

"Of course he did."

"Back then I really was single, plus I was traveling for work and just having a good time. When Tyler invited me to have a glass of wine with him, I did. That led to us taking a walk along The Row, then playing a few rounds of blackjack at his hotel casino. I wound up in his room for a nightcap, and...one thing led to another."

"Meaning?"

"Meaning we ended up sleeping together that night."

Charlotte inhaled sharply, glaring out the window while shaking her head. "I cannot believe what I'm hearing right now."

"Look, not to make excuses or anything, because I know this entire situation is an absolute mess."

"To put it lightly."

"But back when Tyler and I met, he wasn't nearly as arrogant and flashy as he is now."

"It's hard to imagine him being any other way."

Ella paused, swallowing the urge to address her sister's snarky ad libs. "Anyway, Tyler and I ended up spending that entire weekend together. Once the festival was over, he came back to Clemmington, and I stayed in Reno. We did keep in touch and see one another whenever our schedules allowed. And what's interesting, even back then, Tyler talked about how badly he wanted to run Vincent Vineyard. I was always under the impression he'd stop at nothing to take over the top spot."

"Well, it looks like you were right. Because at this point, I'm thinking he's the one who's killing for it. But wait, how did you find out Tyler was engaged?"

"During a moment of eavesdropping here at the vineyard, ironically. A coworker had invited me to a charity event being thrown by Don to benefit underprivileged families. I was so impressed by his generosity that I had to support it. I decided not to tell Tyler I was coming and surprise him by just showing up. Little did I know *I'd* be the one getting the surprise after overhearing a guest discussing Tyler's engagement and elaborate wedding plans."

"Ugh," Charlotte groaned, clutching her chest. "What did he have to say for himself when you confronted him about it?"

"Nothing. Because I never got a chance to talk to him. I immediately stormed out of the event and left him a voice mail message stating that I knew the truth about everything. He never called back, and I never reached out again."

Dead air filled the car as both women sat silently, staring out the windshield.

You've got to tell her the rest...

"And, um…that's not all," Ella mumbled.

"There's *more*? What else could there possibly be?"

"I… I've been receiving threatening messages."

Charlotte reached over and gripped her hand. "What kind of threatening messages, Ella?"

"Texts, emails… It's someone telling me they know what I did and that I'd better get out of Clemmington. Tonight, after Greer's body was found, I received a message saying *you're next*."

"I cannot believe this! Why would you keep all of that from me? You didn't have to go through it alone, you know. I could've helped you. Hell, all of Clemmington PD could've helped you!"

"I know. But that would've meant having to tell Jake about Tyler and me. I just wasn't ready to face everything that would've come along with that."

"Is there anything else I should know?"

"Yes," Ella whispered, staring down at her trembling hands. "That attack at the corn maze? It wasn't the only one. I was chased through Gateway Park after one of our workouts at the track, and assaulted inside the hospital that day you took me to the job interview—"

"*See*," Charlotte interrupted, throwing her hands in the air, "I knew something was wrong that day at the hospital when you got back inside the car! Digital threats are one thing. But physical attacks that you kept to yourself instead of reporting? Not even to me? El! What were you thinking?"

"What was I thinking? I was thinking about Jake, and how he'd just been promoted to chief. I didn't wanna ruin his focus and taint our relationship with news that I'd dated one of his main suspects. I was also thinking about you, and Miles, and everything you'd been through trying to catch the Numeric Serial Killer."

"As if you didn't go through hell right along with us. You're lucky you weren't killed."

Charlotte's grasp on Ella's hand tightened. Through it, Ella could feel the love. She could also see the devastation in her sister's watery red eyes. The sight triggered an unbearable sense of guilt.

"I'm just glad you're okay," Charlotte insisted. "And I will see to it that you stay that way. Now, my guess is that Tyler's behind the attacks. He may fear you're going to ruin his reputation by blasting the news that he's an unfaithful pig to the entire town. He'd be so embarrassed. Also, you're dating the chief of police, whose number one priority is solving this case. If something happened to you, it could throw Jake off and botch the investigation. See where I'm going with all this?"

"I do."

"Oh, and speaking of the chief of police, when are you going to tell him—"

Ella waved her hand in the air. "Please don't start with that line of questioning. I am planning to tell Jake everything."

"When?"

"When the time is right."

A knock on the glass sent both women jolting in their seats.

"Jake!" Ella shrieked, rolling down the window. "You scared us!"

"Sorry, babe. Listen, it looks like we're gonna be a while. I don't want to leave you two in the parking lot waiting for us. El, why don't you go back to Charlotte's place and wait for me there? I'll pick you up as soon as we're done."

She nodded, studying the creases lining his face. The pained expression was a far cry from the look of elation he'd worn as they were heading back from Malibu, before getting Lucy's call.

And now you're about to twist the knife in his heart by admitting to the affair with Tyler...

"How's it going in there?" Charlotte asked.

"It's bad. Really bad. The medical examiner is processing Greer's body now. He's got a bullet wound to the right temple. Lena found a couple of twenty-two caliber shell casings—the same kind that were at Manuel's crime scene—underneath one of the wine racks. And let me say this. While I've got my eyes on everybody, I am having a hard time figuring out who might be behind this. The entire family is distraught. Even Tyler, in his own weird way."

"Chief!" one of the officers called out.

"I'll be right there!" Jake shouted over his shoulder.

"We'd better let you get back to work," Ella told him.

"You two be careful. El, text me as soon as you all make it in and let me know you're safe."

"*Tuh,*" Charlotte uttered, patting her purse. "Don't worry. According to my Glock twenty-two, we'll be just fine."

"I know you will." Jake turned to Ella. "Love you."

"Love you too," she muttered, her lips stinging with remorse as he kissed them softly.

Her eyes glazed over as she watched Jake hurry back inside the distillery.

"Come on," Charlotte said quietly. "Let's get you out of here."

Ella started the engine and pulled out of the lot in a daze, contemplating how in the hell she'd get up the nerve to tell Jake the truth.

Chapter Eighteen

The Daily Herald

OPINION

*Clemmington's Police Department is failing the community.
It may be time to send in the Feds...*

By Lauren Downs

Ms. Downs is a news and entertainment reporter for
WKMD-TV and a former criminal justice professor
at Valley Oak Community College.

CLEMMINGTON—I recently received a personal
invitation to attend a wine tasting event at Vincent
Vineyard in celebration of their newly released tawny
port. With my production crew in tow, I set off on
what was promised to be an amazing experience filled
with exclusive guests, a private tour and, of course,
great wine.

Needless to say, it wasn't.

Before arriving at the vineyard, I spoke with Tyler

Vincent, who at the time was serving as co-vice president of Vincent Vineyard along with his brother, Greer Vincent. We discussed conducting an interview that would air on WKMD-TV, announcing the winery's new dessert wine, exciting plans for the future and more. When I got there, however, our plans took a sharp turn.

I was not greeted by the Vincents. Instead, I was bombarded by the Clemmington Police Department— Chief Jake Love to be exact. He informed me that the vineyard was closed to public access and asked my crew and I to leave without telling us why. I was confused by the request, considering there was a large group of guests bustling about on the back deck.

Then suddenly, chaos ensued. Law enforcement officers came marching out of the business offices carrying electronics, cardboard boxes and brown paper bags. My producer was the first to realize that the vineyard was being raided, which is understandable, considering the recent murder of Manuel Ruiz, Vincent Vineyard's longtime manager, and now Greer Vincent. Connecting the killings to the business is a no-brainer, especially after the owner, Don Vincent, was found stabbed to death in the vineyard's grape fields around this time last year.

Here's where things get interesting. Claire Vincent was set to name one of her sons president of Vincent Vineyard in the coming days. It is no secret that the brothers had been at odds since their father's death, both vying for the top spot. Ironically, Greer Vincent turned up dead right before the announcement. Days later, a press release landed in my email inbox stating that Tyler Vincent had been named president. Instead of humbly (and quietly) accepting the promotion while mourning his brother's death, Tyler and his wife, Jada Vincent, threw an extravagant party in celebration of the appointment. Is it just me, or can anyone else smell the suspicion surrounding such narcissistic behavior?

For most of us, the writing is on the wall. Clemmington PD, however, is turning a blind eye to the truth. While the Love family has somehow managed to attract their fair share of serial killers (from Lena Love's Heart-Shaped Murder investigation to Miles Love's Numeric Serial Killer case), they did apprehend those criminals within a reasonable amount of time. The Vincent Vineyard Assassin, however, continues to elude police more than a year later. Who will be next? Will the murders spread beyond the vineyard and spill over into the Clemmington community? Is our police department capable of preventing that from happening? Unfortunately, my guess is no.

I understand that Chief Love is new to his position and has something to prove. But there comes a time when a man must admit that he is in over his head. Don Vincent's murder occurred during retired Chief Kennedy Love's tenure, who served on the force for over thirty-five years. If he could not solve the case, I highly doubt that Chief Jake Love, who just so happens to be the former chief's son, can.

How can Clemmington PD get justice for these victims, their families and our entire community? The answer is simple: send in the Feds.

Chapter Nineteen

"Thank you so much!" Ella said as she exited Nancy's Country Mart.

Nancy raised her hand feebly, barely looking Ella's way while waving goodbye.

The tone of the town had changed since Lauren Downs's op-ed in *The Daily Herald* hit newsstands. There was a clear divide between the community and the police department, and the Love family in particular could feel the public's disdain.

Jake continued to stand his ground in the midst of it all, refusing to call on the Federal Bureau of Investigation for assistance.

"Clemmington PD does not need help from the Feds," he'd say whenever the topic came up during press conferences. "I believe in this agency. We are perfectly capable of solving this case on our own. We've got three people on the force who helped bring down two prolific serial killers. My officers will utilize those same skills to solve this investigation."

In the meantime, Ella had been doing all that she could to keep Jake's spirits up while struggling through her own private battles. She had yet to tell him about the affair with Tyler, despite swearing to Charlotte that she would.

"Stop making false promises and tell him before it's too late!" Charlotte kept insisting.

"I will!" Ella would always reply. "I'm just waiting for the right time."

What she hadn't realized was that there never would be a right time. Confessing the affair was going to be difficult no matter the moment, place or mood.

Telling Jake tonight was out of the question. Ella had already decided to make it an upbeat evening. He needed it. She'd even nixed their healthy eating agenda and picked up one of Nancy's gourmet meat lover's pizzas and a bottle of Pinot Grigio.

Balancing the pizza box and bottle in one hand and alarm fob in the other, she hurried across the dim parking lot. Her electric-blue Jeep came into view. She clicked the button and reached for the door handle.

"*Ouch!*" she shrieked when a sharp edge of chipped paint sliced her skin.

Ella shook her hand, hoping the cool air would soothe the sting. She took a step back and studied the door. Long jagged white lines had been carved into the paint.

"Now I know my car didn't get keyed..." she griped, opening the door and dumping everything inside. She pulled out her cell phone and tapped on the flashlight, shining it along the surface. The scratches ran from the front to the back doors and all around the perimeter.

She hesitated at the sight of a red mass sticking out from underneath the vehicle. "What in the..."

Fear tore through Ella's limbs as slid her trembling hand underneath the car and poked at the mass. It felt like a lump of satiny material. Pinching it between her index finger and thumb, she gradually pulled the material. Relief hit when she realized it was just a silk scarf.

Holding it up to the phone's light, Ella wondering how the designer piece had landed underneath her car. She figured it had slipped from someone's neck and headed back toward the store to turn it in.

Her fingers skimmed a clump of thick raised stitching. She paused underneath a light pole. A set of initials were embroidered on one end of the scarf.

"JV," Ella read aloud as she continued toward the entrance.

She stopped, staring back down at the initials. "JV, JV…"

Her entire body went numb.

Jada Vincent.

A thousand thoughts flashed through her mind—one being more prevalent than all the rest. Jada was the killer.

It was time to talk to Jake. About everything.

"THIS IS DELICIOUS, EL," Jake said, reaching for a third slice of pizza. "Meat lovers was a great idea. Not to mention a nice break from all the salads."

Ella stared at him from across the dining room table. Shifting in her seat, she whispered, "Hey, there's, um… There's something I need to tell you."

He popped a piece of pepperoni inside his mouth. "Hmm. You know what else was a great idea? Dropping all talk of the investigation. At least for tonight."

"Jake? Did you hear me?"

"Hear what?"

"I said I need to tell you something."

"Oh, no. Sorry, babe. I was too busy blabbering about Nancy's amazing pizza. Go on. I'm listening."

Just say it…

"Remember that day you took me to Vincent Vineyard for the wine tasting?"

"Yeah. Why?"

"It, um… It wasn't the first time I'd been there."

Jake's eyelids lowered, his head tilting in confusion. "What do you mean?"

Ella slid her plate to the side, the sight of food causing a sudden bout of nausea. "I'd visited the vineyard once before. A few years ago, after being invited by someone in the family."

"Hold on," Jake said, dropping his slice of pizza. "One of the Vincents invited you to the vineyard? You never mentioned knowing any of them. Who was it?"

Ella dug her fingernails into her thighs so deeply that she almost drew blood.

Rip the bandage off and tell him!

"It was Tyler."

"*Tyler.* But…why? *How?* You two don't even know one another."

Remaining silent, Ella's gaze fell from Jake's twisted expression down to her plate.

"What am I missing here?" he pressed.

This is it. You've ruined everything…

She looked up and blurted, "Tyler and I had an affair."

Jake's head swiveled, his ear thrust in her direction. "I'm sorry. I think I must've misheard you. You and Tyler *what*?"

"He and I had an affair. And before you say anything, please know that I would've told you sooner, but I didn't want to throw you off the investigation. Not to mention jeopardize our relationship."

Jake pushed away from the table, his glare filled with venom. "You had an affair with Tyler Vincent, and didn't think it was a good idea to tell me?"

His eerily low tone sent a chill straight through Ella.

"Yes," she whispered. "But he wasn't married yet. I had

no idea he was even engaged. And I was going to tell you eventually. I just couldn't seem to find the right time."

"I cannot believe this. It…it doesn't even make sense. Are you still in contact with him?"

"No! Of course not."

Jake stood so abruptly that his chair flipped over. "I'm sorry. I cannot do this," he scoffed, rushing out of the room. Ella reached for him as he flew by. He jerked away and stormed toward the bedroom.

"See?" she yelled. "This is exactly why I didn't want to tell you!"

Bam!

Ella winced when the bedroom door slammed behind him.

"You know what?" she cried out. "I can't do this either!"

She snatched her keys and cell phone off the kitchen counter and ran out the door. Tears blurred her vision as she tore down the stairs and onto the street. Ella turned right, then left, then ran in the direction of Charlotte's house.

The cool night air chilled her skin. Light rain drizzled from the sky while dense fog rolled from dark gray clouds. A jacket would've done her some good. But staying warm was the last thing on Ella's mind.

My worst nightmare is now my reality. Jake and I are over…

A sharp rock dug into the sole of her shoe. She'd left the loft so fast that she hadn't changed out of her UGG slippers. Ella ignored the pain and sped up as sobs ripped through her chest.

Headlights blinked behind her. She spun around, her hair whipping across her face. Jake's dark sedan appeared in the distance. Ella bent down, propping her hands on her knees while heaving uncontrollably. Between the sprints and the stress, she was practically hyperventilating.

It's okay. He came for me...

The sedan slowed down, then pulled to the curb. She waved, tears of relief streaming down her face.

"I'm sorry, Jake!" Ella yelled when the car door opened. "I shouldn't have left like that. I should have stayed back so we could talk. But I'm so glad you came..."

Her voice trailed off when someone stepped out. The silhouette was hard to see through the darkness. But it didn't appear to be Jake.

Ella stood straight up and peered at the car. The headlights had been turned off. She couldn't decipher the license plate.

"Jake? Is that... Is that you?"

The figure remained silent while continuing to approach.

Oh, no. Oh, no... Run!

Just as Ella began backing away, the figure came charging toward her.

"*Ahh!*" she screamed before being knocked to the ground. "Stop! Get off of me!"

Ella clawed at the attacker's face, struggled to remove the black ski mask. Shreds of wool snagged her fingernails.

"Take off that mask! Show your face, you coward!"

Pow!

Blood filled Ella's mouth as a punch to her jaw cut against her teeth. She swung her fist in the air and cracked what she hoped was the assailant's nose. Judging by the guttural scream, she had.

Ella drew back her leg and kicked as hard as she could. The attacker fell back against a tree trunk, groaning, then sliding to the ground. Ella scrambled to her feet and lunged at him, struggling to pull off the ski mask.

"I was ready for you today!" she yelled. "Come on, bitch. Show your face! Is that you, Tyler?"

The killer jumped up and lunged at Ella. This time, she caught a glimpse of a silver blade shining underneath a streetlight.

"*Nooo!*" she screamed, ducking to her left, then charging toward the middle of the street. He chased after her, playing a game of cat and mouse as they dodged in between cars.

"Somebody help me!" Ella screamed. She ran toward the corner, realizing she was only a block away from Charlotte's house.

Make a run for it. GO!

The fog turned her around. Was her house to the right? Or the left?

"You gotta be quicker than that," the attacker growled before lunging at Ella once again.

Her body slammed against the edge of the curb. Ella tried to scream out in pain. But her cries were muffled by the assaulter's gloved hand.

He grabbed the sides of her head, twisting in an attempt to snap her neck. Ella stiffened her muscles and pressed her thumbs into the attacker's eyes.

"You *bitch*!" he hollered, grabbing hold of her face.

Ella rammed her elbow against his temple then jumped to her feet. Just as she jetted forward, he kicked her legs out from underneath her.

"And now you're going to die!" he hissed.

The attacker jumped on top of her, his knees pinned against her arms. He covered her mouth with one hand and gripped her neck with the other.

She gasped for air, willing herself to get up again. Fight back. To no avail.

The veins in her head tightened. Pressure in her throat

mounted as the air grew thin. Her chest heaved, her body struggling for oxygen.

This is it. This time, I really am going to die...

A car engine roared in the distance. Lights blinked while a horn blew. Ella felt her cell phone vibrating against her hip. She struggled to reach for it just as a blade grazed her cheek.

"Touch that phone and I will slice open your throat!"

The car looming in the distance moved in closer. Its siren blared.

The assailant flinched, momentarily letting up on his grip.

"Help me!" Ella was finally able to scream. "*Please!*"

The car jumped the curb and came to an abrupt halt. Someone jumped out. Heavy footsteps pounded the asphalt.

The attacker attempted to hop up and escape.

"Oh, no you don't," Ella gasped. She grabbed his ankle and pulled him to the ground. He responded with a kick to her head.

"*Dammit!*" she screamed as he ran toward Gateway Park's entrance.

"Freeze! Drop the knife and put your hands in the air!"

Jake!

Ella rolled over onto her knees and attempted to stand. "*Go,*" she choked, directing Jake toward the park. "Get him!"

Jake ran after the assailant as he tried to kick open the gate. It was locked. Just when he began climbing it, Jake grabbed the attacker by his hoodie and pulled him to the ground.

"Drop your weapon!" he yelled with his gun drawn. "It's over. You're done!"

The attacker tossed the knife toward Jake's feet. A rush of adrenaline shot through Ella at the sight of surrender.

She rushed over as Jake pulled the suspect to his feet and handcuffed him.

"And now," Jake said, "the moment of truth. We finally get to see who's been terrorizing this town for over a year."

He pulled off the assailant's mask. Shined his flashlight in the killer's face.

Jake and Ella gasped in unison.

It was Faith.

Chapter Twenty

"Thank you, Dr. Allison," Jake said into the phone. "I appreciate you letting me know Ella made it to the hospital. Yes, please call back and let me know how she's doing once you're done with the examination."

He disconnected the call and rushed back toward the interrogation room, where Miles was questioning Faith. On the way there, Jake was stopped by Officer Underwood.

"Chief, Ben Foray just walked into the station and gave us an official statement."

"Oh, really. What does he have to say for himself?"

"Well, after he heard that Faith was arrested—"

"Wait, he already knows about that?" Jake interrupted. "Damn, news travels fast in this town."

"It does. But he wanted to state on the record that he had nothing to do with any of the murders. He did admit to knowing Faith, and said they met when he was performing community service at the school where she was taking computer classes. When she found out he was into fraudulent activities, she hired him to take that tour of Vincent Vineyard and steal the paperwork from Don's office."

"But she works there. Why didn't she just take it herself?"

"Because she didn't want to get caught on camera. She thought Ben could get away with grabbing the documents, and if he got caught during the process, he could pull the whole I-got-lost-during-the-tour stunt. That didn't work, obviously."

The sound of Faith's shrill ranting echoed through the hallway.

"I'd better get back to this interrogation," Jake said, slowly backing away. "Do not let Ben leave here before I speak with him."

"I won't. Oh, and one more thing. You know that amendment to Don Vincent's will that Ben stole? He brought it in with him. Said that Faith wanted him to alter it so that instead of the vineyard being left to Greer, it would be left to Tyler."

Jake stopped abruptly. "But wait…why would Faith want Vincent Vineyard to be left to Tyler instead of her own husband? You must have gotten their names mixed up."

"That's what I'd thought initially too. But I didn't. I'm repeating Ben's exact words. I actually had him run it by me three times. You can verify his statement once you're done questioning Faith."

"Yeah, I will. Because that's weird…"

Jake entered the interrogation room. Faith sat silently across from Miles, the wild grin on her face appearing as though she were in the front row of a comedy club rather than a police station.

"Mrs. Vincent," Miles began, "why don't you share with Chief Love what you just told me?"

She turned in her seat, batting her sparse eyelashes at Jake. "What, that I've been having an affair with Tyler Vincent?"

Instead of seating himself coolly, Jake practically fell into his chair. "I'm sorry. Could you please repeat that?"

She leaned in closer, yelling, "I've been having an affair with Tyler Vincent!"

The room went silent. Jake remained motionless, knowing that if he didn't react, Faith would keep talking.

"I know, I know," she continued, waving her cuffed hands in the air. "I seem too *sweet* and…and *demure* to be with a man so flamboyant, right? It is idiotic, if we're being totally honest here. But that was okay. Because somehow, it worked. You see, I had enough brains for us both. And he had the showstopping presence to represent Vincent Vineyard. Take it to a level far beyond its competitors."

Jake grabbed a bottle of water, his hand shaking as he took several long swallows. He'd seen a lot during his time on the force. But nothing like this.

"You know," the chief began after composing himself, "you're a great actress, Mrs. Vincent. I never would've suspected you were the one behind all this chaos. How long have you and Tyler been seeing one another?"

"Several years," she murmured, her smirk shriveling into a tight scowl. "Believe you me, I hadn't planned on being a mistress for that long. But Tyler tends to make promises that he has a hard time keeping. So, I had to start making moves that would incentivize him to leave his wife."

Miles frantically scribbled down her words, only pausing to ask, "Incentivize, meaning to commit murder?"

"Very good, Detective Love! See, you get me." Faith slid down in her chair, her eyes fixated on the back wall. "Tyler had me doing things I never thought I would. But the goal was to get rid of anything standing in the way of him taking over the vineyard, and us being together. So, I did what I had to do in order to make that happen."

"But why kill your husband?" Jake asked. "The idea of getting a divorce never crossed your mind?"

Faith rolled her eyes. "Murder is clean, Chief Love. In death, you're just...*poof*! Gone. Done. There's no fuss. No splitting things up. No talk of, *no, I get the house*! Or, *you can't have that car*! Divorce is messy. And lingering. Not to mention frowned upon within the Vincent family. Had I left Greer, I would have been ostracized and out of a job. Because who knows when Tyler would've actually left Jada? Plus, everyone sympathizes with a widow. Not a divorcée."

"Damn," Miles muttered. "That's cold. So how did you manage to get Greer's body inside of that wine vat? Did you have help?"

"*Help*? Of course not. I'm not stupid, Detective Love. I work alone. Nothing is a secret if someone else knows about it. I got Greer inside the vat by convincing him that the spout was faulty. Asked him to climb up and take a look, see what may have jammed it. When he did, I shot him in the head. He fell forward, I pushed him all the way in, dropped the lid and that was it."

Despite the heat blowing through the vent, a chill fell over the room. Jake had heard enough. He was burning to throw her in jail. But there was more work that needed to be done.

"Hey, don't look so somber, you two!" Faith quipped. "At least Greer died surrounded by what he loved most. *Wine*. But anyway, back to the reason I did all of this in the first place. Claire was on the verge of naming Greer president of the vineyard. And I couldn't let that happen. He was weak, and way too humble. You all saw him on stage that night at the casino. He was a bumbling embarrassment. Knowing that was my husband, getting upstaged by the man *I* should've been there with, was infuriating. That should have been *me* out there strutting up to the stage, hand in hand with Tyler while singing 'Welcome to the Jungle,' not Jada!"

"Since you mentioned Jada," Jake interjected, "tell me, did she know Ben Foray?"

"No. Well, not until her nosy ass walked in on me talking to him about breaking into Don's office the day of the tour. Once I realized she'd overheard me, I tried to get her in on it, especially since it was her husband's name being forged onto the amendment. But she refused. However, I did swear her to secrecy, and she stuck to her word."

"And she didn't question why you'd want Tyler to take over as president instead of your own husband?"

"Of course not. Jada may be a fool, but she was wise enough to know that a dry, dull man like Greer could not have handled that position. Plus, she had no idea Tyler was leaving her for me."

Probably because he wasn't, Jake wanted to say. But he refrained.

When Faith's voice cracked, he thought she was on the verge of bursting into tears. Instead, she broke into a fit of giggles.

"Wanna hear a fun little fact?" she asked. "When I first met Ben, I had him save my number in his phone under Jada's name. You know, as a precaution, just in case the wrong eyes happened to see me calling."

Jake threw Miles a knowing glance. He nodded, understanding that it had been Faith calling Ben that night at the Hole in the Wall, not Jada.

"It really is unfortunate that you chose to take the lives of Don, Manuel and Greer over greed and lust, Mrs. Vincent," Jake said. "I'm just glad we caught you when we did. Had we not, Ella Bowman would probably be dead, and I have no doubt that Jada would've been next."

He paused, waiting for her to respond. She didn't.

"Did you plant Jada's scarf underneath Ella's car at Nancy's Country Mart?"

Faith stared down at her wrists, running her fingertip along the edge of the cuffs. "Yep. I had to pin the crimes on somebody, didn't I? Look, don't feel bad for Jada. She is not a victim. She's a rotten bully. She doesn't deserve her title as director of *anything*, let alone the honor of being Tyler's wife. With her in prison and everyone else out of the way, Tyler would be president of Vincent Vineyard, we'd get married and live out our happily-ever-after."

Jake recoiled at the flat, cavalier tone in her voice. She spoke as if she were reading through a grocery list rather than confessing to her horrific crimes.

"Why kill Manuel though?" he asked. "He wasn't even in the running to taking over the vineyard."

"But he *was* planning on speaking with law enforcement, now wasn't he? In case you haven't figured this out, Chief Love, I didn't just use those newfound computer skills to design Vincent Vineyard's website. I also used them to hack into Manuel's computer after I saw him chitchatting with law enforcement during the Cabernet Sauvignon tasting, then at the casino event. I knew he was up to something. And I was right. Manuel had secretly audited the vineyard's financial records and *allegedly* found proof that Tyler had been embezzling money."

"Oh, did he?" Jake grabbed his cell phone and sent Detective Campbell a message, requesting that he bring Tyler in for questioning. "So is it safe to assume that you killed Manuel before he could reveal what he'd learned about Tyler?"

A condescending chuckle gurgled in the back of Faith's throat. "Umm, *yeah*. What else was I supposed to do? Sit back and let you find all that evidence, then watch my man go to jail? That would've totally ruined our plans for the future. Manuel left me no choice but to kill him."

As Faith's pupils began to dilate, Jake contemplated placing her on a 5150 hold.

"Plus," she muttered, her head pivoting away from the officers, "Manuel knew about my affair with Tyler."

"How did he find out about it?" Miles asked.

"He caught us making out one night inside the distillery."

"Did Tyler know anything about these murders and the other crimes you were committing?"

"No! He did not. So don't even try and drag him into this. That man is innocent. Leave him alone so he can help assemble my defense team and get me the hell out of here. Speaking of which, when can I post bond?"

"*Bond*?" Jake shot back. "Mrs. Vincent, you murdered three people and attempted to murder a fourth. There will be no bond."

Faith's expression fell into a rumpled frown. Jake thought he'd finally humbled her into facing the ramifications of her actions. But then she stretched out, crossing her legs and looking up at him with a sinister gleam in her eyes. The devilish scowl was unlike anything he'd ever seen.

"I know my actions may be vile," she admitted. "But guess what? It feels good to finally be seen. And heard. And feared. Do you know how hard it is to constantly stand in the background? In the shadows of my inadequate husband, and that disco queen freak show, Jada? I could run that vineyard by myself better than any of the Vincents. But I don't have the looks. Or all that fake ass razzle-dazzle. I'm about the business. Which, unfortunately, doesn't bode well within a sea of superficiality."

Jake's head tilted as he studied Faith's smug demeanor. "Mrs. Vincent, did it ever occur to you that Tyler was just using you for your business acumen? Because I certainly haven't seen any proof that he and Jada were in the process of divorcing. Have you, Detective Love?"

"Nope. Not a shred."

The spark in Faith's fiery gaze dimmed. That curve in her lips straightened as she pulled her feet back underneath the chair. "But I… I know he was working toward it. Privately, I'm guessing…"

"Let's talk about Ella Bowman," Jake said.

"What about her?"

"Why were you targeting her with the threats and attacks?"

"Because of her affair with Tyler."

The words stung like acid seeping through Jake's eardrums. They burned just as badly as they had when Ella first shared the news.

He turned away from Faith, unable to bear her sneering grin.

"*Aww*," she whimpered. "Did hearing that upset you, Jake? I'm so sorry. If I weren't handcuffed, I'd reach out and give you a hug—"

"That's enough," Miles interrupted. "And it's Chief Love to you. Now let's stay on course here. What was your motive behind the attacks on Ella?"

"It's simple. I was jealous. Once I overheard Tyler telling Greer he was worried about her being here in Clemmington and putting their affair on blast, that was it. I knew I had to get rid of her. And before you even say it, I don't care *when* the affair took place. It happened. Plus, how was I to know whether or not Ella came to Clemmington to try and woo Tyler away from me? I wasn't taking any chances. Period."

"Well, how were you able to track her every move?" Jake asked. "Did you hack into her email as well?"

"*Maybe*," Faith purred coyly. "That, and I *could've* placed a GPS tracker on her Jeep as well…"

Leaning back in his chair, Jake crossed his arms over his chest. "Welp, now you'll get to spend the rest of your life in prison over a man who cared nothing about you."

"Without the possibility of parole, I'm sure," Miles chimed in.

"Not only that," Jake continued, "but the woman you and Tyler were hurting the most? Jada? I bet she'll be named president of Vincent Vineyard. Mark my words. Faith Vincent, you are under arrest for the murders of Don Vincent, Manuel Ruiz and Greer Vincent, and the attempted murder of Ella Bowman. Officer Underwood is on his way in to book you." The chief stood, sauntering toward the door. "Oh, and one more thing. Thanks for the tip on Tyler's embezzlement. He'll be facing a hefty fine and three years in prison."

"He'll be facing *what*?" Faith screamed. "No! You can't do that. I didn't even mention anything about Tyler embezzling money. Or did I? If I did, I take it back. And if you didn't record it, I didn't say it!"

"Oh, but I did record it," Miles said, waving his cell phone in the air. "And once we recover Manuel's missing laptop, which I'm sure we'll find at your house, that'll confirm your admission."

"You can't search my house! Where's your warrant?"

"I'll be filing an emergency request to have one issued momentarily," Jake told her before walking out, signaling Officer Underwood over, then calling the hospital to check on Ella.

Chapter Twenty-One

Ella turned off the television and kissed Jake's forehead as he dozed on the couch.

"I knew you wouldn't be able to make it through the entire movie," she murmured.

"What do you mean?" Jake asked, popping up and blinking rapidly. "I wasn't asleep!"

She burst out laughing and stood, pulling him to his feet. "Liar. Come on. Let's go to bed."

"You don't have to tell me twice." He leaned in and kissed her neck on the way to the bedroom. "Plus, I know you've gotta get some rest for your big day tomorrow."

"Yes, I do. Clemmington General Hospital's neonatal unit is expecting me bright and early."

"My girl. I'm so proud of you. Nurse Bowman, reporting for duty!"

Before she entered the room, Jake slipped her hand in his, stopping her in the doorway.

"Listen," he said softly, "I know we agreed to bury certain topics when it comes to the Vincent Vineyard investigation. But I just want to reiterate how happy I am that you've been in therapy, and apologize again for the way I reacted when you told me about you and Tyler's—"

Ella held her finger to his lips. "You don't have to do

that. You've already apologized, and I've accepted it. I understood your reaction. I expected it, really, especially after the way I mishandled the entire situation."

"But I just… I can't help but blame myself for you being attacked that night after I stormed off and you left the house."

"That attack led us to the killer. Getting there may have been brutal, but we did it. And now, you're the hero for finally solving one of Clemmington's biggest cases."

"It never would've happened without your help," Jake whispered, kissing her gently before heading inside the room.

"We do have our cell phone location trackers to thank too," Ella said while turning down the bed. "Thank goodness you were smart enough to suggest we turn them on, and you thought to come after me—" She stopped abruptly when her hand hit what felt like a rock.

"*Ouch*! What was that?"

Jake walked up behind her, wrapping his hands around her waist. "I don't know. Why don't you reach underneath your pillow and find out?"

"Mr. Love, what are you up to?" Ella flipped her pillow over. There, lying on the mattress, was a small red velvet box.

She gasped, her body falling back against his. "Is that what I think is?"

"There's only one way to find out."

Tears sprang to Ella's eyes as she reached for the box. She slowly opened it. A yellow peanut M&M sat in the middle.

"*Jake!*" she screeched, spinning around and banging her hands against his chest. "Why would you trick me like that and—"

The sight of an emerald cut diamond engagement ring propped between his fingertips silenced her.

Jake dropped down on one knee.

"Ella Bowman," he said, taking her hand in his, "once you're done enjoying that peanut M&M, would you do me the honor of being my wife?"

"Yes. *Yes*! Of course!"

The moment Jake slipped the ring on her finger, Ella pulled him to his feet and jumped in his arms.

"Never have I ever thought I'd be this happy," she whispered into his chest.

"Never have I ever thought I'd find a woman like you. Thank you."

"Thank me? For what?"

"For renewing my faith in love."

* * * * *

OLLERO CREEK
CONSPIRACY

AMBER LEIGH WILLIAMS

To rescue animals. Thank you for helping to quiet the noise in our heads just by being.

Chapter One

Luella Decker knew the devil never went down to Georgia. He had set up camp in her hometown of Fuego, New Mexico, for the better part of sixty years.

Now that he was dead, Luella couldn't wait to leave. Fuego was home to more tumult than security—more heartbreak than love—because the devil, Jace "Whip" Decker, had been her father. She'd come home after a six-month sentence in county lock-up long enough to sell her house, pack her things, load up her animals and hit the road.

Soon, she'd leave Fuego in the dust. She knew now never to retrace her steps.

"Turn here," she told the Uber driver.

"Okay," he said obediently. He'd been pretty leery since realizing he wasn't picking up a visitor to Fuego County Jail but a released prisoner. He glanced around. "You, ah, live pretty far outside of town."

"Yes." It's what she'd liked most about the Ollero Creek property. It was on the outskirts, far from prying eyes. She looked across the expanse. The landscape was the only thing Fuego had going for it. In early December, the red sand hills of her youth were dusted white. She could hear the car's tires sluicing over snowmelt that would morph into a muddy mess soon. In the distance, she could see the buttes and mesas that marked the high desert country for the jaw-dropping vista it was. The climate was hot and harsh in summer, but due to its position near the Colorado Plateau, it was cold and snowy in winter.

The driver cleared his throat as they rolled and bumped up the unpaved lane. "What, uh…what'd you do time for—if you don't mind me asking?"

She avoided meeting his eyes in the rearview mirror and chose not to answer. He was likely from somewhere inside the bounds of Fuego County…which meant he'd heard about her father abducting the daughter of a local cattle baron. The daughter, Eveline Eaton, happened to be something of a national celebrity.

That wasn't the only reason Luella's case was newsworthy. Alone, she was no one. When she wasn't working her day job as a trauma nurse at Fuego County Hospital, she lived on the fringes of society. Her father was supposed to have died after killing the Eatons' mother and stepsister in a land dispute seven and a half years ago. He'd disappeared into high desert country. Police had blamed his supposed demise on mountain lions.

It was the promise of living in Fuego without her father that lured Luella back to the town after an extended absence. She'd escaped after high school with her mother to San Gabriel—a clean-cut city far enough away from Fuego for peace of mind.

It wasn't long after she moved back that Luella learned the truth. Her father was very much alive and hiding out in the multitude of caves at Coldero Ridge. He'd come to her over the last seven years in search of food and weapons.

Luella had given him what he'd needed. She'd done whatever it'd taken to survive because nothing scared her more than being at Whip Decker's mercy. Long before he'd taken the lives of Josephine and Angel Eaton in cold blood, he'd knocked her and her mother around the double-wide that had been their home. He drank every afternoon until he was mean with it and condemned both her mother and Luella with words and the brunt of his hand, leaving scars on the surface and deep.

Some of her scars had faded. Others were permanent residents on Luella's skin and mind.

Seven years she'd lived in fear he'd come for her in the night and finish the job he liked to remind her he should've ended the night she was born. He'd brought her into the world. She'd known at some point he'd take her out of it.

That was why she'd been saving. For years, she'd put money away—determined to have enough to escape—from Whip Decker, from Fuego, from the dumpster fire that was her life there.

He hadn't taken her out of the world. He was gone for good this time, and she'd plead guilty to aiding and abetting him. The defense lawyer had argued coercion and self-defense so she'd only served six months but had lost the job she'd had for almost a decade and what little was left of her reputation.

The Uber driver whistled low as he made the turn into the driveway. "That's some house."

Luella's heart gave a tug. She'd painted it white so that it stood stark against the dry, red-stained landscape like the salvation it had been for her seven years ago. It was the first thing that had ever truly been hers.

It was three stories high, box-shaped, with a wide porch braced high above the dry creek bed. There had been no creek at Ollero Creek for half a century but a preserved waterwheel stood as its testament.

What she'd never told anyone—not a soul—was that she'd

bought the house because it was ideal for stargazing. As a girl, she'd been obsessed with the cosmos—mapping them, understanding their pieces and their mysteries...

"Home sweet home, huh?" the driver asked.

She realized he'd parked and she was staring wistfully out the window. She frowned and shifted toward the door. "Thanks for the lift." She started to open it. "Oh," she said, hesitating. "I guess I need to pay you."

"The bill was prepaid."

"Pre..." She narrowed her eyes. "Who paid you?"

He drummed his fingers on the steering wheel, impatient to leave. "Uh, the app didn't say. It just gave me an address. And instructions to be there at ten."

Luella didn't like the idea of owing anyone anything. She opened the door and stepped out. No sooner had she shut it than the tires skidded and the car sped away, fishtailing across the icy, wet road.

She probably should've told the driver she wasn't a hard-core killer—that she'd never harmed another human being in her life. Then again, she thought, this was more fun.

The smile stopped before it started when she heard the restless sounds of her chickens. She took off across the drive and around the side of the house.

The rooster, Caesar, greeted her with a bob of his head and a hoarse croak. As her steps picked up pace, he flapped his wings and skittered out of her path. His grumblings sent the rest of the flock into shrieks and cackles. Inside their coop, wings beat and feathers flew.

She'd check in with them in a minute. First things first: she'd waited six months to see her man and she wasn't going to wait a moment longer.

"Mama's home!" she called as she swung into the barn. There were two stalls. The one on the left had held her sow and its piglets. She'd given them to her neighbor Naleen Altaha and her family in exchange for feeding the others while she was gone.

The stall on the right should have been occupied. Her heart sank like a stone when she saw that the gate was ajar. "Sheridan?" Her panicked call echoed back to her from the rough-hewn rafters.

There was no horse, no hay, no manure—no sign that anything had lived there.

"Oh, my God." Her stomach cramped and she pressed her hand to it.

Her horse was gone.

Her cheeks heated as panic escalated. She kicked the gate farther open so she could pass through it. She trudged back to the house, Caesar squawking irritably at her heels. She reached around the last step on the porch stairs and moved the smooth river rock she'd left there. Grabbing the key underneath, she ran up the stairs, shoved it into the lock of the front door, cranked the knob and flew into the living room.

The phone was mounted to the wall. She pulled down the receiver and dialed Naleen's number.

As it rang, she gave up trying to tamp down the heat in her cheeks. She was a redhead and her horse wasn't where she'd left him.

"Hello?"

"Where's Sheridan?" she said. She did her best to ungnash her teeth but wasn't very successful there, either. "He's not here. Where *is* he, Naleen?"

"Calm down, Luella, okay?"

"Don't tell me to calm down!" Luella all but shouted. "Where *the hell* is my horse?"

"I'm trying to tell you!" Naleen said. "Three weeks ago, I saw him favoring his back right leg. I couldn't get the equine vet out there. He didn't want to come unless he knew you were available to pay for the home visit. So I thought about my ex-father-in-law."

"Griff Mackay? But he works at…" Luella trailed off. *No. She didn't.*

"It was the best I could come up with, under the circumstances," Naleen explained. "You have to admit, Griff is the best with horses."

Luella laid her head back against the wall and raised her eyes to the ceiling. "Why didn't you consult me first?"

"I thought something was really wrong with him," Naleen continued. "And I know how much you rely on that horse. So I didn't hesitate. Once Griff took a look, he said it was a small infection. Nothing major. And he offered to keep an eye on him until you came to pick him up."

Didn't Naleen know what it cost to board a horse? It was why Luella had come up with the arrangement she had with the woman and her husband, Terrence—to drop in twice a day to take care of her animals.

"I hope you're not too upset with me."

Luella braced a hand on her hip as she looked out the window at the empty barn. She swallowed what she wanted to say. "I've got to go get him," she said.

"Hey, Luella?" Naleen said before she could hang up. "Welcome home."

"Thanks," Luella said emptily. She replaced the receiver in the cradle then raked her hands through her hair before heading up the stairs to the second floor.

Her bedroom was on the right—with her bed. She'd desperately wanted to come home, greet Sheridan, check on the chickens, locate her wandering cats then shower under the hot spray in her bathroom tub and crash in her own sheets for a week.

She bypassed the door for the second set of steps. The stairwell narrowed at the top as it spun up and to the left. There was one door on the landing.

She went through it into the dim attic. She took the flashlight off the wall next to the door and turned it on.

The floor was broken up. The boards had fallen away in the middle. The house was old, after all. She'd laid a single two-by-four across the hole to bridge the gap. Putting one foot in front of the other, she slowly made her way across the board to the other side.

There was a loose section of flooring near the end of the attic room. She went down on her hands and knees, removing the rug she'd placed there. She pried away the loose flooring and aimed the beam of light down into the space beneath.

Her money was there, just as she'd left it in even stacks. She breathed a sigh. With the sale of the house, it would be enough.

She had her ticket out of Fuego.

Reaching in, she grabbed the first stack of hundreds. She removed the rubber band from the center and counted out several thousand dollars.

It would have to be enough. If Griff or anyone else at the stable he managed on the other side of Fuego had anything to say to the contrary, her cash stack would dwindle below what she needed. And that was unacceptable.

She'd sworn to herself she'd never go back to Fuego's largest working cattle ranch, Eaton Edge. But she needed her horse. She needed him badly enough she was willing to go against every part of her that told her not to return there.

EATON EDGE WAS nothing short of spectacular. There were those who claimed The RC Resort, a glamorous guest ranch owned by the Claymore family, was better. But Luella knew there was nothing more special than the Edge.

Maybe because she'd once thought she would be a part of it.

She passed the sign with the entwined *E*'s. It had been a girl's dream, one that had come crashing down around her ears along with all the others.

It was better not to dream, she'd learned, turning her Jeep under the naked cottonwood tree with its long, lonely wooden swing. She pulled in next to a line of dirty work trucks.

She ground the shifter into Park and gripped the wheel, letting the heat pump out of the vents. She stared at the hacienda-style ranch house with its long, low porch. In the spring and summer, geraniums hung in baskets along the front. The men hung any shed antlers they found from the eaves. The smells from the kitchen were welcoming, no matter the season.

There had once been a wooden ladder that led from the second-floor balcony up to the flat roof. She'd spent several nights there, flat on her back with the heavens open above her. She'd found planets and traced constellations. She'd witnessed meteor showers and comets.

She'd wanted to go to college to become an astronomer, thanks to endless nights on the Eaton House roof with...

Luella forced herself to look away from the roofline. There was a row of tiny icicles there, drip-drip-dripping. They'd melted down to spikes. When they fell, they'd be razor thin and deadly.

She shut off the ignition and opened the door. She made sure the cash roll was still in her back pocket and hopped down from the cab.

She thought of knocking on the front door. Then she

chickened out. Astronomy and life in some capacity at Eaton Edge may have been her dream, but a lot had happened in the seventeen years since. Her father had killed Josephine, the Eatons' mother, and Angel. He'd recently abducted Eveline Eaton. Whip Decker met his end at the end of an Eaton scope. She'd been sent to jail for her part in it, however unwilling.

She doubted any of the Eatons had bought the coercion defense.

Luella was no more welcome here than she was at Sunday service.

She pulled her hat low over her brow and moved around the house. Trying to stay out of sight of the windows of the house, she wound her way through the empty vegetable patch. *I'm not trespassing,* she told herself. Although that's exactly what she felt like—a trespasser.

Undulating hills rolled into the distance. They were blanketed in timid white. Grass peppered the snow. Icy puddles shined blue green, like mirrors in the valleys. Beyond the hills, she could make out the buttes to the northeast and the cliffs in the northwest. A river, interwoven with thin, broken sheets of ice, ran down the center like a ribbon.

The buildings were all white so they stood stark against the grass and sagebrush in every other season. The barns, the stable, the bunkhouses and workshops…they all followed the same Spanish-style architectural pattern.

She watched a plume of air escape her mouth in a wispy puff. Eaton Edge was the stuff of dreams, all right. She'd reached for them…and had fallen hard in the attempt.

Hunching her shoulders, she approached the stables. Maybe she'd be able to locate Griff without running into anyone else. Especially—

"Lu?"

She came up short of the stable door. She told herself to be strong and cold—like those icicles. Turning on her heel, she faced him—the man she hadn't wanted to face.

Ellis Eaton looked far too good under the clean white brim of his Stetson. He was tall, over six feet, with long legs encased in working-blue Wranglers and a thick buff-colored jacket.

He'd let his hair grow, she saw, like he used to. Needle straight, the hay-colored strands fingered the lids of his eyes. There was a freckle on one of the lids. It'd once driven her to distraction. His face was still tan from being out in the harsh sun day after day. *Honey-toned*, she'd thought.

Every inch of him was lean and long and honey-toned.

She shook herself. She'd learned not to dwell on how good he looked, always, or how a life outdoors had hewn him into the solid butte of a man he was now. She knew not to think how he was the only one of his siblings with a perfect dimple in his chin or how, like his father, Hammond, and older brother, Everett, he'd developed his fair share of laugh lines early.

He carried a saddle over one shoulder. He was wearing work gloves, handy against the cold.

He looked at her like she was as celestial as the moon, stars and planets they'd once marveled at from the roof of his father's house.

Unbidden, the subtle, earthy musk he carried on his skin hit her. He wasn't close enough to smell, or taste. But some memories were so consuming, they came at her like a battering ram whether it was in the middle of the night in her bed at Ollero Creek or the jail yard surrounded by dozens of inmates.

Ellis Eaton had never let her alone, whether he intended to or not.

He stopped staring long enough to set the saddle at his feet. He started taking off his gloves, one finger at a time, as he walked around it, his dark eyes passing from her red waves to her sherpa-lined flannel vest, her thighs in faded, fleece-lined Levis, down to her booted toes. The assessment was thorough. It nearly stopped her heart. "You're home," he said.

She frowned. *You're home*. He couldn't know how the words hurt. And yet…she felt anger and bitterness welling from the deep where they lived—where she'd built them to protect herself. "I'm out," she corrected.

"Today, right? It was supposed to be today." He started to smile.

She dropped her gaze to her boots because she couldn't fight that—his smile. It was sun-kissed and sweet and his eyes…they grabbed. "I came for my horse," she stated.

His chin tipped up. "Ah." He bit down on the middle finger of the first glove as he went to work prying off the other. When he was done, he shoved them both into the pocket of his jacket. "Sheridan?"

She nodded, jerkily. "Naleen said she brought him here. I never asked her to do that. That isn't what I wanted."

He tilted his head. "We were happy to keep him."

"I can't imagine that's true."

"But it is," he told her. "He needed care—a place to recoup. And I think he's enjoyed the company."

"Sheridan doesn't like anybody's company."

A slow smile did creep over Ellis's face and, damn it, her heart missed a whole beat. "Come here," he said, holding out a hand.

She stared at that wide hand with its long fingers and hard-set calluses. She hugged her vest tighter around her, pressing her hands under her elbows when her palms tingled in reaction.

The smile faded by degrees. His eyes tipped down at the corners. It was a shame to watch them turn as sad as they'd been over the last year—a year that had been hell on him, too. He'd lost his father to a third and final heart attack and had gone from second-in-command at the Edge to acting chief of operations after Everett had been shot and nearly killed in the skirmish with her father.

If the rumors were true…and Luella had never asked directly, not wanting to know the answer…it was Ellis who had shot her father, ending his life.

Did he think about it, she wondered, when he laid his head down at night? Had there been any hesitation that day in the box canyon at Coldero Ridge when he'd sighted Whip Decker in the scope of his gun? Had there been time to think about how messed up their lives had all become?

Whose call had that been—for Ellis, with his puppy dog eyes and never an unkind word for anyone, of all people to be the one to kill her father?

Once, he'd had dreams, too—dreams that had lived in lockstep with hers. He'd wanted to be a pediatrician. While he'd gotten closer to realizing his dreams, completing his degree and accepting a residency in Taos, he'd given all that up to be by his father's side through the hard times, to be the dutiful son he was and live the life of a wrangler and cowhand.

As she followed him to the large stable yard, she scanned the horses along the fence. Several hands were there, saddling up. She avoided their bald stares and squinted for recognition among the barebacked mounts.

Ellis slowed, dropping back to stand next to her. He pointed into the near distance, lowering his head toward hers. "That's him over there, I think."

Luella raised her hand to block the angle of the sun. Near the corner of the paddock, she saw the shape of her roan. Light spilled freely inside her. It nearly split her clean through. She broke into a half trot, raising her hand to wave. "Sheridan!" she called. "Here, boy!"

She stopped when she saw two small figures. One wore a powder blue hat, the other fire-engine red. Their mittened hands reached through the slats of the fence toward her horse. "No," she said. She started running. "Stop!"

Fingers wrapped taut around her upper arm, bringing her up short. Ellis leaned in, his warmth burning clean through her clothes. "Hang on," he said. "Just watch."

"He's a biter," she protested.

"Watch, Lu," he murmured, his gold-stubbled cheek dangerously close to hers.

She shivered—from unwanted arousal, from twisted fear…a dizzy cocktail of the two. She moaned as she watched Sheridan lower his nose to those outstretched hands. He nibbled, but not the girls' fingers. He took what he was given, a treat of some kind. The girls broke into giggles. The smallest girl—the one in the red hat—clapped and pet him on the breast.

"I…" She shook her head. "I've never seen him… How long…?"

"Since week two," Ellis said. She could tell by his voice he was smiling again. "It gave me a scare, the first time I saw Ingrid reaching into his stall. But he took to the pair of them. So much so I thought about putting Isla up on his back. I needed your okay first. Is he around other kids often?"

She swallowed the lump in her throat. She watched the girls with their angel faces, their dark eyes like Hershey's

Kisses… They were Ellis's and they were perfect. "Sheridan's never been around children," she managed.

Ellis shook his head. "Well," he said as he straightened, "you're welcome to bring him by whenever he needs a refill on treats. Isla and Ingrid are nothing if not generous."

Luella checked the urge to give herself a hard pinch. "They're sweet kids, Ellis. But Sheridan and I won't be coming back."

His head snatched sideways. After a moment, he said, "You're welcome to."

"We'll pretend that's true."

"Lu—"

Please, stop calling me that. She wanted to scream it. Instead, she said, "I appreciate what Griff has done. And what the girls have clearly been doing for Sheridan. But it's time he and I went home." She pulled the cash out of her pocket.

He grimaced when she extended it to him. "C'mon. Don't do that."

"I'm paying for his feed and board," she stated.

"It's not necessary."

"Don't be ridiculous," she dismissed, pushing the money at him again. "Take the money, Ellis!"

"Keep your money," he said, firm now, too. "He earned his keep by keeping my girls in smiles. I won't be forgettin' that."

She wished he would forget. Why wasn't it easier to forget? They'd lived their lives apart. He'd been married to another woman, for Christ's sake. And she'd made an effort—*such* an effort—to forget what had been.

Fuego was a small town. Run-ins were impossible to avoid. She'd run into him plenty since returning to Fuego seven years ago—and his wife, Liberty, and their sweet, perfect girls with their eyes so like his…too much like his.

It had been impossible to forget. It was one of the reasons she had to get out—leave—never come back. Because how else was she ever supposed to move on?

"Why don't you hate me?" she demanded to know.

"Hate you?" he asked, stricken. "Why would I hate you?"

"He tried to kill her," she said. "Your sister. He almost did kill Everett, just like he killed your mother and Angel. And I helped him. I kept him alive the years that he hid."

"He made you do it."

"You don't know that."

"But I do," he said, softly. Her knees almost gave way when his tone gentled to match the look. "I *know* you. You wouldn't have helped him if he hadn't made you afraid, like he did when you were young." His gaze touched on the hook-shaped scar just visible under the knob of her chin.

"What if you don't know me anymore?" she asked. "What if I'm different? I went to jail, Ellis."

"Doesn't matter."

"It matters to everybody else," she reminded him.

"To hell with everybody else."

Her lips parted. She pressed them together until they numbed. "Do they still talk about us—in town? Do they still talk about our affair?"

"We didn't have an affair," he said, his teeth coming together.

"But she told them we did," she reminded him. "Liberty. And you never told them anything to the contrary."

"It was ugly gossip," he said, "with not one lick of substance. I don't hold by that."

"She's using it, isn't she?" she asked. "In your divorce. Adultery."

"She can say what she wants," Ellis told her. "Doesn't change the truth. Which is that you and I…we never…"

But they had. Just not after Liberty Ferris entered the picture. They'd had one another...on the rooftop...in the cab of his first truck...in his bed...in those spectacular hills that spread out around them. She'd been his.

There was so much water under that bridge, it had swept her away, drowned her, and baptized her as the version of herself she'd had to forge in the aftermath.

Had she drowned—or just been treading water all this time? That could account for why she was so damn tired.

"I'm leaving," she told him. "I'm selling my house and leaving Fuego." Before he could say anything, she went on. "I've made up my mind. There's nothing for me here anymore."

He searched her, and she hardened herself against the torrent of emotions that crossed his features. He began to shake his head. Then, a whistle cut across the yard and he looked around.

Griff was standing outside the barn, motioning him over.

"You've gotta go," she said. "I'll get my horse."

Before she could make a clean break of it, he stopped her again with the same hand.

She closed her eyes. "Let me go."

She heard his long inhale. Then his whisper. "It's that easy for you—goodbye?"

"Why shouldn't it be?" she asked, afraid of the answer—afraid to look at him anymore. It was like staring directly into the sun.

He hesitated for the longest time. Her pulse went off the rails. She stopped breathing. *Don't say it. Don't you dare say it...*

"You can leave," he said, low. "You can go as far away as you like. But a piece of you...it'll always be back here..."

With me. He didn't finish. But she heard it regardless. "It was never enough. That's why I never…we never…"

"Lu."

"Stop saying my name," she snapped. "Stop *saying* it like that. I'm not yours. And I need to be free. I need to be free of you, Ellis! Why can't you just *let me go*?"

His grip loosened.

She jerked herself upright. Rod-backed, she walked away.

The girls had their hands outstretched with more offerings that Sheridan hungrily accepted.

Luella laid her hand on his quarter. True to form, the horse swung his head sideways and sent her a measuring look.

"Hey, boy," she murmured. "Mama's here."

The smaller girl, Ingrid, gasped. "Your hair!"

The older one, Isla, sent her a scandalized look. "Shh, don't be rude! That's Miss Luella, the nurse. Remember?"

"I'm not being rude," Ingrid snapped back. "I love it! It's like fire!"

Luella stared at the wonder in Ingrid's eyes. Her heart gave a tug she couldn't lock down. "Thank you," she replied. "I always hated it."

"Why?" Ingrid asked. She reached up for her own chin-length curls that stuck out from underneath a red knit ski cap. "If I had hair like that, everybody would look at me."

The corners of Luella's mouth quivered. It wasn't quite a smile. But it may have been dangerously close. "That's what troubled me," she said. "Everybody always made such a fuss about it."

Isla studied the waves closely. "I like the curls," she said gingerly. Her face was so serious, and she picked her words carefully. This one was every bit her father's daughter. "Ingrid got the curly hair. Mine's too straight."

Luella sighed. She slid her palm down the length of Sheridan's spine. He nickered, turning his muzzle into her up-turned hand, looking for more treats. "I would've sold my soul for straight blond hair like yours. I guess the grass is always greener." Unable to help herself, she pressed her cheek to Sheridan's neck, breathing in his smell. He had the power to quiet the noise in her head. She needed that now, more than ever.

"Is this *your* horse?" Ingrid asked.

"He is," Luella murmured. "And now I have to take him home."

"Aw," the girls said as one. Isla bit her lip and reached up to give his face another rub. "We'll miss you, boy."

Ingrid's face brightened. "Maybe we can come visit him?" she chirped. "Do you live close?"

Luella stared, blank, at their faces. "I..." She looked away, quickly. "Sheridan and I will be leaving Fuego soon."

"Oh, no," Ingrid said. Her pout was both pretty and devastating.

Isla let her hand fall away from Sheridan's face. "Come on, Ingrid. We should go back inside."

"Goodbye, Sheridan," Ingrid said as her sister tugged her off her perch on the bottom rung of the fence. "I'll miss you."

Luella watched them go, the most precious duo in the world. Then she turned to Sheridan, into him, burying her face in his mane and forcing herself to breathe.

They weren't going to be able to get away from Fuego fast enough.

Chapter Two

Ellis found it difficult to concentrate on cattle, getting them each their winter protein supplement and making sure they were dry and warm in this latest burst of plateau weather. He was distracted enough that he nearly found himself between the horns of two rival bulls the green new ranch hand, Lucas, his brother had taken on had forgotten to separate.

Let me go.

"Goddamn it," he muttered. The conversation with Luella was on a loop in his head. She was leaving Fuego... what, forever?

She'd disappeared once before, after high school. He'd gone early to Taos to settle into his college dorm and to try scoping out a place for her to live, too. They'd planned to attend university together. They'd planned a lot of things.

The sky was onyx, heavy with stars. It looked more inviting than the thick blanket he'd spread across the grass next to the riverbed where they lay in companionable silence. It was so quiet, he swore he could hear her heart beating.

Their hands were joined, his fingers playing through hers. He felt the band on her finger, the one he'd placed there with promises for always...

Always had lasted two months. The engagement had been

so hush-hush neither of their families had known about it. They hadn't wanted to hear how foolish they were.

He hadn't felt foolish. With Luella, Ellis had felt a desperate kind of urgency. It'd been so strong, he'd thought not being with her would gut him.

It had. God, had it ever, however much he'd learned to live with it.

She doesn't want to be found, her mother had told him when, after six months, he'd finally gotten the woman on the phone. *Can't you take a hint, boy? She's moved on. It's about time you did, too.*

"Ellis."

Ellis's head snapped up, alarmed he'd been caught daydreaming again—not by a pair of bulls but by his sister, Eveline. She was a long way from her modeling days in New York and Paris with no makeup and windswept hair. But with her engagement to his friend Wolfe Coldero and her new job as stable manager at the Edge, he'd never seen her more herself.

She closed the distance to him. "Liberty's here."

"What?" he asked, setting aside the pitchfork he'd been using to freshen the hay. "She's not supposed to pick up the girls until tomorrow."

Eveline lifted a shoulder. "She won't say much—only that she needs to speak with you. Sounds serious."

With Liberty, it was always serious—like a self-guided missile. He looked down at himself. He looked like the well-worn cattleman he was—the kind Liberty had made it very clear she hadn't wanted him to be.

She'd wanted to be the doctor's wife. She'd wanted a life in the city. He'd come close to giving her both. But then his father's health went into sharp decline and he'd given that up to be by Hammond's side. He'd brought Liberty along to Fuego, thinking...*hoping* she'd adjust.

Their marriage had gone sour. Her complaints about small-town life and his work hours had been incessant. He'd done his best to bear it. There hadn't been an alternative. His father had been ill, and Everett had needed his help holding up the family business.

The girls had been his saving grace. They loved the Edge. They took to the land, the animals and riding as he and his siblings had as kids.

How could Liberty object so bitterly to something Isla and Ingrid loved with every measure of themselves? Her request for divorce had shocked him to the bone, especially when she'd left the house they'd bought together in Fuego and taken the girls to Taos.

More shocking had been her allegations of adultery, which she'd spread through town like wildfire. The claim that he and Luella had been having an affair...it was nasty and salacious.

She'd hurt him, and by extension, she'd hurt Luella. Why else would Luella be leaving town, too?

I need to be free of you.

Ellis pulled off his hat, turning the band in his hands as he and Eveline approached the house. He felt a scowl on his mouth. It dug deep at the corners. As they climbed the steps of the porch to the back door, kicking the snow off their boots, he glanced up and stopped.

Night had come early, as it did this side of the year. The stars winked.

He released a breath. It clouded in front of him, curling away as he stood and stared at the heavens.

He could see Gemini holding hands on Orion's upper left shoulder.

He hadn't known the names of the stars until Luella. He'd stayed awake so many nights, listening to her tell their stories…

"Ellis?"

He lowered his head, blinking at Eveline.

Her hand was on the doorknob and there was a crease between her eyes. "You okay?"

He was crushing the hat in his hands. Frowning, he dropped them to his sides and tapped the hat against his leg. "Fine."

Her gaze swept across his face, knowing. "You'll tell me the truth later."

No one needed to know what was going on in his head. The best part about being the family counselor was that he rarely had to confess his own thoughts or feelings.

They went through the door, wiping their boots on the mudroom mat. They hung up their hats and shrugged out of their coats, placing them on the pegs lining the wall. The kitchen was to the left. The housekeeper, Paloma Coldero, fed the family and the hands three meals a day. A place at her table was not to be taken lightly.

Ellis smelled chili con carne and his stomach twisted greedily. It was his favorite of all her meals. Regrettably, they bypassed the kitchen for the living room and entry hall where Liberty was waiting.

Ellis stopped when he found Everett there, too. He stood, all six feet five inches of him, his arms crossed, feet shoulder-width apart and his three cow dogs sitting at attention, flanking him. With his hair overlong and the full growth of a beard that had grown unruly over the lower half of his face over the months of his recovery, he looked untamed and intimidating and he knew it.

Liberty faced him, her hands clenched at her sides. Her

long, pencil-straight brown hair fell sleek over the shoulders of her blazer. Her chin came to a sharp point and it was jutting out in defiance. Her back was straight as an arrow, her posture impeccable, and her foot tapped on the floor. As Ellis and Eveline entered the room, her gaze snatched to the pair of them. Not an ounce of warmth touched her features. "You kept me waiting long enough."

"I was in the barn," Ellis explained. "Everett, you can call off the dogs."

"Can I?" Everett asked. He didn't take his eyes off Liberty. There was a dark gleam to them—one that promised hurt.

"I got this," Ellis told him. "Take the dogs. Smells like chili's on."

Everett didn't move. "I'll stay," he said evenly. "You turn your back for a second and something goes missing."

"What would I take, exactly?" Liberty took a scathing look around. "There's not much, is there?"

Everett's lips turned inward. He rubbed them together, carefully. They all knew their father had liked keeping the decor simple on the home front. Since his death six months ago, the family had kept things as he'd liked them. Redecorating wasn't on anyone's agenda. "You've stolen plenty already, haven't you, princess?" Everett asked her. "You've stolen my brother's reputation. You've practically stolen my nieces out from under him…"

"Everett," Ellis said. He wasn't afraid of Liberty, but angering her any more than she already was wasn't wise. Not when the terms of their divorce were still in dispute—primarily custody of Isla and Ingrid. "Let her come in."

The standoff lasted another minute…two. Then Everett eased back, ever so slightly. He gave her a baneful once-over. "Keep the dogs with you," he said to Ellis as he moved away. "Just in case she bites."

"Is he freaking serious?" Liberty muttered as Everett and Eveline moved off.

Ellis looked down at the dogs. Their eyes were on him, waiting for his command. "Lie down," he murmured and waited for them to relax and sprawl across the area rug. "We weren't expecting you until tomorrow. You know Paloma likes taking me and the girls to church on Sunday morning."

She hitched her purse higher on her shoulder. "Change of plans. I'm taking the girls to the children's museum in Taos tomorrow. I promised them we'd go."

"Tomorrow's Sunday."

"So?"

"The museum's closed on Sunday." He spread his hands. "I know enough about city life to remember that."

She glowered at him.

He dipped his head, staring at the points of her shiny black boots. They weren't working boots. They were fancy, soft and buttery—best built for sidewalks. "What do you want?" he galvanized himself enough to ask. "You want to take the girls home early?"

"Yes," she admitted. "But first, we should talk."

He felt a muscle in his jaw twitch as he glanced up the stairs. He could hear giggling. The girls were there, in their room, probably invested in their collection of plush horses or dollies. He was going to have to say goodbye to them sixteen hours early and it was going to hurt.

Easy, he told himself. "Let's talk in Everett's office."

The dogs followed him, obediently. He didn't wait for her to enter before pouring himself a tall shot of whiskey at the sideboard. At the sound of her pointy-toed boots, he knocked the whiskey back, swallowing fire. He was normally slow to anger. He'd always prided himself on that—the glacial slide between his cool and his temper. Since summer, however, circumstances surrounding his family and his divorce had gotten harder and messier. Holding it all together, including his composure, had been almost impossible. He was bound to lose his grip on something eventually and he feared very much that that something was going to be his anger.

"Isn't it your office now?" she asked, shutting the door behind her. "Though, hasn't it been long enough for Everett to recover?"

"He took a bullet to the chest and nearly bled out before they could get him to the OR." He dropped the glass back to the sideboard with a clack. "You don't come back from that. Not whole."

"Some say he's a shadow of himself."

"Talk's preferable to truth for some," he drawled.

"There you go insinuating things again." She paused. "Let's see it."

"See what?"

Gesturing to the chair behind the desk, she said, "You. In the seat of power."

"No."

Her eyes were practically glittering as she walked around the desk, her fingers tracing the wood. "Is it not what you wanted, all these years? To be closer to your father? 'It's my destiny.' That was your excuse for making us leave our life in Taos."

"It's my destiny to be here," he granted. "It's my destiny to work in the family cattle business. But that was my father's chair. Now it's Everett's. Not mine."

"So you're not enjoying any of it?" she asked. "Being in charge. Taking his place."

"It's not about being in charge. It never was."

She lifted her chin. "Then this next part shouldn't be too painful for you."

His jaw had been so tense. He only noticed when it went slack. Unease slithered through him, alongside suspicion. "What do you mean?"

"You should sit," she said and planted herself in his father's chair.

"I like where I'm at," he replied.

"Suit yourself," she said, scooting the chair up an inch. She planted her palms on the desk. "I've spoken to my attorney."

"Greasy."

"His name is Grisi."

"Same thing," he weighed.

"It is not…" She trailed off, catching her command slipping. "I've decided the terms of our divorce."

He tucked his tongue against his cheek and made a noise. "I thought that was something we were supposed to do together."

"You and I don't do anything together anymore," she reminded him.

"Then what is it you want from me?"

She licked her lips, caught herself and firmed them together. "You own twenty percent of shares in Eaton Edge."

"Yeah. And the girls have ten each, to be transferred to them on their twenty-first birthdays, respectively."

"My sources tell me," she said slowly, "that the Edge is worth upwards of around two hundred twenty-four million, easy."

He shifted his feet. He didn't know exactly what the Edge was worth. He'd never been inclined to ask. "What's your point?"

"That means that you yourself are worth somewhere in the neighborhood of forty-four million dollars."

"You want a payout?"

Her hands folded neatly, one on top of the other. "I want the shares. Twenty percent of Eaton Edge and your seat on the board."

He stared for a full ten seconds. Then he barked a loud laugh.

Liberty jerked. "Jesus," she muttered. "*Why're* you laughing?"

"Because you did," he said. "You laughed until you were blue in the face when I told you I was moving back here. Then you spent the next several years letting me know exactly how much you hated everything about Fuego and the Edge, so much so that you pulled up stakes and hightailed it back for the city. And now, after dragging our divorce negotiations out for *eight* months, you're telling me you want my shares?" He laughed some more. "Hell, woman. You are a piece of work."

"I don't owe you anything, least of all an explanation."

"It's my birthright," he indicated. "I think I deserve one."

"It's Isla and Ingrid's birthright, too."

"You wish it wasn't," he said. "You pulled them out of Fuego Elementary and enrolled them in private school fifty miles away." He shook his head. "No. This is about something else."

"What's that?" she asked, tightly.

"You want to hurt me any way you haven't already done," he told her. "You like hurting me."

"You hurt me first," she stated.

"How exactly?" he asked. "I'm still confused on that point."

Her eyes darkened so fast, the flash of blue dimmed and the pupils damn near took over. "You said her name."

Ellis closed his eyes. Leaning back against the sideboard, he lifted his face to the ceiling, doing his best not to take himself back there. But there was truth here—the one truth there was in all of this. "I said her name," he acknowledged. "Once. Doesn't mean I had an affair with her or even thought about doing so."

"You said another woman's name when you were in bed with me," Liberty hissed. She was quiet, deadly so. "That's all the evidence I need."

"It didn't mean anything," he said, more heatedly. He couldn't help it. They'd gone over this ground—a thousand times before. "It meant nothing."

"You say that," she said, nodding, "knowing what I can take. What I'm *going* to take."

"You can't take from me what my father gave. There're previsions. Protections. It's in his will."

"I don't expect to settle this in front of a judge," she admitted. "You're going to give it to me, nicely."

"I'm starting to believe you're not thinking clearly."

"You'll do it," she said. The point of her chin came up again. She smoothed the blazer over her hips as she rose from the desk. "If you expect to get more than a few weekends with the girls."

His head snatched back, as if she'd struck him. "You can't be serious."

"You know me," she said, stepping to him. She smoothed her hand over the collar of his work shirt. She traced the stubble along his jaw with her eyes. Her lip curled. She'd always demanded he be clean-shaven if he expected to share her bed. Anything else was unkempt, unappealing. "I'm never not serious." She hitched her purse onto her shoulder. "I'll go get the girls ready. Come kiss them goodbye and make them your little promises and let's all hope you decide to keep them this time."

As she left the office, Ellis found he couldn't move. Her devastation spread through every part of him, going beyond what her petty gossip and threats had done to this point.

She was determined to ruin him altogether.

Chapter Three

Luella did sleep in her bed. Exhausted, she'd collapsed on the hand-spun quilt after making Sheridan comfortable in the barn and indulging in that hot shower she'd been dreaming about.

She slept twenty hours and woke, as groggy and muddle-headed as she'd felt when she'd closed her eyes.

She hadn't dreamed. That was something. If she had, she was afraid of what she'd see: the back of her father's hand—her jail cell—Ellis's face when she told him she was leaving?

He'd looked like a whipped dog.

She wasn't going to sit around thinking about it any more than she had to. She wasn't responsible for however much her leaving hurt him. She had to leave for her own sake.

She called the Realtor, scheduled a walk-through and appraisal. She sorted her mail, which Naleen had tried and failed to stack neatly on the kitchen table. As her Balinese cat, Sphinx, twined figure eights between her legs, rubbing a long, satisfactory greeting around her ankles, and her American bobtail, Nyx, reclined in the sunny windowsill above the sink, she unsealed billing statements, threw out junk mail and puzzled over a handful of postcards from San Gabriel...

Luella fanned the postcards out, clueless. San Gabriel

was two counties over. Her mother, Riane, still lived there with Luella's aunt, Mabel. Luella, too, had lived there for a time—after her relationship with Ellis had gone belly-up.

The postcards were addressed to her. She recognized the disordered script of Aunt Mabel. There were strange one-to-two-line missives on the back of each one:

Baby.
Mother.
Father.
W.J.
S.G.W.C.
S.9.06.
Nightstand.

Luella scratched the center of her forehead with the tip of her pen. Mabel, an artist, was known for her eccentricities. Luella wondered if her mother, a rigid, unhappy woman who liked to parcel her unhappiness onto others, knew about the messages.

Doubtful. Mabel had been bedridden for the last year. Luella had visited San Gabriel enough to know her mother was taking care of her properly. But she ran a tight ship and did her best to pretend her life in Fuego had never happened by marrying a man from her church and permitting no more than a few cursory visits from Luella, preferably when her new husband, Solomon, was not at home.

Luella contemplated visiting anyway to check in with Mabel and ask about the messages. Yes, it meant a dreaded run-in with her mother. But she had nothing but free time now that the nursing director at Fuego County Hospital had made it very clear she shouldn't return to her nursing job there.

It shouldn't feel like this much of a loss. But it was a sore spot. Going to school in San Gabriel after leaving Fuego and Ellis had saved her from the wells of depression. It'd given her a purpose.

It didn't matter that that purpose had lured her back to Fuego with the promise of a job at the nearby hospital. Neither did it matter that working the COVID unit at the height of the pandemic had pushed her to the brink of despair and burnout. Being a nurse had saved her. It wasn't astronomy, but it had given her a life when she'd thought her life was over.

Wherever she did wind up going this time, there wouldn't be many people who'd hire her with a record.

To avoid thinking about that, she gathered her cleaning supplies and began to dust. She'd left her house tidy. Because she'd lived in the mess and stench of Whip Decker's double-wide, she liked things tidy. Yet being away for so long, there were the cursory cobwebs and dust motes. She scrubbed floors over-hard and washed windows until her arms ached, stopping only long enough to let Nyx out when he roused himself from his respite and yowled.

She wiped the thick wooden beams that crisscrossed over her living area from the top of a rickety ladder and nearly fell off when a knock clattered against the door. She felt the ladder tip and grabbed onto the beam above her for dear life.

The ladder settled back on four legs. She breathed a sigh, loosening her grip on the beam.

The knock came again.

She ground her teeth. Coming down the ladder, she contemplated how long she'd been cleaning. Had she had lunch? Her stomach growled a telltale no. Sweeping her hands over her hair, she dropped her cleaning rag and snatched open the door...

…and nearly shut it again in Ellis's face.

He planted his hand on the door, bracing it open. He didn't look happy.

That made two of them, she thought. "Last time you were here, I tried to shoot you," she reminded him.

"You could have shot me," he remembered. "You chose not to."

"You find encouragement in the damnedest places." She put her weight against the door when he pushed. "Don't. I don't want you in here."

"Don't shut the door in my face."

"Why're you here?" she demanded. "I asked you to let me go."

"You're not gone yet," he said.

She wished she was. Then they wouldn't be doing this. She'd thought she'd said goodbye—the hardest goodbye. "What do you want?"

He reached into his back pocket and pulled out the wad of money.

She cursed.

"You left this on the desk in the office. Take it. I know you need it."

"I don't want to owe you."

"Take the money and we'll call it even."

She wanted to bare her teeth…but she was aching everywhere. Somehow, sleeping hadn't taken the ache away.

He sighed when she didn't reach out. Shifting his feet, he fit his shoulder to the frame of her door and he looked at her, good and long. "What do you want me to do?"

"Go away?" she suggested. Hadn't they established this?

"I can't do that."

"Why not?" she asked.

"Because you don't deserve to be run out of town like this. It's my fault."

She rolled her eyes. "Not everything is about you, Ellis."

"I said your name," he said. "Okay? I said your name once. In bed. With my wife. That's how she got it in her head that you and me had an affair. And now the damn gossips are runnin' you off."

"I'm sorry. Back up." She held up her hands, forgetting to brace the door closed against him. "You did *what*?"

His puppy dog eyes were on full display. He stared plaintively at her until she was forced to look away.

He swung the door farther in. "You got some bread or cheese or something?"

Her mouth fumbled. "Why?"

Ellis stepped inside, unbidden. He veered into the kitchen. "I missed lunch and I'm feeling peckish."

As his boots clomped toward her refrigerator, she lifted her hand in an empty gesture. "Are you really just letting yourself in?"

"Looks that way, doesn't it?"

She stood rooted to the spot. Ellis—in her house… This was inconceivable. Still, her mind circled around one point and one point only. "You…said my name…when exactly?"

His head was in her refrigerator. His voice floated to her, miserable. "It was months ago. In the spring. Liberty and I…we were already having trouble. She hated Fuego. Everything about the place." He straightened, lifting a carton of orange juice. "Is this any good?"

"Sure?" She hadn't exactly gotten around to the shopping since coming home but said nothing of it. *"And?"*

"We talked. I suggested we go to therapy. I couldn't let the marriage break down. The girls deserved a unit. I didn't want to be like my parents. Divorced. Distant. That's *awful* on the kids." He unscrewed the cap and lifted the juice, drinking straight from the jug. He lowered it, smacked his lips. "Ah...that's...that's not right." He capped the bottle and tossed it into her trash. Then he bent into the fridge again. "She countered. She wanted to try for another baby." He stood, a jar of pickles in hand. Turning it around, he looked for the sell-by date. Then he unscrewed the lid and sniffed. "If we were ever happy, it was just after each of the girls were born."

She watched him shut the fridge, open several kitchen drawers until he located a fork. Then he leaned back against the counter and probed the inside of the jar. She reached up for her head, unable to keep up with the onslaught of information. "I'm not sure why all this has to live in my head, too."

"I'm getting to it," he said, biting into a pickle. He chewed, hummed, nodded and took another bite. He offered the jar to her.

Winding her hand, she said, "Get to the point, *please*." *And then get out*. Why had she let him in? Now he was here—in her space—her sacred space where no one else—but especially not *he*—belonged.

"Fine," he said, finishing off the pickle. He peered into the jar, looking for another. "We started trying. We even began talking names. It all went to hell, though, after the spring festival. You remember the festival."

She squinted. It seemed like a lifetime ago. "Do I?"

He stopped moving, his eyes coming to rest on her. "You don't remember?"

"Remember *what*, Ellis?"

"You were there, outside the first aid booth. You were wearing a blue dress. Your hair was down, around your shoulders. You left it free, the way I used to..." He trailed off, looking back at his...*her* pickles. "Anyway... Ingrid needed a Band-Aid. She'd tripped and skinned her knee and Liberty didn't have any in her purse. You doctored her up, the way you do, and we all talked for a minute. Just small talk. Nothing out of the ordinary. Like all the other ordinary conversations we've had since you came back from wherever it was you went after high school. I didn't think I thought much of it—except how goddamn pretty you looked."

Her face was burning—because she did remember. She remembered how she'd thought he'd looked at her. Like he used to. She'd thought it was her imagination. And how could she dwell on it and what it did to her when Liberty had been standing right next to him, her arm through his, her hand in the smaller girl's—Ingrid—while his had been in the other girl's—Isla.

They'd looked like a catalog cover—the all-American family. He'd felt so far away from her... It'd hurt, more than it normally did.

"Liberty wanted to try again that night," Ellis went on. "We put the girls to bed. She lit some candles, put on some lingerie—"

"The finer points you can keep to yourself," Luella ventured.

"Sorry," he said and took another bite. He chewed until he could talk again. "We were going at it. I didn't even know you were a thought in my head. But then your name...it was just out there. Right out in the open. And she looked at me like I'd stabbed her."

"Well, yeah," Luella said with a nod. Any woman could understand that.

"It didn't mean anything," he stated.

"Ugh." She plopped down in a chair around the table. *"Why* are you telling me this?"

"Because if you're leaving town because of the things Liberty has been saying about you and me..." he began, kicking out a chair for him, too. He lowered to it. "It's because of what I did. I said your name and that led her to believe that you and I had been...intimate."

"To say the least," she growled. "According to townsfolk, you and I've been doing it like rabbits."

He grimaced. "It's not right."

"So why didn't you fight it? Why didn't you try to stop the talk?"

"Because I thought people in Fuego—people I've lived near and a good many of whom I've worked with most of my life—would see through it. They know me. They know what kind of man I am."

She paused. "The kind that says another woman's name in bed with his wife?"

He balked.

She did what she'd told herself she wouldn't do—she took pity on him. She knew what kind of man he was—one with integrity. He was a man who settled arguments. He didn't start them. Ellis never started them. He was the one who normally made everything better. His standing in Fuego had been unimpeachable...until Liberty's claims about the two of them. "Your strategy backfired."

"It crashed and burned," he agreed. He pushed the jar away. It slid into Mabel's postcards. "And I wasn't the only one who suffered for it. I came here to say I'm sorry, Lu, for whatever pain and grief this whole mess has caused you."

He reached for the hand she'd laid on the table. She lifted it before he could touch it. Her heart knelled against the wall of her chest at the thought of him touching her.

He made a noise in his throat—one of frustration or longing. She couldn't tell and couldn't dwell on it.

He reached into his pocket and pulled out the money again. When she hissed at him, he held up a hand. "I know there's something you need help with around here. Even if it's getting the house ready to sell… I'll do it. I'll do whatever it takes to settle things with you because I can't leave it like this. You deserve better, however things ended between us all those years ago."

"What do you mean by that?"

"Now, that you have to remember."

"I don't want to remember."

"You remember leaving," he wagered.

She felt a small knot of bile building at the back of her throat and refused to answer.

"You…disappeared. I proposed to you. You said yes. And then, you disappeared."

"It wasn't that simple," she muttered.

"Wasn't it?" he asked. "I meant what I said. I wanted to marry you."

"You don't think I meant yes?" she challenged.

He treaded carefully. "I think you got scared."

She wanted to throw the jar of pickles at him. "You need to leave." She got up, scraping the chair back. "I'll be going to the bank tomorrow morning. If you're not going to leave me be until I give you something to do then you can come back then and fix the chicken coop. The wire fencing is starting to come loose, and I can't have the hens running around all over the place."

"Show me." He beat her to the door, opening it wide for her. "Christ!" he cursed when Nyx greeted him with a startled screech and darted between his legs.

The cat leaped at Luella. She caught him in midair. He

hissed, back arched high. One paw curled over a row of translucent claws and swiped.

"Ah!" Luella cried, cupping a hand under her chin where it stung.

Nyx kicked off her with his back legs and went tearing off under the couch.

Luella turned sideways, away from Ellis, as she lowered her hand. There was a thin stripe of blood across her palm.

Ellis's hand lifted to the back of hers. It hovered, barely there, but it burned more than the scratch. His fingers closed around her wrist and he turned her to him. "Let me see."

"I'm fine." He smelled like nights on the plain and spring rain and shiny golden dreams right where they'd fallen. When his touch rose to her jaw, she torqued her chin away. She pressed it into the soft flannel of her shoulder, closing her eyes tight. "*I'm fine*, okay?"

Her pulse was high in her ears and the ache was back, full-force.

Stop it, she told herself. *Just stop.*

"We should clean that." His fingertips feathered across her cheek. "Where's your peroxide?"

"Ellis." She took several steps back from the warm line of his body. "I worked in an ER for years. I know how to take care of a scratch."

"'Course, I know you're capable, but it's a bad spot."

"I've got it."

"Does that cat act like that all the time?"

"He was just scared," she said. "Animals react differently to fear."

Words brushed softly across the tip of her ear. "I know some humans who behave that way, too."

She flushed hot and red. Breathless, she backpedaled, desperate for air. "Get out, please."

"Exactly," he said. "You still want to show me that coop?"

She heard his boots retreat to the door. She forced herself not to watch the way he fit his hat over his head, dipping his crown low instead of bringing the hat up to it. It'd always been Ellis's way—to open doors, to bow from his height to put on a hat or a shirt or…

She used to love watching him dress. She'd loved watching him piece together what she'd unraveled, always with the lazy, satisfied smile that came from their loving. It had been enough to take her breath away.

He still was.

He'd said her name—with Liberty?

"Close the door," she said.

"What?" he asked, pausing on the stoop.

"Just…" She planted her hand against his jacket shoulder and pushed him farther out. Then she yanked the door from him and shut it.

With him safely on the other side, she took a leveled breath. She planted her hands on the door, closed her eyes again and worked to knit the pieces of herself back together. She'd done it so many times, she only had to close her eyes to imagine them weaving their broken selves back together—like Mary Shelley's *Frankenstein*. Not pretty but functional.

When she was certain-ish that she was okay, she opened the door.

He stood on the porch with his hands on his hips, confusion all over his face.

She moved around him.

"You forgot your coat," he said, chasing her with it.

She snatched it, aware of the fact that the cold was slapping her in the face. Her teeth were chattering by the time she punched her arms through the thing. When he stepped up to help her zip, she waved him off. Her Frankenstein seams were starting to tear already. "I don't need you."

He lifted his hands. "Sorry," he said. "I don't want you to catch anything."

"The chickens are back this way."

"Lu?"

He was so close at her back, she could practically feel her name rolling off his tongue. She hugged herself.

He touched her, his hand on her arm like yesterday.

She kept her back to him but found her feet stopping in the sludge of ice and snow on the ground.

She felt his breath cascading across the hair. "I want you to be okay," he said.

"I'm okay," she said defensively.

"So why're you leaving?"

"I have to," she told him. "I moved back here because I got hired at the hospital. Now that that job's gone, I've got nothing to keep me. And you should've fought what Liberty said—what everyone in town said. You should've fought for—" The words *me* and *us* battled for dominance on her tongue and she swallowed them. "You should've fought. Period."

"I'm sorry."

"Ellis," she said, exasperated, "it's not just about the gossip. I'm leaving because I'm a Decker. No matter what I do, people will always see me as Whip Decker's daughter. I can't live with that legacy."

He came around her front. She tried taking a step back but his touch held and she was forced to stare at his shirtfront. "He's gone this time. He doesn't have power over you anymore."

"His name does," she said. "I'll never not be Luella Decker to these people."

"You were always Lu Decker," he murmured. "And it meant something different. You made it mean something different. You built a life here. Why can't you do that again? Why do you have to leave?"

"Because…" She shook her head and turned her face upward. It was daytime—no stars. But she could see the moon. She closed her eyes to it, too. "I'm tired of hurting. Whether it's from you or his legacy, I'm just tired, Ellis." She tried to throw him off. "You always had to be there, didn't you—with your puppy dog eyes and your white hat? You've always been there, everywhere I look. How is anyone supposed to move on—to just learn to *be*—when you're *everywhere*?"

"I know," he breathed.

"Do you?" she asked, derisively.

"I do," he said. "You're everywhere for me. Waiting in line at the Tractor Supply. Or buying a watermelon at the roadside stand. Whether you were in your blue dress or your blue jeans…it didn't seem to matter. I looked and I wanted."

"Too far," she said, accusingly. "You've taken it too far."

"Yeah," he said with a small nod. His whisper-soft gaze passed from her left eye to her right. He was down to a whisper. "With you, I've always done that, haven't I?"

When his feet shifted toward hers and his front nearly buffered her, she pulled in a strangled breath. "This can't be happening. It's—"

"Crazy," he said. "Stupid. Reckless. Just like before. When it comes to you, I will never not be crazy, stupid, reckless."

His head lowered and she pressed a hand to the center of his chest to back him up short. She felt his heart beating and froze. For a moment, she counted the beats. She absorbed the way his breath snagged and his shoulders lifted and fell in rapid succession. To know she still had this effect on him—it was potent. "You better not kiss me, you fool."

"Why not?" he asked, the flat of his brow coming to rest against hers.

Don't answer that. Don't you dare answer that, Luella. "Because…"

"Because?"

Her hands had fisted in his collar. Now, when had they done that? "Because I want you…to shut the hell up." And then she did something crazy, stupid, reckless and all other manner of mixed-up things she didn't understand.

She kissed *him.*

Ellis stumbled back a step. "Lu."

"I said shut up," she demanded, dragging him back to her. She raised her mouth to clash with his.

Hell, she was leaving, wasn't she? She'd never get the chance to kiss Ellis Eaton again. She'd dreamed about it for so long…him—his kisses. Why not one last sip for the road?

"Mmm," he groaned, eyes seamed tight. There was a burrowing line between them. "You taste so good."

"No talking." She grabbed him by the ear. "Just kiss me, once, and never again."

"The hell I can." He spread his hands over her hips as his mouth swooped to hers. The fool man licked and teased, fumbled and smoothed. He breathed into her.

It was like an electric current, from him to her. She'd felt dead for so long. Depression had come back to bite over the course of her sentence. She'd started sinking back into the tangled net of numbness that was as familiar as it was discomfiting. It'd been ready when the bars rolled into place, locking her in her cell. She'd been flirting with it long enough, thanks to her time in the COVID unit and her father's ugly secrets.

She'd been numb for six months. So why all of a sudden did she feel electrified, from her head to her toes?

Shocked, she stumbled over her own feet and the soles of her boots skidded on the icy drive.

He yanked her up by the forearms like she was weightless. When she still couldn't catch her footing, he backed her up to a point near the house where the snow was packed. When her boots gained traction finally, she realized her back was up against a trellis with bare, dry vines and there was nothing in front of her but him.

He planted his palms on her face, framing it gingerly. He kissed her, lovingly, then again in the same indulgent fashion until she didn't know which way was down and which way was Ellis. And all the while, that current sang up and down her body. She felt every nerve dance, every jet flame of her pulse... She'd wondered if this part of her had shriveled up and died.

She wondered if being struck by lightning would be as devastating...

He broke away so they could catch their breath but he didn't back down. "It's still there," he said in disbelief. "It's all still right here."

She shook her head automatically.

"Yes," he argued.

"No." Did he not realize it was too much—too much for a body to handle?

"Do I need to prove it?" He touched his lips to hers, just barely—enough. He nibbled and sipped and her legs were jelly. She had to hang on to keep from losing her footing again.

"I don't want it." Her voice shook. She couldn't stop the trembling. She felt so much, tears punched through and threatened to spill.

He raised his head enough to gauge her expression. He smiled, slowly—a crooked smile that was real and sexy and had lived inside her head for years. "Now that's something *you're* going to have to prove."

"I will," she pledged. "Just as soon as you back off."

"Honey, you grabbed ahold of me. You *still* haven't turned me loose."

Studiously, she untangled her arms from around him. They fell to either side of his hips before flailing in reaction and she was able to drop them away. "Back off, Ellis."

He waited a beat, licked his lips. Her blood sluiced, slow and molten. She'd lost it—lost herself all over again. *Son of a bitch.*

The sound of a whinny broke through the quiet. It was the high-pitched, distressed kind of whinny that brought Luella to attention. "Sheridan," she said, pushing Ellis back and sprinting around the house for the barn...

She stopped in her tracks. Her momentum nearly carried her topside over and she wavered over the spot.

The yard was littered with hens. They lay, limp, on the frozen ground. Feathers lifted on the breeze but otherwise there was no movement.

Luella pressed her hand over her mouth to hold back a scream. Every single one of them was dead.

Chapter Four

Ellis stared at the scene. The hair on the nape of his neck and arms lifted. As his gut tightened, he grabbed Luella before she could take a step forward. "Stay back."

"They were fine." The way she said it wasn't right. Her voice was too flat, almost a monotone. "I fed them, changed their water… They were laying."

"Lu," he said, planting himself in front of her. "Go back inside."

"They were fine," she said again, her gaze level with his sternum. She didn't blink. Her voice, again, didn't sound like her own.

What the hell? "Lu, honey," he said evenly. "Their necks are broken."

She blinked, finally. Her gaze, glassy, lifted to his. "What…?"

"They didn't just keel over," he explained. "Somebody did this."

"Somebody." The first grasp of understanding broke through. The first emotion bubbled behind it. Her breathing hitched. "Who would…?"

"Go on inside," he urged, walking her backward. He couldn't let her study them any closer. "I need to look around."

"Sheridan," she said. "He's in the barn. I have to—"

"I'll check on him," Ellis assured her. Her face was perfectly heart-shaped. The skin of her cheeks was like ice when he touched them. Moments before, they'd been red as cherries. "Lock the dead bolt and don't let anybody in but me."

She panted over several breaths then closed her eyes. She gave a quick, jerky nod.

"Go," he said. When she broke away, he added, "Run."

He was pleased to see that she did. As soon as he heard her feet clatter up the stairs, he went to his truck and pulled the rifle down from the rack behind the cab. Glancing out over the landscape, he broke it down. Then he loaded several shells and reassembled it. He strapped it across his shoulders and took the safety off.

None of the hens lay together. Their bodies didn't overlap. There was a perfect halo of snow around every one of them. He trod carefully around the edges, trying not to disturb any footprints. Moving to the barn, he could hear the roan kicking the gate. He pushed the door open, swinging the rifle up.

It was a small building—just big enough for two stalls and a short hayloft.

Sheridan's ears were back and the whites of his eyes were showing. His tail, too, was high, and his hooves danced in the hay Luella had freshened for him only hours ago, from the look of it. "You see something?" Ellis asked him.

The horse showed his teeth in answer. He snorted and kicked the gate again.

Ellis peered into the shadows of the other stall. Taking several steps back, he swung the barrel up and tried to get a look in the loft.

Luella was low on hay, which made it easy to see that there was nobody hiding out here.

A loud bang brought him up to his toes as he swiveled the rifle toward Sheridan's stall.

The feed bucket knocked against the metal gate once then again. The horse knocked it off its hook in a show of displeasure. It fell to the ground.

Ellis blew a breath out sharply and lowered the gun. "What's with your mama and crazy animals, huh?" he asked.

Sheridan braced his neck upward. He looked tough, but Ellis could see him quivering. He wanted to soothe the horse but knew he'd lose his fingers if he reached over the gate.

Ellis moved out of the barn and did two turns around the perimeter. He edged around the workshop then tiptoed through it. There were several deer hides hanging from the low rafters that had been cleaned, tanned and dried. He shifted through them slowly, making sure every hiding place was empty.

He frowned as he made his way around the house, inspecting the shadows of the large waterwheel closely. The benefit of Ollero Creek was that it was flatlands as far as the shining cliffs to the north—miles of open country impossible to hide in.

At least, it was that way to the north. To the south was town. Ellis knew neighbors were sparse out this way.

How long had he been inside? Was it long enough for someone to sneak in by truck, break two dozen chicken necks, position them just so in the yard then make a clean getaway?

Ellis went up the stairs to Luella's porch.

She was waiting outside the door. "What'd you find?" Her shotgun was in her hands. "Is Sheridan okay?"

"I asked you to wait inside," he said warily.

She eyed his gun. "Sheridan," she said again, plainly.

He put the safety on the rifle. "Your horse is all right. Just spooked."

She studied his face before deciding the truth for herself. She lifted her chin though he saw little relief. The glassy note was back in her eyes.

He didn't like it. "Let's get inside," he urged. "Come on." He placed a hand on the small of her back.

It was only after the door closed and it was bolted that Ellis laid the rifle down on the kitchen counter. He then leaned over the sink to get a good look out of the window. The cat lounging on the sill flicked its tail but didn't try to take a swipe at him.

"Did you see anything?" she asked. "Anyone?"

"No." Her windows faced north. Prairie grass peeped through snow, dotting the landscape as far as the cliffs. Nothing spoiled that view but shadows from passing clouds.

"Who would do this?" she asked in the same even tone from before.

He rounded to see that she had lowered to the couch. The shotgun was across her lap. "They didn't leave a calling card, other than maybe footprints and tire tracks."

She frowned. "Someone from town then."

"I think it's most likely."

She turned the disconcerting, dead-eyed stare to the window close by, eyes roving over the terrain.

He walked to her. "Are you okay?"

"Fine," she said, too quickly. "What do I do?"

Stop looking like that, he thought. He needed that odd mannequin stare to stop. "You're not going to like it."

"Say it anyway."

"We need to get the police here."

"No," she said decisively.

Her eyes were too blue in her face. She was white as

snow. Lowering to the space next to her on the couch, he didn't touch her. He was afraid to. She was so still, he was afraid she'd fracture. "Lu, I can't do anything about tracks. But they can."

"I don't want them here."

Ellis scouted for patience. It was the sheriff who'd hauled her to jail shortly after they'd found her tied up on the edge of a road. She'd been hogtied by her father, the same man that Sheriff Jones had claimed she'd aided and abetted. As a result, she'd spent the last several months behind bars. Ellis couldn't blame her for not wanting the police involved. "You don't trust Jones," he said.

"You're damn right I don't."

There was some heat behind the words. He latched onto it. *There you are, Lu.* "What about his deputy, Kaya Altaha?"

"What about 'no police' don't you understand?"

"When Jones wanted to haul you in after we'd found you on the road that night," Ellis remembered, "Altaha was the one who told him you needed medical attention. She was the reason you were treated first. I don't think she believed you could have been involved with your father. She's a friend. I can call her, personally, and have her come out on her own to check out the scene."

Her spine was straight. Her posture hadn't caved, and her jaw was strong and set. She pressed her lips inward. "You really think it's going to do any good?"

"Yeah, maybe," he said. "Somebody's got to know someone's hurt you."

"They hurt my chickens."

"They hurt you!" As her eyes swung to his, he heard the words echoing back to him. He didn't try to take them back or the agitation that had escaped with them. "They hurt you," he said, more quietly. "And they're going to pay for it. That's why we need to get Altaha down here, so she can help us catch 'em."

She scanned his face. When her eyes settled on his lips and hers parted, he felt the warm feeling around his navel that was always present around her heat to a torch.

"You better be sure about this," she whispered. She placed her hands on her weapon. They wrapped around it, white-knuckled.

She'd withdrawn into herself again. Ellis cursed and dug the phone out of his coat pocket to place the call.

ELLIS OWED THE deputy a lot. Not only had she become a personal friend—she'd practically saved his brother's life. When Everett had been shot by Whip Decker at Coldero Ridge during the man's last stand, Kaya Altaha had been the one to administer triage on scene and call in a rescue helicopter.

His brother had come too close to dying. The surgeons at Fuego County Hospital may have saved him from the brink of death, but it was Altaha who'd been responsible for his getting on the operating table to begin with.

The Jicarilla Apache Native thought fast on her feet. Not much got past her, from what Ellis had seen. Her work wasn't swayed by personal judgment or local politics. As she peered from underneath the wide brim of her deputy's hat at the chicken-strewn yard, her full mouth turned down at one corner. Her dark eyes were narrowed to slits. "How long did you say you were inside?"

"Twenty to thirty minutes, max," Ellis answered.

"And you didn't hear anything?" Altaha asked, kneeling in the sleet to examine the closest hen.

"Only the horse when we were outside," Ellis said. "He's been spooked by something."

"That horse acts strangely in the best of times."

"He stayed with us for a while at the Edge. I never saw him like this."

They both could hear Sheridan kicking the gate again and Luella's soothing tones from inside the barn.

"You're right about them," Altaha said about the chickens. "Looks like their necks have been broken. Luella was in the house with you the whole time?"

Ellis weighed the question then sent a sideways scowl to Altaha. "Don't do that."

"It's just a question."

"The kind that made her nearly talk me out of calling anyone out here," he noted. "She thinks everybody's out to get her."

"Answer the question, Ellis," she said, standing again.

"Yes, I was with her."

"The whole time?"

"The whole time!"

"Doing what exactly?" When he didn't answer immediately, she added, "I can't put the pieces together without knowing the whole picture. What's your business with Luella Decker?"

"She's leaving Fuego," he answered reluctantly. "I had to know why."

"Luella's leaving Fuego?" she asked. "When?"

"She didn't say exactly."

"Did she give you a reason why?" Altaha wanted to know, picking up the bag she'd set nearby. She took out a digital camera and checked the lens.

"She doesn't feel that she's welcome," he replied.

"One could argue that, as the town villain's daughter, she's never felt particularly welcome," Altaha considered. "People have made certain of that." She raised the camera to her face, angled herself over the first hen and snapped a picture. "Why leave now?"

Ellis surveyed the dead. "Guess she's had enough."

"Sounds like some part of you wants her to stay," Altaha muttered, leaning over the next hen for another shot.

"That doesn't sound like a deputy," he observed.

She raised herself to her full height. With the hat, she was no more than five-two. "No. But I hope it sounds like a friend."

He contemplated that as she went about taking pictures of the entire scene. He trusted Altaha. But he'd never admitted his feelings about Luella—to anyone. His family had speculated about his relationship with her, he knew. But they'd never openly discussed it.

"When the snow's melted like this, it's difficult to get anything solid from tracks," she observed.

He knew she'd parked at the mailbox and walked to the house from there. "What about tire treads?"

"I took some pictures," she replied. "I'll need to take photos of yours and Luella's so we can compare."

"She didn't do this, Kaya."

At the sound of her name, Altaha straightened from a crouch. "It's good you called me. Whip Decker snuck around in plain sight for years. Jones didn't see it. It's made him look bad."

"Now he's got it out for Lu?" Ellis asked.

"When he got word of her return yesterday, he didn't have much good to say about it." She shifted her weight. "And he's not the only one."

"Who else?" Ellis asked thoughtfully.

"I'll make a note," Altaha assured him. "Cross-reference it with whoever lives on this side of town. See what comes back."

"Thanks," Ellis said, "for coming out."

"Can't say it's my pleasure," she said, tilting her head over the sleek black feathers of a plump hen. "This doesn't feel impulsive or random. It's calculated…"

"Planned," Ellis agreed. "Some sick bastard planned this."

The rooster made hoarse croaking noises as he peered at one of his prone ladies. Altaha made a noise. "You got lucky, didn't you, Big Bird? Say cheese." She raised the camera and took the rooster's picture, too.

"His name's Caesar."

Ellis looked up and saw Luella. She was still a shade too pale. Her mouth was drawn in a grim line.

Altaha examined Luella, doing well not to make it obvious. "Did they all have names?"

Luella stared across the debris field. Ellis could see the shaded half circles under her eyes. "Yes. I bought half of them as chicks and raised the others from hatchlings."

"I'm sorry," Altaha said, sincerely.

Luella studied her with a neutral expression. Then she gave a nod.

"Do you hunt?" Altaha questioned.

"A nurse's salary doesn't always cut it. Times get lean. I hunt in season."

"So do you have any game cameras?" Altaha wondered.

Luella looked toward the eaves of the house. "I do… but they've been off since I was away. I never turned them back on."

Ellis saw the game camera high above them. It had been mounted underneath the eaves of the house. "You should turn them back on," he told her.

"Can you think of anyone who knows of your return?" Altaha asked.

Luella glanced at Ellis then quickly away. "This one, obviously."

Altaha took her notebook from her back pocket. She made sure the camera was strapped around her neck and started to jot Ellis's name. "He give you any trouble?"

"Usually," Luella replied.

Ellis tilted his head in return but kept his mouth shut. He'd seen the flash of emotion on her face. Even if it meant she was annoyed or angry at him, he'd take anything above the hollow shell she'd disappeared into.

"Other than that," Luella went on, "the Uber driver who dropped me off. He said somebody had prepaid." She asked him, "You didn't do that, did you?"

Ellis shook his head.

"Somebody else anticipated your release," Altaha decided aloud, making quick notes. "Anyone else?"

"Naleen," Luella said, "your sister."

Altaha nodded. "Have you been to town? To the market or feed store?"

"No," Luella said. "But I did go to Eaton Edge yesterday."

"Anybody see you there?"

"I did," Ellis noted. "I saw her."

Luella held his stare, brooding.

Altaha frowned. "Anyone other than Romeo?"

"The girls," he said. "You talked to the girls."

"I did talk to them." The line of Luella's mouth softened. "They were precious."

"Hard to believe they're Liberty's kids." Altaha stopped and checked herself. "That was uncalled for."

"Not entirely," Ellis muttered. "Griff saw her, too."

"I called Ms. Breslin at the realty company, too," Luella said, "to see about putting the house on the market. Other than that, I can't think of anyone."

Altaha tapped her pencil against her pad. "This'll make a start." She flipped the cover down then tucked it into her pocket. "I'll make some calls, get these pictures back to the office and call if I need to know anything else. Is that okay?"

Ellis fought a smile. The question was simple, but it would mean something to Luella.

"Yes." Luella paused. "Thank you, Deputy."

"Of course," Altaha said. "I'll need to take two or three hens, for autopsy so we can confirm how they died. Do you need help—taking care of the rest?"

"I'll see to that," Ellis told her.

"No," Luella argued. "I will."

"Lu—"

"They're my chickens, Ellis," she said. "I'll bury them."

"You need protection," he noted.

"You've got a ranch to run, as I recall."

"I'd keep my doors locked," Altaha advised. "And cameras on in case whoever did this comes back."

Luella's brow furrowed. "It's Sheridan I'm worried most about."

"I can come back for him," Ellis said. "I can bring him to the Edge."

She scanned him for a long time, considering. Then she shook her head. "I can bolt the barn door, same as I can bolt my own. We're both better off here."

Ellis wasn't so sure about that. But she was right. He was still chief of operations at Eaton Edge as long as Everett was in recovery. He didn't think that had changed since he'd left an hour ago. It put a foul taste in his mouth, leaving her. But he didn't see as he had much of a choice. "I'd like to help you bury them, Lu," he said quietly.

Altaha tucked her pen into her breast pocket. "Hell, bring me a shovel. I'll help, too."

Chapter Five

Luella had to leave the house again. She wished there was someone she could call. For the first time in a long time, she wished she had friends—not just neighbors like Naleen and Terrence.

She couldn't get the scene out of her mind—her hens dead in the yard—or how she, Ellis and Altaha had had to fight to dig a hole deep and wide enough in the hard-packed ground they'd uncovered beneath melted snow to bury the lot. The morning after, there was nothing but scattered feathers and Caesar wandering dolefully around an empty coop.

It'd been frightening—how quickly the numbness had grabbed hold of her again. She'd hidden behind it. The shock, the anger, the grief…they were emotions too big to handle shoulder to shoulder.

There were times she had to admit she turned to the numbness for consolation. She'd had to do that after she escaped Fuego the first time for San Gabriel. She'd gotten far too comfortable in the numbness. She'd sought it more recently during her time working in the COVID unit…

The worst of it was that he'd seen it—Ellis. He'd seen what the numbness did to her once it had a chance to grab hold.

A part of her hadn't wanted him to leave. After they'd

buried her chickens and she'd watched him drive off, she'd been afraid to go back inside her own house without the warmth of him beside her.

That was something else she'd had to contemplate as she lay next to her shotgun all night long.

She set her game cameras back up to stream and alert her to any movement around Ollero Creek. If she, Sheridan, Caesar and the cats were going to get away, she had things to take care of in town first.

She stopped by the feed store for hay. Rowdy Conway had come out of his auto repair store to gawk at her and even lifted two fingers to his brow to salute her. She stared at him hard until he crawled back to where he came from.

Had he done it? Had the lewd town mechanic killed her chickens?

She looked around the parking lot and saw that she'd drawn attention. People were looking and talking in small clusters.

She's back. Luella Decker's back.

She slammed the tailgate of her truck and went around to the driver's door to get inside. She shut it with a hard yank.

She was pulling into the bank when she saw the sheriff and the deputy coming down the sidewalk toward her.

Luella put the truck in park and wondered briefly what would happen if she simply bypassed the two of them.

The sheriff's hard expression brought her hand up short of reaching for the jacket on the passenger seat. As they made a beeline, she rolled down her window. "Sheriff," she greeted.

Sheriff Jones had a heavy brow, a muscled jaw and clear blue eyes that cleaved. Next to Altaha, he looked ridiculously tall. There was a settled paunch around his middle, just large enough to rest on his gun belt. When he swept off his hat, his head was shiny and hairless. "Ms. Decker."

She didn't flinch at the way he said her last name. It took a lot. She moved her eyes to Altaha. "Deputy."

"Luella," Altaha returned. "How are things?"

"Busy," she noted. "I should really get back to—"

"We'll only take up a moment of your time, Ms. Decker," Jones said, widening his stance.

When he refused to elaborate, she knew he was waiting for her to get out of the truck. She set her mouth carefully in a neutral line, shut off the ignition and opened the driver's door. Stepping down to the pavement, she faced them, weaving her arms across her chest in what she damn well knew was a defensive stance.

Jones spoke first. "My deputy tells me you're on your way out of town."

"That's the plan," Luella admitted.

"There's been trouble at Ollero Creek."

"Yes. Someone murdered my hens."

He ran his tongue over his teeth. "No leads."

Luella looked to Altaha, who rushed to clarify, "Not yet. The vet had a chance to look at them, though. Their necks were broken, for certain."

Luella grimaced. "What about the tire treads? You said you took pictures."

"We're still going over those," Altaha said. "I canvassed your closest neighbors and questioned everyone on the list you gave us. We have a pretty clear understanding now of who knew of your return."

"Ellis Eaton was with you when the incident occurred."

Luella scowled at Jones's statement. "He was."

"So you've got yourself an alibi," he surmised.

She nearly rolled her eyes but stopped just in time. "Whoever did this, Sheriff, snapped the necks of twenty-three chickens. *Snapped* them. In a very short period of time.

You may think I'm capable of that, but I find that kind of violence toward animals abhorrent."

He raised a brow. "You'd like that on the record, wouldn't you, Ms. Decker?"

"All right," Altaha intervened. "We just wanted to drop by and update you on the case."

"Sure," Luella said, not breaking Jones's stare.

"You got business at the bank?" Jones asked.

"No," Luella lied. "Just casing the joint."

If she wasn't mistaken, she saw Altaha's mouth curve just before the deputy cleared her throat and shifted her feet.

"We're watching you, Ms. Decker," Jones warned.

"I'm sure, Sheriff," Luella replied as the two took off across the street. As soon as they disappeared into the pawn-shop, she opened the truck door again. Reaching over the driver's seat and console, she pulled the jacket off the passenger seat and grabbed the handle of the duffel bag she'd hidden underneath. She locked the truck then went into the bank.

And was nearly mowed down by Paloma Coldero.

"Luella Belle Decker."

Panic struck Luella like a high-speed train. She felt her feet moving back toward the door. Paloma was a formidable figure. How else could she run the house at Eaton Edge and keep Everett in check as she had for the better part of his life?

The woman had cared for him, Ellis and Eveline when their mother, Jo, ran off with Paloma's brother, Santiago, to Coldero Ridge. The scandal had rivaled Luella's own family's. Paloma was practically Ellis's adopted mother and was one of the few who knew how deep his attachment for Luella had gone.

Paloma had caught her once, Luella remembered—sneaking downstairs just after dawn from Ellis's bed, mussed and carrying her own boots.

Nobody intimidated her quite like Paloma.

Bracing her hands around the duffel strap, Luella tried to read the woman's face. "Ms. Coldero."

Paloma made an unfavorable noise. "It's Paloma to you and always has been. Let's not pretend otherwise."

Luella's mouth fumbled. "Thank you?"

"No trouble," Paloma said. She had painted brows, wide hips and a swinging walk. She was either the warmest person in the world or the most discerning. There was no in-between. "I'm pleased to see you've returned. I knew about it, of course. You know Ellis. He can't keep a secret to save his life."

Luella opened her mouth then carefully shut it, unsure what to say to that exactly. She and Ellis had many secrets.

"I hear Ellis came to see you yesterday," Paloma said.

"Well, sure," Luella said for lack of anything better. Who *hadn't* heard Ellis had been at her place?

"Tell me, Luella Belle," Paloma said, "*did* the man behave himself?"

Kissing. Kissing entered her mind like a solar flare. She'd kissed Ellis. He'd kissed her. They'd decidedly not behaved themselves together.

Her mouth worked around several explanations in the space of a moment but none of them made it out.

Paloma lifted her chin, knowing. "I see. Well…you tell me if he should be punished and I'll see to it."

"Him?" Luella heard the word eject. She closed her eyes. "I mean…that's… No, you don't need to… We both…"

Paloma surprised her by laughing. It was deep and rolling. "I'm teasing you, *niña*. I hope the rumors about you leaving Fuego aren't true. You're a good girl, despite the

talk. It's a shame so many people choose not to see it—
see *you*."

Luella gaped at the woman.

"I see you," Paloma said, leaning forward slightly. "You
know that. Keep it with you. Know you got somebody in
your corner."

Luella blinked several times. Shocked by the sudden rush
of kindness, she shook her head quickly. "I…"

Paloma's warm hand covered her cold, fisted one. "Don't
let them chase you off. Not unless it's what you want, deep
down. Know what you want, Luella Belle. And you take it."

Luella could say nothing as Paloma replaced her bank
card in her wallet. "Is leaving what you really want?"

Luella looked away quickly. "Um… I'm unable to really
justify an alternative." Her voice wavered. It shocked her,
almost as much as the line of questioning. "I'm trying to…"
She milled her hand, fishing for answers that weren't there.
"Trying to figure things out…"

"You let me know if you need help moving, if that's the
answer. I know a few good-ish men. You come to the Edge
sometime. I'll feed you. You need some more meat on your
bones."

Luella braced her hands on her hips and did her best to
breathe through the kindness. More meat on her bones?
She'd always been on the round end of pear-shaped. The
stress of the last few years hadn't helped. "Okay," she said
weakly.

"Take care."

"Mmm-hmm," Luella offered. When the bells over the
entrance tinkered and the door closed behind Paloma, she
let out a shuddering breath.

Why did kind words hurt as much as an open-handed
slap? Luella had never understood it. But she was just as

powerless against unexpected words like Paloma's as she'd ever been.

She hadn't cried after losing her hens. Not because it didn't matter. Crying meant opening herself up and opening up was a terrible, horrible idea she couldn't afford any more than kissing Paloma Coldero's adopted son's sultry mouth.

Her stomach hurt from holding everything—*too much*—in. She didn't grieve—her animals, the dregs of her family or her childhood, her first love…anything anymore. Life had given her far too much to grieve. It was impossible to do it without unraveling. Maybe that was why she welcomed the numbness sometimes, even if it scared her.

She slapped her forehead with her palm—one good, hard slap. Then, thinking again, breathing carefully, she went about stitching herself together once more. She counted the threads, made those stitches nice and tight so they'd hold for more than a few hours at a time. *Maybe?*

Please.

Go back to Eaton Edge? Was the woman crazy?

She caught the wave of the bank teller. She walked to the little window at the counter. "Hello, Mrs. Whiting. How are you?"

"Luella," Mrs. Whiting said. She didn't smile or offer near as warm a greeting as Paloma had. "It seems talk's true and you have returned."

"Yes." Luella cleared her throat, tightening her grip on the handle of her bag. "I was hoping to speak to Mr. Monday. I'd like to open an account."

"What kind of account?"

"A savings account," Luella said.

"I'm afraid Mr. Monday retired this October," Mrs. Whiting said. "You wouldn't have heard that. Not while you were in prison."

Luella fought the urge to sigh. "I wasn't in prison."

"I beg your pardon?"

Luella raised her voice. "I wasn't in prison, Mrs. Whiting. I served my time in the county jail."

"It's apples and oranges, isn't it?" Mrs. Whiting asked, tightly.

"For some," Luella said wearily. "Who can I speak to about opening an account?"

"You'll have to make an appointment with the new bank manager," Mrs. Whiting stated. "Jedidiah Gravely."

"Jed," Luella said, fighting the urge to curl her lip in distaste. "Fine."

"How's your mama doin'?" Mrs. Whiting asked as she consulted her computer screen about that appointment.

"Fine, I guess," Luella said. "We haven't really spoken."

"Your own mother," Mrs. Whiting admonished, looking down the sharp blade of her nose.

"My own mother," Luella said back.

"She's a good woman, your mother," Mrs. Whiting said, writing something down on a bank card. "Despite who she married the first time."

"Despite that," Luella echoed emptily.

Ms. Whiting handed the card over. "Come back tomorrow morning. Mr. Gravely will see you then."

"Thanks a lot," Luella said as she turned away from Mrs. Whiting.

"You have a nice day," Mrs. Whiting returned, emptily.

Luella stuffed the card into the back pocket of her jeans and began to walk back to the doors.

Something hit the floor behind her. Someone cried out in alarm. She glanced around and froze when she saw the man spilled out on the black and white tiles and the woman bent over him, cloaked in worry. "He's not breathing!" she cried. "Somebody call 911!"

Luella dropped the duffel. She crossed the lobby. She put her fingers to the man's neck, felt for a pulse. There wasn't one.

She took off her coat. "Ma'am, is this your husband?"

"Yes," she said, frantic. "Ben. Benjamin Tate."

"Was Mr. Tate having any trouble this morning?" Luella asked, working quickly to unbutton the man's jacket over his chest. His torso lay still. No respirations. Luella positioned him until he was flat on his back. She tipped his chin up, made sure his mouth was open, checked for obstructions. "Shortness of breath, chest pain?"

"He said it was indigestion," Mrs. Tate said, crying freely now. "He took some Pepcid. That's it."

Luella glanced around, saw that Mrs. Whiting was on the phone with the emergency dispatcher. She had to work quickly to give the ambulance time. Placing both hands just below Mr. Tate's breastbone, she interlocked them then straightened her arms and began chest compressions. She kept them coming, hard and fast, counting under her breath. When she got to one hundred and ten, she stopped to do several rescue breaths.

Mrs. Tate was sobbing now. Mrs. Whiting and the other tellers were crowded around her, doing their best to console her.

Come on, Luella thought when Mr. Tate's ribs didn't rise. She quickly switched back to chest compressions, making sure to press in a full five centimeters with each one. Sweat began to roll down her hairline. She heard a rib break, but she kept going, repeating the process even after Jones and Altaha rushed in.

She saw Mr. Tate's ribs rise after another set of rescue breaths.

"Ben!" Mrs. Tate shrieked. "Oh, Ben, come back, sugar!"

"Paramedics are here," Altaha said, placing her hand on Luella's shoulder.

Luella looked around to see them rushing in with the stretcher. "Code blue," she said, stepping back and giving them free rein over the situation. They asked quick questions, she gave quick answers. Then she followed them out with Mrs. Tate to the ambulance.

Once husband and wife were loaded and the doors shut, Luella watched the ambulance disappear.

The sirens faded. Only then did Luella see that the crowd had thickened. Not only was everyone from the bank on the street with her. Everyone from the laundromat, the pawnshop, the bakery and barber shop was there, too.

She cleared her throat. It was a raw. Pushing her hair back from her face, she felt the dew on her skin.

"You did good," Altaha said on her right. "You may have saved his life."

Luella took a breath. "We'll see."

"Did you lose this?"

She looked around to find Sheriff Jones with her duffel. She took it. "Thank you."

His gaze wasn't any friendlier than before. She looked around and found discerning looks. She hugged the duffel to her. "Excuse me," she said as she picked her way through the bystanders to her truck.

Eveline Eaton stood in her way. Luella felt the collective

breath of the crowd and heard the whispering as she stood toe to toe with her father's last victim.

"Luella," Eveline greeted. "I was hoping to run into you."

Did Luella hear that right? She was tired now and there was ringing in her ears.

"I'm glad the Tates found you before I did," Eveline said. She was blonde, polished even in snow-and-dirt-encrusted boots. She was slim and leggy, every bit the model she'd once been. "We should have lunch sometime."

Luella stared at her for what she was sure was a full minute. "If you say so."

"I do," Eveline said with a smile. It was genuine, with a flash of straight white teeth. "It was me, by the way."

"You who?"

"Who paid for the Uber," Eveline revealed.

Luella shook her head. She shook herself. *She did?* "Why would you do that?"

"That's a talk for another time," Eveline told her. "Preferably, when the entire town isn't eavesdropping on us."

Luella glanced around. No one had moved. On cue, Altaha raised her voice. "What is this, a block party? Back to your business, people!"

Luella watched them scatter like roaches when the light comes on. "You think they'd have better things to do."

"It's been six months," Eveline said with a shake of her head. "I figure another six years and they'll start talking about something else."

Luella almost snorted a laugh but stopped.

Altaha approached them. "I'll let you know about Mr. Tate," she told Luella. "They'll notify us of his status at some point this afternoon."

Luella nodded. "I appreciate it."

Altaha looked to Eveline. "And I guess I'll see you and Wolfe later."

"Maybe," Eveline said. At Luella's cautious frown, she explained, "It's poker night at the Edge. You could join us."

Luella shook her head. "I best be getting back to my animals."

"Any more trouble at Ollero Creek?" Altaha wondered.

"Not that I know of."

"Give me a call if anything changes. Normally, we ask people to call the station but Jones is real sensitive about you, for some reason."

"For some reason," Luella muttered, frowning.

"He saw the money in the bag."

Luella swore out loud. "After my crack about casing the joint, I guess he thinks I robbed the bank."

"Mmm," Altaha said. "I know you're not liable to put a foot wrong, but I'd be extra careful. There wasn't anybody happier to hear that you're skipping town than the sheriff."

"You're leaving town?" Eveline asked. "Why?"

Luella thought about answering, but she settled for: "A conversation for another time."

Eveline gave a slow nod. "Give me a call, too, when you're up for a lunch date."

Luella lied, "I will." Then she retreated into the safety of her truck and locked the door.

Chapter Six

Ellis felt as if he were juggling bulls, heifers, calves, tractors, one touchy ATV that didn't get up and go like it used to, and a stack of paperwork he desperately wanted to set fire to. Still, he stayed ensconced in his father's office long after he'd left the barn. Night pressed against the windows. There was a nice fire crackling in the hearth. Paloma had brought him a plate of enchiladas verdes and sat with him while he ate.

Now Ellis pressed the office phone between his ear and shoulder while he filled out pay stubs, checking off the names of their winter team as he went. He took a sip of water from the glass Paloma had brought him, swallowed, adjusted the phone again and said, "So when you add to one side of the equation, what do you have to do to the other addend?"

There was a slight pause. Then Isla said, uncertain, "Add the same number to the other side, too?"

"Almost there," Ellis said. His pen hovered over the checks as he thought about it. He sat back in the chair, giving his back a stretch. Who knew sitting for hours at a desk could cause just as many aches and pains as being on a horse all day? "You know Lady Justice and her scales? One side can't level with the other until they balance each other out."

"Uh-huh," Isla said. He heard a wet sniffle.

Ellis's heart ripped. Isla was a marvel at so many things. She was an accomplished rider on her horse, Boon. Her nimble fingers could race across piano keys like they were made to do so. She liked to write poems and songs.

The enemy was math. If not for math, Isla would have nothing to weigh her down. "It's okay, baby. We're going to get this," he said.

"It's so hard, Daddy," she cried. It was as soft as a mouse—not the lion's roar he knew it was inside her.

"I know," he murmured. "But I want you to think about those scales and the best way to even them out. When you make one number bigger, you have to make the other..."

Another pause. "Smaller?"

He closed his eyes and gave into a proud papa smile. "And how do you do that?"

"By subtracting the other addend by the same number?"

"Yes," he said, beaming as he sat up. He grinned at the room at large, then stopped when he saw there was no one to share his pride with. "Baby, you got it."

"Daddy?"

"Yes?"

"Ingrid got in trouble at school today."

Oh, boy, he thought. Where Isla's weakness was math, Ingrid's was curiosity. A scientist trapped in a child's body, she'd snuck small animals into her bedroom for study. She'd given up on piano in favor of deep cloud contemplation. She liked nothing better than lying in the grass of the park outside the studio where Isla practiced once a week, watching the clouds shift or trying to find insects.

She didn't suffer fools, either. She could charm just about anybody with a grin but one foul word from someone at school was cause for retaliation. And it'd only gotten worse since the separation. While Isla never complained about her new school in Taos, Ingrid did so regularly and with increasing volume. She wanted to come back to Fuego. She wanted to ride, too. While form and hands were paramount to Isla, Ingrid just wanted to clamber up on her pony, Dander, and go. She would ride all day if Ellis let her.

He braced himself and asked, "Do I need to talk to her?"

"I don't know," Isla said, rife with anxiety. Isla carried too many worries—far more than a seven-year-old should. Her voice dropped to a whisper. "You know those tiny ketchup packets?"

"Yeah," Ellis said, apprehensively.

"She squirted one in a boy's eye."

Don't smile, Daddy, Ellis told himself, tipping the receiver away from his mouth. He worked to keep his facial muscles at half-mast. There was pride here, too, but… *Straight face.* "Well…did he do something to her first?"

"Yes. He said a bad word at her."

Ellis squinted. "He's in kindergarten, too?"

"Yes."

"Jesus," he muttered, pulling the phone away from his ear and gathering a steadying breath. Bringing the phone up once more, he asked, "What does Mama say?"

"Oh, she's mad," Isla said, still in hushed tones. "She says if she gets called to school one more time, she's going to…"

When she trailed off, Ellis dipped his chin. "Isla?"

Liberty's voice cut across the line. "It's time for bed, Ellis. You've kept her awake long enough."

Ellis checked his watch. "She needed help with her homework. And since when do they go to bed at seven thirty?"

"Since Ingrid started dozing off in Bible school," Liberty said.

"That's because she's bored and she wants to run around

outside," Ellis said. "What's this about Ingrid being in trouble? You're not going to punish her?"

"Why shouldn't I?"

"Because the kid cussed at her," Ellis said. "You can't blame her for—"

"I *can* blame her for behaving like a—"

"An Eaton?" he finished for her.

Liberty sighed. "I've been called to the principal's office three times this semester."

"Maybe if you brought her here more," he said, "she could run and play and be with the animals. She could get her energy out. You've got them wrapped up so tight with music and Bible school and homework, she doesn't have a chance to get it all out. It builds up. Maybe this accounts for some of her negative behavior."

"You want more time with them?" Liberty asked. "Okay. Sign those shares over to me first."

Ellis dropped his face into his hand. He scrubbed. "There's got to be something else you want—"

"Not if you want shared custody."

He checked the urge to throw the receiver across the room. "This is extortion and you know it."

"Maybe next time try not sleeping with someone else."

"I never…" He rubbed his teeth together. If he yelled, it was only more ammunition for her. If he yelled, she'd hang up and her feelings for him would tank further, if possible. He released a long breath. "I need you to reconsider. Please."

"You need more time," she surmised. "You take all the time you need. In the meantime, the girls will remain in Taos with me."

"You can't—"

"Do you want to tell the girls good night or not?" she asked pointedly.

A knock on the door brought his head up. It opened and the Edge's head wrangler, Javier Rivera, peered in. "You're missing all the fun, *amigo*. The deputy's robbing us blind. She and Everett just went all in. They're the last ones standing."

Ellis nodded mutely. He waited until Javier shut the door. Then he told Liberty, "Put them on."

"Good night, Daddy," Isla said.

Louder, Ingrid called, "'Night, Daddy! I love you! Give Dander a kiss for me!"

"Will do." A smile stretched across his mouth. "I love you, too. Both of you. Okay?"

"Okay!"

"Okay, Daddy."

"Good night," Liberty said, then the line went dead and Ellis stared into the fire, feeling burned like kindling.

"YOU PLAY LIKE you used to race cars," Altaha said as she and Everett slapped cards onto the table one after the other.

"Yeah?" Everett asked. Ellis had found them alone at the kitchen table. The others had left. The game had been won by the deputy, apparently, and now she and Everett were engaged in an intense, late-night round of War. "How's that?"

"Badly." Altaha whooped when she won a set. She scooped his cards and her cards her way. "Thank you!"

"Woman's a goddamn con artist," Everett said to Ellis. "Why do we invite her?"

"Because you Eatons," Altaha said, stacking her side of the deck, "you don't back down from a challenge. Right?" she asked Ellis.

Ellis thought of Liberty's demands and badly wanted a stiff drink. "Even if it kills us." He focused on his brother. There was color in him tonight. Maybe a little light in his eyes and it was good to see, Ellis had to admit. Everett needed a challenge other than the one he'd been fighting with himself. PTSD had been a hard battle. Trucks and tractors backfiring sent him right back to summer and the box canyon and the shot that had shattered his sternum and nearly put him in the ground.

His brother was leaner, harder and had been lost for the better part of six months. Ellis had said nothing out loud about working late on those pay stubs and the rest of it because his brother needed this: this simple interaction with others to bring the light back—the fight back. His brother, who'd always thought on his feet and juggled cows, papers, ranch responsibilities like a king and now was fighting something bigger than himself. Not physically, anymore, but a mental battle that was just as treacherous.

I can't punch something I can't see, he'd told Ellis one particularly bad night a few months back.

Ellis and Paloma had fought to get him into therapy. He'd dug in his heels, but after confining himself to the ranch for weeks at a time watching reruns of *Yellowstone*, avoiding town and people in general, he'd finally broke. He was now seeing a therapist once a week in San Gabriel. Paloma and Ellis took turns driving him. They'd both watched Hammond Eaton let his health slide away. They weren't going to do the same with him.

Poker nights helped, too, Ellis thought. Paloma hated gambling but even she had to admit these bimonthly gatherings were good for Everett.

"Ah!" Everett cried when Altaha took half the deck in another close battle. "You're a card sharp, sweetheart."

Altaha raised a brow and sent him a deputy's glance.

"Deputy," he quickly amended. Then fumbled again. "Sweetheart. Deputy sweetheart."

She stared at him for several seconds. Ellis counted them, watching his brother sweat it out and enjoying it. There weren't many people who could make Everett perspire with a look. A slow smile worked its way across Altaha's mouth. She slid her eyes over Everett's form. "You didn't eat. Paloma wasn't pleased."

"She lives to complain in my ear," he muttered, tossing his cards onto the table—what was left of them. "I gotta give her something."

"I'm starting to understand why a rancher like you has remained decidedly single," she said, lifting her glass from the table. It was half-full of beer that was no longer frothy. "You're a perfect ass."

"Thank you," he said with a tip of his hat. "It's been a while since I've gotten a remark like that."

She snorted. "Oh, they make hats for asses like you. You know that, right?"

"I've got plenty of hats," he drawled. "You wanna see 'em?"

Altaha laughed. It sounded remarkably like a giggle and Ellis froze. Was this… Were they…flirting? She waved her hand. "I'm going to take a pass on that. Maybe some other time."

"I'll hold you to it," Everett said. There was a smile on his face. It was sly, as it'd once been. Around the edges it was soft as it never was.

Ellis was inexplicably starting to feel like a third wheel. "Any updates on the case at Ollero Creek?" he inquired.

Altaha made a noise. "Nothing solid. Tire treads are pretty common. They were newer, though. Definitely a four-by-four."

"Everybody's got a four-by," Everett commented, reassembling the deck.

"That's true," Ellis said. "So it's a dead end?"

"The case isn't cold," Altaha said. "I'm not giving up on it, Eaton. A little faith, huh?"

Faith had been hard to come by. He was still raw from the phone call. Picking up an abandoned beer glass, he took a gulp of the lukewarm contents. He winced, set it down with a clack and tried not to stew over the idea of Isla going to bed sad or Ingrid in trouble with her mother or Luella alone at Ollero Creek. "Has Luella reported anything?"

"No," Altaha replied. "I checked in with her this afternoon. She saved Ben Tate's life at the bank. He's in stable condition."

"I heard," Ellis said quietly. He'd also wondered over the enormous sense of pride he'd felt when he had. Not surprise. Of course, she'd saved a man's life. Just a strange well of pride in the woman that hadn't been his in seventeen years. He looked around for the Bluetooth speaker that was blaring country music out in deafening waves. "You should turn that down."

"I like this one," Everett opined. He'd been watching Ellis closely in the talk of Ollero Creek. "Who doesn't love a good ditty about a man pining after some girl he left behind?"

Altaha made a gimme motion with her hand. "May I?"

Everett eyed her once then unlocked the screen of his phone and slid it her way.

"Thank you," she said, hands busy scrolling. She grinned. "This one," she said when the country music cut off, "is for you, sad boy."

"Me?" Everett asked as a piano intro flooded the room.

Altaha stood, pushing back her chair. As Gloria Gaynor started crooning, she started to spin.

Everett leaned into Ellis. "What's happening here?"

"I think…" Ellis raised the beer to his mouth again "… the good deputy is dancing."

Everett's jaw loosened as Altaha's braid went flying and her hips started to move. "I feel like I'm seeing Darth Vader without his mask."

Ellis found himself smiling at the display. "She's got moves. Maybe as many as you used to. Oh," he added when Altaha crooked her finger. "I think you're being summoned."

Everett raised his hands. "Ah, no. I don't think so."

Altaha rolled her eyes. "Come on! I hear Everett Eaton used to tear up the floor at Grady's Saloon."

"Before he was banned," Ellis mentioned.

"Banned," Everett said with a decisive nod. "For life."

"Then you're past due," Altaha insisted. "Get your boots over here before I sit on you!"

Everett pursed his lips. "That's not a threat, sweetheart."

"Now!" Altaha said, grabbing him by the hands and yanking him to his feet.

Next to her, Everett looked as tall as a tree and just as awkward. "You do know hootin' leads to hollerin'?"

Altaha beamed. "That's what I'm counting on, cowboy."

AS ELLIS SAW the good deputy out to her truck some time later, he said, "I can't remember the last time Everett smiled."

"Your big brother's going to be fine," Altaha assured him. "He just needs to remember who he is. That guy who used to race cars and cut a rug at Grady's. The same guy who punched True Claymore in the teeth at my sister's wedding."

Ellis laughed. "Yeah. We're still paying for that one. You know the Claymores tried to sue? Even when he was recovering from his gunshot wound."

"Annette and True Claymore are a pox on this town," Altaha said. "If not for True's brother, the reverend, I'd say run them all off. But you didn't hear that from me."

Ellis raised his hands to show he wasn't listening.

Altaha stopped moving toward her truck. "I heard a rumor."

He crossed his arms. "We love those around here."

"If this one's true, I've got something to say about it. Word is your ex is asking for your shares in Eaton Edge in exchange for custody."

He sunk his hands into the pockets of his jeans. The night was cold. He blew clouds into the cutting wind. "Where do you get your sources? They're uncanny."

"As a matter of fact, it was Annette Claymore bragging at the barber shop," Altaha said. "Every chair was full. Four cosmetologists, one barber and eight customers heard every bit of it. Now it's spreading like a virus." She paused. "You're saying it's true?"

Ellis sighed. "Yes."

"May I speak as your friend now, not your deputy?"

"After all that hootin' and hollerin' in there, it's hard to see you as anything else," he remarked.

"Fight her," Altaha said. "Fight her to the teeth."

He groaned. "I can't lose my girls, Kaya."

"You can't lose your birthright either," she said. "If not for your sake, then for your father and your brothers. It'd kill them both. And if you are willing to fight, I've got someone you ought to speak to."

"You know a good divorce lawyer?"

"No, but I do know the man your wife was having an affair with."

He took that. It went down like a serrated pill. "You... What?"

"Walker Sullivan," Altaha supplied.

"The...bronc buster?" Ellis had a laugh. "I thought that was just..."

"Careful, moon-eyed looks and talk over the last seven years like you and Luella Decker?" Altaha asked. "No. It was more than that."

"Do you have proof of this?" he asked, trying not to wince at how much she'd been able to discern about him and Luella. "Of Liberty and Walker?"

"They were screwing in the bed he shared with his wife, not yours, if that makes you feel any better."

Was any of this supposed to make him feel better?

"You recall they separated, too. Last Christmas."

Ellis shook his head. "Hang on. Liberty hates cowboys. The whole lifestyle, everything about them. Why would she want another one?"

"There are some forces greater than all of us. It doesn't need to make sense. It just is. Or was. Seeing as Liberty's living in Taos now, I'd say the affair's over."

"Jesus. Did you learn all this at the barber shop?"

"No. Walker's ex, Rosalie, is friends with Naleen. They talk. Naleen passes on pertinent information. She was in the shop the day Annette told everyone about Liberty's evil plans for you. I think she told me about Liberty and Walker so I'd pass it along to you. Not everybody sided with Liberty during the separation. I hope you see that now. And I hope you fight fire with fire."

He studied her. She was angry. Maybe as angry as he was. He gave a slow nod.

"Does your family know what she's trying to do?" Altaha asked.

Ellis shook his head. "Everett's got enough on his mind. Eveline and Wolfe are planning a wedding. And Paloma worries enough already."

"They need to know," she advised. "Here." She dug into her small, battered handbag and pulled out a card. "This guy—he lives an hour away but he helped Naleen get primary custody of Nova in her divorce from Ryan Mackay. There was infidelity involved in that case, too." He hesitated. "On both sides. It was ugly but this guy helped."

Ellis took the card with some reluctance, read the name and practice and realized he was in this now, all in.

"Call Rosalie, too," Altaha added. "She still lives in that house by the Tractor Supply. Even if she did burn that mattress."

"I guess I should say thank you."

She patted him firmly on the shoulder. "Do it later when you feel less like a man scorned. Oh, and somebody needs to say it. Spending your free time with Luella Decker might not be the best look for you if you're going to tell the judge you didn't sleep with her."

Ellis's brow furrowed. "But I didn't sleep with her."

"I believe you. But a judge may not if you're sleeping with her now."

"We're *not* sleeping together."

She flicked the strap of her purse over her shoulder. "Tell me right here and now if the opportunity presents itself you won't touch her for the next twelve months."

Unbidden, Luella's mouth entered his mind. Her sweet mouth in her heart-shaped face. Her taste—like muscadines ripening on the vine.

He had touched her. He'd chased her across her yard and touched her and now he was burdened by the knowledge that all that'd been between them before was still there. It was right there—ready and waiting like fruit on the vine.

When his mouth opened and stayed that way, she pointed at it. "You see that right there? That's trouble."

"It doesn't mean I'm going to sleep with her," he claimed. But the words sounded unconvincing in his own ears.

"Hell, Ellis," she said, walking backward to her truck, "I'd have jumped on your brother tonight to cheer him up if you hadn't been here after everybody else went. And he and I have a lot less history."

The idea of Everett and the deputy together alone long enough to make these decisions for themselves made Ellis's head hurt a little. "You mean well, I guess. Good night, Deputy."

Chapter Seven

Luella frowned at the postmark on the large manila envelope in her mailbox. She lifted it to the light.

San Gabriel.

Luella stared at the writing—her name, her address.

Aunt Mabel's handwriting again.

Luella carefully tore the top of the envelope. What had her aunt sent her now? Would it make more sense than the short-worded postcards still sitting on her kitchen table?

She reached in and pulled out a photograph.

Confused, she opened the envelope wider. It was empty. Turning the five-by-ten over, she frowned at the faces on it.

She didn't recognize either one.

Luella leaned back against Sheridan's warmth. She'd saddled him for a ride around her property where she'd surveyed fences and looked for signs of entry around the perimeter. She'd found nothing out of place.

Luella studied the photograph in closer detail. She did recognize something. The sign for the Fuego Horse Arena was in the background. The couple, embracing around the waist and smiling for the camera, was in the foreground. In the middle ground were various people, out of focus, milling here and there in hats and chaps.

The rodeo, she discerned. The man was wearing chaps,

too. No hat. He had a full head of dark, shaggy hair and he was tall. Stupid tall. Very *Smoky and the Bandit*.

The woman wasn't dressed for an event like he was but she was sporting boots and a flat-brimmed hat as well as a printed blouse that looked like something made in the eighties.

There was a date in the bottom right corner of the photograph. Luella squinted because it was a bit smudged.

03-11-87.

"Eighty-seven," Luella mused. She offered the photo for Sheridan to have a look. "Year before I was born. Fifteen years before you, handsome." She kissed him above the nose.

He chuffed, turning his nose against her torso to blow his breath across her.

She ran her fingers through his forelock. The woman had red hair, she saw upon closer inspection.

Red hair.

Luella's fingers tangled in Sheridan's mane. She studied the face of the woman again, hard. It was heart-shaped, like her own.

Her jaw dropped. "Mom?" she said out loud. Then she shook her head, unable to relate the smiling woman in the photograph to the bitter woman in San Gabriel who answered by the same name.

Luella flipped the photo over again. Nothing but blank space on the other side. No message. "What the hell, Mabel?" she asked. The man in the photograph might be a mystery, but it was most definitely not her father. Too tall, dark and good-tempered. "What are you trying to tell me?"

The sound of a truck approaching had Sheridan's hooves dancing back on the driveway. Luella grabbed his bridle as she looked in the direction of the highway.

It was one of the trucks from Eaton Edge. She braced herself, stuffing the picture back in its envelope and tucking it under her arm. The truck slowed and the window rolled down.

Luella balked at the face of Eveline Eaton in the driver's seat. "Hell."

Eveline laughed. Her breath plumed out the window from the warm cab. "I think you meant hell*o*. A little out of practice?"

"Yeah, sure," Luella said. "What are you doing here?"

"I don't expect you to call me about that lunch you said we'd arrange. And I've got something to say to you."

"You want me to invite you into my house?" Luella asked, doubtfully.

"That is the way to do things," Eveline considered. "Maybe we could even do something crazy like have a cup of coffee together."

"I don't have anything to go with coffee."

"Then we'll just have to starve," Eveline drawled. She eyed Sheridan. "Hey, big boy. We've sure missed you at the Edge."

Luella covered his nose in defense. "I'll let you in," she said, resigned.

IT WAS ODD, leading Eveline inside after stabling Sheridan. Luella took her time supplying him with fresh water and bolting the door. She checked on Caesar. He'd taken to lingering in the coop. She pretended it didn't break her heart. As she mounted the steps to the porch, she jumped at Nyx as he chased her feet across the boards. "Scoundrel," she hissed when his claws sank into the jeans over her calf and he worked his way up her leg. She shook him off. "Go on, now!"

Digging her keys out of her pocket, she shoved one into the first dead bolt. "Watch him. He strikes without warning."

"Oh, most men do," Eveline gauged. She eyed the key going into the second dead bolt but didn't say a word about the strong security measures.

Finally, Luella shoved her way into the house, letting Eveline come in, too. She shrugged out of her jacket, hung it and her keys on the peg and made a beeline for the coffeepot.

"Aw," Eveline cooed. "What's this one's name?"

Eveline saw her take off one soft leather glove to raise her hand to Sphinx's back. The feline was reclining on the back of the couch. "Sphinx. She won't swipe."

Sphinx purred at Eveline's attentions. Luella found two clean mugs and poured coffee. She set the mugs on the table, set out napkins with them then sat down. "What'd you want to talk about?"

"You don't believe in small talk?" Eveline asked, stroking the line of Sphinx's spine one last time before taking off her other glove. She pulled out a chair at the table and settled.

"As a rule," Luella decided.

Eveline nodded. "Talk's cheap when it's common." She lifted her mug and blew across the surface. "I think that's something we've both learned the hard way."

Luella frowned. If Eveline was trying to find common ground between the two of them, she'd need to keep searching. Eveline Eaton was a ball of sunlight who no doubt could still squeeze into those size two runway outfits she'd once dazzled the world in.

Next to her, Luella felt like a rock in comparison. Her cable-knit sweater was a neutral color and a bit drab. Her boots were battered and her size twelve jeans had wide tears around the knees. In contrast, Eveline wore a warm wool coat that looked new and Ariats that had barely been scuffed.

"Postcards," Eveline said, picking one of Mabel's messages off the top of the pile. "Someone has an admirer."

"Hardly," Luella murmured, taking a sip of her coffee. She held the mug in her hands because she'd forgotten her gloves on the ride. The heat soaked clean through her skin.

Eveline frowned at the message. "'W.J.'?" She made a face. "Whoever this is from has just as big a gift for gab as you."

"It's my aunt," Luella said, reaching out to take the postcard. She pulled the stack closer. "She lives in San Gabriel. My mom's been afraid her mind's been slipping for years. This seems to confirm it." She eyed the manila envelope she'd set on the side table by the door.

"Is she ill?" Eveline asked, unwrapping her scarf.

"Not that I've heard," Luella said. "I don't talk to my mom much anymore."

"Maybe you should go see for yourself."

"The last time I went, my mom and I couldn't sit in the same room for more than a few minutes at a time."

"Why not?" Eveline asked. "I remember your mother. Riane, right? She was always the nice lady at church who handed out peppermints."

Luella remembered the woman who'd hidden under that one. The one who'd take a beating from Jace Decker and make sure her daughter knew she was the one to blame for it. *Devil's spawn. Bad seed.* And later, *Hussy. Jezebel. Whore.* "She forgot how to be nice a long time ago."

"I'm sorry to hear that," Eveline said.

Luella shifted in her seat, uncomfortable. "Why did you pay for the Uber?"

Eveline lowered her eyes to the table. She traced a parting in the wood with a neat fingernail. "Because I met your father. Like my mother and half sister before me, I met him in the worst way. I survived where they didn't. And over the last few months, I've come to understand that you did, too. You survived that, somehow—as a girl and a woman. I survived one day with him. I can't imagine the strength it took for you to live through all that you did."

Luella stilled.

"Also," Eveline said, bringing her hands together on the table, "you tried to warn me about him this summer. You said whoever was stalking me didn't want to be found and I should leave it be. I get what you were trying to do. You were trying, in your way, to save me from him because you knew what he was capable of. If I had listened to you, Everett might not have been shot and you might not have gone to jail."

"And my father would still be out there," Luella stated. "He'd be alive. In a way, I owe you and yours for taking care of him."

"It wasn't me," Eveline said. "Not directly."

"But you didn't quit and he's dead and we're both here alive to talk about it, apparently."

Eveline offered her something of a smile. "If you *are* going to leave Fuego, I wanted you to take my gratitude with you, and I wanted you to know how much I admire you."

Luella closed her eyes. She shook herself slightly. Was she dreaming? Ellis's sister…admired *her*? "Did…did Ellis put you up to this?"

Eveline's expression went blank. "What does Ellis have to do with anything?"

"Nothing. Never mind." Luella pushed herself up from the table. "Thank you… I think."

"Likewise," Eveline said, rising. She reached for her gloves and scarf. Her brow knitted as she pulled them on, one finger at a time. "I was sorry to hear about your chickens. What a horrible thing. They think it was someone from town?"

"That's the working theory, I believe," Luella said, leading Eveline to the door. "Someone who wants to make it known that I'm no longer welcome here, most likely."

"And you're all alone out here?" Eveline said, looking around.

Luella's gaze fell on the cat stretching itself as it walked lazily across the back of the couch. "I have Nyx and Sphinx and Sheridan. Caesar the rooster, too, even if he is downhearted."

Eveline laid her hand on Luella's arm. "This is rough country to be a woman alone in. I know that now."

"I have a gun," Luella told her. "How's Wolfe? I haven't seen him."

Eveline's grin blazed. "He's fine. Busy. He's wanted to visit but we just finished the house. He's been trying to get Santiago's wing ready so he and his caretaker can move in."

"It's nice that you're bringing him home to Fuego," Luella commented.

"It'll be good for everyone," Eveline said. "Wolfe hated him being so far away in the mental facility. Paloma can visit him whenever she likes, and he'll be able to see the desert and the mountains he loves."

"When is the wedding?" Luella asked, a bit awkwardly, surprised she wanted to make the effort. Something had eased between her and Eveline, however, which made it easier.

"March," Eveline said. "A spring wedding at the Edge. With Wolfe and Everett's feud finally over, it'll be perfect. It's the place that brought Wolfe into my life."

Luella hissed when a bracing wind laced across the porch. She'd forgotten her jacket inside.

If Ellis were here, he'd be chasing her with it.

She nearly smiled. It made her stop and scowl. "There's a storm coming. Another blizzard. Drive careful."

"Sure." Eveline's teeth flashed. She fit her sunglasses into place. "You do know my brother's in love with you. Don't you?"

Luella's pulse skittered. She felt her breath hitch. From far away, she heard her voice. "Which one?"

Eveline's laugh tittered into the air. As she waved and went back to her truck, Luella stood frozen at the top of the steps, glad of the cold snapping her cheeks.

When Eveline drove off, Luella beat feet down the steps, needing the cold a bit longer to pipe down some of the heat inside her.

My brother's in love with you.

Ellis, young and smiling—carefree and golden—filled Luella's mind. The star-shaped diamond ring he'd given her, missing for over a decade now, was an itch at the base of her finger.

"I wish this could last forever," she told him as they sat underneath the shadows of their horses. The clouds were passing fast. She could hear thunder on the horizon. They'd have to ride soon—ride hard for the ranch house or the nearest shelter. The need to linger, to stretch time so that his shoulder pillowed her cheek and the circle of his arms remained unbroken, was too much for her to give up, even for a storm.

"Who says it won't?" he asked, turning his lips against her temple for a brushing glide.

There was a smile in his voice. She could tell. Hers faded by gradual degrees as thunder knelled again. It was too perfect to last—the moment. This. Some part of her knew. She'd known from the moment he smiled at her in class over a chemistry book. She'd known the second he'd asked her out under the guise of stargazing on his roof.

She had known it from the moment she'd realized she loved him—how hard *she loved him—and when he'd told her he loved her in return.*

From their first dance—it was supposed to be at home-coming but he'd taken her into the hills after her father had knocked her around. And the first kiss, shortly thereafter. Their first time inside a sleeping bag near a crackling fire under the stars not long after spring thaw. And all the times after—she'd known she couldn't keep him. How could he be hers when he was so perfect?

She'd never had anything perfect—not until Ellis. If her mother was right and her father, too, she wasn't meant to.

She was so afraid of breaking his heart—in quiet moments like these where she felt the rush of time against the sweet, languid undercurrent of longing and love, it broke hers.

The moments were slowly, quietly breaking her heart, because she knew they were inevitably bringing her closer to when time won and everything fractured.

How could she keep him when she and her world were so imperfect?

She'd do anything, she realized, to be perfect for him...

She'd tried to be perfect. When he dropped down on one knee and proposed, she'd felt relief beyond measure. This would be her way of keeping him. No one could argue with a ring. It meant she belonged, to Ellis and the Eatons, and she'd never have to go back to her father or her mother.

Luella stopped short, the memories falling fast at her feet as she faltered.

The chain she'd used to lock the barn door was lying in the mud. The bolt had been cut.

The door hung open and she didn't hear Sheridan inside.

Chapter Eight

Ellis stomped on the gas. Visibility was growing worse by the minute. Snowflakes batted the windshield as the wind funneled them in at an angle. He put on his headlights and veered in the direction of Ollero Creek.

The phone call from Luella had been unexpected. It had also been hysterical. Sheridan was gone and he didn't have much hope that she'd done as he'd asked.

Wait, he'd told her. *Wait for me. Don't go looking for him yourself.*

He nearly took out her mailbox, cranking the wheel to the left when he finally saw her driveway creep up. The tires bounced in and out of ruts, but he didn't slow.

He braked in front of her house. Her truck was there. He ducked out into the weather, keeping his head low as he raced up the steps to her porch and knocked on her door.

No answer.

He peered through the window. The cat, Nyx, stared back at him, lifting its paw to bat at his face on the other side of the glass.

Ellis cursed, going back down the steps. He went around the house to the yard. The barn was just as she'd left it, closed and empty but for the rooster.

He studied the ground. There were tracks, but they were fading.

He ran back to his truck. The flakes were starting to grow fatter and fall faster.

He opened the door of the horse trailer behind his truck. "Come on," he urged to his horse, Shy. He was already saddled and ready to ride, as he had been at the Edge. Ellis zipped his jacket, put on his gloves, pulled his bandanna up over his nose and mounted. Then he set out around the yard to follow both the woman's and the horse's tracks.

They'd gone north, in the direction of the cliffs, across the long empty prairie. Because of the snowfall, he couldn't see the cliffs or anything more than ten feet in front of him. The house quickly faded behind him as the storm swallowed him and his mount.

He frowned when he noticed another set of tracks alongside Sheridan's. About fifty yards from the house, he saw the first signs of blood. He pulled on Shy's reins. His stomach hit the ground before his feet as he dismounted.

The blood trail was thin, but it traveled with Sheridan's hoofprints as far into the distance as he could discern. He followed on foot a ways, just to be sure.

The boot prints going forward were jumbled. Was there a confrontation? Or had Luella stumbled? Was she hurt?

The tracks grew lighter, barely discernable. Ellis stayed on foot, leading Shy one step at a time.

The blood trail was the only thing that remained consistent. "Son of a bitch," Ellis said as the prints nearly faded out altogether. He was about to lose them. Snow crusted the brim of his hat. It gathered on his shoulders. Squinting, he tried to pick shadows out of the white haze. "Lu!" he called, cupping his hands over his mouth. His voice was absorbed by the falling snow. There was no echo. When no sound came back, he raised his voice further, straining his vocal cords. "Luella!"

Panting, he laid a hand over the horn of Shy's saddle. Before he could lift his foot to the stirrup, he heard the distant sound of a whinny. Then, a woman's shout, followed closely by the sharp report of a gunshot.

He mounted fast. Bringing his rifle around to his front, he urged Shy forward at the gallop.

Shadows did take shape in front of him. The horse. Ellis grew closer and the red of Luella's hair broke through the snowscape. She was belly-down on the ground. For a split second, he thought she was hurt and he nearly lost his mind.

Then he saw her shotgun in her arms, aimed in the direction of the horse.

"Lu!" he called.

Her head swiveled. "Ellis, stop! He's armed!"

Before Ellis could react, another gunshot rang out, louder this time.

Shy bucked a split second before impact. Ellis felt the burn across his arm. Then he felt himself falling away as Shy bucked a second time. The reins fell from his hands.

The ground jarred him. He kept his head up. He tried sucking air into his lungs. They refused to work. The wind had been knocked out of them.

Stay calm, he told himself when the urge to panic mushroomed. He did get his breath back, siphoning it in and out in steady puffs and thinking through the situation.

The rifle had fallen a few yards away. He tried to orient his surroundings. It was difficult with the wall of white around him. Shy. Rifle. Luella. Sheridan, fifteen feet away.

He crawled through the brush and snow to the rifle. He took off the safety then tilted his head, trying to sight. His arm screamed. He felt the warm wet growing inside his jacket. He breathed carefully, aware that his pulse was jacked up. If he could keep his breath steady…

He didn't wait in vain. The shadow of a man stepped out from behind the horse.

"Son of a bitch," Ellis breathed. Holding the rifle steady, he squeezed the trigger.

A cry flew out of the flurry, along with twin whinnies from the horses. Luella cried out, too.

Ellis lay very still, watching the shadow in his sights. It folded over. For a moment, he thought it would crumble to the ground.

It straightened instead and fled into the white wash.

Ellis got cautiously to his feet. "Lu?" he called, bringing the rifle up in front of him. He sidestepped to her, watching for the figure through his scope. "You all right?"

"Am *I* all right?" she called, getting cautiously to her knees. "You fell off your horse. Are you hit?"

He made a noise. The blood was running down the inside his sleeve. The wound was little fire torpedoes dancing up and down his arm. "I saw blood in the snow. Is that you or—"

"It's Sheridan," she said, urgent. "He's been hurt."

"Call him," Ellis said. "He doesn't look tethered."

"The bastard was using him for cover," Luella moaned.

"I know," he replied. "Call him. He won't come to me."

Luella lifted her fingers to her mouth and released a shrill whistle. "Here, boy! Come!"

Sheridan milled across the far point of their vision. Then his shadow grew stronger against the white.

"That's good!" Luella called. "Come here, boy! Come to mama!"

Ellis breathed a sigh of relief when Sheridan trotted the rest of the way to Luella. He kept himself between them and the last point he'd seen the man's shadow disappear into the storm.

"Oh, God, Ellis," Luella cried. "He's hurt. He's hurt real bad."

"It's all right," Ellis soothed, brushing his hand along the horse's flank. It was sticky with blood. "You can ride with me. We'll lead him back to the house and see if we can't get the doctor out to look."

DR. WILSTEAD SHOOK her head as she leaned over Sheridan's prone form. The horse lay sedated on the floor of the operating room at her office in Fuego. She patted the wound on Sheridan's croup with gauze. "This is a travesty," she muttered. "I hope they catch whoever did it."

Luella's hands were like ice even though she'd been indoors for over an hour now. Weariness was heavy in her bones.

Her baby was bleeding. Not to death. She knew that. Still, her mind went places she'd rather it didn't as she assisted Wilstead with the operation.

She swallowed. Her throat was bone dry. It was lucky Wilstead had agreed to let her into the OR. The doctor had needed an extra pair of hands and her regular assistants had all been snowed in. Lucky for Sheridan, Wilstead lived above stairs of her practice with her family. If not for her... what would she have done?

"We nearly did," Ellis said on Wilstead's far side. He was also assisting. "If it wasn't for this godforsaken storm, we'd have had him."

"I'm just going to sew Sheridan up now," Dr. Wilstead told them. She'd already located and extracted the bullet.

"It's small caliber," Luella said, studying the bloodstained slug in the petri dish at Wilstead's elbow.

"Nine millimeter," Ellis added.

"It's going to take a while for him to heal," Wilstead informed them. "But he's going to be all right."

"You'll keep him here," Luella surmised.

"I think that's best," Dr. Wilstead replied. She read Luella well. "He'll be safe. I promise."

Luella nodded, wishing she could believe just for a moment that either she or Sheridan could be safe again. "Thank you."

"There's water in the mini-fridge at the nurse's station," Wilstead revealed, stripping off her gloves. "You both look like you could use something to drink."

Luella felt fatigue pressing down on her eyelids. As she cleaned her hands in the sink in the corner of the room, she couldn't get the scent of Sheridan's blood from her nose.

She glanced back at him. His eyes were open, blank and staring.

Luella turned away when her stomach churned and nausea brimmed. She couldn't lose him. She just couldn't. Wilstead said he'd live, but Luella knew there was no going back to Ollero Creek. At least, not for Sheridan. And how was she supposed to face it without him?

She fled the operating room, wending through the halls of Wilstead's practice without direction. Everything ached—every muscle and joint.

She'd felt so alone out there. The storm had swept across Ollero Creek so quickly. She'd lost her way. If not for the blood in the snow...

But then the fear—the desperation, the despair. If anything happened to Sheridan...

Seeing Ellis come out of the whiteout like the fairy-tale knight he was had rocked her to her core.

He'd come for her—fighting cold and wind and snow. He'd come.

She tried to hold on to that feeling, the tidal wave of relief and faith and…well, she was very much afraid that the appropriate word was *love*. However, the fatigue crushed her. Her boots felt like they were lead-lined. Her head ached.

She felt like a soda can under a steel-toe boot, shrinking under pressure.

It was a familiar feeling. She remembered well how burnout had chased her through her graveyard shifts of the pandemic. This felt too close to that. And the numbness lurked, a blanket of shrink-wrap she knew she wouldn't be able to dislodge once it wrapped around her.

"You okay?"

She closed her eyes at the voice behind her at the nurse's station. Wilstead's practice was normally a hive of activity. Now there was no one in the hallway between the OR and the station.

Again, though, she found she wasn't alone.

His touch passed over her arm, then the other in long, soothing sweeps.

She felt her head tipping back to the warmth she knew was there—the warmth he'd offer in a heartbeat. Her pulse quickened at the promise of something that wasn't numb or bleak.

Ellis. The promise of him. Would it ever not be there if she did the impossible and stayed in Fuego? Could she really give up the promise of him?

When she didn't move or answer, she felt him close in. She didn't step away. She didn't even think it. *Tired*, she thought. It was the fatigue.

She could almost believe that. But as his head tipped down to hers, she felt his lips in the nest of her hair, then his cheek.

A shiver, infinitesimal, shimmered through her, lighting the way for him.

Closer, she thought.

It was inexplicable. But with Ellis came heat and she was so damn sick of being cold.

She wanted to feel. She wanted to feel him.

"He's okay," he murmured, mistaking her shiver for a sob. "Hey…" His hands trailed down her wrists until they found hers. He cupped her palms in his. "He's going to be okay."

She watched his long fingers twine with hers, interlocking. The texture of his skin was rough. She welcomed the friction. She felt her lashes flutter as his ribs pressed into the line of her shoulders on a long inhale.

He was breathing her in.

And, just like that, he flipped the switch and turned her on.

She didn't pull away like she should've. She didn't do anything like she should've.

My brother's in love with you, his sister had said just hours ago.

All this time? she wondered. Through it all—marriage, fatherhood, the life he'd lived apart from her?

He let go with one hand, tightened his grip on the other, bringing her around.

She was out of regrets and fresh out of excuses.

There was a contemplative bar between his eyes. He didn't quite meet hers, either. Instead, he studied their linked fingers, how they blended. How they fit.

She wanted to smooth that line. She wanted too much.

It didn't help at all when he raised her knuckles to his mouth. His eyes closed and the freckle on his eyelid flashed as he skimmed a kiss across them.

She felt so small and so full. The light of him pulsed

in her blood. It choked out of the emptiness. It shined so brightly it burned.

Her breath left her in a scattered rush. She pulled her hand from his and waited until his eyes snapped open and he began to understand what she wanted from him. Her arms twined around his neck.

His lips covered hers. She demanded that vital body-to-body contact. She opened her mouth to his, tilting her head and amping the kiss up until she forgot about storms.

Hunger gnawed and twisted low in her belly. His hands cradled the back of her head and his lips turned against her cheek then her ear, into her hair.

She tipped her head when his mouth found the sensitive place on the side of her neck they both knew was there. Shuddering, she opened her eyes and let the fluorescent lights on the ceiling blind her. She was soft and weak, alive and undone. It felt *so good.*

He made a deep, sexy noise in his throat. "You still shiver when I do this," he breathed against her throat. The words were hot against the damp circle his mouth left behind. "I can't… How am I supposed to *think* knowing you still shiver…?"

"Think?" she repeated. There was no thinking with Ellis—only churning, burning, aching…

He suckled that point on her throat.

Her nails dug into his shirt. If he didn't stop, he'd break her down. She'd be nothing—no strength left, no sense or pride.

She planted her hands on his shoulders and pushed.

He stumbled back a step. He was panting. A flush crawled up the length of his long, muscled throat. His open mouth closed, his lips turning inward as if to lock her taste in. His eyes were hooded and…

Oh, God. His eyes were the worst part. In them she saw everything he made her feel.

She told herself to look away. She didn't need to know what she did to him. She didn't need to know what he felt. As she touched her tingling mouth and watched him recover himself over the course of several ragged breaths, she realized she couldn't stop.

Later, she pledged. Later she'd blame it on the gunfight, and nearly losing her horse to a madman. But a smile bloomed, unbidden and absurd, on her lips.

His gaze tracked its progress. His eyes measured the wide curve of her mouth then the flush she felt on her cheeks. They circled her features then rolled back as he closed his eyes. "Oh hell," he cursed under his breath, bracing his hands on his hips as he turned a half circle away. "You're too much."

She'd seen his answering smile. It was shy and knowing, all in one.

Would he do this to her forever? She had to wonder. Was the answer to all her bad days, her dark moods...was it always going to be the one she'd abandoned?

She thought about tracing that flush with her fingertips. Better, her lips. But she found the wet black stain on the elbow of his jacket. Her lips parted, once, then released a distressed sound when the scent of blood again washed across her senses. "Ellis..." She gripped his shoulder, accessing the area. "You're hurt?"

His eyes, still steeped in her, touched on his sleeve. "I'm fine," he said. Then he grinned. "Honey."

She shook her head, all the good feelings gone. "You've been bleeding. You've been bleeding for a *while*."

"It's nothing, Lu," he said. "Just a graze."

"Graze..." Her thoughts flew back to the snow-covered

prairie. He'd fallen off Shy and hit the ground just after the second gunshot…

She began to tear at his jacket.

"What're you—"

"Uh-uh," she grunted, breaking off buttons and yanking down the zipper underneath to get to him. Her heart was in her throat. She yanked the collar loose over his shoulder, torqued it down his arm until she could get a decent look.

There was blood everywhere. It was hours old, but the smell of it and sweat stung her nostrils. Her stomach clutched. "Oh, *God*, Ellis! Why didn't you *say* something?"

"You were scared out of your mind about your horse. What was I supposed to say?"

"I don't know," she said with a sneer. "Maybe something like, 'Hey, you know what, honey? I've been *shot*!'"

He laughed and she checked the urge to deck him. When she tugged at the sleeve once more, trying to remove the jacket completely, he grimaced. "Easy, easy," he urged.

"Goddamn it," she growled. Grabbing him by the wrist, she trudged the rest of the way to the nurse's station, dragging him behind her. "Take off your damn clothes."

"The doc's in the next room," he warned. "I'm not sure we should—"

She whirled, planted her hands on his chest and knocked him back against the counter. "I'm not trying to get into your pants, you idiot! I'm trying to dress your wound! Take them off!" She started digging through cabinets and drawers, taking what she might need and muttering as she did.

"We need to have a conversation about your bedside manner," he considered.

"You really don't know when to shut up," she remarked, dumping her supplies on a tray. She washed her hands in the sink thoroughly before grabbing a pair of gloves from the open box next to it. She tugged the first one on, grabbing it by the wrist to fit it tight between her fingers as she turned back to him.

His jacket and shirt were gone. She saw the bloody mess of them on the floor. More, she saw the long line of his torso, the sprinkling of golden fuzz over the expanse of it, and the hard muscles under it, the wide, hard points of his shoulders and the stark line of his collarbone.

The wound was a few inches above the elbow. It glared red and was more than an inch in length.

She swallowed. "You've been carrying this. This whole time."

"It's fine," he said. There was no humor left on his face. "The blood makes it look worse than it is."

She glowered. "I'm a nurse, Ellis. I know what this is and it is *not* fine."

He blew out a breath and leaned his hips back against the counter she'd shoved him toward.

"Sit up there," she demanded, bringing the tray.

He hesitated, but at her approach, he eyed the tools and decided to comply. He pressed his hands down on the counter and boosted his hips over the edge, his triceps popping out at her as he did. His hair fell over his brow and she saw the pain contort his face. His eyes met hers, honest for the first time with the level of discomfort he was in.

Her irritation drained. Keeping her hands steady even when they wanted to shake, she starting mopping up the mess.

The corner of his mouth trembled in the upward position. "Be gentle with me," he whispered.

His breath washed over her cheek. She swabbed, daubed, discarded and repeated then angled his elbow so the lights shined on the gash. She cursed, long and dirty. "You need sutures."

"Bandage me up and I'll be—"

"If you say 'fine' one more time, Ellis, I swear to God—"

He lifted his free hand to stop her. "I get it. Sorry. Just… do what you've got to do, sweetheart. I trust you."

She glared at him for a handful of seconds before she went looking for more supplies.

It took a while to get him sewn up. He didn't make a sound, but she saw sweat beading on his brow and upper lip. The flush was gone, along with a good bit of his color, and his breathing was a touch labored.

When she was done, she stood back and studied her work. She gave a satisfied nod even though the smell of his blood was still strong in her nose.

What if the killer's aim hadn't been off? What if Shy hadn't bucked at the last second? What if that nine millimeter had gone in above the sternum, the same place his brother had taken a bullet six months ago?

"Thank you," he said.

"Don't," she said, pulling off the other glove. Turning to the sink, she disposed of the gloves then cranked the tap to scrub her hands. "You know the drill. Keep them dry. You should probably talk to your doctor and get an antibiotic. You don't want infection. Give the sutures two weeks. And try not to use that arm." When she'd washed her hands thoroughly, she dropped her face to the sink and splashed water on it.

She felt his hand low on her back. It feathered over her spine before coming to rest just above her belt. "I'm all right, Lu. You did a good job."

She shut off the water and reached blindly for the paper towels.

He handed her a wad. She patted her face dry. "Don't

you think too much Eaton blood has been spilled because of a Decker?"

"No more blood will be spilled on account of this guy. We're going to get him. I promise you."

"You've promised too much in the past," she reminded him. "It backfired. I don't want it to be that way again."

"I don't regret my promises," he stated. "I only regret letting you out of yours."

She straightened, wishing he'd step back, give her some room. "I shouldn't have called you tonight."

"God knows what would have happened to you out there if you hadn't."

"I should've called the deputy instead," she said. "I should've—"

"Do you know what it'd do to me," he asked, "to lose you like that?"

He sounded anguished. "You're the one who's hurt."

"Takes more than that to kill a man like me," he said, tugging her around to face him. "I think my brother's living proof of that."

"You may be an Eaton," she said cautiously. "But you're not imperishable."

He smiled once, a furtive movement that vanquished some of the trouble in his eyes. Then his gaze turned down over her mouth, following its curve.

She turned her face away. "Don't do that."

"What?"

"Kiss me again."

"You kissed me again, honey."

"Why did you let me?" she said, her voice rising enough to echo through the clinic halls.

He let out an unsteady laugh. His words dipped low. "Because it was worth it—*so* worth it."

"This is Fuego—where *everybody* talks."

"We're alone."

"People find things out. What if us kissing gets back to Liberty? What if she uses this to hurt you?"

His eyes darkened, growing troubled again. She hated it but did nothing to stop it. "One of us," she said heavily, "has to start thinking clearly again."

"Sure," he said with a small nod. He braced his hands on his hips. "You want me to apologize?"

"You're sorry?"

"You really want me to answer that?" he asked, hoarse.

No. Knowing exactly how un-sorry he was wouldn't be good for her at all. She sighed. "You have to stop."

"Stop what?"

She gathered her strength because his sexy drawl wasn't helping. "Stop kissing me back. Stop looking at me like… like you can't live without me—because we *both* know you can."

He stared, his gaze dark and conflicted.

"Just…stop," she finished with little breath or energy left. "Promise me that. Not for my sake…but for your own."

His eyes rolled up and around. They closed and he nodded, tipping his head to the side to ease the tension in his neck. "I promise," he returned.

She tried telling all the dark, downtrodden parts of herself that this was the way it had to be. This was the way things should have stayed between them. She'd let him shift the status quo. She'd let him move it a mile up the road and continue doing so until she lost every ounce of wherewithal she'd built. "Thank you."

"Just remember," he warned, his gaze coming back to hers with grim finality. "I keep my promises. You know that, Lu, better than anybody."

Her heart started to pound. She had to get out of here…

"You can't go home to Ollero Creek," he said. "We barely got out of your driveway to get here. I'd say it's a far sight worse now. The storm hasn't let up."

Her shoulders slumped. What was she supposed to do if she couldn't go back?

"Don't hit me," he asked of her.

She began to shake her head. "Why would I…"

"You need to come home," he said, "to the Edge. With me and Shy."

Automatically, she crossed her arms over her chest. Why did he have to say it like that? *Come home.* "I can't."

"Where else have you got to go?"

"The motel."

"Where's your wallet, Lu?" he asked. "Besides, I don't like the idea of you being alone someplace off the highway when the guy who took a shot at you and Sheridan is still out there. I called Altaha. She can't meet with us until tomorrow morning. She's trapped 'til morning on the rez visiting her mother. And I know damn good and well you don't want me calling Jones…"

She thought about that and shook her head.

"The road to the Edge will be clear. Everett and the hands will have made sure of it. They always do."

"Listen—"

"Sheridan's safe here with the doc and her family above stairs," he continued, unhindered.

"I know. I just—"

"I've promised not to kiss you or touch you or *look* at you. You know I'll hold by that."

"Ellis—"

"Come on home with me, Lu," he persisted, unrelenting. "I'll drive you back to Ollero Creek first thing in the morning. I promise."

When he broke down her excuses like that, what choice did she have?

Chapter Nine

Ellis knew how painful it must be for Luella to enter Eaton House after so much time. She hesitated on the threshold, eyeing the room beyond him with a wariness that slayed him.

He held the door open wider. "Come on, honey," he murmured. "It's cold."

She remained on the doorstep. He could see her building her weaponized defenses, one by one. The stillness was taking over, bricklaying the panic until she started to look glassy, just as he'd seen her look before.

He reached for her, but Paloma swooped in. "Ellis, where have you been? We were worried sick. And shut that door. You're letting the cold in." Before she could close the door for him, she found the woman on the other side. "Oh." Her demeanor changed. "Oh, you poor thing."

Ellis watched Paloma throw a strong arm around Luella's waist and guide her in, leaving her no choice but to enter. "Did you get snowed out instead of in, *niña*?" Paloma shut the door with a loud bang. Luella jumped. Ellis wanted to soothe her, but Paloma snapped her fingers at him. "Take her coat."

"Yes, ma'am." As Paloma rattled on about a warm meal and a hot bath, Ellis positioned himself behind Luella. He knew what he'd promised. What he wanted was to put his hands in the auburn waves of her hair. It'd fallen out of its strict braid and was messy and wet.

He made himself take her jacket by the shoulders as she unzipped and slipped her arms free. Paloma led her in the direction of the kitchen and Ellis hung her jacket on a rack on the wall next to his brother's. He was surprised to find both Eveline's and Wolfe's there as well. They had a full house.

Instead of slipping off his own jacket and joining his family in the kitchen, he went out the door again. Shoving his hands into the pockets of his jeans, he ducked his head low and trudged back to his truck. Shy needed to be stabled. He could do with a good grooming session and a blanket as well as his fair share of treats. He wished Isla and Ingrid were there to see to that. Shy ate up their attentions and they showered him with them, knowing he was Daddy's own horse.

He wondered what it would be like having them all at the table together—his girls and Luella. He unlatched the door on the horse trailer and walked Shy out onto snowy ground. As they came around the truck, a light hit his eyes. He raised his hand to block it.

Everett's voice came out of the dark, stringent. "I oughtta kill you."

Ellis blew out a breath. "After dinner. I'm starved."

"What the hell were you thinking?" Everett asked, dogging him step for step around the house. "I had to hear it from frickin' Wilstead that you tried to get yourself killed. Was this summer not enough? Has our family not lost enough?"

Ellis turned on him. "You think I don't know what this family's lost, Everett? I was there—waiting outside surgery for the doctors to tell us whether you lived or died. I was there beside you when Dad took his last breath. And I was there when Eveline was dragged into that frickin' hellhole. I have watched every remaining member of my family come up against death in the last year."

"So why'd you decide to go chasing it, too?" Everett wanted to know. "If I'd known you'd leave the ranch and run off to risk your life for that woman, I wouldn't have kept you in charge."

"Her name's Luella, you son of a bitch," Ellis snapped. "You *know* her name! And you want me out as acting chief, you say the word."

Everett glowered in the light from the porch. It crossed streams with the light from the stables, casting odd shadows in the thickening sludge around their boots. "You know what it feels like to almost lose a brother. Did you need me to know, too?"

"I didn't do this to scare you," Ellis said. "I did it because—"

"Oh, hell, Ellis, don't say you love her," Everett intervened. "There's no coming back from that stupidity."

"You're right," Ellis said, walking on with Shy. "There's not."

"Seventeen years," Everett said, on his heels. "Seventeen years and you still can't let go. Not if your life or your family depends on it."

Ellis was done with the conversation—so done.

"I know you tried to hide her here," Everett revealed. "When Whip beat her so bad, she couldn't go to school for two weeks. You hid her in the rooms above the stables. You took her food, soap, clothes and blankets."

Ellis didn't say anything. It was too hard a place to revisit, even if he did wonder how Everett had found out when no one else had.

"I know you looked for a place for her in Taos," Everett continued, dogging Ellis and Shy into the stable. Out of the wind, his voice grew louder. "Near your dorm where you two could be close to each other. Maybe even live together."

Ellis led Shy into his stall. He went about the process of uncinching and unsaddling.

Everett hung on the gate, his arm long over the top. "I know you gave her a ring."

Ellis's hands stopped for a second—only a second—before he recovered himself. He carried the saddle out of the stall when Everett opened the gate for him and walked it to the tack room.

"Whatever happened to that ring, anyway?" Everett asked. "A whole carat, right? Set you back around fifteen grand."

Ellis lifted the saddle into its place. "How the hell do you know that?"

"I have eyes," Everett said. "I have ears. More, I know you. I know how your mind works, and your heart. Where Luella's concerned, you've got too much of one and not enough of the other."

Ellis blew past him again, grabbing a grooming tote while he was at it.

"You don't think you need to ask my permission?" Everett asked. "To keep her here."

Ellis checked the urge to kick the gate open, but only just. "She's got nowhere else to go. And I own twenty percent of the Edge, same as you. You want me to get Eveline so her forty can stack up against you too?"

"She'll stack 'em against me on principle," Everett muttered. He spat in the hay. "Both of you. Thorns in my side. Liberty called, by the way."

That did stop Ellis. The brush in his hand fell to his side. He shuffled from Shy to the gate and reluctantly looked down the row of stalls at his brother's long form.

"When were you going to tell me?" Everett asked. "I might be looking across the table at her instead of you during board meetings next year."

"It's not going to happen."

"So you're giving up on your girls, then? Just like that?"

Ellis swung the gate open. The brush dropped to the ground. "Is that what you think of me?"

"Man's too much a fool to stay away from his mistress?" Everett questioned. "There's not much else he wouldn't do."

Ellis's strides quickened. "I don't care what kind of shape you're in. I'm going to kick your ass."

Everett pushed off the wall, shoulders high. He made a come-hither motion. "Come on, boo. I'm ready."

Ellis's hand curled into a fist, eyeing the smug line of Everett's mouth. Before he could do something about it, a loud whistle cut through the stables. Several horses startled. They stamped their feet. Ellis's feet came up short when he saw the figure of his future brother-in-law, Wolfe Coldero, in the doorway.

He frowned at the pair of them and raised a brow underneath the brim of his old black felt hat. Mute since childhood, he raised his hands in a question.

Everett sneered. His and Wolfe's feud had been long but had finally cooled when it had been Wolfe who had gone into the depths of the box canyon to rescue Eveline from Decker. Still, there was some lingering resentment on Everett's part that was unlikely to be put to bed anytime soon. "Always the frickin' hero," he muttered, backing away from

Ellis. "Maybe you can talk some sense into him," he added as he passed Wolfe on the way out.

Ellis took several breaths to calm himself. He never came to blows with Everett. It was Ellis who deescalated things before they could get that far.

The pain in his arm gnawed at him. He relaxed his fist and avoided Wolfe's gaze as the man approached, patting each horse on the nose that stuck its head out to greet him. He had a way with horses and Ellis's sister that was uncanny.

Ellis picked up the brush and grabbed Shy by the bridle. He'd followed Ellis halfway out of his stall. Ellis steered him back in then went through the motions of grooming him.

Wolfe stopped at the gate, observing. He lifted his shoulders.

"Fine," Ellis responded. "On edge, is all."

Wolfe lifted his hand to his own arm.

Ellis recognized it as the place he'd been shot. "It's just a graze."

Wolfe tipped his chin up but stopped short of a reassured nod. His hands moved in a language both he and Ellis had made up as children and young adults. *Luella's shaken up.*

Ellis considered, picking the hair out of the brush bristles. "Probably from being back here more than anything."

Wolfe nodded. *Were you really going to fight him?*

"I wanted to," Ellis said, truthfully. "What does that make me—kicking a man when he's down?"

Wasn't that what he was doing to you?

Ellis chose not to answer. "I'm not giving up my girls. He has to know that."

I know you won't.

"Liberty was having an affair," Ellis revealed. "A real one with Walker Sullivan. Did you know?"

I would have told you.

Wolfe would have told him, Ellis knew. "I can fight her. I don't have to give her anything, if I play my cards right."

We'll help.

Ellis nodded. "Thanks. How is she, other than shaken up?"

They both knew to whom he was referring. Wolfe had witnessed more of Ellis and Luella's relationship than others had. They'd even taught her a good deal of their sign language. Wolfe's hands moved to show him. *Settling some. Paloma's helping.*

Wolfe pushed his way into the stall. He clapped Shy on the chest a few times, ran his large hand along his withers. He held out his hand.

Ellis stopped and looked at the man's face.

It was broad-planed and maybe more familiar than his own. He eyed the brush.

"I can finish," Ellis protested.

Wolfe's hands milled in explanation. *You're dead on your feet. I'll finish up.*

Ellis blew out a breath. He *was* tired, damn it. The events of this afternoon were catching up with him. It wasn't just his arm that hurt, he found, but the line of his shoulders and spine from being unseated. Blowing out a breath, he relinquished the brush to Wolfe. "Thanks."

Wolfe patted him on his uninjured arm then went about the chore of tucking Shy in for the night.

LUELLA STOOD BY while Eveline and Paloma made her a pallet in front of the fire in the office. "I can just sleep on the couch."

"Nonsense," Paloma chided. "You need something better than that on nights like these. Especially after what you've been through."

Luella felt at a loss. It was an empty, aching feeling she couldn't suppress any more than her fatigue. "I don't have to sleep in the house. I know there's room above the stables."

"They're being renovated," Eveline revealed, patting a pillow to flatten it. "My father left the rooms to Paloma so she wouldn't have to commute from town anymore." She glanced up at Luella, tossing the hair out of her face. "Besides, Ellis wouldn't want you so far away as that."

Luella couldn't think about what Ellis wanted, any more than she could think about what she wanted. She'd seen the stairs. Did the eighth tread up still shriek like it had when she was younger? Did Ellis still sleep in the third bedroom on the right?

"I'll loan you some clothes," Eveline offered as she stood up. "I keep some things here for nights like this."

Luella bit her lip. Then she remembered herself and said, "Thank you." She looked to Paloma. "You've done too much."

"Think nothing of it," Paloma said, standing with some help from Eveline. "We're just glad you're okay after that mess today."

Luella opened her mouth to respond but was interrupted by a knock on the door. When she saw Ellis at the door with his good arm raised against the jamb and his tired eyes, she closed it quickly. He hadn't had a chance to change, either, and he looked as ragged as she felt. His gaze skipped past his sister and Paloma and landed squarely on her. "You doing okay?"

"Fine," Luella said.

Ellis eyed the pallet. He stepped in. "I'll sleep here. You go upstairs."

"No!" she protested. "No, this is fine. There's nothing wrong with—"

"Lu," he said, quietly. "I am too tired to argue. I'm sleeping here. You take my room."

"I don't want—"

"It's one night," he said, near exasperation. "I won't be able to sleep if you don't."

Luella felt both Paloma's and Eveline's gazes. She wanted to turn away from all of them. *Sleep in Ellis's room?* How could she possibly?

Paloma decided for her. "Right this way, Luella Belle." She eyed Ellis after taking Luella's hand. "You need a shower."

Ellis's mouth quirked in a ghost of a grin. "You sweet thing."

As Luella followed Paloma out, she couldn't help herself. She raised her eyes to his. They held for one second—two too long. His gaze flickered briefly over her mouth before Paloma tugged her gently on.

The eighth tread didn't just shriek anymore. It screamed. On the landing, Paloma turned to the right.

One, Luella counted as she passed the first door. Her heart picked up pace, just as it had when following Ellis through the darkness when she was eighteen. *Two. Three.*

Paloma flipped on the light and went about tidying while Luella stood frozen in the doorway. "I just changed the sheets this morning. He hasn't slept in them."

"Slept in them?" Luella repeated numbly, eyeing the bed. Everything was just as it had been.

"You'll want a shower," Paloma said. "I'll get you that change of clothes from Eveline. You didn't eat much at dinner. Do you want me to bring something up? Some comfort food to help you settle?"

What was this, a luxury hotel? Luella shook her head faintly.

Paloma sighed over her. She trudged back to the door, took her by the hand and made her sit on the bed.

Luella watched Paloma take off her boots, as if from far away. Her head was floating. This couldn't be happening. She couldn't be back...

"It'll all be all right," Paloma said, patting and rubbing her hand. "Are you sure you don't need anything else?"

Luella stared at her. "I... I don't know what I'm doing here."

Paloma squeezed her hand. "You need sleep," she murmured. "That's what you're here for. Remember?"

Luella found herself nodding, latching onto the simplicity.

"You'll get yourself cleaned up," Paloma said, "because when your head hits that pillow, Luella Belle, you won't have to think about it. You'll just rest."

"Are you sure?" Luella asked, her voice wavering. She was shocked by the weakness.

"Absolutely," Paloma said with a smile. "And if you don't believe me, I can send up something to help you do so."

Luella thought about it. Then she shook her head vigorously. "No. I'm... I'll be fine."

Paloma's smile turned into a full-fledged grin. "Thatta girl." She patted her hand some more like she was a child again. "Morning's the time for all those pestering thoughts."

"Right," Luella said, nodding. "You're right." She squeezed Paloma's hand back. "Thank you. You've been..." She didn't know how to finish without breaking down completely.

"We'll talk, if you like," Paloma said. "In the morning."

"In the morning," Luella parroted. When Paloma got up to start the shower in the adjoining bathroom, Luella released a long breath. She tried not to look at the pattern of the bedspread—blue and green striped—or the antlers over the door—Ellis's first buck. She tried not to look at the bookshelf with the medical journals or textbooks…or the shirts hanging inside the open closet.

She did her best not to see or smell anything. Because too much of it would force her back into all the tender, loving memories she'd tried so desperately to suppress.

PALOMA HAD BEEN right, thank God. Luella slept a hard, dreamless sleep that put her out of her misery. When she woke, groggy and wondering briefly if she'd been drugged at some point, she felt a familiar weight on her chest. Opening her eyes, she stared into a set of unblinking yellow ones and frowned. "Sphinx?"

She sat up in bed. Sphinx shrank to her belly at the sudden movement. Her purring ceased.

Luella let out a shuddering breath, scooping the cat into her arms. "Where did you come from?" she asked, bringing Sphinx's cheek to her own.

The cat's purring set off again with a vengeance. She bumped her head against Luella's hand and arched her back under the glide of a stroke.

Luella looked around. She was in Ellis's room. The sun was gleaming through the slight parting in the curtains. Cradling Sphinx, she swung her legs over the side of the bed. In the bathroom, she brushed her teeth with the toothbrush and toothpaste Paloma had loaned her. She tried finger-combing the curly mass on top of her head but gave up.

She was stunned to find her clothes from yesterday clean and folded on Ellis's dresser. As she dressed, letting Sphinx twine around her ankles, she studied the two hand-drawn illustrations taped to the mirror. The one signed *Isla* in tidy cursive was a sweet rendering of three cartoonish figures on horseback. The other signed *Ingrid* in uneven print letters was what appeared to be a picture of three dragons. The largest dragon with its wings wrapped around the two smaller ones was labeled *Dadee.*

Luella blinked several times. She shoved her feet into her boots. Then she picked up Sphinx and opened the door.

Three large dogs waited outside. They were belly-down on the floor, having had their noses pressed to the parting between it and the hardwood. As one, they jumped to their feet when she appeared.

"Now, now," she warned when they lifted their noses toward the cat for a curious sniff. She felt Sphinx tense. "Stay back."

One did a small bunny hop onto its back legs, getting far too close for comfort. Sphinx hissed and Luella took a step back into the room.

"Down," called a voice from down the hall.

Luella peered around the jamb. She felt her stomach clutch at the sight of Everett. He closed the door of his room smartly as the dogs came to greet him with a scritchity-scratch of claws. His hand reached down to pat each of their heads. "Outside?" he asked and they quickened, ruffing in whispers from their long throats. He finished buttoning the cuffs of his shirt as he led them to the stairs. "Should've figured you for a cat person," he muttered as he passed.

Luella narrowed her eyes but said nothing as his steps and those of his furry companions clattered down the stairs together. Tucking Sphinx under her chin, she gave him time to get all the way down before starting downstairs, too.

She followed the smells of breakfast into the kitchen. There she found Wolfe, Eveline and Everett, having just let his dogs out the back door, around a large butcher-block table and Paloma hovering over all of them.

Luella felt like an imposter.

"Lu."

She closed her eyes briefly as the low word trickled down the length of her neck. Turning, she found Ellis. He was already dressed, clean-shaven and smelling of aftershave. "Good morning," he offered.

His dark eyes shined in such a way that made her warm and toasty. "Morning," she returned. She thought of his arm. "How are you?"

"Riding high on Mexican coffee and anti-inflammatories," he said wryly. "Did you sleep?"

"I did," she said. "You shouldn't have given up your bed for me."

"It was worth it," he said, "to see you looking so rested. You found a friend."

"She found me," Luella said, petting Sphinx on the head. "How did she get here?"

"Naleen Altaha," he said, braving a scratch under Sphinx's chin. "She and Terrence stopped by Ollero Creek to check on you early this morning. When they didn't find you, she called after me to see if I knew where you were."

"Why would she call you?" Luella asked.

"Because her sister, the deputy, told her if anybody knows where you are, it's me."

Luella frowned. "Oh."

"She brought the other one, too," he muttered, "in a cat carrier with some choice words. He seemed more interested in the stables so I let him go out there. That's okay?"

Luella nodded. "He's a free spirit."

"He's somethin'," Ellis opined. "Caesar's out there, too."

She gaped. "She brought my rooster?"

"And your purse and phone," he said. "And some extra clothes and toiletries, if you need them."

"Does she think I'm moving in?"

"Until we find out more about whoever's trying to attack your animals, I have a mind to keep you."

Keep you. The words echoed from far off. When she'd recovered from a beating from her father after recouping above the stables at the Edge, Ellis had wanted her to stay—permanently. *I could keep you*, he'd said, his brow touching hers. *My father kept Wolfe, for a time. He can keep you.*

Wolfe didn't have a home, she'd reminded him. *I do.*

You're not safe there. If you stay, nothing will ever hurt you again. I promise.

She shook her head to stop herself from going through the rest. She hadn't stayed. She hadn't been safe. And all that was good about her life—Ellis, college, everything—had fallen away from there.

"She won't feed us until you both sit."

Luella glanced back at Everett's complaint and saw, alarmed, that everyone at the table was watching. She stepped away from Ellis. "I'd like my things," she told him.

He nodded to the counter. "That's your bag there."

It was. And Naleen was blessedly thorough. Luella found clean jeans, shirts, underwear and socks. There was her own toothbrush, toothpaste, deodorant...

She was going to have to send Naleen something in return, though she had no idea what.

"Do you have everything you need?" Eveline asked.

Luella stuffed her things back into the bag. "It seems so."

"If you need anything else," Eveline told her, "let me know."

Everett groaned then threw his head back and shouted, *"Breakfast!"*

Paloma swatted him on the shoulder. "Manners!"

"We're coming," Ellis said. He pushed something at Luella.

It was a mug. "Oh," she said, looking down into the murky contents. "Thank you."

He winked. "Milk and honey."

She placed both hands around the cup of coffee. Milk and honey was how she used to take it. She lifted it to her nose. The aroma curled up her nostrils.

Paloma piled her plate high with *huevos rancheros*, salsa fresca, fried potatoes, avocado, and refried beans. Wolfe looked amused when she glanced up at him with wide eyes. "Wow," she mouthed.

He unrolled his fork and knife from his napkin and placed them on either side of his plate. He put the napkin in his lap and, with his hands, signed, *Eat up, little sister.*

Luella followed his example, unrolling her utensils and placing her napkin on her lap before digging in. She caught Ellis observing her from the corner of his eye. He only started eating after she did.

It was delicious. She noticed none of the others talked. Was it because the food was that good or because she was there?

She'd never had breakfast with the Eatons—not in all the months she'd been with Ellis in high school. He'd snuck her out the front door a few times while Everett and Eveline sat down to the early-morning meal with their father. Other than some snatched leftovers from Paloma's table, Luella had never been privy to a place at it.

"*Hola*, Eatons!" someone called from the front of the house.

Ellis dropped his fork, lifted his napkin to wipe his mouth and started to rise. "That's the deputy."

"Deputy Sweetheart?" Everett asked.

"Deputy Altaha," Paloma corrected him. "You'll be good."

Luella frowned at the food left on her plate. Taking one last sip of coffee, she started to rise, too.

"Ellis," Paloma said, "carry Luella's plate to the office. If the deputy's going to question the both of you, you might as well do it on a full stomach."

Luella began to shake her head. "That's not necessary..."

On her left, Everett made a noise. "Rule number one— don't argue with Paloma. She'll make your life a living hell."

"Language," Paloma barked.

"Number two," Everett continued, "swear all you like at the dinner table so someone can be further up her hit list than me."

Luella didn't know how to take this. She narrowed her eyes.

Eveline helped her out. "Rule number three—never listen to Everett. His interests are completely self-serving."

ALTAHA FROWNED BEHIND the office desk. "I'm still confused as to why *you're* here."

Everett reached up to take the toothpick from the corner of his mouth. "I'm his representative."

Ellis exchanged a glance with Altaha and looked studiously back down at his written statement from yesterday's shootout. "I'll plead my own case, if it's all the same to you, brother."

"Nobody here's a suspect, cattle baron," Altaha explained to Everett. "I'm just taking statements. And some details of the case are being kept under wraps for investigative purposes."

"What's Jones's take on all this?" Everett asked curiously.

Altaha eyed him over the length of the room. It was similar to the long, cool look she'd extended him over cards.

"Ellis, is your representative suggesting he wants a second opinion on this case?"

"Not my representative," Ellis repeated. "*So* not my representative."

"If you have a complaint about my performance," Altaha went on, "please do feel free to kiss my ass."

The corner of Everett's mouth quirked. Maybe to hide a grin, he stuck the toothpick between his teeth again. "Damned if I don't like you, Deputy Sweetheart."

"Are they...?" Luella began under her breath.

"I think he's trying?" Ellis muttered back.

The door opened at Everett's back, knocking him off balance. He scowled when Eveline poked her head in. "What are you doing?" she asked him.

"Leanin', if it's all the same to you," he grumbled.

She rolled her eyes then sought the others in the room. "Luella, this is for you."

Luella reached out for the phone. Everett gave in, taking it from his sister and walking it across the room.

"It's been ringing," Eveline revealed.

"Thanks," Luella said. She unlocked the phone and checked her call list. She frowned. "Oh."

"What is it?" Ellis asked.

"Nothing," Luella said. "It's just...my mother. She never calls me."

"Riane?" Ellis watched her stand and pace to the far corner of the room. As long as he could remember, Riane Decker, or Howard or whatever the woman went by now, had given Luella the cold shoulder. Where Whip's wrath had been all fire and brimstone, Riane's answer to that had been torrents of shooting ice.

"Paloma needs you," Eveline chided Everett.

"Now?" he asked.

"Now!" Eveline said.

Everett groaned and followed her out.

"You'll need to sign that," Altaha said, bringing Ellis's attention back to his statement.

He scratched his signature across the bottom and handed it over the desk. "We never got a good look at the guy."

Altaha tapped the edge of the documents on the desktop to straighten them. "We know the assailant carried a small caliber weapon."

"But other than that, no leads."

"Apart from the fact that he's escalated from breaking necks to using a handgun," Altaha commented, looking over their statements carefully. "It's a man. We know that now from both your and Luella's descriptions. He also likes to strike when Luella is home at Ollero Creek."

Ellis nodded. "That's what concerns me."

"It's ballsy, too," Altaha said. "Ballsy criminals are my favorite."

"Why's that?" Ellis asked, bewildered.

"Because they normally have an abundance of overconfidence. That leads quickly to recklessness and that leads inevitably to mistakes. If the storm didn't knock them out, Luella had her game cameras turned back on for this one."

Ellis thought about it. "Damn. You're right."

"We might have an APB out on this sucker by the afternoon. The sooner we get an arrest, the sooner Luella can go home again. I hope Liberty's not stopping by before then."

"Not until next weekend when she's supposed to drop off the girls," Ellis answered. Though who knew if she'd be doing that, after the threats she'd been making about his parental rights?

"Hmm," Altaha said. "Have you spoken with Rosalie, the former Mrs. Sullivan?"

"I've been busy," Ellis said.

"I see that," Altaha said pointedly.

He tried to think of a retort but heard a curse from Luella's direction. "What's the matter?"

Luella stared at her phone. "It's my aunt Mabel. She's just...passed away."

Altaha folded her hands as compassion took over her face. "I'm sorry to hear that."

Ellis rose but stayed back when Luella lifted a hand. "No," she anticipated him. "I... I need a minute."

"When is the service?" he wanted to know.

"Tomorrow," Luella said. She lifted the phone then lowered it. "She's been gone for a couple of days. My mother's just gotten around to telling me."

Frickin' Riane. "I'm sorry, Lu. I know how much you loved Mabel. Do you need a ride?"

He noticed she didn't meet his eye. "This is something I need to do alone. I need to check on Sheridan before I go..."

Altaha placed their statements together in a folder. "I can drive you there and back to your house."

Ellis shook his head. "I don't like the idea of you being there on your own."

"She won't be alone," Altaha informed him. "I'll be there."

"What about Sphinx, Nyx and Caesar?" Luella asked. "They should come home, too."

"No," Ellis said. "They stay here. I told you. Until this guy is caught, you all need to stay here."

Luella sighed. "I don't think it's up to you to decide what it is I need."

Chapter Ten

Luella spent most of her time at the funeral looking at Mabel's self-portrait, a colorful abstract painting. It didn't have one straight edge or line. Mabel had had an abhorrence for straight edges and lines—neutral palettes. Realism.

It was a wonder she and Luella's mother, Riane, the bitter pragmatist, had lived together for two decades. Part of that was Mabel's disabilities, Luella knew. Mabel had had Treacher Collins syndrome, a rare disease she had suffered from even through childhood that had caused facial deformities. Because of negative reactions from people in the community of both Fuego where she grew up and San Gabriel where she moved to be closer to doctors, she had developed a strong aversion to leaving the house.

Luella remembered holding Mabel's hand as they walked down the sidewalk. Her fingers had been so tense. Normally bubbly and loquacious, Mabel had been reticent, as if fear had given her lockjaw. Even as a teenage girl, Luella had known her hand was a lifeline and had refused to let go, especially when people pointed.

People who knew the real Mabel couldn't help but fall in love with her. She was a kind soul who liked to paint people against her signature abstract backgrounds. She'd especially loved working with the physically and mentally disabled and in later years had taught art classes to them in her backyard. She'd liked to laugh until she cried, always smoothing over Riane's harsher points with cheer and encouragement. Riane complained constantly about how Mabel saw the world through rose-colored glasses.

"Why didn't you tell me she was sick?" Luella muttered at her mother in the front pew of the church.

"Shh!" Riane replied. "We're in the middle of the service!"

"I had a right to know," Luella said, unhindered.

Riane glanced over each shoulder. The organist drowned out Luella's voice. No one was listening. "You've been busy, haven't you—in jail?"

She breathed the last two words in a scandalized undertone. Luella frowned at her. "I was allowed mail and phone calls. And I've been back now for two weeks. I'm sure it was in the newspaper."

"She didn't ask for you."

Riane knew that would be the deepest cut of all. Luella looked down at the program for the service. There were no pictures of Mabel's face. Shouldn't there be pictures? "I think you're a liar. She sent letters to my house—"

"Letters." Riane turned her head to look at Luella fully for the first time. "What letters?"

"Postcards," Luella said. "Photographs."

Riane visually flinched. "What did the postcards say?"

"Wouldn't you like to know?" Luella challenged.

Riane's lips firmed and she looked away.

"How did she post the letters if you didn't know about them?" Luella asked, confused. "I thought she was bedridden."

Riane stared rigidly at the altar. She spoke out of the side of her mouth, her voice vibrating with fury. "That nurse.

The one from the hospice service. She must've snuck them out under my nose."

Luella scowled. "You denied a dying woman's wish to talk to her niece," Luella said. "I'd pray harder if I were you."

"If we're praying for our sins," Riane said through hardened teeth, "then you'll have to rush to get ahead of yours."

Devil's spawn. Harlot. Whore. Luella felt the sting of the words as if they were more than memories—as if Riane had spoken them here in the church. The satisfied smile that settled over Riane's mouth made Luella's posture cave and her will to stand up for herself wilt altogether.

WHILE A GOOD many people had turned up at the church service and subsequent burial, particularly Mabel's old students, Luella found herself alarmingly alone with her mother and stepfather at the old house on Tesuque Lane.

For a time, Luella stood outside the two-story abode. It was much like all the other houses on the street. Luella remembered how Mabel had made it different—a brighter coat of paint, untrimmed garden flowering most of the year in plumes and spikes with wacky wind-spinners galore. It had looked like an artist's haven.

Her mother had taken out much of the plants, leaving only square hedges along the house front. The house had been repainted a neutral tone, and the wind-spinners—where were they? Had Riane thrown them out, and if so, when—before or after Mabel's passing?

Was it even the same house? When Luella entered, would she be able to feel Mabel's spirit at all?

It was painful crossing the threshold, far worse than entering Eaton House. Not just because Mabel was gone, either. She didn't want to remember being eighteen in this house and all the disappointment and anguish she'd brought with her. No bags but far too much baggage. If not for Mabel…would she have survived any of it?

The mismatched, shabby-chic decor had indeed been replaced by a carefully culled assortment of antiques. There was no artwork anymore. Mabel's abstract world had been erased.

Biting her tongue, Luella veered into the kitchen, where she found Riane and Solomon. The former was making coffee while the latter read the newspaper. "Luella," Solomon said. He looked cautiously at Riane. "This is a surprise."

Luella reminded herself she had nothing against the man her mother had married—only how Riane had used him and his fine community standing as a means of covering up every aspect of her previous life in Fuego with Whip Decker. "Nice to see you, too, Sol." She placed her purse on the counter and noted that her mother's back was still to her. "I ran into the hospice aid you mentioned. Betty. She said something about a box for me?"

When Riane didn't answer, Solomon hefted himself to his feet. At three hundred pounds, he couldn't do this so easily. "I believe it's upstairs. You girls catch up. I'll go hunt it down."

"Thanks, Sol," Luella said. "You weren't going to tell me about the box," she surmised when she and Riane were alone. "Just like you didn't tell me Mabel wanted to see me—so much so she had to sneak messages out of the house."

"Don't be dramatic," Riane muttered, taking down two mugs. She poured coffee into the first, then the second. She sugared them both, poured in cream. Setting the second mug next to Solomon's newspaper, she faced Luella over the length of the kitchen table. Eyeing her in the detached way she'd grown so accustomed to, she lifted her mug to her lips and drank.

Run. The message always came—a scream of adrenaline after any small amount of time spent in her mother's company. Luella felt the stir of minute hairs on the back of her neck and the sharp twist behind her navel that made her feet itch for the exit. It wasn't just the biting words and dirty looks that made Luella want to head for the hills. Something in Riane's manner never failed to make Luella feel not just like the unwanted daughter but prey.

Riane sighed. "That man's slower than Christmas," she muttered. "It's a box full of junk. Nothing of value. You could leave without it."

"Mabel wanted me to have it," Luella said. "That means something."

"Don't expect anything from the will. She left the house to me and Solomon."

"What about the art?" Luella asked.

"What about it?"

"It's missing," Luella said. "What have you done with that? What were her wishes for it?"

Riane's mouth folded into a thin line. "It's being stored in her studio outside. Once we convert it into a garage, however—"

"Let me guess. You'll put it on the street."

"I'm sure her students will collect some of it."

Luella shook her head. "You're unbelievable."

"What would you have me do?" Riane challenged. "It's not worth anything. She wasn't a celebrated artist."

"She was known well enough regionally," Luella said. "You could open a gallery. Do showings. Sol's got some savings, hasn't he? Or have you blown it all on renovations and antiques?"

"Solomon's money is none of your concern," Riane said tightly. "None whatsoever."

"I don't want his money," Luella said. "I don't want Mabel's house. I want what she left me. And then I want never to speak with you again because the only reason you and I have interacted over the last ten years was because of her. Now she's gone and, I'm sure you'll be happy to know, so am I."

Riane searched her. "Where will you go?"

"I don't know," Luella said. "Somewhere where I'll never have to think about you or my father again, preferably."

"A sinner can't run from her sins," Riane opined.

Luella narrowed her eyes. "It's a sin to be born, Mother—or a sin to be your daughter?"

"It's a sin to carry a man's child out of wedlock," Riane retorted plainly enough.

Luella seamed her mouth shut to keep in the cry that wanted to pierce the jagged silence. She said nothing as twin wails of grief and anger keened inside her.

Riane was moved to smile by Luella's inner turmoil. "You forget… I know all your nasty secrets. It was me who brought you to Mabel's so that you could be saved."

"Is that what happened?" Luella whispered, her voice lost.

"What happened was willed," Riane said pointedly, "by God, and no less than you deserved, whore that you are."

Luella blinked several times. She looked around the kitchen—at the oversized wooden knife, fork and spoon on the wall, at the large unadorned cross over the kitchen table. "Somebody should go check on Sol," she muttered. Before her mother could, she backed away. "I'll go. It'll give me a chance to say a proper goodbye to Mabel. Is her room still the one on the end with the windows?"

"Mind you don't slip anything in that bag of yours on the

way there and back," Riane warned, taking several steps after her. "I'm not afraid to call the authorities."

Luella didn't dignify that with a response. She practically fled up the stairs to Mabel's room and almost bowled over Solomon on the landing.

"Careful there, darlin'," he said with a chuckle. "Don't want you taking a tumble down those stairs."

The comment was completely innocent. He couldn't have known. There was no way her mother would've told him anything. But nothing could be more devastating for Luella to hear. She accepted the box, cradling it to her. "Excuse me," she said and veered around him.

She shut herself inside Mabel's room. The medical bed was still in place but it had been stripped. Bouquets of flowers were packed across the raised surface of both the armoire and dresser, some on the floor. They were in various states of decay. The smell was heady, almost overwhelming. Luella set the box on the bed, along with her bag, and absorbed the silence.

Bracing her hands on her hips, she tried to find some semblance of Mabel.

Not even here, she thought. Her mother worked fast. Not one paintbrush lay scattered across the floor. The grains of the wood panels had been scrubbed of their paint flecks. There were no knickknacks—nothing.

She took the lid off the box. Pulling out the contents, she spread them across the blank canvas of the mattress.

They weren't Mabel's things, but her own—things she'd left when she departed the house after her convalescence. Books, she found. Comfort reads she'd found little comfort in at the time. Notebooks. She opened them not to find writings but pressed wildflowers from desert walks. She pulled out a sketchpad and flipped it open without thinking.

Charcoal sketches leaped out at her. They had been done at Mabel's tutelage. She let the pad fall away from her hands to the mattress, unable to touch the profile of Ellis's face, or any of the others she knew followed.

She'd sketched other things—thickets of rough Indian paintbrush, the gnarled twists of an old Colorado pinyon, constellations, mountains and clouds... But she'd always come back to Ellis's face like the glutton for punishment she was. She'd never drawn him from photographs. She hadn't had any. She'd sketched him from heady, passionate memory.

Mabel had begged her to go to art school. Luella hadn't been able to drum up the energy for more dreams. She'd seen too many tattered. So she'd rushed headlong into nursing school, determined to drown her grief with the busywork that came with being a trauma nurse.

The baby's layette made her hands fumble, too. Mabel had chosen things in fragile yellow, white and mint... The blanket they'd spent many a night cursing viciously over hooks and slip stitches had somehow managed to turn into something soft and delicate, if not perfect.

Luella raised it from its folds and pressed it to her cheek. *There's no end to a good mother's love*, Mabel had told her soothingly when she'd returned home to Tesuque Lane, arms and womb empty. *You're a good mother, 'ella. You cry. I'll sit here with you as long as you do.*

She carefully placed everything back into the box. She did so neatly, in the same order as she'd found it.

When she put the lid on, Luella reached into her purse and took out the postcards. *Baby. Mother. Father.* Those were the first three messages. Luella set them aside, trying not to think of the broken triangle that pointed from her to Ellis and the life she'd hidden from him and lost.

W.J.

Luella bit her lip. Were these initials? She racked her brain and couldn't see how they connected to her, Ellis or the baby.

S.G.W.C.

The abbreviation was too long to be initials. Maybe it were an acronym—for an organization or a place...

S.G. could stand for San Gabriel. And *W.C.*.... Luella thought hard.

Baby. Mother. San Gabriel.

Luella stared at the letters as something dawned. Her lips parted. "San Gabriel Women's Center," she whispered to the walls.

She'd been taken to San Gabriel Women's Center by her mother the day she fell down the stairs here on Tesuque Lane.

As she looked at the next postcard and the letter and numbers scrawled across them, she lost her breath. *S.9.06.*

September 9, 2006. The date it had happened.

How had she not seen it before? *Baby. Mother. Father. San Gabriel Women's Center. September 9, 2006.*

Mabel had needed to speak to her about her baby...or the day her baby had been brought into the world via Cesarean section without a heartbeat.

But why?

And how did that tie into the remaining messages—*W.J.* and *Nightstand*?

She eyed the nightstand close at her hip. Reaching out, she gripped the little round knob and pried it open.

Empty.

Damn it. Her head was starting to hurt but she went back to poring over the messages, willing them to make sense.

Nightstand.

Her gaze fell on the door. She'd been undisturbed by her mother or stepfather. She listened, trying to hear them in the hall and only found silence.

Her pulse quickened as she stood. She stuffed the cards back into her purse and lifted the box from the bed. She took one last look at the room that was no longer Mabel's then opened the door.

Studying the length of the hallway, she couldn't glean any signs of inhabitants. From downstairs, she heard the everyday echoes of kitchen dishes clanking together, water running, a man's voice then a woman's answering.

Luella edged down the wall to the master bedroom, feeling like a thief. The door was open. She peered inside.

It was clear whose side of the bed was whose. The nightstand on the right held a pair of thick reading glasses, a bestselling hardback crime drama and a framed photo of an unsmiling Riane. The nightstand on the right held a Bible, a bottle of hand lotion and a sleep mask.

Luella made sure again that Solomon and Riane were downstairs before she set the box down and moved past the door.

Was she really doing this? She had no doubt her mother had been telling the truth when she'd said she'd call the police. She'd likely find no greater satisfaction than watching officers take Luella away, maybe following it up with a restraining order. The more distance Riane could put between herself and her past with Whip Decker, the better.

However, if there *had* been something in Mabel's nightstand for Luella...where was the most likely place Riane would have stored it?

It was a long shot. Still, Luella's breathing was all too audible, practically thunderous, as she went down on her knees before the nightstand. Her hands were shaking as she lifted them to the drawer pull. Forcing it open, she was relieved to hear it whisper and not squeak along the tracks.

She peered into the dark contents. Here she found trinkets where she'd found so few in the rest of the house. A watch that looked expensive, a pretty paperweight prism that would shoot rainbows if it ever saw the light of day again, a thin book of psalms and blessings, a cross on a silver chain...

Luella didn't recognize anything. Nothing set off warning bells. She nearly shut the drawer again, defeated.

Then she saw the ring box. It was blank—no brand—black and velvet. Still, something niggled Luella to reach in and pick it up.

She checked the door. It was still open—still empty. Sitting back on the floor, she opened the box with a soft creak...

...and nearly keeled straight over.

The diamond glittered in the lamplight. It was etched in a star shape. Four points—north, south, east, west.

Polaris, Ellis had told her when he'd given it to her for the first time. *True north, holding steady all through the year while the sky moves around it. That's us.*

The sob was tumultuous. It broke like a wave and the diamonds blurred.

She'd thought she had lost it. She hadn't been able to face him—not after losing his ring...and his baby.

"What is going on in here?" Riane came into the room. She saw Luella on the floor next to the bed she shared with her husband and fury hit her face. "How dare you?"

"How could you?" Luella said simultaneously. She held up the ring box for Riane to see. "You stole this! You *stole* it from me! Why?"

Riane stared at the ring, then Luella's red, hot face and narrowed her eyes. "It never should have been yours."

Luella laughed bitterly through the tears. "Here we go."

"You weren't meant for anything that fine," Riane told her. "It shouldn't have been given to you to begin with. It wouldn't have been if you'd given that boy time to think—if you'd shown him who you really are."

Luella's stomach cramped as her breath hitched, but she got to her feet and straightened to her full height. "You had no right. No right. This is mine. It was meant for me. There's nothing you can say anymore that can convince me otherwise."

"But I did convince you otherwise," Riane said. "You didn't tell him about the baby. You ran away, tried wearing his ring and hiding yourself and your bastard away because you were ashamed. You were ashamed you led that fine boy astray with your wiles."

"The only reason I left Fuego and Ellis behind was because Whip found out I was pregnant and threatened to kill him if I didn't take care of it. But what you did—it was worse! You spent the next six months convincing a vulnerable eighteen-year-old girl that she never deserved any of it—Ellis, his ring, the life we would've had together or the child that we made. You stole it all from me, starting with this!"

Riane made a grab for the ring box.

"Don't!" Luella was beyond sense or any vestige of calm. Where was the numbness now? She was somewhere beyond it. "If you try to take it from me again, I will give you a reason to call the cops on me."

Riane's eyes lit with malice. "Look at you! Every bit Jace Decker's daughter. It disgusts me, how you ever could have thought you could have it all."

"I could have," Luella realized. "You may have convinced

me I couldn't have him…but I could have had a piece of him. You didn't take that from me. Fate did."

"It was God!" Riane argued. "He took what you should never have tried taking for yourself!"

"Shut up!" Luella yelled, covering her ears. "Shut up, shut up, shut up!"

The screams echoed off everything and nothing.

Solomon entered, brows high on his otherwise hairless head. "What is all the fuss about?"

Luella gathered the box from the floor. "Hey, Sol, did you know Riane here tried to give away her own grandchild? She didn't ask me to kill him like my father did. But she did try to sell him to some rich couple in Sante Fe. They offered a sight more than the couple in Lubbock."

"We don't have to listen to this, Solomon," Riane said, placing her hand on his shoulder. "In fact, I don't feel safe with her in our house. Please do call the police for me."

"Please do know when to get the hell out," Luella advised the man on her way to the stairs. She couldn't leave fast enough. "The devil's a lot closer than you think. She wears stringed pearls and a twinset and likes to blame little girls for her mistakes."

Riane called over the rail of the landing, "Don't trip and fall on your way out like last time!"

Luella fled into the foyer, rounding the corner with speed enough to foot-race an elk…

…and ran headlong into Ellis.

Chapter Eleven

"Wh-what are you doing here?" Luella asked, stricken.

Ellis stared up the long stairwell. He felt like his heart was outside his body. What the hell had he just heard?

She put her hands on her head. Her fingers sank into his hair. She tugged on it as her eyes wheeled. "Ellis, *what are you doing here*?"

Ellis opened his mouth, closed it then remembered how he'd wound up on her mother's doorstep. "Everett. He had an appointment with his shrink in San Gabriel. It was my turn to drive him and I thought I'd check on you—make sure you're okay… What you said up there…about a child…"

"Nope," she said and darted around him before he could catch her. She opened the door and fled.

Ellis cursed and went after her.

"I have to get out of here," she said numbly as she made for her truck. It was parked in front of his in the driveway. "I have to…"

Ellis grabbed her by the arm. "Lu, I need you to look at me."

"No, I need to go, Ellis," she said, snatching out of his grasp. "I have to go, now!"

"We need to talk about this," he said, chasing her around

the driver's side. He beat her to the door and planted his hand on it. "Just look at me, all right? Tell me what I just heard."

She yanked on the handle of the door to no avail. "You heard *nothing*. Let me go!"

He'd had enough. He took the box from her, set it on the hood of the truck then grabbed her by the arms and held. *"Look at me!"*

She shook her head, closed her eyes but he glimpsed the wet over them anyway. "I can't," she chanted. "I can't. I can't…"

"Calm down," he said. It was as much for him as for her. "Just…calm down and let's talk about this rationally, okay? You said Riane had a grandchild." He ignored her when she shook her head again, frantic. "I heard it plain. You said she tried to give it away, sell it? You're going to have to clarify. I won't let you loose until you do."

"He was going to kill you." It bubbled up from somewhere inside her, the words tumbling over each other. "He said he would gut you like a fish, pull out your insides and tie them together. He said he'd make me watch!"

"What?" Ellis said, shocked. "Who?"

"My father." Her eyes were glassy. "Whip Decker. He was going to kill you if I didn't kill our baby. And he wasn't lying. I know he wasn't lying, Ellis. Look what he's done— to your mother, your sisters. He was sick and sadistic but he didn't lie."

"Okay," he said, trying to soothe when he felt like the world was tumbling, over and over in a sickening lurch. "Okay," he said again, running his hands over her arms. "When…when was this? When…did you find out?"

She went slack, leaning against the truck for support. "I can't. It's too much."

"I need to know, Lu," he insisted. "Please. I need to know."

Her face screwed up and she took a tremulous breath. "May. Just after graduation. He found my test in the trash. I was already far enough along I felt sick and heavy… I waited so long to take it. I was in denial—and not thinking straight otherwise I never would've left it in the trash like that. I never should've taken it at home—"

"Slow down," he said, catching her face in his hands. "Slow down, honey." He touched his brow to hers, trying to breathe calm into both of them. "It's okay," he murmured, trying to believe it. "It's okay."

"I'm sorry," she said. He felt her hands balled in the front of his shirt. "I'm so sorry. I lost him. I lost our baby—"

"Shh," he soothed when the brittle, broken words trailed away like smoke. "You didn't… You didn't mean to. I know you didn't."

"I felt him kick," she said, "and I knew I couldn't let her give him away. She tried—tried talking me into it. She tried forcing me to sign the papers. But I couldn't… I couldn't give him away. He was yours."

"Mine." Ellis absorbed it, like a highway armadillo absorbs the impact of a four-by. "He?"

She nodded slightly. "Yes," she whispered. "I wasn't supposed to know. Mother didn't want me to find out. She said I would get too attached to it. But Mabel took me to my appointment. I heard his heartbeat. They told me it was a boy. I saw the shape of him. His feet. His hands. His toes. And I knew he could never be anyone's but my own."

"What happened?" he asked, lifting his head from hers. When she balked, he rushed to soothe. "This is hard for you, sweetheart. I know. But I need to know."

"I was leaving," she mumbled. "I wanted to leave. Not to go back to Fuego. I wanted to go to Taos to find you. I thought we could go somewhere far enough away that neither my mother nor father would find us. I had a bag packed. I tripped at the top of the stairs and…"

He let loose a breath to relieve some of the screaming pressure inside him. It didn't work. Not in the least. "How… how far along were you?"

"Seven months," she said. "By that point, it was September. I'd had enough of her talk. She chased me to the stairs and I fell…all the way down. I started to bleed."

"God Jesus, Lu." The words had gone thick.

"Mother took me to the local women's center," she said. "The doctor there… He said I was in labor. It was too early. There were complications. The baby's pulse wasn't right. I wasn't in my right mind—scared and confused. I think I might have been in shock or…maybe I lost my mind. I don't know. They had to sedate me. I woke up and…he was gone. Just gone."

He took several careful breaths. The coping mechanism he always fell back on…it wasn't working. Why wasn't it working? There was too much inside him—too much building. It was going to come out—in all its messy, dark glory. "You should have told me," he said, sounding small even to his ears. "I could've been there. I could've helped you."

"He was going to kill you," she replied. "Gut you like a fish…"

"Your old man was a killer," he acknowledged. "You were right to believe he would've done it. But you forget. I had my brother, my father and half a dozen good ranch hands at my back. We would've taken care of him. I would've happily taken care of him, Lu, so that you and I could raise our child together and live the life we wanted in peace. The one I promised you. Remember?"

She was too lost to speak. He'd lost her, somewhere in the realms of past traumas. He pressed her face into his shoulder so he could wrap her up and hold her like he'd never had to stop. Giving in, he buried his face in her hair and tried to cull something of himself out of the scent of her.

Luella had been pregnant when he'd left for Taos. She hadn't fallen out of love with him. She hadn't wanted to break things off. She'd left to protect him from her father's cruelty, which she'd known all too well by that point. And Riane...

Riane had done the rest.

"I never should've let you go back to them," he said. "I never should've let you go home after that last time he beat you. None of this... You would've been okay..." He raised his face and lifted hers so he could see. "You watched me have children with another woman."

Her eyes remained closed. "You have two beautiful children, Ellis. The sweetest."

"I know I do," he said and nodded. "I love them. God, but I love my girls, Lu."

"How could you not?"

"And you and I—we had a son?"

"Yes, Ellis. You and I had a son."

He let out of laugh that wasn't a laugh. It was breathy and compromised. He was compromised—completely and utterly compromised. "I wish I could have held him."

"Me, too," she said and he saw the tears leak through, the wet getting caught in her lashes. "They never let me... I don't even know where he's buried. I don't..."

Something burned his throat. It was tight and things were trapped there, broken and ragged.

"The hell is going on?"

Luella turned her face away at the sound of Everett's caustic voice.

Ellis couldn't bring himself to look at him either. "You okay to drive?"

Everett paused. "Sure."

"Take the keys," Ellis said, digging into his pocket and tossing them Everett's way. "We'll follow you."

"Are *you* all right?" Everett asked. "You don't look so good."

"We'll follow you," Ellis repeated, leading Luella away from the driver's door. She didn't stop him from steering her around the front of the truck to the passenger side where he boosted her in and closed the door.

"Ellis?" Everett said. "Am I hearin' things right?"

"We'll talk about it later," Ellis said. "I need to get her home."

Everett waited a beat. "Watch the road." Without further argument, he stalked to the other truck.

LUELLA WOKE LONG after the witching hour. The room was dark, but the light beaming from the adjoining bathroom told her it was Ellis's and the silence said that the house was dead around it.

As she lifted her head, Sphinx stirred on the pillow next to hers. Luella reached out to drag her fingers through her fur. She felt drained. Her face felt tight, as if she'd fallen asleep with tears on it and they'd long since dried.

She stilled when she found Ellis's silhouette sitting on the bed's edge, his back to her. He was still fully dressed. Her box from Mabel lay open at his feet. The little ring box was clutched in his hand.

Luella turned on her side. As she stirred, his head swiveled in her direction. "Did I wake you?"

She shook her head. Fitting her hand under her cheek, she tried to gauge him.

He'd been quiet, too, when they'd come back to Eaton Edge. Over dinner, neither of them had eaten or said anything despite Paloma's and Eveline's attempts to pull them into conversation. Everett, at least, had known not to engage them. He'd eaten and kept his mouth shut, for once.

No one had said anything when Luella chose to turn in early. She'd made some excuse about needing to visit Sheridan early—and that was true. She did want to visit him at Dr. Wilstead's. Though mostly she'd just needed to be away from everyone.

It seemed grief would never be done with her. Watching Ellis grieve, too, for what was—for all that might have been—made it worse.

Shouldn't it have felt better—to have someone to grieve beside?

Luella swallowed. Her throat still felt raw. She knew she'd be hoarse when she spoke but she had to know. "That day in the box canyon this summer…was it you who killed my father?"

Ellis looked at her long before answering. "Yes."

She ran her eyes over his profile, so like the charcoal sketches of the boy he'd been in the sketch pad at his feet. "How did it feel?" she asked.

His brow knit a second before he looked away. His shoulders lifted and fell on a long inhale and exhale. "It should've been Wolfe," he replied. "He wanted it. He had a vendetta. When he missed his chance and I had Whip in my sights, I didn't hesitate. Now I wish I could go back and squeeze the trigger again and again, like I should've done when you came to me beaten. I wanted to kill him then and I should've."

"You're not a killer, Ellis."

"Then why did it feel so good," he asked, "ending him?"

"Because he was a monster," she said. "A real, living, breathing monster."

"There've been too many of those between us," he observed.

"I wish it'd been me," she told him. "I had plenty of opportunity. Plenty of reason. Especially when he showed up at Ollero Creek expecting me to keep him alive. He told me he'd take me out of this world. I should have at least tried to do the same to him. A lot more people might've been saved."

"Maybe we both are better off not thinking about what should have been," he said, the words dredged from deep in his chest. "Though that's a lot harder now…knowing. I gave up finding you too easily when you disappeared."

"You did try to find me." She wanted it to be a question because she'd never been sure, entirely, how hard he'd looked for her once she escaped to San Gabriel.

"I went to the police. I went to your father's house."

She closed her eyes. "No. Ellis."

"He was too drunk to do anything more than laugh in my face," Ellis said. "I never knew what he was laughing about—until now. The sick son of a bitch. It was the police who told me. They knew where you were and they weren't saying, for your protection. They gave me Riane's number and when I got her on the phone, she made me feel so stupid. She said you didn't run away from him, like everybody thought. You ran away from me."

"She's an excellent liar," Luella told him. "She always has been."

She saw the weariness in his shoulders, the way they hung, in the way he scrubbed the lines in his brow with the back of his hand. She reached out for him, touching the place between his shoulder blades where she knew strength lived. "You're tired," she whispered.

He said nothing. Instead, he turned to look at her again. The light from the bathroom bathed her face. She knew he could see everything. He searched it for some time. She could feel his eyes roving in gentle glides and didn't want to hide.

She moved her touch down his arm, tugging. "You don't have to watch over me anymore."

"I want to."

"Ellis," she said softly. "Come to bed."

He wavered, watching. Then he reached down and pried his boots loose, one at a time. He set them next to the box of her things. Then he stood and unlatched his belt. He removed it, rolled it up and set it on the nightstand. Then he walked into the bathroom and she heard water running and him brushing his teeth.

He turned out the bathroom light. She heard him come to the bed. She lifted the covers so he could slip underneath. She moved Sphinx closer to her.

The bed shifted and she felt his toes touch hers. He turned to face her. She felt his breath on her face, then his fingers in the thick coils of her hair. "Tell me what happened to you," he told her. "There were a good few years there you spent in San Gabriel…after what happened."

She licked her lips. "I wasn't well. Mabel tried to bring me out of it, but I spent a year in this…numbness. Sometimes, it was so much I couldn't breathe through it. It felt like this weight on my chest. I was either overwhelmed with grief or completely turned off from everything. I didn't have the energy to feel. And since that felt safer than grieving, I kind of stayed there and got to know it."

"You were depressed," he surmised.

She nodded. "I know its name now. Though it took me

years to understand…and by then, it was like my shadow. Where I went, it came."

"How long did you stay in that house with your mother?"

"Too long," she admitted. "It did get to the point where I couldn't stand it. I got a job, worked days to rent a place above a pizza parlor. I went to night school. Nursing school. I worked in the emergency room of the hospital there for a time. And then, I got the call from the nursing director at Fuego County Hospital with a job offer. They needed a trauma nurse."

"You came back," he remembered.

"I thought my father was dead," she told him. "And I thought you were living in Taos."

"That was around the time Dad's health started going," Ellis remembered. "Everett asked me to come back. And I did, Liberty and the girls in tow."

"By that point, I'd already bought Ollero Creek and started working. It was too late to run again. Even after Whip started showing up at my door, demanding a handout."

She felt him tracing the lines of her throat in feathery strokes. "Do you still get depressed?"

Unsure of how to answer, she opened her hand and closed it. She wanted to touch him. "Something's wrong with me. It's off. There are times I feel dead."

"You're not dead," he murmured.

"Maybe it's regret," she said, under her breath. "It's like Jacob Marley. He had to carry those chains through eternity."

"You're not dead," he said again. "And I don't regret anything…unless you count every man who's touched you since the last time you slept in this bed with me."

"I haven't…" she started to tell him. She pressed her lips together. Could she let go of this—her last remaining secret?

"You're the only one who's touched me," she told him, so quietly she almost didn't hear her own admission.

His breath shuddered across her face. "Lu." His hand cupped the back of her neck and she knew what that meant before his mouth closed over hers, hot and wet and sweet.

His arms wound around her. His lips nipped ever-so-gently to part hers. After a moment's resistance, hers opened on a whimper.

"You're not dead," he breathed. "Say it."

She sighed, reaching for him. "I'm not dead."

"Good girl." He kissed her slow, dipping deep when her head dropped back into his open palm. Submission took hold. "Now say my name, here in the dark."

Her breath grew ragged. She spanned her hand across the length of his throat, trailing her nails up to the hairline at the nape of his neck.

He shivered, involuntarily, creating little fires in her blood. "Say it," he whispered again, his hand flattening against the heavy bottom curve of her breast.

She closed her eyes, feeling all those little fires take hold. "Ellis."

He groaned, taking his time unbuttoning her plaid button-down. He parted it, pushing it back from her shoulders. Underneath, she wore little and felt exposed. She was rounder than she had been before in this bed. It had been so long since she'd felt the glide of a man's gaze—Ellis's gaze.

She could see enough of his dark eyes in the dim light from the window. His touch followed the path of his eyes and undid her. She tugged the shirt over his head and pulled him back to her. She felt heady, alive, urgent for his mouth on her. Her body rose under the firm line of his.

"Mmm-hmm," he said in approval. His hands spread through her hair, smoothing it over the pillow until it crowned her head. He pressed a kiss to the center of her brow then between her eyes, down to the bridge of her nose. He touched his lips to the point of her cheekbone, then the other. He turned a kiss underneath the line of her jaw.

Her head dropped back, urging him to wind his way around. He followed suit, teasing her with kisses up the length of her throat to the lobe of her ear. The sensitive nerves there made her body bow in a fluid, involuntary motion as the furnace lit around her center.

She let him keep spreading kisses, weaving them in star maps over every hard point of her collarbone, down. She arched as his kisses trailed between her breasts and his hands followed, over peaks and into valleys. They were barely there and everywhere. His lips followed the center line of her abdomen, her navel.

Luella panted, crazy with kisses. He tugged her panties and she shrugged them down her legs, kicking them away.

The heels of his hands nudged her knees outward and his head lowered between her legs. His mouth covered her.

She reached up to grip the iron post of his headboard. He didn't stop and her cries grew loud in the quiet dark. Her palm was damp around the metal as he indulged her in hypnotic pulls in tune with the beat of lust alive now inside her.

She began to make little keening cries and covered her own mouth to stop from waking the house. "Stop," she moaned. "Stop, please. I'm dying…"

He made a noise, somewhere between longing and protest and pulled himself away.

"Oh, my God," she sighed.

"Look at you shinin', honey."

His voice was rough and sexy. He unsnapped his jeans. She let out a shuddering breath at the promise of more.

He was hard and she was hungry for that weight. The

space between her legs ached, pulsing like he was inside her already.

He came down to meet her, laughing silently, breathlessly, as he kicked to free his legs from his jeans. The smile felt foreign on her face, but it wasn't a lie. She hadn't had to work for it. The giddiness of being here in the dark with him—it was memory bubbling to the surface, bursting to meet and match the reality of tonight.

I'm not dead.

He scooped his hands beneath her and hitched her into his lap. His hands ranged over her back from waist to shoulders and back in a possessive wave. His gaze had a gleam to it that was hard and soft. It echoed need and promised things deeper—things she couldn't contemplate. He was smiling. He knew he had her—all of her.

So not dead.

A sigh of relief and pleasure fell as he slid inside her. His, hers? She wasn't entirely sure. Her arms hemmed around his shoulders even as his bracketed her waist. She blazed, hot for him.

He lit a goddamn fire—another fire she'd never be able to put out.

He began to churn, fine strokes that drove her up in increments and took her apart. When the cries hit her throat again, she turned her mouth to his. She was definitely going to wake the house.

The heat built to a flash point, the finest point imaginable. *Polaris*. He made it worse when he said her name. He said it like a prayer and she was done. She let her nails dig into the skin of his shoulders until he grunted and she skittered over the brink.

Ellis stilled. She could feel his heart slamming against

hers. For a second, she worried neither of them was breathing anymore.

His lungs released in an immense wave, rocking them both. He came, too, just as hard.

"Look," he said. When she didn't lift her head from his shoulder, he steadied his voice and tugged lightly on her hair. "Look, Lu."

She managed to lift her head and look at him.

His hand stroked her cheek. His eyes were hooded. She expected him to kiss her, but he held back—looking.

The intimacy came to a staggering point and she understood. She was his woman. She'd long been his woman. In that moment, it didn't matter—all the years in between.

He'd devastated her. He always did—so much so she was afraid of how little she'd find of herself in the morning.

Chapter Twelve

"We can't keep meeting like this, Deputy Sweetheart."

Ellis rolled his eyes at his brother as Deputy Altaha propped one hand on her uniformed hip in the kitchen the next morning. Everett leaned against the counter, a cup of coffee in his hand and a large grin spreading across his face.

Altaha sized him up, slowly. "You know...when most people find an officer of the law on their doorstep before breakfast, they tend to react differently."

Everett thought about it. "I like a challenge."

She lowered her chin. "You *are* the challenge."

"That is a compliment, Deputy," he drawled, "of the highest caliber. I thank you."

Altaha exchanged a look with Ellis, who shrugged helplessly. Paloma saved them all by shoving a *sopaipilla* in Everett's mouth on her way to the table with a platter. "Chew, *niño*," she advised. "*Buenos días*, Deputy."

Altaha took off her hat. *"Buenos días, Señora."* She looked to Ellis. *"Cómo estás?"*

"Bien," he replied. "Join us for breakfast?"

Altaha eyed the setup on the table with intrigue. "I'm supposed to drop in for a quick word and return to the station, but I see Paloma's made her sopaipillas."

"Later," Everett announced. He grabbed Ellis by the

elbow and tipped his head toward the door for Altaha to follow. "I've got some business to discuss with the both of you."

"Business?" Ellis mumbled. It was unlike Everett to want to discuss any sort of business before breakfast. And since when did their business involve the deputy?

"Okay," Altaha said slowly as Everett quickly ushered them down the hall and all but pushed them through the door to the office. As he shut the door, she rounded on him. "What's going on, cattle baron? I thought it was Ellis who needed to speak with me. Not you."

"Hmm," Everett said, feigning ignorance as he walked around the brawny desk. "That's odd, as it was me who called."

Altaha narrowed her eyes. "Pretending to be your brother?"

"We do sound a lot alike on the phone," Everett considered, distracted now as he riffled through desk drawers, brows drawn together.

"We sound nothing alike," Ellis argued. "On the phone, or otherwise."

Altaha stopped talking to study Everett more closely as he located a flash drive. He drew up the chair behind the desk and sat. In his big, working hand, the drive looked tiny. It looked downright foreign there as he turned his head sideways to try fitting it into one of the ports on the desktop PC.

"Oh, for heaven's sake," she muttered. She took the flash drive and easily found the correct port to plug it into. "You're liable to break it at this rate."

He sat back, wiggling the mouse insistently. "What's happening here?"

"Your monitor's off." She reached across him to turn it on then halted, bringing her eyes around to his.

Everett stared, somewhat innocently—as innocent as Everett could manage, in any case.

She pursed her lips, easing back into a professional stance. "Real smooth, cowboy."

Everett didn't have the decency to keep up the charade. "Got to give a man points for trying."

"Or," she considered, "I could arrest you."

He hissed through his teeth when her hand went to the small of her back to palm the set of handcuffs. "I almost wish you would."

Ellis had had enough. "Look, as much fun as this is, I'm going back to my breakfast." He wanted to see if Luella had come down yet. He'd left her wrapped in his bed, her red hair a fan around her face.

He'd wanted to wake her and had only just checked the urge to trace the parting of her lush red lips with his fingertips. There was more inside him. He had more to show her, more to give.

But she'd needed rest. And he'd wanted a bit of time to process what was and what had been.

How could so much change in one day, past and present?

Everett, sobering, turned to the computer screen. "The trip to San Gabriel joggled some memories."

"What kind of memories?" Ellis asked, coming around the desk to see the monitor. His brother was viewing the files from the drive. There were hundreds. "What could you possibly find in this mess?"

"Dad might not have taken care of himself," Everett ventured, "but he was an excellent businessman and an even better record-keeper. He kept everything he wrote down."

"I know this," Ellis said, remembering the nightmare that had been his father's file boxes. They'd all been meticulously organized, but there had been *so many*.

"When I heard the word *baby* yesterday from Luella," Everett elaborated, turning to stare at his brother pointedly, "I remembered a meeting Dad had around the time of her disappearance—the summer after you graduated high school."

"Whoa," Altaha said, holding up her hands. "Time-out. What about a baby?"

Ellis frowned at Everett. "It's not public knowledge."

"What exactly?" the deputy asked. Her eyes widened slightly when Ellis could say no more out loud without Luella's say-so. "Oh."

"Good." Everett nodded, satisfied. "We're all on the same page now."

"Against our will," Ellis noted.

Everett leaned toward the screen, slowing his scroll. He chewed his lower lip as he got closer to what he was looking for. The file names were dates, Ellis saw. These went back over a decade. "You remember a meeting Dad had with someone seventeen years ago?" he asked in disbelief.

"It stuck out," Everett weighed. "We don't get many people doctors at the Edge."

"The meeting was with a doctor," Altaha said, trying to string together the details.

Everett growled low in his throat as he highlighted a file name with the mouse and double-clicked it. "Right around this time… We were sending off a truckful of heifers. I was about to see it off when this guy arrived, white coat and everything—said he was from San Gabriel."

The file opened and filled the screen with an overhead shot of a desktop planner.

"Hell," Ellis groaned. "I forgot he used to keep notes by hand."

"Little ones," Everett acknowledged, "that spilled into the margins when he was feeling wordy. Like this one…"

He double-clicked again and the screen zoomed in on the bottom right corner of the calendar.

Everyone leaned in, trying to read Hammond's tiny, precise lettering.

Altaha read out loud, "'Transport at 10:00 a.m. Fence check. Payroll. Dr. Bridestone, no appointment, 9:20 a.m.'"

"I'll be damned," Ellis said with a shake of his head. "Seventeen years ago."

"When did Luella say the baby was born?" Everett asked him.

"She didn't," Ellis said. "She lost the baby."

"When?" Everett persisted.

The urgency in him spooked Ellis. "September. What does this have to do with Dr. Bridestone?"

"The good doctor wanted to know if Dad was interested in adopting an orphaned kid from San Gabriel."

Altaha stared openly at Everett. "I'd say that's something to remember."

"He…wanted to give Dad a baby?" Ellis said. He shook his head. "Why, exactly? What were his reasons?"

"He said it was well known that Dad liked to take in the odd kid or two," Everett revealed.

"Was it?" Altaha asked.

Ellis thought it over. "He tried to adopt Wolfe but backed off when Santiago claimed him. I thought about asking him to take in Luella…after Whip nearly killed her. I think he would have said yes. But I don't know anyone who would've known that other than her."

"What else did this doctor say?" Altaha inquired.

"He said Dad could have the kid by Christmas," Everett explained.

"Did Dad seem interested?" Ellis asked.

"He didn't turn the man out," Everett said. "Dad didn't have a habit of turning anyone out."

"Especially not a kid in need," Ellis considered.

Everett nodded. "Yeah."

"How could any of this have been legal?" Altaha asked.

"Well, that's the part of the conversation that struck me as off," Everett said. "Dad wanted records, paperwork, permissions from the parents or system so that if—and, frankly, when—he chose to accept the child into his home, there would be no pushback. No chance a young mother might come looking for him."

"A boy," Ellis repeated and his heart dropped out from under him.

"Sit down," Everett said immediately.

"I'm fine," Ellis replied with a shake of his head.

"Sit down," Everett said through his teeth. "You look like you did when she dropped the bomb on you yesterday—like you've been torpedoed."

"I can stand," Ellis informed him, shifting his feet just to prove he could.

"Was there anything else?" Altaha asked. "Any other details that could be important?"

"Only that there was a price," Everett explained. "The baby came in exchange for a five-figure lump sum, paid up front in cash."

"Jesus," Ellis uttered.

Altaha shook her head. "The cost of adoption is up there, even by traditional means. This whole thing stinks, however. Who was Dr. Bridestone? And what business did he have leading the adoption process like this? And why Hammond? Why Fuego and Eaton Edge? There's far too many red flags."

"I'll leave that with you," Everett said, selecting the print function so that the machine in the corner began to whir to life. "Though I have some theories of my own."

Ellis thought about it, then automatically rejected the idea. "No."

"It's no less than finding out I'd have a seventeen-year-old nephew if Luella hadn't miscarried," Everett pointed out.

Ellis turned away. His was sweating at the implications. "You changed your tune toward Luella last night," he remembered. "You stopped barking at her and me. Is this why?"

"No," Everett noted. "Blood's thicker than water. If she's the mother to one of ours, whether or not the kid lived, that means something."

"It means everything," Ellis murmured.

"Ellis," Altaha said slowly, "I'll look into this, starting with Dr. Bridestone in San Gabriel. We'll see where that leads."

He nodded.

"Will you tell Luella?"

He rejected the idea. "Not until we know more. All this… it could lead to nothing. You said you were looking at Luella's game cams from the night Sheridan was kidnapped."

Altaha frowned at the pivot. "Snowfall made the picture unclear."

He cursed, louder than he wanted to. "Did you canvass? Were there witnesses?"

"There was a blizzard," Altaha reminded him. "How far out in front of you could you see? Farther than Luella's neighbors, I'll wager."

Ellis ground his teeth. The frustration gnawed at his cool.

Everett watched him with more understanding than Ellis liked.

Altaha patted Everett on the shoulder. "It's good to see you behind the desk again, cattle baron."

Everett looked down at his hands, which were both clamped around the arms of the chair. "Feels good, I guess. What do you say, Deputy Sweetheart? Fancy joining me for breakfast?"

A distant smile flirted with the corners of her mouth, but before she could answer, the phone on the desk rang.

"It's probably the buyer from Bozeman," Ellis said. He reached for the receiver.

Everett beat him to it and answered in a bark. "Yeah?"

Ellis's hand fumbled to his face where he scrubbed. Before surgery, his brother's business demeanor had always been more Billy Goat Gruff than Ellis thought necessary. It appeared postsurgery wasn't going to be much different.

Everett frowned as he pulled the receiver away from his mouth. "For you," he said, pushing the phone at his brother.

Was that resentment in the lightning-blue flash of Everett's eyes—or was he just being his normal, recalcitrant self? When Ellis did hand the reins of Eaton Edge back to Everett, he hoped it would be a smooth transition with no hard feelings on the part of his big brother and rightful boss. Ellis and Paloma had prevented him from ignoring his therapist's warning of not returning to work too soon during his journey toward physical and mental recovery.

Ellis made a mental note to assure Everett that when the time was right for him to return to his position of chief of operations that Ellis would happily return to the support position their father had wanted for him. He cupped the phone to his ear. "This is Ellis."

"Ellis," a brisk, feminine voice greeted. "I'm so glad I reached you. This is Rosalie. Rosalie Quetzal—from town council?"

Ellis lifted his chin. Rosalie Quetzal...formerly Sullivan, he realized. He turned his gaze to Altaha with a lift of his brows. "Of course. How are you, Ms. Quetzal?"

"Fine." Her tone was strained around the edges. "Listen, I know this may seem out of left field, but I was wondering if you'd like to get together sometime and talk."

Talk, Ellis mused. The only thing he and Rosalie had to talk about that he knew of was their respective spouses' apparent habit of jumping into bed together. "Yes. I've been meaning to call, too. Things have been crazy."

"I could come to Eaton Edge," she offered. "Would that be better for you?"

He thought about it. "Why not Hickley's BBQ?" He shifted so he could read the desk calendar where he'd taken to scrawling notes, just like their father had. The calf didn't fall far from the dam. "Is eight o'clock this evening too late for you?"

"That sounds just fine," Rosalie noted. "But, just for kicks, let's make it Mimi's—same time, my treat."

"I'll see you there," Ellis agreed though he had other thoughts about letting a lady pay for a meal.

"Bye now," she said and hung up quickly.

Ellis let the phone dangle from his hand for several seconds before he replaced it in the cradle. "You put her up to this."

"I did nothing of the sort," Altaha claimed. "But I may have put a bug in my sister's ear."

"What kind of bug, exactly?"

"The kind that goes, 'Buzz-buzz, his ex-wife's a con artist,'" Altaha drawled.

"It's been on my mind," he told her, "contacting Rosalie."

"I'm sure it has," she granted. "You've had a lot going on."

"Speaking of ex-wives," Everett said, leaning back in his chair, "is she bringing the girls this weekend? It's your turn."

"Last time I spoke to her on the phone, she made it sound like my visitation rights are over unless I sign my shares over to her," Ellis explained.

Everett muttered something uncomplimentary. Then his gaze flicked to Altaha. "Pardon."

She pulled a face. "Hey, I'm with you."

His eyes narrowed and his mouth softened toward her. "You want to help us out with this little problem?"

It took her a moment to soften toward him in return. "I like how you think sometimes, I've got to admit." Looking to Ellis, she said, "I think I'll give the former Mrs. Eaton a call."

"You're not going to threaten her," Ellis said. "You could lose your job."

"Did I say I was going to threaten her?" Altaha asked. "She just needs to be reminded that she's in violation of your rights and that won't reflect well on her when her case goes in front of a judge."

"It won't make her happy," he warned.

"You want to see your girls," Everett guessed. "You need to see your girls. Hell, we all do. The place isn't right without them. Do it," he told Altaha. "I'll owe you one."

"I like that, too, I think," Altaha weighed. If Ellis wasn't mistaken, she sent him an infinitesimal wink on the way out.

Everett looked far too smug for Ellis's peace of mind. "Careful there," he cautioned.

Everett laced his hands behind his head and grinned. "Don't piss on my parade, *mano*."

No, Ellis thought, seeing his brother more relaxed than he had in a long time. *I couldn't.* "We need to check fences in the southwest quarter. Ride with me?"

Everett shifted to his feet. "Only if you're on gate duty."

"That means you're driving," Ellis said, pulling a face. Everett was notorious for being a terror behind the wheel.

"You're damn right I am. While we're out, you can tell me what the nature of your business with sexy town-council lady is."

Ellis heaved a sigh. "You're incorrigible."

LUELLA DIDN'T KNOW what to think, much less feel, when she came out of Dr. Wilstead's office and saw Ellis holding the door open across the street to Mimi's Steakhouse for Rosalie Quetzal.

Rosalie was a single woman again after her divorce. She'd quickly gone back to her maiden name and was a lot like Eveline in the looks department. Tall, blonde, regal, she was a woman who carried herself well and enjoyed her high standing in the Fuego community.

She was on the city council, as her father had been before her, and could be mayor if True Claymore would loosen his hold on the position. For a rodeo cowboy's wife, she'd gone far beyond any buckle bunny Luella had ever heard of.

As they disappeared into the restaurant—Fuego's finest—Luella stood on the stoop, all the warm, fuzzy feelings she'd felt after her last few hours helping Wilstead care for Sheridan wafting away like smoke. An involuntary exhale left her on a rush. The emptiness that followed was insurmountable.

Last night. Last night, he'd touched her and tasted her, claimed her. It had only been last night that she'd realized she was his woman. She was Ellis's woman, unequivocally.

Had she forgotten what she'd had to go through years before and the harsh understanding that had come with it?

She might be Ellis Eaton's woman. But he would never

be her man. She had worn his ring. She'd planned for a future with him. She may be his lover again, the mother of his child, the woman he'd thought about even when he was with his wife…

But she couldn't think of him as her own any more than she could think of the moon and stars as her own.

She started to cross the street to the windows of Mimi's, but then thought of the pathetic picture it would make with her face pressed to her glass—the cold without and the warm within with Ellis and Rosalie wrapped up in it over wine and appetizers.

Stumbling back a step, she nearly tripped over the curb. "Luella?"

She looked around and was distressed to find witnesses. "Eveline," she said, sounding dull even to her own ears. "Paloma."

"Oh, *niña*," Paloma murmured, reaching up with a gloved hand. She cradled Luella's cheek. "You've forgotten your hat."

"Come with us," Eveline invited, closing in on her other side. Luella didn't know what to think when her arm linked through hers. "We were going to see what the new axe-throwing place is like."

"I don't think so," Luella said, digging in her heels before they could think about urging her in the direction of people and lights. "I'm not sure I'm in the mindset for axe-throwing."

Eveline studied her. A knowing light hit her eyes. "Oh, I think you might be. And it's not every day I convince Paloma to leave the sanctity of her kitchen. Come on. Let's try it."

"Okay," Luella said unwillingly as she was coaxed along. They tuned off Main Street together and onto 2nd Avenue and approached the adobe-style building that had once been a run-down furniture store. A neon sign read Hatchet House. It buzzed busily over the double-door entrance. Luella frowned when she saw the mash of people inside.

"I reserved a time," Eveline said as they took off their coats and gloves. "I'll talk to the owner, see if we can't cut the line."

Luella and Paloma were left to stare at their surroundings. The place had been refurbished to look like a saloon with snack booths in deep red leather and the same rough wood furnish on everything from the floors to the ceilings, tables and chairs. "Well, they certainly did improve on the place," Paloma opined.

"I don't think I can do this," Luella said, her feet itching for the doors.

Eveline swooped back in. "We've got the target on the end. It just opened up. This way."

Luella once again found herself practically frog-marched, this time through a tight clutch of people, most of whom openly stared at the unlikely trio—the model, the housekeeper, the home-wrecking felon who had no business here or anywhere else in Fuego, if you asked them.

"Drinks, ladies?" the waitress asked as they hung their coats on handy hooks nearby.

Eveline was already rolling up her sleeves. "Three beers?"

Paloma chuckled in her throat. "It's my night off. Margaritas, all around. I'm buying."

Eveline whooped happily. She grabbed an axe from the sideboard then stepped up to the mark. "Now, how do you do this, exactly?"

Paloma pursed her lips, eyeing the target. "I think we can all assume you just chuck the blessed thing."

Eveline turned toward the far wall, lifted the axe and

heaved it. It didn't hit the mark. It buried itself beneath the outermost circle. "Oh," she said with a grin. "That was satisfying. Give me another."

Paloma made a disagreeable noise. "Let Luella have a turn."

"Oh, yes," Eveline said, stepping back to let Luella have a throw. She handed her the next axe. "You have to try it. It's fantastic."

"Erm, okay," Luella said, unsure. The axe didn't feel foreign in her hand. She'd chopped her fair share of wood at Ollero Creek and had the arms to prove it. Or she had, before her incarceration. Feeling silly nonetheless, she tried to ignore the people around her as she faced up to the target and eyed the center. She planted her feet, lifted the axe in both hands and released, throwing her weight into it.

Eveline cheered and Paloma applauded soundly when the blade found the middle ring. "Look at you, Luella Belle," the latter said with a shake of her head. "You're a natural."

"She's a Viking," Eveline said admirably. She hugged Luella around the shoulders. "I knew you'd love it."

"I…" Luella stopped, wondering what the odd sensation was around the lower half of her face. Jesus, was that a smile? The adrenaline she recognized and there was plenty of it. It *was* satisfying, she found, surveying her axe on the board with something akin to pride.

"Margaritas," the waitress said, returning with a tray full.

"Wow…" Luella couldn't believe her eyes. "Are those glasses or fishbowls?"

Eveline cackled, raising one. She clinked it first to Paloma's then handed Luella hers and clinked it, too. "To girls' night out."

"Girls' night out," Paloma repeated.

Luella stared, wide-eyed, at them both as they drank.

She blinked several times, smelling all the sweet and salty goodness in her bowl. Then she lifted a shoulder. *What the hell?* she thought and drank, too.

LUELLA CLOSED ONE EYE, trying to sight that center circle like she had before. It wavered and she frowned. "You know... I don't drink a lot. Alcoholics are a pox on my family tree, my father being the biggest and loudest and ugliest..."

Eveline snorted a laugh. She was leaning against the nearby wall, nursing the remains of her fishbowl and looked a little worse for wear despite the happy flush on her cheeks.

"I'd forgotten how great margaritas are," Luella went on. She was rambling. She knew she was rambling. And slurring, slightly—only slightly. "It's no fun to drink them alone. Drinking in company...*so* much better..."

"Damn right," Paloma said, raising her glass.

"Paloma!" Eveline said, overloud. "You swore!"

"It's you children," Paloma opined. Her words leaned heavy on her Latin accent. "Bad influences. Your brother, especially."

"Which brother?" Eveline wanted to know.

"The one who didn't spend last night cozy in Luella Belle's arms," Paloma noted.

Luella threw and missed. "Beg pardon?"

"Oh, *please*!" Eveline said, grabbing the next axe for herself. She didn't relinquish her drink as she stepped up to the line again. "Ellis came down all dope-faced this morning. Like he had sunshine beaming out from between his ass cheeks."

The *s*'s ran together, making Luella grin loudly. The mental picture of Ellis's cheeks helped. She picked up her drink but hiccupped before she could get it to her mouth.

She placed it carefully back on the table with both hands. "That's enough, I think."

"Oh, no," Eveline said after another ill-timed throw. Sober or drunk, she had no talent for axe-throwing. "Another, *please*. I never do this. And I love you guys." She hugged them both around the neck and pulled them in for a squeeze.

Luella found herself laughing even as she choked on Eveline's designer perfume. "I can't do another. I'm sorry."

"Don't be sorry," Paloma said, patting her on the hand and leaning toward her in an empathetic way. "You sweet girl. You've come a long way tonight."

"I have," she said in wonder. "God. I never did this with I was younger. I never had girlfriends."

"Not one?" Eveline asked, stunned.

"Not one," Luella said with a shake of her head. "When I was little, I knew making friends meant playdates and sleepovers, right? All the normal things. But what mama or daddy would let their little girl spend the night in Whip Decker's double-wide? Plus, playdates would only ever bring questions about the bruises I carried like a patchwork quilt. The kind little girls with normal fathers don't have…"

Eveline and Paloma fell silent. Luella was distressed to see Eveline's eyes swell with tears. "Oh, no. I didn't mean… I told you I'm no good at this. Damn, I'm *such* a downer."

"No," Eveline said even as a wet, round drop escaped down her cheek. "No, Luella. Don't you dare apologize. You're doing so great."

"So great," Paloma echoed. "I wish you'd run away to the Edge, like Wolfe did. I would've taken care of you. Like my own."

Luella felt tears of her own stinging her eyes. "You would have?"

"Without question," Paloma said. "Aw, *niña*. Come here to Paloma."

She found herself enveloped in a warm hug. The circle of Paloma's arms felt safe. She pressed her face into her wide shoulder. Her eyes closed. There was warmth inside her instead of the devastating emptiness that had been there on the street.

"You shouldn't leave," Eveline said, patting Luella on the back as she pulled away to wipe her face on a napkin. Paloma used hers to blow her nose. "Whip Decker is finally gone. You're free now to do whatever the hell it is you want. What have you always wanted to do, Luella? Why did you come back to Fuego after being away so long?"

Luella sighed. "Oh, I don't know. At first, I told myself it was because I got a job at the hospital and it was just convenient. But after being back at the Edge... I'm starting to think it's because I wanted to be close to it again. I fell in love with it, every bit as much as I fell in love with...you know who. Some part of me never forgot that feeling of being there or...belonging to it. I just wanted to belong to something, in the permanent sense."

Paloma nodded. "I know exactly what you mean, *niña*. When I came to the Edge, I was a young woman. I've never left—and not just because I have people there who need me. The land...the sky...the way they reach for each other...the way the river comes down out of the mountains and never ceases, no matter how hot or dry the desert country is... It's miraculous. It's vital. It grabs you by the soul, and it doesn't let you go."

"No," Luella agreed. The land—that sky—those stars... so many stars...she'd fallen in love under those stars in more ways than one, she realized.

"It brings people together," Eveline mused, cupping her

chin in her hands, axes and margarita forgotten. "Normally, land drives people apart. It is the most coveted resource on earth. But the Edge is different. That's why I wanted my wedding there. If not for the Edge, I'm not sure Wolfe and I would've ever been together."

Paloma nodded. "The land draws the right ones in and it holds them. They may go away, like the both of you did, but it never stops calling them back."

Luella ran a hand under her nose. "I want to belong there. But I don't."

"Bite your tongue, girl," Paloma snapped, stern for the first time that night.

"It's true," Luella said. "Ellis and I… Things didn't work out. Now everything's so complicated. There's too much there—too much hurt and too much grief. It's like a friggin' mountain I can't use my hands to move, just my heart and my mind and I'm not sure either of those are strong. And even if I could use my hands, they're not strong enough either. It's a no-win scenario."

Eveline put her cheek on Luella's shoulder. "I told you, didn't I, that Ellis is in love with you?"

"Oh yeah?" Luella asked. "Then why did I just see him going into Mimi's with Rosalie Quetzal?"

She saw Eveline and Paloma exchange a significant look. Her heart turned over. "What?" she asked. Could she handle the portents behind that look? She was already on the edge. The bubble of warmth and friendship they'd created was a fragile thing with the emptiness just below—an ill-fated net waiting to catch her when she tripped and fell on her face once again…

Paloma made a face. "Rosalie was married to Walker Sullivan. The rodeo king."

"I know," Luella said. "What does that have to do with—"

Eveline cleared her throat, lowering her voice. "He was sleeping with her."

"Rosalie?" Luella said. She shook her head, trying to clear it. "Wait. I've had too much to drink…"

"Not with Rosalie," Paloma said, patiently.

"Well, not exclusively," Eveline clarified. When Luella still couldn't grasp the meaning behind any of it, Eveline threw her a bone. "With Liberty."

It was spoken under Eveline's breath but it rang through Luella head like a gong. She sat up straight. *"What?"*

Paloma nodded. "Unbelievable. We know."

"Sh-she… Hold on." Luella raised her hands and stared hard at the tabletop, making the wavy age lines in the wood fix themselves in place. She needed absolute clarity here. "That…that…"

"Minx," Paloma supplied.

"Hussy," Eveline offered.

"That *bitch*—"

"Oh, that's good," Eveline agreed. "I like that better."

"—she waltzes 'round town telling everything that breathes that Ellis is a no-account cheater who's been sleeping with me, his ex-girlfriend, for all these years and watching everyone tear the two of us down piece by every little piece and all that time…the whole *damn* time, she's the one who was having the affair? With a *married man*?"

"Mmm-hmm," Eveline agreed, widening her eyes for effect. "She's a real class act, right?"

"She's a phony," Paloma added. "She's a…oh, what's it?"

"Use your words," Eveline encouraged, nodding fervently.

"She's a…" Paloma snapped her fingers. "A *hypocrite*!"

"Yes!" Eveline said, raising both hands. "Preach!"

"For Christ's sake," Luella said, grabbing her head in both

hands. It was starting to hurt—really hurt. The anger...the shock...it pulsed and writhed. "I... I need to get out of here."

"Ohmagod," Eveline cried, grabbing her by the shoulders. "Are you going to yak? Here, I'll take you to the restroom. I'm actually feeling a little queasy myself... Too much Cuervo."

"No," Luella said, rising quickly. "I need to... Too many people... Too many axes... Too *mad*. Do you *know* what I'm saying?"

Paloma hefted herself to her feet. "I know *exactly* what you're saying, *niña*." She slapped money on the table. "We're leaving." She picked up her glass, downed the remains of her margarita in one go then let it clack back to the table. "Eatons out!"

"Yeah, we are," Eveline said as she hooked her purse over her shoulder. She gathered their coats off the hooks and followed close on their heels.

The crowd between them and the door parted, miraculously. They cut a fine swath through the Hatchet House patrons. Luella was proud of the fact that she didn't stumble or appear too tipsy.

They were just about to reach the exit when something blocked their path. Or, someone.

Eveline groaned. "Not now, Conway."

Rowdy leered at them all from his medium height. He had a medium build to match his coveralls. Luella's nose curled. He smelled like it'd been several days since he'd changed out of them. "Barf," she moaned.

He drew his head back on his neck. "That's not very nice, is it?" His eyes did a dive over her knit sweater. "You look plenty nice. You smell plenty nice. But you ain't nice. Are you, devil's daughter?"

Paloma stuck her finger in his face and shook it. "You

will watch your mouth, Theodore Conway, or I'll knock the Rowdy right out of you the way your mother should have the day she decided to call you that instead."

"Let's go," Luella begged, trying to vie for the exit. "I want to go."

"We're going," Eveline agreed, sneering at Rowdy as they went.

Luella touched the handle. Behind her, Eveline shrieked. Turning back, Luella saw Rowdy's hand cupping the back of Eveline's jeans in a firm hold.

Eveline whirled on Rowdy, who was grinning like a fiend, dislodging his grip. "Ah," he said, pressing a hand to his heart. "It feels just as round and sweet as it looks in the pictures." And he laughed.

Eveline balled her hand into a fist and brought it up, humming with fury. Luella stopped her, grabbing a bottle off the nearest table. She brought it down with a great deal of force on Rowdy's head.

There were screams. The music stopped. All eyes were on Rowdy as he slumped stupidly to the ground, then Luella, who held the neck of the broken bottle in her hand.

"You did that so well," Paloma murmured as Luella tossed the offending bottle away.

"I wish I could've done something like that," Eveline said. "Heaven knows he deserves it."

"Next time," Luella promised.

"Hey!" The owner, a large mountain of a man named Homer, barreled down on them. "You're not going anywhere!"

"We are, too," Paloma said.

"You can't knock out my patrons and leave," he argued, pointing to the coveralls that were Rowdy slumped across the floor like a lumpy potato sack.

"We *are* your patrons," Paloma informed him. "Good paying ones, too, who were enjoying themselves just fine until Theodore here copped a feel on Ms. Eveline."

"I'm going to have to ask Luella here to wait for the sheriff," he told them, banding his arms over his chest. "The rest of you can go."

"You can't arrest her," Eveline said. "She was defending me."

"I can't," he granted. "But the sheriff can."

"We're not leaving without Luella," Eveline said, getting right up in his face. Or as close to it as she could. He was a really large man.

"Fine," he said, dipping his red face down into hers to drive the word home. "I'll tell them you tried inciting a riot in my place of business. *All* of you."

"Fine," Paloma volleyed back, nonplussed. She drew Luella and Eveline back toward the bench by the door. "We'll wait right here. Won't we, girls?"

As Eveline and Paloma both settled in with determined faces, Luella wondered, dazed, why she'd waited until she was leaving Fuego to make friends there.

Chapter Thirteen

Being taken down to the station again in handcuffs was another low point, Luella would admit. But sharing a cell with Paloma Coldero and Eveline Eaton was a high one. When Ellis, Everett and Wolfe appeared on the other side of the bars, they found the three women in fits of laughter as they recounted how Rowdy had looked as he sidled to the wooden planks at Luella's feet.

Everett raised his hand to the bars over his head. "Well," he drawled, pushing his hat up from his brow. "This is a turn of events."

That only made Paloma and Eveline laugh harder. Luella's laughter fizzled at the sight of Ellis's quiet stare. She cleared her throat, remembering how quiet the room had gone when she'd smashed the bottle over Rowdy's head. She also remembered how for about an hour—a entirely miserable hour—she'd thought he'd been going into Mimi's with Rosalie for a date.

How could she doubt him when she was the one locked up in a jail cell again? And she'd gotten his sister and housekeeper thrown in here with her...

She licked her lips. "It's my fault they're here. They didn't do anything. Homer's a liar. Nobody incited a riot. Rowdy copped a feel on Eveline—"

"Wait, *what*?" Everett barked.

"There he goes," Paloma said, amused.

"Zero to rage in three milliseconds," Eveline measured. "That can't be good for his health."

"What are we going to do about him?" Paloma said, eyeing Everett with pity.

"Get him a woman?" Eveline suggested.

"You'd wish that on a woman?"

Eveline narrowed her eyes. "She'd have to be as strong as you."

"Stronger, *niña*."

"Y'all 'bout done?" Ellis asked, sounding maybe a little amused, too.

"Oh, I don't think so," Paloma said. "This is the most fun old Paloma's had in a long time."

"Aw," Eveline cooed, tipping her head to Paloma's shoulder.

Wolfe blew a low whistle.

"What are the charges?" Luella asked. "Jones wouldn't tell us." What she didn't ask—what made her heart pound in dread—was whether her night in jail was going to be a violation of her parole.

"He wouldn't tell us either," Everett said. "He may hate you more than he hates me. And here I was thinking that wasn't possible."

"Jealous?" Eveline teased.

"He's threatened to charge the three of you with drunk and disorderly," Ellis revealed.

"Ooh, nice," Eveline said.

Luella frowned because she sensed there was more.

"And disturbing the peace," he finished.

"It's an axe-throwing place," Eveline said, humor vanishing in another upsurge of indignation. "It's not exactly a peaceful establishment."

"It was Theodore who disturbed the peace," Paloma added. "We were trying to make an exit."

"When he groped you," Everett said, dropping the words like grenades.

"Yes," Eveline said, thrusting her chin in the air. "And I would've given him the what-for if Luella hadn't stopped me by dropping a bottle over his head."

Ellis raised his brows. His gaze passed over her face first in a considering sweep before feathering over the points of her torso.

Her navel gathered the heat of that. It helped tamp down on the shame, somewhat. She wanted his warmth. She hated what she'd done. But she hadn't wanted Eveline to get in trouble and Rowdy had needed the comeuppance.

"The lawyer will take care of all of it," Everett said with a shrug. "From the sound of things, Jones will have to drop the charges."

"Even against Luella?" Paloma asked.

Everett exchanged a glance with Luella. He must've seen the way she was gnawing her lower lip. "Yes," he said without question, surprising her.

She opened her mouth to say "thank you," but stopped at the sound of footsteps. Altaha nudged the men out of the way. "Make a space, people. Geez." She fit the keys in the lock. "Ladies, your bail's been paid. You may go now."

"Thank you, Deputy," Paloma said, coming to her feet as the others did. "My purse?"

"See Officer Jenkins," Altaha suggested. She looked tired. Then again, it was near midnight. "He'll get your things back to you."

"Might I suggest some cushions for those benches?" Paloma advised her.

Altaha tucked a smile behind the pursing of her lips. "I'll look into it, ma'am." She let Eveline out but stopped Luella from passing. "A word?"

"Okay," Luella said, apprehensive.

Eveline grabbed Wolfe by the face and mashed a kiss to his lips before he escorted her out, every bit the doe-eyed intended. Everett groaned but followed. Ellis hung back with Luella and Altaha. "What's the trouble, Kaya?" he asked.

"You should know, too, I guess," Altaha informed him. "Jones has taken me off the Ollero Creek case."

"What?" Luella and Ellis said as one. "How could he?" Luella asked. "You've been working on it for weeks…"

"He doesn't feel I'm making enough headway in the investigation," Altaha revealed, grim. "He also feels that I'm too close to the family."

"What family?" Luella asked.

"Our family," Ellis murmured.

She glanced up and caught his gaze. It was round and dark and bursting with meaning. Her stomach flipped and she looked away quickly.

"I'm sorry," Altaha said in an undertone. "But you'll have to deal with him now on this."

"Isn't there anything you can do?" Luella asked.

Altaha eyed her with sympathy. "Look, Luella, I'm surprised the sheriff let me take this case to begin with. He's been trying to push me out for a while now."

"Why would he do that?" Ellis asked. "What's he got against you?"

"I don't know," Altaha said slowly. "Could be that I have breasts, a badge *and* a brain. Could be I'm Jicarilla. All I know is I've had to work four times as hard as everybody else in this station house to make any kind of ground and I get no reward for it where others who do half the work do."

"That's bullshit," Ellis muttered.

"He's the sheriff," Altaha reminded him. "And until that changes, I don't see things being any different."

"You're a good cop," Ellis pointed out. "A damn good cop. The best we have in this county."

"Thanks," she said with a little smile. Turning her attention to Luella, she said, "You need anything, don't hesitate to call. He can take me off your case but he can't stop me from answering a distress call."

Luella thought about it. "There may be something I could use your help with. Something I can't and won't discuss with your boss."

"Sure thing," Altaha said. "I'd say step into my office but he's got eyes all over this place. We can meet tomorrow, lunchtime, if I don't get any calls away from the station."

"How about at Ollero Creek?" Luella asked.

"Lu," Ellis said in warning. "It's still not safe."

"She's the deputy," Luella reminded him.

"I am the deputy," Altaha said with a nod. "Oh, by the way, I called your ex in Taos."

Ellis's eyes opened up with possibility and, in equal amounts, dread. "Yeah?"

"Expect to see your girls the day after next. She'll be bringing them for the weekend."

He released a heavy breath. "I'd hug you, Deputy, but your boss may frown upon that."

"Oh, he'd definitely frown," Altaha stated. She patted him on the arm. "Enjoy them, will you, and see if you can't end this thing with the missus?"

"Already on it," he said, taking Luella by the wrist. He tugged her toward the exit.

Ellis escorted her out of the station. They rounded the corner where they found his truck waiting. The others had gone, probably in another Eaton Edge truck. Before she could reach for her door handle, he used the circle of his hand around her wrist to tug her around.

She gasped, her front buffered suddenly by his.

His arm hooked around her waist and he brought her to her toes for a firm kiss.

She fumbled for his shoulders. "Wh-what…"

"Did you really break a bottle over Rowdy Conway's head?" he asked.

His eyes were glittering in the dark. She licked her lips, trying to tamp down on the mystifying urge to grin. "Yes."

He made a noise in his throat then brought his mouth back to hers for a kiss as thorough as it was disarming. She felt the door of his truck at her back and embraced the feeling of being trapped between it and his body. She moaned when his hips churned against hers. Gasping, she turned her face away from his but kept her hand firmly thatched in the hair on the back of his head. "We're in the middle of town."

"I don't give a hot damn where we are or who sees," he whispered. The words breezed across her cheek. He touched his temple to her cheekbone. "I could get lost in you. Right here."

She'd lost herself to him a long time ago. She closed her eyes. "Say my name."

"What?" he asked, touching her chin. "What'd you say, honey?"

She gathered her voice above a whisper. "Say my name, Ellis." *Like you said it with her. Show me how you said my name.* "I need to hear you say my name."

It was ridiculous but she could almost hear him smiling. She could feel it. "Luella," he said.

She sighed, turning into him again. "Again."

"Luella," he said. He tugged her into another kiss, this one soft as rain.

"Again, damn it," she said, bringing herself up to her toes to reach the lines of his face… "Say it again."

"God Jesus, I like you strict," he breathed across her mouth. He groaned when she fished his bottom lip between her own, his hands flat against the windows of the truck. "Luella, honey. My always."

"Oh," she sighed again, this time giving in—just throwing in the whole damn towel. Who was she if she didn't need him?

A car passed on the street and she broke away. She was hidden from view by Ellis's breadth and found distraction in the fragrant hollow of his throat. "Let's…let's think for a second."

"Why?" he whined.

A smile dangled from her lips. "Because your girls are coming home."

He lowered his head. There was light in his eyes. "Thank God."

"I shouldn't be there when they do."

"You can't go back to Ollero Creek," he told her.

"I'll find somewhere to go," she told him. "Someplace safe."

"Where's safe when I can't be there to protect you?"

"I'll be okay, Ellis," she told him. "I want you to focus on the girls this weekend. Enjoy them." She pressed her lips together for a second and inhaled, unsteady. "And…if it comes down to it, I need you to promise me something."

"What?"

"If Liberty tries to take them from you again," she said slowly, "and you come to a point where you have to let me go to keep them, I don't want you to hesitate. I want... I need you to keep your girls."

"Lu—"

"Don't," she said. "I didn't get to spend one single moment with my baby...our baby. You can't miss a single moment with your girls. You know that."

"I know that," he told her. "I'd do whatever I could to get those moments with our son back for you. You know that?"

"I do," she whispered. "You didn't promise me."

"I promise," he said with a nod. His hands cupped her hips, tugging her against him once more. They slid around to the small of her back and crossed and he leaned the side of his head against hers. "I'm working my hardest to take it all back."

"What?"

"My life," he said. "My parenthood. My standing. Yours, too. Redemption. The girls need the Edge, their lives there, just as much as I need them."

He was a wonderful father, she saw—such a good daddy. She hated Liberty all the more for trying to erase him from his daughters' lives.

"What do you need to talk to Altaha about tomorrow?"

"Oh." She eased back, spanning her palms across her chest. "Just some decoding. My aunt left me postcards and a photograph of my mother. I've been able to figure out some of the messages. But I was hoping she could help me with some of the others. They helped me find my ring. Did I tell you that?"

"Good old Mabel," he said running his hands over her back.

"Dear old Mabel," she murmured.

"Come home to my bed?" he asked. "Once more at least. Please." When she thought about it, he added, "Don't make me beg." It wavered out of him on a nervous chuckle. "I'll do it on my knees—right here on the pavement."

It might have been the dregs of tequila that made her say it. She'd definitely blame it on tequila in the morning. But she smiled, sly, and said, "I can think of better things for you to do on your knees, Ellis Eaton."

A satisfactory rumble sounded in his chest. "Keep talking like that, sweetheart, and I may not make it back."

"ELLIS, WHERE ARE *YOU?*"

Ellis exchanged a wary look with Eveline over the long line of Shy's back in the stable two days later. The horse jerked at the shout from somewhere near the stable entrance. He set aside his hoof pick and brushed his hands off as he peered into the aisle.

Liberty was looking for him.

Unlatching the gate, he left his sister to see to Shy's care. "I didn't think you'd show," he revealed. "Did you bring the girls with you?"

"I have a bone to pick with you!" she shouted. Five stalls down, the young ranch hand, Lucas, poked his head out, brows raised to the ceiling. "Why are you in cahoots with Rosalie Sullivan?"

Ellis took off his hat in a weary motion. He frowned. "I take that as a no. And I see you're still in touch with the town gossips."

"You met her at Mimi's Steakhouse," Liberty accused. "What did you discuss?"

"That's not really any of your business, is it?" he contemplated. "You wouldn't be so worried about it, either, if you hadn't slept with her husband."

She balked. Turning red as a poppy, she went up to her full height. "How dare you—"

"Let's talk truth for once, shall we?" he intervened neatly. He was stunned he could sound so level when everything inside him came up to a wicked point. "I have something you never did."

"What is that?" she wanted to know.

"Clear and present evidence of my spouse's infidelity," he stated. "You waited for the right moment to pin this whole mess on me. When I said Luella's name, that was your opportunity, to get out of the marriage and take something for yourself. You never thought it'd come back on you like this—not after getting the entire town to side with you and spread your rumors to the far corners of the county and back. You'd have gotten away with it, too, if it hadn't been for Rosalie."

"What're you, sleeping with *her* now, too?" she accused.

Ellis nearly smiled. It was a petty response. "Say goodbye to my shares and that seat on the board and have my girls here tomorrow morning, eight o'clock sharp. Then you're going to call Greasy and tell him the new terms of our divorce."

"Fine," she grumbled. "What do *you* want?"

"Split custody," he said. "I'm not going to take them away from you completely, even though you threatened to do that to me. They need you every bit as much as they need me. I'll even cut you a check, and a generous one to pay for their tuition should you decide they need to stay in private school. But they will have a life here at the Edge. They can have the best of both worlds and when it comes time, they can choose for themselves where they want their lives to unfold. That's the arrangement we should've had from the beginning. They need to come first, Lib. It always should've been them first."

Her eyes moved from his left to his right and back and

forth in quick succession. When she looked away, around at the hands that had gathered to watch the spectacle, she released a breath. "I did bring the girls. They're in the house with Paloma."

"Good."

"Your deputy didn't leave me much choice," she said. "I'll be back to pick them up Sunday morning."

"Sunday afternoon," he countered. "You forget Paloma likes to take us to church."

"Fine, if you tell me how long you've been seeing Luella Decker again," she snapped back. "You were spotted outside the police station the other night—"

"That's a real nice surveillance team you've got on my tail," he remarked.

"—and some say she sleeps here most nights now. Is that true?"

He rocked back to his heels and crossed his arms. "As our marriage has been over for some time now, I'd say that's none of your business, either."

"It won't help you," she warned. "You have to know that."

"I know I'm done playing your games," he replied. "I'll see you Sunday afternoon."

"I don't want her around the girls," Liberty warned. "I won't have it."

He tilted his head. "Sure. If you can look me in the eye and tell me neither of the girls ever saw you flirt with the rodeo king."

She knew he had her. It was why she set her teeth behind her lips. She turned away quickly.

When she reached the open barn doors, Luella's cat Nyx snuck like a black wraith out of the shadows and attacked her ankles. Liberty cursed and shrieked and shook him off.

The cat went flying with a yowl and she pushed her hands through her hair, her steps quickening with every stride.

IT WAS ONLY after Luella told Ellis that she was staying with Altaha that he let her go. The deputy lived not far from downtown Fuego in a one-bedroom house with a chain link fence around the front yard and a screen door with decorative iron over the front. "It's cozy," Altaha said as she led Luella inside. "A little too cozy at times but, hey, I'm single. What do I need the room for?"

Luella assured her it was fine. She slept on the couch the first night, Sphinx curled against her belly.

She turned twice in the night toward phantom warmth that wasn't there. Already she'd grown used to having Ellis beside her.

Over breakfast the following morning in the little windowed space off the kitchen that the deputy called her conservatory, Luella tried to figure out if that was going to be a problem.

She still expected more chaos. If she'd been able to count on anything in life, it was that.

Altaha joined her with a plate of toast. Her reams of glossy black hair were piled messily on top of her head and her gel sleep mask was still wrapped across her forehead. A buttered knife rasped across the surface of her bread. It clattered to the tabletop and she reached for her coffee with a deep frown. "Look, I got something to say and it isn't good so I'm going to have to ask you to brace yourself."

Luella, her feet in her seat and knees between her torso and the table, set her mug aside. "Is this about the postcards I gave you?"

"No," Altaha said with a shake of her head. "Though that photograph does bug me something fierce."

"What about it?"

"I don't know," Altaha said, contemplative. "The man. He rattles something." She gestured to her head. "I can't put my finger on what."

"Okay," Luella said cautiously. "Is what you wanted to tell me something about Ollero Creek?"

"No. Jones has really shut me out of that one. The man's a steel trap when he wants to be."

"What then?" Luella asked. "It's not Ellis…is it?"

"Your boyfriend's fine," Altaha said. "I got a phone call saying Liberty showed up with the girls as instructed so that's something. No, it's…more to do with you and what happened to you in San Gabriel seventeen years ago."

"What?" Luella asked. She lifted her napkin and wiped her mouth, setting her feet down on the floor where they belonged. "Why would it be about that?"

Altaha looked uncomfortable. She turned her gaze to the ice-entrusted backyard that was about the size of a postage stamp and seemed to gather herself. "Everett asked me to look into something that happened back then. A visit his father had on July 20—from a doctor named Dr. Bridestone. Does that name ring a bell?"

Luella thought about it. It did sound familiar in some vague, distant way. "I… I don't know. It might."

"We'll cover that in a minute," Altaha said. "The first thing you need to know is that Hammond Eaton was offered a large sum of money for a newborn baby that would have been delivered to him in December of that year if he met the demands of the closed adoption."

Luella's eyes had gone wide. "A newborn."

"Yes," Altaha said. "So I looked into it. I dug back through your records from the time of your hospitalization without asking. As a friend who isn't on this case in any official capacity, I have to say I'm sorry."

Friend? Luella nodded, distracted.

"Do you remember the name of the obstetrician who happened to be on call that night?" Altaha asked.

Luella squinted down the long lens of her memory. "Dr. Gladbreed? No, that's not right. Dr. Stonewell." A frustrated noise escaped her. "Damn it. It was something along those lines. Some combination of the two."

Altaha waited for Luella to piece it together, watchful.

Luella rubbed her lips together, thinking fast. She snapped her finger. "Dr. Bredston. That was it. Sorry. It was so long ago…" She fumbled to a stop when she saw Altaha's brows drawn together, concerned. It didn't strike her like lightning, as some ideas did. It unveiled itself in slow, utter horror. Luella shoved her chair back from the table and stood. "Oh, my God. Dr. *Bridestone*."

Altaha took a careful breath. "I'm afraid so. You see, I tracked down his wife. His records stated he died eight years ago. Heart attack. She didn't give me much, but it was enough for me to piece some of the puzzle together, for the most part. She admitted that in September of 2006, he came into some hefty cash. She asked him where it came from. He wouldn't tell her, initially. But she managed to needle it out of him. He admitted to his part in exchanging a baby he'd delivered via C-section at the women's center to Fuego County Hospital into the waiting arms of his adoptive parents for the money."

Luella had to open a window. She tried releasing the nearest one from the jamb. It wouldn't budge.

"It's stuck shut." Altaha rose and went to the little patio door. "Here." She pushed it open and let the cold in, propping it open with a potted snake plant. "Just breathe for a second."

Luella made a noise. *Just breathe?* Her baby had been born—alive. Her son had been stolen from her by a corrupt obstetrician and given to complete strangers for a heap of cash.

Heap of cash. Heaps of cash...

She lifted her head slowly. She turned to meet Altaha's gaze and saw something hidden there. Missing information that Luella knew... "Did my mother, Riane Howard, have anything to do with this?"

Altaha licked her lips in a furtive motion. "Luella, your mother arranged the entire thing from start to finish."

A sob bubbled forth. "Oh, God," she cried. There were bitter, bitter waves of grief and horror building inside of her. She turned away quickly and raced from the room.

Down the little hallway, she found the door to the powder room. She closed the door then went down on her knees and rocked herself through waves of sickness.

It reduced her to dry heaves—uncontrolled, gut-wrenching dry heaving that left her weak as a kitten. At that point, she lay on the floor and pressed her brow to the cold tile, trembling and wet with sweat. Her stomach cramped and her mind took her back not to the emptiness it was familiar with when trauma came for a visit...but to those long, long months in her mother and Mabel's house seventeen years ago when she'd felt trapped and panicked and helpless.

She thought of her mother then shut her eyes to hide.

She *was* the devil's daughter, in more than one regard.

Chapter Fourteen

Ellis, Isla and Ingrid spent the weekend riding together, going for long walks and stargazing. He took them up to the roof where he'd set up the old telescope and talked about the stars until they fell asleep on either side of him, their little heads slumped to each of his shoulders. He took them into town for lunch at Hickley's. He took them into the hills to find the little bits of crunchy snow left over for a snowman and then the inevitable iceball fight.

They returned to Eaton House hungry as trolls. Everett, also hungry, colored in coloring books with vigor alongside them while they waited at the table for Paloma to finish dinner. Eveline brought them new boots to try on as they were rapidly growing out of their current ones. They modeled them up and down the entryway, mimicking their aunt's supermodel pout and gliding walk. Wolfe taught them how to build fires in the fire pit on the bricked patio and watched over them as they roasted marshmallows, making sure they didn't burn their hands or any other part of their bodies.

There were reams of laughter around the dinner table again. Paloma told stories from Ellis, Everett and Eveline's youth that Ingrid in particular couldn't seem to get enough of—perhaps because she shared whatever chromosome that had led them on their misadventures.

At night, he missed Luella but soon found himself crowded into the center of his bed when Isla and then Ingrid snuck in from their bunkroom down the hallway and joined him. He listened to their breathing slow and then deepen into repose, almost in sync, and tried not to count the days he had been away from them—and how many more they were going to spend apart before this was all over.

No one came to wake him the following morning—not Paloma, not Everett, not even the restless dogs he kept at his heels. They slept in then tromped downstairs, Ingrid still sleepily invested on his shoulder, to scrounge up a late breakfast.

Sunday afternoon caught up with him all-too-quickly. After church, they had time enough for one more ride across the Edge. He helped them strap on their helmets and mount their ponies and he and Shy led them out into open country air.

"Yeehaw!" Ingrid whooped to his right.

He snuck a glance at Isla. Her form was still superb. Better still was the broad grin on her face. "Faster?" he asked.

"Faster!" Ingrid chirped. "I want to fly!"

"Faster," Isla agreed with a certain nod.

"Yah!" He gave Shy a tap with his heel and the horse broke into a near gallop. The girls' mounts followed suit until they were all in flight.

"That was fun," Ingrid said with a sleepy, smug expression as they walked the horses back to the stable half an hour later.

"I wish we could ride all day," Isla said with a touch of melancholy.

"Me, too," Ellis agreed. "When it gets warm, I want to take you camping on the back of Ol' Whalebones."

"Ol' what?" Ingrid asked.

"The mountain you see to the north," he said.

"It's where the Edge ends," Isla said sagely. "Everybody calls it Ol' Whalebones because it looks like the backbone of a whale."

"The Apaches have another name for it," Ellis told her. "Do you remember it?"

Before Isla could answer, Ingrid stood up in the stirrups. "What's that?" she asked, pointing over her pony Dander's ears.

Ellis looked ahead and saw the black spot in what was left of the ice. He drew back on the reins. "Whoa."

The girls followed suit as he sat and looked at the smudge against the white landscape. He shifted back in the saddle, flicking the reins over Shy's head. "Stay here. Understand?"

"Yes, Daddy," Isla said obediently.

"Yes, Daddy," Ingrid echoed.

Ellis dismounted. He grabbed the reins and led Shy behind him as he approached the figure.

Shy's feet began to dance backward. He whinnied, his nose turning up once, then again.

Ellis stopped long enough to pat him on the neck. He could get closer, but he didn't have to.

Inside, he cursed. It was a black cat.

It was Luella's. The one that had attacked him and then her at Ollero Creek and Liberty just the other day. The cat had been skulking around the stables, chasing mice and boots to his heart's content.

He watched the cat's belly, willing the bastard to breathe.

Instead, it was eerily still against the ice-and-dirt-strewn grass.

Ellis looked around. He scanned the fence to the east and the shadow of the river to the west. His eyes fell on the buildings in the near distance.

The cat was alone out here. More, it had died inside the bounds of the Edge—meaning that whoever had brought harm to Ollero Creek had penetrated the safe harbor that was his home.

He cursed a stream, unable to help himself.

"What is it, Daddy?" Ingrid called. "Is it hurt?"

He glanced back at his girls. He scanned the shape of their pale faces, the little tufts of air that escaped their mouths.

He was going to send them away this time. They wouldn't be able to return until he hunted down the killer and finished this.

ELLIS KNOCKED ON Altaha's door that evening, hat in hand. He studied the worn texture of her welcome mat, hating the news he carried.

The door behind the screen opened. Altaha appeared in plainclothes, her hair braided black over her shoulder. "What are you doing here?" she asked.

"I need Luella," he said without preamble.

She pushed the screen open. "Now's not a good time."

"Why not?" he asked. "Has she been talking to someone at the Edge?"

She tilted her chin. "No. Why?"

"Something's happened," he told her. "Another animal attack."

Altaha lifted a brow. "How do you know it's related to the others?"

"It was Luella's cat," he said.

"Just hers?"

"Yes." He took a step forward but she didn't budge. "Damn it, Kaya, let me in."

"It's not a good time," she repeated.

"What's going on?"

"She's had a hard few days," Altaha revealed. "She's had some news… It's been difficult. She's processing."

"What news?" he demanded.

"You can't come in," she told him, "until she says you can. Do you understand?"

He met her stare and knew he wasn't getting past her. "I just want to talk to her. She needs to know about her cat."

"Jones," Altaha said in realization. She nodded. "He's the lead on this now. He'll want to talk to her, too."

"I need to warn her," he told her.

"Leave it with me."

"Kaya," he said before she could close the door. "I can't walk away not knowing what's hurt her."

She frowned. "Look, lover boy—"

"Let him in," Luella said from behind her.

"Lu," he started then stopped. She looked like actual hell. Her hair was a mess around her face and her cheeks were splotched with red and white in patches. The red had washed down her neck to the open collar of her chambray shirt. Worst of all, her eyes—they were rimmed with dark circles and they didn't so much look at him as through him.

"I'll make coffee," she said before shuffling into the depths of the house.

Wide-eyed, Ellis looked to Altaha for answers.

She heaved a sigh and held the door open. "You heard the woman."

Carrying his hat, he stepped over the threshold, knowing on some level the news that waited for him was twice as bad as the news he'd come to deliver.

"I COULD GET fired for this," Altaha said as Ellis sped past the sign for San Gabriel.

They'd been driving for some time with Luella riding

quiet in the backseat. He glanced in the rearview mirror at her remote face. She'd remained motionless for much of the drive, staring out the window.

That empty stare was scaring the hell out of him.

As the speed limit signs narrowed to the town limit, he didn't lift his foot from the gas. "Nobody asked you to come," he told the deputy.

"Damn it, Eaton. I'm a cop. Slow the eff down!"

He did—but only by a fraction. "Tell it to me again."

"We've been over it three times," Altaha told him wearily. They blew past the police station and she gave a little wave.

"Once more," he insisted.

She sighed. "I know *some* of the timeline."

"Starting with?"

"Luella had an accident at the home she was sharing with her mother and aunt," Altaha recounted, turning to look into the backseat for confirmation that didn't come.

"She fell down the stairs," he remembered, filling the silence delicately. God, if she'd just say *something*—let him know she was going to be okay. The news that their baby had been stolen was enough. But the silence was crushing him.

"Riane took her to San Gabriel Women's Center where she was admitted around five o'clock in the afternoon," Altaha continued. "The doctor on call at that time was Dr. Bredston. He arrived shortly after, clocking in around half an hour later, which is pretty impressive considering it was a Sunday and he lived some forty-five minutes outside of town. The RN who first attended Luella that evening was one Scott, Lacey. She was the only nurse in the room."

"The whole time?"

"From what the file said, yes. Luella corroborated that."

Ellis thought about it. "There were at least three in the

room when each of the girls were born—plus the obstetrician. Not to mention the anesthesiologist and interns. Weren't there any other nurses on staff that night?"

"There had to have been," Altaha reasoned. "It's the largest women's center in the county. Even on a Sunday, you'd think they'd need at least two or three."

"Go through the rest of it," Ellis said, turning down the road toward the residential side of town.

"According to Luella, she was sedated an hour or so after she was admitted," Altaha went on. "The reason being that she was hysterical. When she woke up, the doctor had gone home. The only people with her were RN Scott and her mother, Riane, who told her her baby had been stillborn."

"But the files tell another story?" Ellis prompted.

"Yes. They took her into the OR not long after she was sedated where Bredston performed an emergency C-section. The baby's time of birth was reported as seven twenty-two that night."

"From there?" Ellis asked, his pulse swimming in his ears.

"A bus was called from the nearest hospital—that's Fuego County Hospital—and arrived around eight thirty. The baby was taken directly to the NICU."

"What was the reason?" Ellis wondered, the words punchy. His hands hardened on the wheel.

"Premature birth," she said. "Other than that, no medical reason was noted in the file. From there, the baby's whereabouts taper off. I'll have to quibble with the hospital for those. Luella, however, was discharged from the women's center three days later. Bredston discharged her with a script for a high dose of ibuprofen and an antidepressant. She followed up with her post-op appointments."

He ground his back teeth together as he pulled onto Tesuque Lane. "I don't buy that the nurse, Scott, wasn't in on it, too."

Altaha grabbed the panic bar over her head when he swerved into Riane's driveway. "Christ," she muttered.

He'd unclipped his seat belt and opened the driver's door before he'd shut off the engine. He eyed the front line of the tidy two-story, scowling at the curtains over the windows. He reached for Luella's door but she'd already opened it and was climbing to the ground. Grabbing her arm, he muttered, "Easy there, honey."

"I'm not made of glass, Ellis," she informed him.

The blotchiness he'd seen on her complexion yesterday had been replaced by an almost translucent pallor. She *looked* like glass. "You don't have to come in. You can wait out here, if you need to."

"I want to see her," Luella said. "Hear what she has to say for herself."

"It's not going to be easy."

"What part of this is?" she asked. "What part of our lives has *ever* been easy?"

He could hardly breathe. Everything he had to say seemed too paltry an offering in the face of her disillusionment.

Altaha led them up the front steps to the front door. She pounded on it several times with a closed fist. As they waited, she asked him, "So, you wanna be good cop or bad cop?"

Ellis eyed her blandly before the door opened and a large man in a polo shirt and khakis barely hanging on by a belt answered the door. He looked from Ellis to Altaha, who was in her official uniform and hat, and frowned. "Can I help you, Officer?"

"Deputy Altaha," she greeted, extending a hand for him

to shake. When he did, hesitantly, she asked, "Are you Solomon Howard?"

"I am," he said, reaching up for his browline. He stopped to scratch it. "Is there some kind of trouble?"

"We just have a few questions," Altaha explained. "Is your wife, Riane, home?"

"She is," Solomon said, glancing over his shoulder. He tapped his fingers on the edge of the door.

"Let us in, Sol," Luella said at Ellis's back.

"Luella? What are you doing here? Your mother's not going to be happy to see you. I can tell you that."

"She can deal with it," Ellis told him.

"Ellis," Altaha said, setting her teeth. "I do have to insist," she told Solomon. "It's official business."

"I guess." He narrowed his eyes on Ellis. "Can I ask what this is about?"

"We're following up on a case," Altaha noted as they followed him through the foyer into the kitchen breaking off to the left, "to which she was a witness some years ago. We have a couple of follow-up questions then we'll be out of your hair."

"Riane? There's some people here to see you."

Riane was sitting at the table with a pair of scissors and what looked like coupons spread across the table. When she looked up from her business, she stiffened first at the sight of Altaha then stilled completely when her gaze locked on Ellis and Luella standing shoulder to shoulder. She got to her feet, the chair moving back with a screech across the floor. "What are you doing with him?"

"Long time, Moms," Ellis greeted cheerlessly. There was a muscle ticing in his jaw incessantly. "How's it hangin'?"

She scowled at him then Luella, the scissors clamped

in her fist. "What's she told you?" she asked, staring hard at Altaha's nameplate on her shirtfront. "My daughter's a pathological liar. Always has been. You know that, Ellis."

"Shut up and sit down," Ellis said, pulling out a chair for himself.

"Now," Solomon said, inching forward, "you can't speak to my wife like that."

Altaha raised her hand to him. "Sir, I'm going to have to ask you to wait outside."

"You said you were just going to question her," Solomon said, eyes peeled.

"Be quiet, Solomon, and go call the lawyer," Riane snapped. "Make yourself useful, for God's sake."

"What do you need a lawyer for, Riane?" he asked, bewildered.

"Go on!" Riane yelled.

Ellis ran a hand down his shirtfront, contemplative. He waited until Solomon left the room, chastised, before he pulled a chair out for Luella and gestured for her to sit beside him. When she did so, facing her mother again with silent reluctance, he decided to take the lead. "You were ready with that lawyer bit, weren't you?" he asked Riane.

"I don't have to speak to you," she said.

"You are wrong about that."

Altaha had been poised between the only exit and Riane. She moved the only remaining chair, motioning for Riane to sit back down. "It's like we told your husband, Mrs. Howard. We'd like you to answer a few questions about the night your daughter went into labor. That's all."

"Luella never went into labor," Riane sneered. "She miscarried. They had to go in and get the baby out. It was stillborn."

"Nope," Ellis put in. Luella flinched and he laid his arm across the line of her shoulders, steadying.

Altaha spared him a glance. "Please, sit down, Mrs. Howard."

"What if I don't submit to these questions of yours?" she asked.

"Then we can take this down to the station," Altaha told her, evenly. There was a finality behind it, though, that made Riane's head snap back. "It's up to you."

Riane's eyes followed Altaha's hand as it reached around on her belt. She shoveled out a breath then pursed her lips in an unhappy pout and dropped unceremoniously to her chair.

"The real story this time," Ellis said with a hurry-up motion. "Come on. Take us through it, step-by-step."

"I don't know what you want from me," Riane claimed.

"You could start with whatever relationship or arrangement you had with Dr. Graham Bredston," Altaha suggested.

She made a disgusted noise. "We didn't have a relationship. He was the doctor in the delivery room that night."

"Dr. Bredston, did you say?" Solomon asked, coming into the room. His phone was in his hand. He shuffled to the table, his temples lined. "Isn't that the obstetrician from church who died a few years ago?"

"Be quiet, Solomon."

"He was a big donor for those fundraisers you do every year. The ones for the foster children."

"I said quiet, Sol!" Riane screeched.

He stopped and looked from his wife's stern expression to Ellis and Luella. His mouth formed an *O*. "Sorry. I called the lawyer."

"Is he coming?" Riane asked.

"Ah, yes," Solomon said. "But he's an hour away. There was some court case in Santa Fe he had to attend this morn-

ing. I could sit with you until he gets here..." He trailed
off when she quailed him with another one of her looks.
He jerked a thumb behind him. "All righty then. I'll be out
back..."

They waited for him the shamble out again. "Idiot," Riane
muttered.

"So your relationship with Dr. Bredston," Altaha picked
up. "It was monetary, in some fashion."

"He donated money to a good cause," Riane supplied.

"How long have you been attending the same church as
him?" Altaha asked.

"I never attended church here in San Gabriel," Altaha
claimed. "Not before I met Solomon."

"That's a lie," Luella said, under her breath.

"Shut up, girl."

Ellis went cold. "I've never hit a woman in my life, but
you say that to her again and I might."

"You've got your own family now, don't you?" Riane
asked him. "Why're you getting so worked up over my
daughter? She left you, remember? Ran away, hid her baby
so you wouldn't have to worry yourself over it."

Altaha cleared her throat. "Everybody remembers you in
Fuego for your perfect attendance at church every Sunday.
First to get there. Last to leave. You organized fundraisers
there, too—as well as luncheons, bazaars... You practically
ran the nursery. Reverend Claymore describes you to this
day as the incredible one-woman show."

"Did you try to sell those babies, too?" Ellis wondered
out loud.

"Ellis," Altaha said. It was a low warning.

He didn't want to back down. He didn't want to settle
back and watch. She'd sold his and Luella's baby. He was
sure of it. He eased off only because he knew if anybody

could get a confession out of her, it was Altaha. And they needed it.

"Mrs. Howard," Altaha said, carefully, "I've already warned you. You can cooperate or you can answer these questions at the station. We have evidence that Luella's newborn was born via C-section at San Gabriel Women's Center before being rushed to the NICU at Fuego County Hospital. We also are certain that Dr. Bredston and the nurse on staff that night, Lacey Scott, lied to Luella about the baby's whereabouts."

"Sounds like they're the ones you need to question," Riane said. "Not me."

"So when we question Lacey Scott," Altaha continued, "she won't confess to having colluded with you to make this happen?"

Riane was silent on that point. She turned her face to the window. The sun fell harshly against the creases of her face.

"How did you convince them to do it?" Ellis pushed. "Were you paid that much for the baby that you were able to cut them both in on it?"

Her nose twitched. She stared at nothing, motionless.

Ellis sat back against the ladderback chair. He wanted to flip the table over. He wanted to break something. He wanted to scare the truth out of her.

He needed to know where his son was.

Reaching for Luella's hand, he used it to bring himself back. Her fingers were so chilled, he curled his around them and tucked them against his navel. Looking around, he noted the glass-front cabinets, the fine china, silver and crystal on display at every corner. "It was enough, wasn't it—to fix you up for life? How else could you afford this? Mabel taught art classes. You work at the church, like you always have. Solomon doesn't fetch much at the grocery store he manages."

When Riane again said nothing, he shook his head. "Hell, at least tell me why you did it—how you could sell your own grandson like that. You owe us that much, at least."

At first, he thought she wouldn't respond. He thought they'd sit the whole hour in silence waiting for her damn lawyer. Then, quietly, as if from far away, he heard her say, "I didn't want my daughter to raise a bastard, like I had to."

Ellis stared, wondering if Riane had said it or he'd imagined it. Luella whimpered.

Altaha leaned forward. "Can you repeat that, Mrs. Howard?"

"You've got ears, Deputy," she hissed. "I'll say nothing more until the lawyer comes." Her arms knit across her chest and she closed her eyes, as if exhausted.

Bastard. Ellis heard the word over and over.

He didn't realize he was grinding his teeth until Luella's hand turned into his, reaching. She met his gaze. Shock penetrated the blank wall of her composure. Her eyes were big and blue and desperate. Tears filled them and he nearly broke.

"You two should go outside," Altaha told them. "Walk it off."

He never should have brought Luella back here. He never should've made her sit through this. Keeping ahold of her hand, he brought himself then her to their feet. His hand on the small of her back, he ushered her toward the door.

Before he left Riane's kitchen, he turned to face her. "If there is a hell, you're going there. And when you get there, I hope you meet your ex-husband. It's nothing less than you deserve after what you've put her through."

"Ellis," Luella said at his back.

He followed her urging, opening the door for her. They escaped the house together.

He watched her sit on the front steps and, after a moment, drop her face into her hands.

Heavily, he sat next to her. He sat with her as the weight of everything came to the surface. He put his arm around her, soothing as best as he could as he heard her cry. She'd suffered so much here without him.

Not anymore, he thought. She wasn't going to be without him anymore.

Fighting his own emotions, he rocked against her. "Hey," he said, sounding gruff.

She lifted her face and wiped away the wet. She'd cried silent tears, the only sound her breath hitching every few seconds. He wished she'd wail until there was nothing left of it—until she was free of it, the whole terrible weight of it.

He waited until her eyes came back to his. "I love you," he said.

Her lips trembled. She shook her head.

"No," he said. "You'll hear it here, where you ran from Whip and your mother hurt you. You'll hear it because it's still true. I love you, Luella. I'll say it however many times I need to. I will work until I make a believer out of you, like I did before. I love you. I will never stop loving you. No matter what comes."

She stared, her eyes softening as they circled his face. It was her only response, beyond the biting of her lip.

He touched his lips to the center of her brow. "I'm sorry," he said, reaching up to wipe away her tears. "I can't change the fact that you were born to her. But I can tell you every day that you're worth ten of her. More. You're worth more." He traced the curve of her ear. "Remember? 'All the stars and the ones we can't see...' That's you."

She closed her eyes. He'd said it before when he'd proposed. Her hand slid up his arm, clutched his wrist then touched him palm-to-palm. Fingers lacing through his, she brought his hand to her cheek and pillowed her head there. "I always knew I was yours," she said after some time. "I never thought...you could be mine, too."

"I never wanted to be anything else."

"Stop," she said automatically.

He turned his hand to her cheek, bringing her focus back to him. He made sure he had it, before he challenged her. "Why?"

Her lips parted. She eyed his mouth. She exhaled quickly. "I'm not sure anymore," she murmured.

"Me either," he said. "I will make this right. If our son's out there, I will find him. And I will bring him back to you. I swear."

Chapter Fifteen

Luella walked Sheridan around the paddock on a lunge line in a wide circle, wary of the crazy look in his eyes. "Walk," she instructed. He'd been cooped up in a stall too long, waiting for his wound to heal enough for sport. Until he could be ridden again, the lunge line was his best means of exercise. And until she was sure he was limbered up, he would have to walk. "I know, baby," she cooed. "You're doing great. Just…walk."

It did her good to see him walking. It must be nice, getting outdoors again. As soon as she'd led him out of the stall and into the paddock, he'd bobbed his head as if to say, *Yes! Yes!* She found a smile on her lips as she gave him subtle urgings through the rein. "Turn. Good boy. Let's walk the other way."

He snorted, tugging lightly on the line.

"It's boring," she granted. "I get it. But you're a good boy and you're doing great."

She'd debated whether to bring him back to Eaton Edge or not. Since she and Ellis had buried Nyx, it had become clear to her that whoever had been able to hurt her animals at Ollero Creek could hurt them here, too. She couldn't help but question whether Sheridan would be safe.

Extra security measures had been stepped up. Hands

were posted outside the barn at all times. She didn't envy those on the graveyard shift, and she knew them all. Wolfe and Eveline took it in turns as well as Everett, their head wrangler, Javier, and Griff MacKay, the stable manager.

Luella knew each of them personally. It helped that they were the ones who Sheridan seemed least likely to take a bite out of.

"He's almost ready for tack."

Luella found Ellis standing at the gate. His gloved hands were wrapped around the top rung, but he kept himself on the other side. Sheridan had come a long way since leaving the clinic, but he still wouldn't let Ellis near him without nipping. Luella had started to wonder if it was because he sensed how much Luella liked him.

Loved him.

Her stomach fluttered. The sun was bright in the midday sky, casting shadows under the brim of his white hat. But she saw the intensity beyond the smile—the deep portals of his eyes. It transported her to someplace diverting. There was safety there and heat—so much heat, it made her knees weak.

She was back in his bed. Their nights had been filled with everything his eyes promised—intensity, sweetness, need and safety.

My always.

It was a wonder she managed to get any sleep at all. If not for exhaustion, she'd lie awake thinking how she was going to handle loving him and leaving again.

She went back to watching the placement of Sheridan's hooves. Ms. Breslin had stopped by yesterday. The inspection at Ollero Creek had gone well. She'd worked up a list price and had wanted Luella to approve it and the listing so it could finally go on the market.

Luella had panicked. She'd waited until Ms. Breslin left before escaping outdoors into the fresh air, wondering why her flight reflex had kicked in.

Isn't this what she'd wanted? She'd *wanted* to sell, leave Fuego, start over. And someone wanted her gone, enough that he'd killed just to get that message across.

Luella pivoted toward the gate as Sheridan completed his next circle. Ellis knew her moods. He fell into companionable silence.

Perfect, she thought. He was so damn perfect…for her.

It was a strange thought. She'd never thought of him that way. Perfect, yes. But not perfect *for her.*

The idea was like candy. Hell, it was a drug.

Should she really think of Ellis in those terms?

Perfect. For me.

Whether she should or not, she couldn't seem to stop.

"Ellis!"

The stare broke, leaving Luella with a pleasant shiver as she shortened the lunge line, bringing Sheridan to a slow stop. "Whoa," she murmured, shortening the rein until he was within reach. As the young hand, Lucas, came to the gate to meet Ellis, Luella stroked Sheridan's winter coat, checking his wound to make sure it hadn't torn with any of the new activity. She couldn't help but eavesdrop, especially when the words *the sheriff* fell from the boy's mouth.

"Thanks," Ellis told him. "You're on gate duty today?"

"Yeah," Lucas said. "With Everett."

Ellis made a face. "Good luck with that."

"Any idea when I'll be able to call him chief again?" Lucas asked.

"Not sure why you stopped," Ellis replied. They heard ringing in the distance. "That's the lunch bell. Head in for a bite. We'll be there shortly."

As Lucas trudged back in the direction of the house, Luella walked Sheridan to the gate. "What about the sheriff?"

"He's here," Ellis said. "In the house."

He gauged her reaction. She set her jaw. "Maybe there's news."

He nodded though she could read his doubt for what it was. "Do you want me to stable him?"

He reached for Sheridan's halter. The horse pulled away.

Ellis sighed but offered something of a smile. "I'm not going anywhere, partner. You're going to have to learn to put up with me."

Luella made soft noises until Sheridan relaxed. She pressed her cheek against his face.

Ellis watched, looking hard and soft and all manner of wonderful, forbidden things. When his glove closed over the top of her hand on the gate, she stilled.

He smiled, using the hold to bring her close.

She followed his bidding, coming up to her toes. The gate was between them but it didn't matter. Despite Sheridan pushing his nose at her hip for attention, she accepted the bidding of Ellis's mouth.

It was so tender, she felt her legs buckle. They'd made his iron bed frame rock the night before. How could something this demure be just as effective?

"Mmm," he murmured, thick tawny lashes coming down to reveal the freckle on his eyelid. His sigh blew across her mouth. She shivered again and he grinned. "Who needs lunch? I've got you, honey."

She sank her teeth into her lip to stop herself from moaning. "If you're still planning on taking that ride into the southwest quadrant, kissing won't sustain you."

"I don't know 'bout that," he said, sly. "It sure keeps me toasty thinking about this mouth." Her lips parted under the urging of his thumb. She checked the urge to insert it into her mouth. "Other things about you, too. All the other things."

She closed her eyes, turning her cheek to his palm. "You're making me blush."

"That helps, too," he said, "as I know all the little places that blush leads me when I'm taking off your clothes, one layer at a time."

He was touching her now through the gate, hands soft on her curves. She stopped thinking—just stopped. How was she supposed to concentrate or, hell, function on any level when she knew he thought about her like this? She had hay stuck to her sweater, rips in her jeans and mud on her boots. This morning, she'd tied her hair back in a tangled mess at the base of her neck. She smelled like horse—horse hair, horse sweat, horse slobber. Still, this was how he thought about her. "You can't take off my clothes here."

"We could go skinny-dipping," he suggested, framing her hips as his mouth turned its attention to the column of her throat. "Like we used to. You remember."

She did, vividly. "It'd be more of a polar plunge at this point. I'm not sure you could perform after a shock like that."

"Ain't no harm in trying, sweetheart."

It brought a laugh out of her, as he'd intended. She pushed him away. "Recall that the sheriff's here."

"I'm going to have to have a word with him," he said, hanging his head as she opened the gate and guided Sheridan through.

"About?"

"Wiping away that smile," he said. "I'm helpless when you smile. You know that, don't you?"

"You need to stop talking."

He'd fallen into step as she made her way to the stable yard. The easy way his hand found hers, linked and held, didn't go unnoticed. It was natural to walk hand in hand with him. "To you? Never."

"Sheridan's going to take a bite out of you," she warned.

"Tell me it's not worth it."

She started to laugh again. It died in her throat when Sheriff Jones came around the side of the building. "Uh-oh."

Ellis growled. "I'll take care of him."

"No," she said. "I'll see what he wants."

"What he wants is to rattle your cage." His hand tightened on hers. "Let him try it. I might be in the mood for a misdemeanor."

"Ellis," she said. As they drew closer, the sunlight glinted off the sheriff's sunglasses. Something stirred in her blood. She frowned when she recognized it as a frisson of fear.

"Can I help you, Sheriff?" Ellis asked.

"Eaton," he greeted. "I'd like a word with Ms. Decker, if you don't mind."

"Oh, but I do," Ellis said in a tumbled rush that spoke of his irritation.

Luella frowned at them. "What can I do for you, Sheriff?"

"You can give me your whereabouts from last Sunday," he said, drawing his writing pad from his back pocket. He flipped through. "The eighteenth, around noon."

"What is this about?" she asked as Ellis shifted his feet, impatient.

"I'd like your whereabouts," he stated again, stubbornly.

"I was at Kaya Altaha's house most of the weekend," she answered.

"My deputy's?"

"She let me stay a couple of nights there," Luella explained.

"And you'd say that's your alibi for the time in question?"

"Alibi?" Ellis snapped. "You mind telling us what your meaning is exactly?"

The frisson of fear had started to drench her in a cold sweat.

"Rowdy Conway," Jones said.

"What about him?" Luella wondered.

"Somebody tried to run him off the road between the southeast pasture here at Eaton Edge and town," Jones said. He planted his hands on his belt. "It was a truck driven by someone that matched your description."

"He saw *me*?" she said doubtfully.

"He said he thought it was you," Jones explained. "And since it was you who assaulted him at Hatchet House days before—"

"Oh, for God's sake—" she began.

"—I'd say he's got his reasons for assuming so."

She shook her head. "It wasn't me, Sheriff."

"You're certain?"

"Pretty darn," she drawled.

"I'll be checking with Deputy Altaha to ascertain your whereabouts," he said, stuffing the notebook back in his pocket. "Until then…don't leave town."

"Jesus Christ," Ellis muttered.

Luella narrowed her eyes on Jones's back as he strolled in the direction of Eaton House. "What was Rowdy Conway doing near the Edge's southeast gate the same afternoon Ellis found my cat dead out there?" she called after him. When he stopped and rotated halfway around to study her again, she shrugged. "Did you think to ask him that question when he came to you with these claims?"

Jones considered her. Then he lifted a hand to pinch the brim of his hat in parting and kept going.

"Son of a bitch," Ellis groaned. "Surprised he didn't arrest you, just for the fun of it. Give it time. He'll be back."

"Yes," she said wearily.

"We'll be ready."

She glowered at the determined glint in his eyes. "Don't do anything stupid."

"I'm an Eaton, honey," he argued. "We don't call it stupidity. We call it defense, and there's nothing we take more seriously than defending our own." His gaze was a hot, dark lance as he snuck a kiss over her stunned lips. "You're mine. My own. Nothing's going to stand in the way of that. Not even the goddamn sheriff of Fuego County. Let him come. I'm waitin'."

As he walked away, too, she released a heavy breath. Why did he always say the words that were bound to disarm her most? She closed her eyes, briefly, before petting Sheridan on the neck and leading him into the safety of the stables.

She jumped when she nearly ran into Everett. "Make some noise, why don't you?" she suggested.

"He's right," he told her.

"Which part?" she asked. "There's a lot there to digest."

"All of it," Everett said. "We're Eatons. We defend ours— all of ours. Doesn't matter who from."

"*You'd* defend me?" she challenged. "From the sheriff?"

"In a heartbeat."

There was no hesitation. Luella was stunned beyond belief.

"I'd have done it," he claimed, "had you let him keep you seventeen years ago. We might've been better off if we'd finished off your father then."

"And I'm the one who has to live with that," she assured him.

"We all live with it," he told her. "Ellis has carried it for almost twenty years. You'll remember that before you think about leaving him again. When he says he's all in, he's all in, baby. There's nothing more certain in this world than my brother when it comes to his kids and his woman." She opened her mouth to reply, but he intervened. "*You're* his woman. It was never that other one. Let him give you the life he wants to—the life he's always wanted to give you. I'd say he's earned it."

Before she could offer any sort of reply, he stalked off in long strides. She heard him holler at Lucas.

It was hard enough trying to figure out her own heart and mind—never mind having to deal with two tall, dark and brooding Eaton men.

LUELLA AND ALTAHA had taken to meeting at Ollero Creek a couple of mornings a week. It was the deputy's opportunity to update her on the San Gabriel case as well as try taking another crack at Mabel's messages. It was Luella's chance to sit with the rooms and try to figure out if she really wanted to sell them.

She didn't take her panic attack after speaking to Ms. Breslin lightly. Did she really want to leave Fuego—or was she just being chicken about the final plunge? Once the house was on the market, that was it. No turning back. No changing her mind. But she wasn't going to do it unless she was absolutely certain it was the right choice.

The trouble was, she had no idea what was right anymore.

She stood in front of the window overlooking the plain. The snow was all melted. In the distance, she could see clouds, but not the kind that brought snow from the mountains. It would bring cold rain and thunder. By nightfall, everybody in Fuego would be sheltering from the storm.

Deer were visible, she saw with a start. She stepped closer

to the glass, squinting. Three does. Or perhaps a mother and two large fawns. She saw the smile in her reflection and blinked.

She'd caught herself doing that quite a bit over the last few days.

A few days of contentment—were they enough to make the decision that would determine where she should spend the rest of her life? A few days of happiness amid a lifetime of chaos.

She couldn't count on happiness. Or, at least she hadn't thought she could. After the lecture from Everett and Ellis's intimate attentions of the last few days... Well, she was starting to believe. That was a hell of a lot scarier than a storm. Her whole belief system was in upheaval and it was all their fault.

It wasn't just the brothers. It was Eveline, who she'd been sharing stable duties with. They'd discussed her dream of opening a horse rescue either at the Edge or on the property she now shared with Wolfe just outside Fuego city limits. It sounded not just like a noble pursuit but an important one. Her excitement had been tangible.

Hell, it was contagious. Luella bit her lip. Wouldn't it be nice helping rehabilitate horses who'd had a rough start in life? Horses like Sheridan.

The kitchen door opened and Altaha breezed in with a burst of cold. "Wind's picking up," she noted, stomping her feet on the rug. "It's going to get wicked."

"Yes," Luella said, frowning at those storm clouds on the horizon. "Did you find anything out there?"

"Nothing," the deputy said, removing her hat. "Everything's clear."

Luella breathed a little easier as Altaha joined her near the window. On the long expanse of wall next to it, the deputy had already started an elaborate link chart. Mabel's postcard messages had been tacked amongst various names—Luella, Ellis, Hammond, Everett, Dr. Bredston (aka Bridestone), RN Lacey Scott, Mabel, Riane and Baby. Altaha had used Post-its to make notes under each name. The messages Luella had already figured out also had Post-its with the meaning written on each.

In the center hung the photograph Mabel had sent her of her mother and the mystery man.

Altaha bounced on the balls of her feet. "I feel closer."

Luella narrowed her eyes on the board. "Nothing's changed here. How could you feel closer?"

"I feel it," Altaha repeated with a bob of her head. "Starting here." She tapped the face of the mystery man in the photograph. "Why would your aunt send you this particular photograph?"

Luella lifted her shoulders. "I don't know."

Altaha pursed her lips. "You remember what Riane said during our sit-down at her house."

"She said a lot of things," Luella remembered. "None of them good."

"She said she did what she did with your baby so that you didn't have to raise a bastard…"

Luella's stomach clutched. "Like she did," she finished dimly. She had mulled over the words. Had Riane meant that? Was Luella a product of a relationship other than the disastrous one Riane had had with Whip Decker…or had Riane said it simply to hurt her?

It was a toss-up, really.

Nonetheless, Luella found her focus returning to the mystery man. "You believed her. And you think this man may be my father."

"It's a theory I've been working," Altaha admitted. "You

have to see it makes sense." She pointed to Mabel's post-cards, one by one. "'Mother.' 'Father...'"

Luella stared at the third. "'Baby.'"

"Maybe Mabel was wiser than any of us thought," Altaha suggested. "Maybe everything about this comes full circle."

"Maybe..." Luella let the possibilities hang in the air. "She hasn't led us wrong with any of the others. 'Night-stand.'"

"The date," Altaha added, nodding to the card with *S.9.06.*

"And the abbreviation," Luella said, frowning at *S.G.W.C.*

"We'll need the testimony of Lacey Scott to charge Riane as most of Bredston's wife's statement is supposition and probably won't hold up once Riane's lawyers sink their teeth into it..."

"Have you had any luck finding the baby?" Luella asked. In her mind, her son was still a baby. It'd taken a while to bring herself around to fully accept the miracle that he was alive, much less a teenage boy fast approaching adulthood.

"No," Altaha said. "Adoptions have a lot of red tape around them, particularly closed adoptions. It may take weeks. Maybe months before we get through it."

Luella nodded. "We'll keep trying."

"Of course, we will," Altaha assured her. "Until then, we should figure out what the last message means."

"'W.J.' It's got to be initials," Luella stated.

"I ran a search through county residents to see how many people with the initials W.J. there are around here."

"What'd you come up with?"

Altaha made a face. "Roughly a hundred."

"Wow," Luella said. She shook her head. "That's dis-couraging."

"I printed lists from both San Gabriel and Fuego in 1987,

2006 and now, but I've only just started combing for names that are familiar. I want you to take a look at them, too. Something, or someone, might pop out at you. We just need to narrow it down. Once we get fifteen or so, I can start knocking on doors, asking questions…"

Luella nodded. "I can do that." She stared at the *Baby* card again. "I wish we knew his name. If I just knew his name…all this would be better."

"We'll find it," Altaha told her. "I won't stop looking for your child. Not until he's found."

"Thank you," Luella said, "Kaya."

Altaha's mouth formed into a warm smile. "You're welcome, Luella. Hey, I forgot to mention. I checked your game camera footage again this morning."

As the deputy pulled out her phone and logged into Luella's security server, Luella leaned over her shoulder. Altaha backtracked through the footage from the night before. "At approximately two twenty-two…"

Luella made herself take a steadying breath as she watched a large figure lumber across her empty yard. "His back's to the cameras."

"Look at the way he's walking."

Luella hated how ghostly the image of the man looked in night vision. Everything was pixelated in shades of gray while the killer's form floated like an apparition.

No, *floated* was the wrong word, Luella realized, looking again. "He's limping."

"Mmm-hmm," Altaha said, her smile fixed. "The injury's to his right leg or hip."

Luella's eyes grew round. "You could check the hospital—see if there's been someone admitted for an injury."

"I did, before I knew where Ellis's bullet hit the guy," Altaha informed her. "There were no gunshot wounds reported within seventy-two hours at Fuego County Hospital or the urgent cares around here."

"Oh," Luella said, deflating.

"But knowing it's his right side… If he knows how to work the system then he may have convinced a doctor to supply him with pain meds, anti-inflammatories, antibiotics."

"What was he doing, do you think—at the house?"

"I think he was checking to see whether or not you were home."

"If I had been?" Luella wondered, quietly.

"Best you not dwell on that one," Altaha said. "You're not leaving Eaton Edge anytime soon, are you?"

"I don't know what I'm doing." The words spilled faster than Luella could catch them. When Altaha only stared, Luella licked her lips. "Well. It's true. I don't know what I'm doing…or what to do."

"About your living situation…" Altaha asked, "or the other thing?"

The other thing was Ellis, of course, and his feelings for her. Her feelings for him. Their feelings for each other. "It's hard to think about leaving," Luella admitted in a low voice, "when I don't know where our son is. How would you contact me if you did find him?"

"*When* we find him," Altaha amended. "Is that the only thing keeping you here?"

"I don't know," Luella lied, pacing to the other end of the kitchen. "It would be easier to sell everything…start over somewhere new. Somewhere no one knows who I am… who my family is…"

Altaha gave a nod. "That would be easier. I know I haven't had it as hard as you. But if you'd told me a year ago that Wolfe Coldero—that kid who showed up on the

Edge beaten and silent and nearly broken—could be living life as good as he is now, I wouldn't have believed it."

Luella thought about it. "Wolfe's lucky. And he deserves a good life."

"You deserve one, too," Altaha insisted. "And if anybody in this town disagrees with that, they can go straight to hell."

Luella laughed in a sudden burst. Miracles did happen, she was finding, one confidante at a time.

Before either of them could speak, Altaha's phone rang. She frowned at the caller ID. "Well, well. Lacey Scott found us." She glanced at Luella. "I need to take this."

"Go ahead," Luella said. "I'll be outside."

Chapter Sixteen

The wind stung her eyes but she stared nonetheless at the land. Now that the ice was gone, the grass stirred. It whispered.

So much space, she thought. How many times had she thought about buying a telescope, building some sort of shed out in the open so that she could observe the heavens from its roof?

The thought had brought too many memories of her and Ellis at Eaton Edge. She'd always dismissed it.

Space, she considered. It wasn't the cosmos, she realized. It was right here, on Earth.

Why *had* she bought all this space? It was too much for one person. She'd wanted to make use of it, somehow. But the thought of her father lurking out there somewhere when she'd known he was alive had scared her enough to give up any ideas or possibilities…

Possibilities.

"Eveline," Luella said. "Eveline's horses."

Eveline had admitted that her and Wolfe's place was too shrubby. The desert terrain out near them was too unfriendly. It would require a lot of work to turn it into a horse haven. And the Edge was already a multitiered operation in and of itself. The Eatons and their cowboys had their hands full.

But here… Why not here, where the grasses ran wild… where there was plenty of room to build and for animals to roam?

It was be a risk. But Luella had known it would be worth it, from the moment Evenline had mentioned it.

Risk. Possibilities. Dreams.

Luella grinned until her cheeks ached. Her heart beat a little faster, a little lighter. *Finally*, something she wanted. Something she could do. Something she could be passionate about other than Ellis and the search for her baby… This might be the thing—like Sheridan, the thing that quieted all the noise in her head, that brought her back from the edge of numbness and disquiet…

And if she could reach for that…was it really that much more of a stretch—reaching for a future with the man she loved?

She'd done it once. She'd fallen on her face—but not because he hadn't loved her.

They would have built, too. She and Ellis…they wouldn't just have dreamed it. They'd have built it—the lives that they'd mapped out in words.

Castles in the sky were real, Luella knew now. With the right amount of intention and the love she knew she felt for him and he felt for her, those castles became homes. And they'd live in one together, with Isla and Ingrid and maybe— *oh, God*—one day, their son, too.

She heard Altaha coming down the porch steps. She turned, beaming. "I know what I want now. I know *everything* I want. I…" She stopped. "What? What is it?"

"Lacey Scott," Altaha said, lifting her phone in indication. "She says she had knowledge of the con your mother and Bredston ran. She lied to you in the delivery, but not because your mother got to her or the doctor. She refused them both when they approached her."

"Then why did she do it?"

"She was coerced," Altaha stated, "by a cop."

"A cop?" Since when was there *a cop* in this story? They should have been narrowing down the perpetrators, not chasing new leads. "A real cop?"

"A deputy, as a matter of fact," Altaha revealed. "A Fuego County deputy."

"Does she remember his name?" Luella asked.

"He didn't give one," Altaha said. "But she gave a description of him. Luella, I'm sorry. It's been right in front of me."

"What?" Luella asked. "*Who is it*?"

"It's Jones," Altaha said.

Luella faltered. "The...sheriff?"

"It fits," Altaha said, moving with her thoughts. Her feet took her around in circles as she laid it all out. "He wouldn't have been a sheriff in 2006. He was a deputy, like me. He's been around since then. Born in Taos, moved to Fuego with the wife in the mideighties. 'W.J.?' His name's Wendell, for God's sake. Damn it, I'm such an idiot. I mean, look. Look at this!"

She was holding Mabel's photograph. With new eyes, Luella stared at the mystery man next to her mother. Full head of hair, slim hips, mustache...but she saw it now, too. She saw Sheriff Jones all but screaming at her out of the man's face. "Oh, my God." She felt sick. All her good feelings from moments before were gone. "Wh-what do we do?"

"I'd like to visit his wife, Katie. She should see the photo. We can't confirm it's him in the photograph...not until she does."

"Okay," Luella said. She trailed Altaha to her police vehicle. "This is my fight. If Jones is involved in my baby's disappearance, I'd like to see you bring him in."

"I'll allow it," Altaha decided. "Your head's cooler than your boyfriend's. I don't think I have to worry about you running off doing vigilante nonsense."

JONES SHARED A pretty cabin with his wife, a dental hygienist. Altaha knocked on the front door. There was a wooden sign hanging underneath the peephole. It read *The Jones Family, Est. 1985*. Luella had gone to school with the sheriff's son, Mark. He'd been quarterback of the Fuego football team.

He'd called her *devil's daughter*, just as Rowdy Conway did.

Luella felt light-headed. She rocked herself from side to side.

"Do you need to wait in the truck?" Altaha asked without turning her head.

"I'm good. Just…weird feeling, is all."

"Hold it together for me," Altaha urged. She straightened when the door unlocked from the inside and Katie Jones peered out. "Mrs. Jones."

"Deputy Altaha," Katie said, pulling the door back from the jamb. Her smile started then stopped when she found Luella next to her. "Oh. What—"

"Is the sheriff at home?" Altaha kept her tone even.

"No," Katie said. "As far as I know, he's at the station house today."

Altaha relaxed. Luella felt it more than saw it.

"I'd invite you in," Katie said, glancing over her shoulder, "but we've got the kids home for the holidays."

"That's a fine thing," Altaha said. She was trying to set

Katie at ease, Luella knew. "It's been a while since the both of them have come home at the same time, hasn't it?"

"Yes." Katie's dimples flashed in a brief smile. "Yes, Mark and his wife, Keegan, flew in last night. Sybil and the grands have been here for several days. Her husband, Jim, will join us over the weekend."

"A full house for Christmas, then?"

"Yes. Isn't it wonderful?"

"Absolutely. Listen, Mrs. Jones, I know you're busy and I don't want to take up too much of your time, but I was hoping you could help me with something."

"Okay," Katie said. She stepped out on the porch, closing the door behind her. Luella didn't miss how her eyes strayed to her and the smile dimmed.

Altaha took the photograph out of a manila folder. "I was wondering if you could identify this man here for me."

Katie took the picture in both hands. "Oh," she said, a quick grin flashing across her face. "Oh, Wendell. Look how handsome. It's been so long since…"

The grin tapered off little by little. Her eyes raced across other details in the snapshot. She shook her head. "Why…?" She stopped, cleared her throat and thrust the photograph back at Altaha. "When was this taken?"

"March 11, 1987," Altaha explained. "It was taken by Luella's aunt, Mabel Brinkley. We're certain the woman in the photograph with him is—"

"Riane," Katie said. She rubbed her lips together, as if she'd blurted it out by accident. "Riane Decker." Her frown strengthened. "This one's mother."

"She was a Brinkley, too, at the time," Luella threw in. "She married my father in February of the following year."

"A shotgun wedding," Katie remembered.

Altaha studied her closely. "I'm sorry, Katie, but I have

to ask. What was the nature of your husband's relationship with Riane at the time this picture was taken?"

"We were friends," Katie murmured, her mouth drawn. "We were good friends...for a time. Riane...she was good fun. Always at the rodeo. She liked the men. The cowboys. She fancied herself a buckle bunny."

"My mother?" Luella said, shocked by the idea.

"Oh, yes," Katie said, drawing her sweater around her. She didn't meet Luella's eye. "She... I... Well, we were all different back then."

"What do you mean by that?" Altaha asked.

Katie rolled her eyes. "Oh, come on, Kaya. You weren't born yesterday." When Altaha only continued to wait for an explanation, she blew out a breath. "We were swingers, all right? Wendell and I. Hell, all us newlyweds were."

"Was Riane involved in this lifestyle, too?" Altaha ventured.

"Very much so," Katie said with a nod.

"Were she and your husband involved sexually?" Altaha asked delicately.

Katie closed her eyes. She brought her forehead down to her hand and scrubbed her temple. "It was so long ago. So damn long ago. What does it *matter* anymore what they were?"

"It's important, I'm afraid."

Katie dropped her hand. She kept her eyes closed. "Yes. They were involved."

"How long, would you say?" Altaha asked.

"Long enough."

"Can you be a little more exact?"

Katie cursed impressively. For the first time, she raised her voice. "I don't know, Deputy. I don't know. For a while, it was just harmless fun. I slept around, too, but no one shows up on my doorstep asking about that."

"So you knew about the affair."

Katie's expression grew frosty. "Did I say it was an affair?"

"My mistake," Altaha said.

Katie's shoulders rose and fell quickly. Her breathing had quickened.

Altaha gave her a moment to gather herself. "You knew they were sleeping together."

"I did," Katie said. "It meant little."

"I'm trying to establish a timeline," Altaha said, carefully. "When would you say they stopped? They did stop. Didn't they?"

"He said they did. I found out I was pregnant with Mark. He was Wendell's child. I never had any doubt about that. But I wanted to stop. The parties...the drinking... I don't mind telling you, the drugs that came along with it...it wasn't healthy. I wanted us both to be healthy. Stable. So we stopped being swingers."

Altaha waited, as if she could smell more.

Luella tried to fade into the background. Was there more?

It came slowly, the distress. First, Katie's breathing increased once more. Then she blinked, and there it was in her eyes. She looked to Luella, accusation painted there.

Luella's lips parted. "It didn't stop," she realized in a whisper. "He went back to her."

"She chased after him," Katie returned. "Like a *bitch* in heat. She practically stalked him, for Christ's sake. I caught her in the house once. He said she'd been waiting when he came home...in our room. It's disgusting."

"Did he indicate that the encounter was nonconsensual?" Altaha asked.

"No," Katie said. "Not exactly. But...he told her he was done. And she couldn't accept it."

"Okay," Altaha said. "One more question and I'll let you go back to your family."

"That would be nice," Katie said irritably.

"How long was it between Riane's last encounter with your husband and her marriage to Jace Decker?" Altaha wanted to know.

Katie shook her head. "I can't answer that."

"Why not?" Luella found herself asking.

Katie scowled at her. "Because I don't know when the last time was! The doctor put me on bed rest and Wendell said he wasn't going to the rodeo anymore. But sometimes he'd come in late, drunk or high as a kite and smelling of her cheap perfume...like he was addicted to her. It was horrible—absolutely horrible. It only stopped after Jace entered the picture. He put a stop to it. Your father wasn't a good man, but at least he put a stop to Riane's exploits. Once he entered the picture, Wendell stopped going to the rodeo. Once she stopped chasing him, he had a chance to straighten out—to become the husband and father I knew he could be."

Luella didn't know where it came from, but the question leaped out of her mouth. "Has the sheriff been acting oddly over the last month?"

Katie shook her head. "In what way?"

"Coming in late at odd hours," Luella elaborated.

"He's a police officer," Katie said. "Of course, he comes in at odd hours."

Altaha took up the line of questioning. "Yes, but has he seemed off to you?"

Katie scoffed. "No. I mean, he's been in some pain. But other than that—"

"Pain." Altaha latched onto the word, a dog with a bone. "What kind of pain?"

"You know he was hurt on the job," Katie said. When Altaha said nothing, she added quickly, "A few weeks ago. He said there was some scuffle out in the county. A domestic dispute that got out of hand. He took a bullet."

"Where?"

"What?"

"What part of his body, Katie?" Altaha insisted.

"His leg."

"The right or the left?"

"The right!" Katie shrieked. "Jesus, you *know* this!"

Altaha exchanged a look with Luella.

Luella felt her color draining. Little black spots floated around the edges of her vision.

The sheriff wasn't just the cop who had most likely coerced Lacey Scott to participate in her baby's kidnapping. He'd had a blistering affair with her mother. And he was the one who'd killed her chickens, her cat, and who had abducted and shot Sheridan and Ellis.

"You say he's been at the station," Altaha clarified with Katie.

"That's what he told me." As they both moved off the porch in quick strides, Katie came after them. "Wait. What is this about? Why is Luella here? And why do you need to find him?"

Altaha spoke into the radio on the shoulder of her uniform. "Hey, Wyatt. Do you read?"

Some static screeched over the line then the voice of her fellow deputy. "Ten-four, Altaha."

"Switch to Channel Two, will you?" Altaha asked him, opening the door to her truck and piling in. She waited until Luella joined her before cranking the engine. Katie stood outside the truck, her face a map of questions. When Deputy Wyatt replied that he had changed channels, she asked, "Are you at the station?"

"Root and I just left."

"Was Jones there?"

"That's a negative."

Altaha cursed. "Has anybody had eyes on him today?"

"Ah... I haven't. Root says he hasn't. If you open the channel, I'm sure you could contact him directly."

Luella straightened in her seat. "She's making a call." She pointed at Katie outside of the truck. Her cell phone was in her hands and she was dialing.

"We're out of time," Altaha agreed. She turned her mouth to the speaker again. "This is an APB. I need a location on the sheriff, boys."

"An APB? On *Jones*?"

"I believe he is armed and dangerous," Altaha reported, putting the truck in reverse.

Luella grabbed the handle over her head as the tires skidded across the driveway and Altaha backed out to the highway, jerking the wheel. Luella glanced back in the direction of the home. "Three miles," she muttered. "His house is three miles from Ollero Creek."

"If that."

"But...why did he kill my animals? I don't understand *anything*."

"We'll find out," Altaha asserted, "if we catch him before he flees town. Hang on." She toggled the siren and mashed on the gas.

Chapter Seventeen

The clouds fretted and flickered. They swept in sideways across the Edge, bringing a downpour. It was too hard a rain to spit sleet, and the sky was far too hot-tempered for snow.

This storm had been building. It'd worked itself into a fine fury, one that made the horses out in pasture spook and the cattle low fitfully.

"Get 'em all in," Ellis instructed. "Make sure the gates are locked. I don't want to be chasing them in this mess. Lucas, watch that bull. He'll take the hide off of you. Javier, make sure Eveline and Griff have a handle on the horses."

Everett sprinted up. "A moment?"

"We don't really have one," Ellis said. "You see what's coming."

"It's Jones," Everett said.

That got Ellis's attention. "What about him?"

"He's back, looking for Luella."

"Is he?" Ellis considered. "Did he give a reason?"

"No. He's not leaving without her."

Ellis exchanged a meaningful look with his brother. "It might be time he stepped into my office, for a change," he said, nodding toward the barn.

Everett's grin was sharp. He rocked back on his heels, considering. "I like where your mind's at."

As Everett walked back toward the house, Ellis scanned the yard. The others had a handle on things. Even Lucas. The boy was coming along. When he saw Wolfe come out of the stables, he waved him over. At his approach, Ellis said, "Trouble's here. Stick around?"

Wolfe raised a brow but didn't question him. He nodded.

Ellis ushered him inside because he could see Jones, his head low to stop the wind from carrying off his hat, making his way around the first corral.

The sound and smell of cattle would've been oppressive had Ellis not grown up with it. He checked in with the other hands, made sure everyone had a handle on their business. He reached through the rungs of a fence to check the hay. It was dry.

Wolfe tapped Ellis on the back. He turned and saw the sheriff duck inside. "Be ready," he muttered before he stood up. "Sheriff."

"Eaton," Jones returned.

"You interested in joining the cattle business?" Ellis wondered. "You can't seem to stay away."

"I'm looking for Ms. Decker," Jones said briskly. "Your brother said you know her location."

"I do," Ellis said, reaching back to scratch his neck. "Unfortunately for you, I'm not willing to share it."

Jones's gaze had been roving over the restless heifers in the nearest pen. It seized on Ellis. "She's a suspect in my case."

"She's nothing of the sort," Ellis rebutted.

Jones shifted his weight.

Ellis stilled when the sheriff's hands went to his gun belt. Behind him, he could all but feel Wolfe's readiness.

"What're you a cop now, too?" Jones asked him.

"No," Ellis said. "But I know the truth and that's that you're making her life difficult. I think it's time you admit why."

A humorless smile touched Jones's mouth as he scanned Wolfe. "You Eatons. You're all the same. You think you're above the law, one step ahead of us... Before all this, I thought you may have been the sane one. But you live so long with crazy, you become it. You crossed the line, right around the time you started screwing Luella again."

"You don't get to say her name, Sheriff," Ellis warned. "Not in my house."

"I can call her what I damn well want. And I can make her life harder."

"Can you?"

"You have no idea what I am capable of, Mr. Eaton," Jones said. "No idea."

Before the two men could square off, the chirping of a ringtone reached Ellis's ears. Jones stopped. His teeth showed as he took a step back, dug into the pocket of his slacks and pulled out his cell phone. He scanned the screen. "We're not done here," he said before turning halfway away to answer.

"I sure hope not," Ellis returned.

As Jones took the call, Ellis risked a look back at Wolfe.

Wolfe may have looked unflappable to anyone else. But Ellis recognized the ticing muscle in his jaw, the flexed tendons of his neck. The tension was enormous.

His friend sensed exactly what he did. Something about Jones was off and for once it had little to do with Wolfe's or Ellis's personal aversion of the man.

"What?" Jones snapped. His face hardened. Ellis saw the sheen of sweat on it for the first time as he cast a fur-

tive look in their direction. "When? When did they…" He listened. His free hand fisted, the knuckles white. "Listen carefully," he said, lowering his voice. He turned on his heel and retreated toward the door.

Ellis let him go. Then he saw the hitch in Jones's gait.

With every step, Jones favored his right leg.

Ellis's mind flew back to the snowstorm—the shadow in his scope—how it had bowled over after Ellis squeezed the trigger before it disappeared into the whiteout…

His heart racked his ribs as he told himself to stay calm. Following Jones, he thought quickly.

The sheriff lived on the same side of town as Ollero Creek.

He'd been dogging Luella since her return.

You have no idea what I'm capable of.

I'll be goddammed, Ellis thought. He caught sight of Javier near the door. He gave him a tip of the chin.

Javier did the same in response then shut the barn door soundly, blocking the sheriff's exit.

Jones's feet faltered. He stopped muttering instructions into the phone, bringing his hand up to block sound from entering the receiver. "Open that door," he demanded of Javier.

"I don't think so, Sheriff," Ellis answered for him, putting himself, too, between Jones and the exit.

Jones looked around, found Wolfe ready at his back. He pulled his hand away from the phone. "I'll call you back," he said before he shoved the phone in his pocket. "Open the door and this will end peacefully."

"Fine," Ellis said. "Tell me why you did it."

"Did what?" Jones snapped.

"Tell me why you slaughtered Luella's flock," Ellis told him. "Tell me why you shot her horse and killed her cat."

Jones's expression went carefully blank. "Stand down," Jones said and he reached for the Glock strapped to his hip.

Ellis reached around, too, to palm the pistol he kept nestled in the waistband of his jeans. "You first."

Jones didn't move but for the beads of perspiration creeping down his cheeks. Then his grip on the gun tightened.

Ellis swung his around and up as Jones raised his. Shots rang out. The herd moaned and milled, straining against the fences, as the hands ducked down with shouts of "Get down!"

ALTAHA AND LUELLA tracked Jones to the Edge, thanks to a 911 call. The words *shots fired* rang in Luella's head as Altaha drove her truck right up to the front porch of Eaton House, killing the siren.

The deputy unbuckled, her weapon ready in her hand. "Stay here."

"Like hell," Luella said, grabbing her shotgun and scrambling out the passenger door. She saw Paloma. "Are you okay?"

"They're in the barn," Paloma said. "Is it true the sheriff—"

"Stay here," Altaha instructed. "If any other deputies arrive, tell them what you told me. Luella, you stay, damn it!"

"I'm coming," Luella said and cocked the shotgun for good measure. As they rounded the house, she choked back a scream when Everett nearly ran into them.

"Deputy," he said, breathing hard. He, too, was carrying a weapon. "Sweetheart. You seen Paloma?"

"She's that way," Altaha said, pointing. "Give me a rundown."

Everett opened his mouth but the sound of gunfire made

them brace themselves against the wall of the house. "Get down," he said, pressing a hand into Altaha's shoulder.

She shrugged it off. "*I'm* the police officer. *You* get down."

"Ellis has got him pinned in the barn," Everett stated.

"Ellis?" Luella asked, distressed. "He's in there?"

"Him, Wolfe, Javier, Lucas and one or two more of our men," he explained.

"How did it start?" Altaha asked.

"The sheriff came looking for you," Everett said of Luella.

"How long has the standoff been in progress?"

"Fifteen minutes."

"Is anyone down?"

"I'd be surprised if everyone's still standing after all the shots we've heard."

Altaha placed a hand on his arm. His attention came back to her. Luella noticed for the first time the line of sweat along his upper lip and his unnatural pallor.

"Are you okay?" Altaha asked, quietly.

"I need my brother and my men out of there," Everett said in no uncertain terms.

"How many access points does that barn have?" she asked.

"One on the east side. There's a weak spot on the north side. We did a quick patch on it a few weeks ago with plywood. With the right tools, we can breach it in seconds."

"That sounds like the best bet. Wait here for backup. Send them my way."

"You're not going alone," Everett asserted, jumping to his feet as she did. "Those are my men in there."

Luella stood, too. "I'm coming with you, too."

"Don't either of you understand?" Altaha asked. "Jones

is armed and dangerous and we now know he's capable of murder."

"Come again?" Everett asked. More gunfire made Altaha take off running. Everett and Luella didn't stay behind. He took the safety off his pistol and frowned at Luella as she kept pace with him. "Nice weapon you got there. You know how to shoot it?"

Luella groaned at him. "Just stay out of my way."

"Likewise."

ELLIS STAYED LOW behind a large rolled-up section of barbed wire. As cover, it wasn't ideal but it was working for the moment. He tried to listen over the frantic sounds of the cows for Jones's movements. As far as he knew, they still had him pinned behind a stack of lumber.

At least their position was between Jones and the door. Ellis glanced over at the sound of a pained moan.

Wolfe was tending to Javier. He'd been hit in the first exchange of gunfire. The bullet from Jones's gun had been meant for Ellis but had bounced off the wall and hit Javier instead. "How much time do we have?" he asked, concerned by the amount of blood on the shoulder of Javier's shirt.

Wolfe's hands were strained with it. They moved quickly. *Need a doctor. Now.*

Ellis tried peeking out from behind his position. Another shot volleyed from Jones's position. It hit somewhere over Ellis's head. He ducked back down. "I don't have enough ammo left for the cover fire you need to get him to the door." He narrowed his eyes in the direction he knew Lucas and the other young ranch hand Mateo were hiding out some twenty feet away. He hoped to God they stayed there. "We need a distraction."

As if on cue, the wall near to Jones's position splintered.

More, the plywood over a weak section of wood caved in. An unmanned Polaris buzzed into the arena, sending heifers scattering, their eyes whiting. "What the hell?" Ellis said a split second before Altaha rushed in with Everett on her heels.

Wolfe made a noise. Ellis waved him on as Altaha and Everett drew Jones's fire. "Go," he said. "Go!"

Wolfe hauled Javier onto his shoulder and, in a crouch, headed for the door. Ellis's heart was in his ears as he counted the seconds it took for the two of them to get through. When the door closed behind them, he breathed a sigh of relief.

They weren't out of the woods yet. He looked around the wiring, trying to get a sense of what was happening.

Jones was shooting in the direction Everett and Altaha had taken toward an alcove where they could hunker down.

Altaha didn't make it. Ellis saw her go down, heard her cry over the din. Everett didn't miss a beat. He scooped her up and got her behind the wall before Jones squeezed off another round.

Ellis heard the sound he'd been anticipating for the last few minutes.

The empty click from Jones's weapon's chamber. There was a curse that followed. The sheriff was out of ammo.

Ellis thought about advancing then hesitated. Did Jones carry an extra clip on him?

Ellis wet his throat and called, "I know you're out! Stand up and let me see your hands!"

There wasn't an answer. Nor did Ellis see those hands.

Gritting his teeth, Ellis thought quickly. "We'll lay down our weapons, all of us, if you come out nice and slow." A shadow crept through the opening in the wall near Jones's position. Ellis squinted. His eyes went wide when he saw Luella's silhouette.

JONES'S ATTENTION WAS on his belt. His Glock was on the floor between his knees, empty. His baton was in one hand and he was searching for something else.

Keeping to the shadows of the wall, Luella kept her shotgun out in front of her, her finger on the trigger. Putting one foot in front of the other, she crept like she'd seen a mountain lion creep through the tall grass at Ollero Creek. It'd been stalking a family of pronghorns.

Ellis raised his voice. "I'm going to give you to the count of three, Sheriff! One...two..."

The barrel of her gun came up against the side of Jones's head just as he pulled a Taser out of his belt. "Drop it," she told him.

Every muscle in Jones's body froze.

"I said drop it!" she hollered. "Now!"

His fingers loosened around the Taser. It bounced to the barn floor.

"Hands," she said, kicking the Taser away. "In the air. Now."

His palms came up, reaching for the sky.

"Stand," she said, taking a few steps back, enough space so he couldn't snatch the shotgun barrel from her.

He stood, slow and obedient.

"Now turn," she instructed. As his feet shuffled around, she saw him favoring his right side. "Take off the belt and toss it this way. Then empty your pockets—all of them." As he started to, throwing everything out of reach, she shook her head. "It was you."

"It was me," he admitted.

"Why?" she demanded. "*Why* did you do it?"

"For your mother."

Luella's chin dropped. She planted her feet again, to keep herself fixed. "After all this time...she still has a hold on you?"

"Not the kind you're thinking," he argued.

Ellis appeared, his weapon in his hand. He kept it trained on the center of Jones's body. "You got him, honey."

"Are you okay?" she needed to know.

"I'm fine. Javier and Altaha need medical attention."

"I called it in," Everett said from somewhere beyond her. His voice didn't sound right. "Luella..."

"Go," Ellis said, bringing himself around to her position. "I've got this guy."

Luella lowered her weapon slowly, backing away. She found Everett near the alcove he and Altaha had discussed before breaching the wall and dropped to her knees beside him. His hands were pressed, one over the other, on Altaha's left thigh. "I can't stop the bleeding," he said.

"You're doing good," she told him. "Keep pressure on it. Use your knee, if you have to."

"She can't stay awake."

Luella heard the quaver underneath what he said. She leaned the shotgun against the wall after putting the safety back on. It was only as it slipped out of her hands that she realized how slick her palms were. She unclipped her belt and pulled it off quickly. Working in quick, steady movements, she fashioned a tourniquet around Altaha's leg and secured it. Then she checked Altaha's eyes, prying back each lid. "Kaya." She tapped her on the cheek.

Altaha's eyes rolled from the back of her head. "Hm?"

"Hey, friend," Luella greeted. "You've got the hard-ass cattle baron out of sorts over here."

"Mmm," Altaha mumbled. Pain worked over her face and she hissed.

"Sorry," Everett said quickly. "I'm sorry. My hands are only good for cattle branding."

Altaha tilted her head to look at him. "Geez, Eaton," she said, dull. "Go lie down somewhere."

"Once you stop bleeding, sweetheart, I'll do just that."

She closed her eyes, started shaking her head listlessly. "…love your hands…hate it when you call me that…"

Luella tapped her cheek again. "Stay with me. Help's on the way." She kept her voice even, but she breathed a tumultuous sigh when she heard the paramedics rushing in. "Gunshot wound to the left thigh." She rattled off Altaha's status and anything else that might help. Then she pulled Everett back so they could go to work on her. He winced when the deputy cried out in pain. "It's the tourniquet," Luella explained. "It's supposed to hurt." She found herself rubbing his arm, up and down. "She's in capable hands."

When Everett remained silent, watching them place Altaha on the stretcher, Luella brought her attention back to him. "You're not hurt, are you?"

Everett shook his head.

Luella remembered suddenly what had happened in the box canyon the summer before—how he'd been dealing with PTSD episodes ever since. "You ran into the line of fire," she realized. "That must've been difficult."

"My people were in here. I couldn't sit back and let them…" He trailed off as the medics carted the stretcher out.

Luella gave him something of a smile. "You should be proud of yourself."

He cleared his throat. "I guess we've both made some strides today." At a grunt of protest behind them, they turned to see Jones up against the barn wall. Ellis was cuffing his hands behind his back. "That must do you some good."

Luella's lips thinned. "The police are coming. But I'd like to hear what you have to say, Sheriff—about my mother. You said you did what you did because of her. Explain that."

When Jones hesitated, Ellis pushed him harder against the wall. Jones cursed. "Riane wanted you to leave town," Jones said, his cheek mushed against the plywood. "When you returned from jail, she wanted you gone as fast as possible."

"Why?" Luella asked. "She left Fuego years ago. Is San Gabriel not far enough away?"

"That husband of hers had to leave a good-paying job when news of Whip Decker and his accomplice daughter hit the papers and Riane's connection to it came to light. That was when she contacted me and said if I didn't find some way to get you to leave Fuego after your sentence, she would tell Katie…"

Luella felt her heart in her throat, beating wildly. "Tell her what?"

"…that I'm your father," Jones said. "Your real father."

"How do you know she was telling the truth?" Luella wanted to know. "My mother lies. Don't you know that?"

"When Riane met Whip Decker, she was already pregnant," he revealed, "with my child."

"And you didn't tell your wife any of this," Luella said.

"She was pregnant with Mark," he said. "She was late-term, on bed rest. Her blood pressure was through the roof. How could I tell her I'd put another woman in that position?"

"The woman she didn't want you anywhere near," Luella added.

"Riane was like a fever I couldn't break. She wouldn't let up until you came into the equation."

No wonder Riane had resented her so much. She'd been

the other woman and, suddenly, a mother with no means to raise a child. "So she never saw anything in Whip Decker... other than a means to an end."

"She got the short end of that stick," he said.

"You'd have me pity her?" she wondered. "After she made you kill my chickens, my cat and almost my horse?"

"I admit to killing the chickens," he said. "A chicken's nothing more than a meal, when it comes down to it. I couldn't kill the horse. She asked me to. She said that would be the jumping-off point for you. But a horse is another animal altogether. As for the cat, I had nothing to do with that."

"Then who did?" Ellis asked. They could hear people again rustling outside the barn.

"Rowdy Conway all but confessed to it the day he said Luella ran him off the road," Jones stated.

"But you didn't charge him."

"No."

"Why?"

"Because I needed you scared," he said. "I needed you gone. If you'd have just left, none of this mess would've happened."

"If you'd just have come clean with your wife, my chickens and my cat would still be alive," Luella argued. "Ellis wouldn't have been shot. Javier or Altaha, either. You've got a lot to answer for, Sheriff. I hope you're prepared to live with that."

The deputies, Root and Wyatt, filed in. They faltered when they saw the sheriff cornered and restrained. "What... what happened here?" Wyatt asked. "Sir?"

Jones waited several beats, long enough for Ellis to make a frustrated noise behind him. Then he closed his eyes. The muscles around his mouth trembled, making the bristled hairs of mustache vibrate. "Put me in the back of the wagon and take me to the station, boys. You can lower your weapons. I'll come quietly."

Luella watched them lead Jones away through a wide swath of Edge employees. It was raining buckets and running off the men's hats in streams. She stayed under cover of the barn, the smell of animal and hay and blood thick in her nose.

Warmth cloaked her shoulders as hands draped over them. They massaged. Ellis's words flowed over her ear. "I just about lost my mind when I saw you sneaking up on him. He could've had an extra clip on him. He could've tased you, swung at you..."

"I was ready," she said. "It felt how I think you might have...in the box canyon this summer when you had Whip in your sights."

His arms slid around her. They knitted against her belly, gathering her hands in his as his cheek came to rest against hers. The line of his back was damp from rain or sweat or both. Nothing had ever felt that good. "Whip Decker wasn't your father."

She closed her eyes, turning her temple to his cheek, seeking comfort against the cold. "No."

"You never were the devil's daughter."

Riane's harsh features formed in her mind. She shivered. "That depends on your perspective."

"I'll need to get to the hospital soon to see how Javy's doing. Someone needs to let his wife, Grace, know what's happening, if she doesn't already know."

He'd see to all of that, she thought. He'd see to everything. That was Ellis's way. She gripped his arms tighter, bringing him in closer.

"Do you think Altaha's going to be all right?"

"I don't know," she said, truthfully. "It could just be tissue damage, but if the bullet punctured a bone or a major vessel…"

He nodded off the rest. "What do you want to do, honey? Do you want to go to the hospital or the station?"

She was so tired. She couldn't imagine doing anything but curling up in bed…with him. Tipping her head back to his shoulder, she swayed with him in their little space over the hay. "I want…" she began in a whisper.

"Yeah?"

She pressed her lips together as the certainty washed through her—a fresh, hot wave of excitement. "I want to get married."

He stilled. They stopped swaying. "Do what?"

"I want to get married, Ellis," she stated again, surer.

He turned her to face him, his grip on her upper arms as insistent as his gaze. "Are you serious?"

"We just came out of a gunfight," she said. "We're both covered in blood, sweat, gunpowder and God knows what else… How could I not be serious?"

"You want to marry me," he realized, surprise bleeding into naked joy.

"I want to marry you," she said—because it felt good, so good, to say it again.

He expelled an unsteady breath. His hands reached for her face. "Lu," he whispered.

"I know you aren't free," she said. "But once you are, I'd like to make you mine. I think we've both waited long enough to belong to each other."

"Yes. Yes, we have." He grinned widely. "You just proposed to me."

"I didn't get on one knee like you did," she said with a sentimental smile. "Should I have?"

"Nah. And I like that we've come full circle."

"I'm tired of circling—running, hurting… I want to take up my place here with you. You'll be my constant?"

"It'd be my honor," he said, kissing the point of her cheek, then the other, "and my pleasure to be your constant, Luella Decker."

"Not Decker. I don't have to be a Decker anymore." She smiled, her eyes wet with tears. "That's not my legacy anymore—and it won't have to be our son's either once we find him."

"You're damn right. But what do I call you?" he asked, weaving his hands through hers. "When we get up to the altar and I take you as my own, finally."

"I'll be your Luella Belle," she told him. "Always."

"Always," he said with a satisfactory nod. "Luella Belle Eaton."

She grabbed hold of him. "I like that very much."

ELLIS WAITED OUTSIDE the police station. He'd wanted to be there when she arrived. He'd needed to be there when it all came to a close.

When he saw the car coming down Main Street, he pushed off the building. Taking off his hat, he waited on the curb for her to bring the vehicle to a slow creep then a complete stop. He tapped the hat against his leg as she stretched her long body out of the driver's seat and looked at him across the hood.

"What's this about, Ellis?" Liberty asked.

"Did you drop the girls off?"

"With Paloma," she stated, shutting her door. She tucked her handbag against her hip.

"Everett delivered my message."

"With relish," she said, lips curling in distaste. "Looks like he's back at the helm."

Ellis nodded. "He's back in his rightful place."

She shook her head. "You could've been so much more."

"I am what I am," he told her. "I'm a brother. I'm a father. I'm my father's son. This is the life he wanted for me, and it's the life I love, the life that I fight for."

"Is it really safe to have the girls at the ranch?" she said, doubtfully. "Gunfights. Cat killings. I didn't feel comfortable leaving them there."

"It's funny you mention cat killings."

"Why's that?"

He tilted his head, wanting to watch the trapdoor shut. "Because a cat killing was never part of the official report," he explained. "It was never part of any news story. It was kept under wraps by Sheriff Jones. He was responsible for all the other killings. It unsettled him when he realized there was a copycat killer running around town, too."

Briefly, Liberty bit her lower lip. She stopped herself, glancing at some point over his shoulder. "You sound like you're accusing me of something."

"Of killing Luella's cat?" He shook his head. "No. You never did like to get your hands dirty. But you knew what was going on with Luella's animals. You knew she was staying at the Edge. And when you left the stable that day you dropped the girls off, the cat, Nyx, attacked you on your way out. You kicked him halfway across the yard."

"So?" she asked, jutting out her chin. "How am I the guilty one, all of a sudden?"

"Because Rowdy Conway isn't the steel trap you thought he was when you told him to do it," Ellis explained. "Deputy Wyatt never had to lean on him. He cracked, just as soon as they brought him into the station for questioning. He says you sought him out on your way out of town that day, having heard that Luella broke a bottle over his head.

You targeted him because you knew he'd be feeling humili-
ated. You even threw in a few hundred dollars, just to make
it worth his while."

"I didn't do anything wrong," Liberty claimed. "My
hands are clean. I didn't kill the cat. He did."

The door to the station opened. Deputy Wyatt and another officer, Deputy Boot, stepped out into the white winter sunshine. "Ms. Eaton?" Wyatt said. "We'd like you to
come with us."

She drew up straight as a pencil. Her jaw worked sound-
lessly. She took a step back. "What for?"

"We need to ask you a few questions about where you
were Friday, December 16."

"This is not happening," she said, looking wildly around
for Ellis as they escorted her into the building. "Ellis! Are
you just going to stand there and let them do this?"

Ellis bent his head as he lifted his hat. He set it on his
head and pulled it low over his brow. "Good luck, Lib," he
said simply before the door closed behind them and he was
left alone on the street. Sinking his hands into his pockets,
he walked back to his truck so he could get back to building the future he wanted for his girls and Luella.

The storm wasn't gone. He wasn't sure it ever would be
completely. But he'd found peace in it. He'd made his peace
with it. As long as he had the three of them, he was content.

Epilogue

"Open the door!" Eveline called to Wolfe as she held the gate to the open pasture.

Wolfe unlatched the door to the horse trailer and opened it wide.

Luella waited, holding on to Ingrid's shoulders so the little one wouldn't rush toward their new arrival. She felt the girl go up on her toes in anticipation. "Why doesn't she come out?" she asked.

"She's scared," Isla said. Her hand threaded through Luella's elbow, comfortably. "Isn't she, Lu?"

Luella couldn't stop the smile. It always came whenever the girls referred to her by the pet name. "Yes. She's been through a lot."

"Doesn't she know she's home now?" Ingrid asked, all but dancing on those toes. "She doesn't have to be cooped up ever again like she was in that stockyard. She can run and play and canter and race however much she wants and she never has to stop!"

"She'll learn all of that," Eveline told them. "She just has to give it a chance."

"Baby steps," Luella agreed. "She's going to take one day at a time, each moment in baby steps, until she learns to trust us. We just have to be patient and let her go at her pace."

Eveline called to the horse. Wolfe offered his soothing noises, the ones that normally worked.

Luella sighed. "I think it's time we brought him out."

Eveline nodded. "Call him. Let's see if we can't tempt her out."

Luella unclipped the radio from her belt and raised it to her mouth. "Ellis, do you read me?"

The radio crackled. Then Ellis's voice smoothed out. "Always, honey."

Another grin she couldn't fight, Luella thought as it spilled across her face. "Bring him around, please."

"Ten-four."

They waited. Ingrid started to squirm. Luella rubbed her shoulders. Patience was not one of Ingrid's virtues but Luella loved her spirit. Isla leaned her head against Luella's hip. "I can't wait to see her run," she breathed.

Luella put her arm around Isla and hugged her close. Over the last three months, things had moved much slower in her relationship with Ellis's oldest. Luella and Isla had bonded over quiet walks at the Edge and quiet talks.

Baby steps, Luella thought again.

They heard the far-off sound of a neigh. In the trailer, Luella heard the shuffling of curious hooves. She looked in the direction of the house with its retired waterwheel and dry creek-bed and saw the man and horse coming up the lane. She leaned down to the girls' ears. "It's your daddy," she whispered.

Ingrid cackled. "Sheridan's not trying to bite him in the butt today."

"It's early," Eveline drawled. "Give it time."

Luella watched her horse and shook her head when she

saw how he'd come to accept Ellis's lead. While Sheridan still liked to take the occasional nip out of her man—and, really, how could she blame him—they'd come to understand one another, at least. It helped that, as the weather warmed toward spring, Ellis had been taking him on cattle runs, first on a lead rope next to Shy so he could get the lay of the land. Then, in the saddle, where Ellis had let him follow the herd and put his biting to use on the stragglers.

Luella had to admit it had worked to temper Sheridan's aggression, his restlessness, even bolster his confidence.

Ellis and Sheridan came to the gate, where Ellis paraded the roan in front of the trailer. Sheridan sniffed in the direction of the mare, gave an intrigued bugle and danced a little in place.

Isla gasped when, finally, the mare's nose poked out into the open air.

"Come on," Ingrid murmured. "Come on, girl."

Ellis looked to Luella and winked. "Should I let him be wild?"

She nodded. "Let's hope she follows."

"Easy," Ellis said to Sheridan when he came around to his front. He unlatched the bridle, loosening it enough to get it over his ears and off. "Show her how it's done," he said, patting his withers before he let out a rallying "Yah!"

Sheridan's front legs waved once in the air before he took off through the gate, the wind catching his mane and tail, just as it caught the prairie grass.

From the mare, there came a nicker. Sheridan, at a distance now, slowed and whinnied, arcing in a half circle.

"What's happening?" Ingrid asked.

"They're talking," Ellis said, coming to stand with them at the fence.

"What's he telling her?" Isla asked.

Ellis met Luella's gaze. "He's saying, 'Come on, girl. Live this life with me.'"

"What's *she* saying?" Ingrid asked, tugging on Luella's hand for an answer.

Luella couldn't look away from Ellis. "'Give me a second. I'm trying to catch my breath.'"

He laughed quietly, laying his arm across the top rung of the fence so that his hand could splay across the surface of her hair. She felt the sun warm on her face and had to catch her breath, as well, as she thought about how long it'd taken them to get here.

"Here she comes!" Ingrid said, giving in to a hop.

The mare came down the ramp in hesitant steps. She was a paint horse. Luella and Eveline had wanted to bring home all the horses in the stockyard. And that was the long-term goal. But the paint...after hearing her story, they'd wanted her to be the first.

She moved through the gate, skittish of the humans on the fringes. Then she took off into the pasture, moving like lightning.

Eveline closed the gate. Wolfe came to stand with her and they all watched as the paint let the wind take her. As Sheridan turned and galloped toward the cliffs in the distance, on some unspoken plane where only the purest beings interacted with each other, the mare turned, too, in unison.

"She's free," Isla said as she and Ingrid climbed the fence to watch.

"She sure is," Ellis murmured. He turned his head and dipped a kiss to her head then Ingrid's. "Aren't they a picture?"

Luella made a noise. She feared if she spoke, it would come out all watery and she didn't want the girls to think she was upset.

She and Ellis had worked to shield the worst of what had happened over the last months from them. They knew that their time with their mother had been limited by the judge in the custody case.

In the future, they would have more time with Liberty. Ellis had never wanted them to be apart from her completely. Split custody was still what he had his sights on. But after being charged with the cat killing after her arrangement with Rowdy had come to the surface, the judge had thought it best for the girls to live at Eaton Edge for the time being.

More change was on the horizon. Ellis and Liberty would have to reach some co-parenting arrangement. And there would be a wedding.

Luella ran the tip of her thumb over the ring band on her left ring finger. She'd finally gotten used to wearing Ellis's engagement ring again, though it still made her blink in surprise when she saw the Polaris diamond winking light at her.

The Eatons had refused to accept Luella's suggestion of a city hall ceremony. There would be a wedding, they insisted, at the Edge or Ollero Creek—wherever she wished. It helped that the girls had taken the news of the engagement well. They wanted their father to be happy, and they had grown to accept Luella's place in his life. They'd accepted her in their lives, as well, which was the greatest gift of all, she thought, gathering Ingrid's golden strands of hair in her hands gingerly.

She'd wanted the two of them to feel as if Ollero Creek Horse Rescue was theirs, too. It would be their job to name the paint, and others who came to live here. Luella was determined that they would never miss a release.

Luella did what Isla had done for her. She rested her head on Ellis's frame as they watched the pair become specks against the backdrop of the plateau and sandstone cliffs. She had a family. She would have a wedding. She was going to live this life with Ellis and his girls and the horses she, Eveline and Wolfe were going to rescue together.

Second chances were the stuff of dreams and she was living them.

The sound of a truck rumbling toward them brought her head around. She laid her hand on Ellis's back when she saw the sheriff's vehicle.

He tensed, too, automatically. Then, he relaxed. "It's a friend."

It was easy to forget that the weight of the Fuego County police was no longer stacked against her. Wendell Jones was serving his time. His reputation had saved him from a long sentence. It had helped him that both Ellis, Javier and Altaha had survived their gunshot wounds. His reputation as a sheriff and his exemplary record as a police officer with over thirty years on the job had gone a long way, too.

Jones wouldn't be gone forever. But now wasn't the time to dwell on that.

Luella walked with Ellis to meet Altaha.

The sheriff's badge on her uniform gleamed as she removed her sunshades and smiled in greeting. "Howdy, Eatons," she called, hitching only slightly on her bad leg as she walked to them. "How was the first release?"

"Perfect," Luella admitted. "I'm sorry you missed it."

"Me, too," she said, squinting to find the paint and Sheridan in the distance. "I got held up at the station."

Ellis studied her. "What can we do you for, Sheriff? No more bad news, I hope."

"Nope," Altaha admitted. "Though there is news and I wanted you to know immediately."

Luella felt her heart pick up pace and didn't know what to feel, exactly.

Altaha took an envelope from her back pocket and held it out for Luella. "This came via fax this afternoon."

"From who?" Ellis asked as Luella lifted the flap of the envelope and took out the contents.

"Odessa," Altaha answered.

Luella was having trouble reading Altaha's expression. "Texas?"

"Read it," she urged.

Luella unfolded the fresh-printed papers. She read the first few lines. Her hand trembled as it came up to meet her mouth. "Oh, God, Ellis."

He took the papers and scanned the first few lines. His arm went around her shoulder immediately, drawing her close. "You...found him."

Altaha tilted her head. "Told you I would."

Luella couldn't speak past the knot in her throat. Instead, she stepped to Altaha and enveloped her in a hug.

Altaha patted her on the back. "I'm just sorry it took so long."

When Luella stepped back, wiping her eyes, Ellis took his turn, bringing Altaha in for a strong-armed embrace. "Thank you, Kaya."

"This is the best thing I've done on the job yet. Believe me when I say it's my pleasure. You'll have to be the ones who establish contact."

"His adoptive parents are open to that?" Ellis asked, stepping back to scan the paperwork.

"They are," Altaha said, "just as long as you contact them first."

"This is incredible," Luella breathed. "It's got his name."

"Look at that," Ellis said with a soft smile. "Our son's name is Kai."

She lifted her face to his. "We have a teenager."

"I'm old, Lu," he said. "You still want to marry me?"

"If you can handle these fine lines," she told him. "And ignore the wrinkles."

"Puppies have wrinkles, too," he said, touching his brow to hers. "Nobody can say no to them any more than I can say no to you."

"I've got to be getting back to the station," Altaha said, shifting toward her truck as the two kissed. She stopped, however, and turned back. "Oh. Could you do something for me?"

"Anything," Luella said.

Altaha pursed her lips. "Tell your brother I've thought about it. I've thought about it a lot. And my answer is yes. He'll know what it means."

Ellis narrowed his eyes. "Do *I* want to know what it means?"

"Probably not," Altaha said with a smirk. "You'll deliver the message?"

"Yes," Luella said before Ellis could think twice.

"Thanks a lot." Altaha tipped her hat. "See you around, lovebirds."

"See you," Ellis said. As she walked off, he opened his mouth.

Luella touched her finger to his lips. "Whatever's to come of it, let it be. He did, for us." She rolled her eyes and added, "Well, eventually."

His smile came slowly but warmly. "Dang. My wife's going to be so much smarter than me."

"Maybe." She held him close as she looked back to find Isla and Ingrid playing tag in the grass with Wolfe and Eveline. "You make up for it by being such a good man and an even better daddy."

"This is all I need in life," he explained, resting his cheek on top of her head so they could both watch. "You. This family. This chance."

"It's more than I ever wished for," she said.

"And I won't ever let it get away from you again."

"I know." She rested her ear to his chest, closed her eyes and listened to his heart.

His voice rumbled through the wall of his chest. "How 'bout we celebrate tonight with some stargazing?"

She grinned freely, running her hands down the long, strong line of his back. "Absolutely."

* * * * *

COMING SOON!

We really hope you enjoyed reading this book.
If you're looking for more romance
be sure to head to the shops when
new books are available on

Thursday 7th December

MILLS & BOON

LET'S TALK

Romance

For exclusive extracts, competitions and special offers, find us online:

f MillsandBoon

𝕏 @MillsandBoon

⬛ @MillsandBoonUK

♪ @MillsandBoonUK

Get in touch on 01413 063 232